"MAYDAY! MAYDAY! MAYDAY!"

Brenna swallowed a painful lump in her throat as she watched the final moments before *Prototype II* began its test to beat the speed-of-light barrier. This time, her cousin Morgan would be the pilot. "Take her, Morgan, out to the stars!"

Morgan's image vanished from the screen. Countdown began. The time hit zero. And suddenly monitor graphs became green smears and readouts refused the incoming data. Such velocity was not possible—not in space as mankind had traveled it—until now!

Then alarms shrieked, and Morgan's voice came, roaring frantically. "Field instability! Overload! We have hull collapse and are losing life support..."

A high-pitched scream pierced Brenna's brain through the receivers. "Fire!" Morgan was crying. "We have fire!"

Explosion!

Another voice was shouting: "Mayday! Mayday! Mayday!"

D1041253

By Juanita Coulson
Published by Ballantine Books:

Children of the Stars:
Book One: TOMORROW'S HERITAGE
Book Two: OUTWARD BOUND
Book Three: LEGACY OF EARTH
Book Four: THE PAST OF FOREVER*

THE DEATH GOD'S CITADEL

THE WEB OF WIZARDRY

*Forthcoming

OUTWARD BOUND

BOOK TWO OF THE SERIES
CHILDREN OF THE STARS

JUANITA COULSON

A Del Rey Book

BALLANTINE BOOKS • **NEW YORK**

A Del Rey Book
Published by Ballantine Books

Library of Congress Catalog Card Number: 81-67846

ISBN 0-345-28179-9

Manufactured in the United States of America

First Edition: May 1982
Second Printing: April 1989

Cover Art by David Schleinkofer

Author's Acknowledgment

With sincere thanks — again! — for invaluable
help, advice, and encouragement to:
Kay Anderson, Harry J.N. Andruschak,
Gary Anderson, and Terry Adamski.

Through an agony of distance
   I have gazed on other stars,
Where the roadways of the heavens
   Reach beyond the course of Mars.
I have seen the stellar glories
   And the darkness in between,
Where the gods have left their planning
   To mankind and his machine . . .

           —*Apodosis*, Canto IV
           Anonymous

Table of Contents

THE SAUNDER DYNASTY

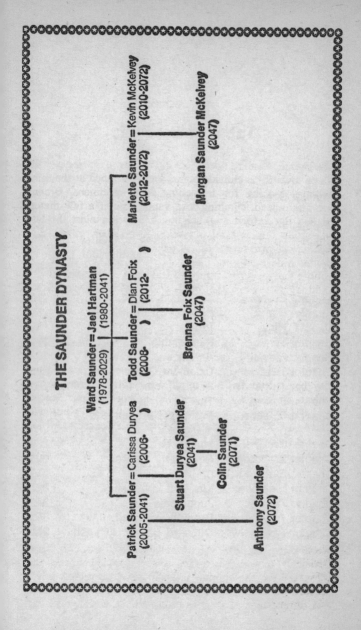

Ward Saunder = Jael Hartman
(1978-2029)   (1980-2041)

Patrick Saunder = Carissa Duryea
(2005-2041)   (2006-)

Todd Saunder = Dian Foix
(2008-)   (2012-)

Mariette Saunder = Kevin McKelvey
(2012-2072)   (2010-2072)

Stuart Duryea Saunder
(2041)

Brenna Foix Saunder
(2047)

Morgan Saunder McKelvey
(2047)

Colin Saunder
(2071)

Anthony Saunder
(2072)

✪✪✪✪✪✪✪✪

CHAPTER ONE

Separate Paths

As Brenna Saunder and Derek Whitcomb started up the slope toward his cliffside home, Derek stopped at the mine tailings, looking for interesting rock specimens. Brenna went on ahead, climbing to a vantage point a few meters higher. She turned and, shading her eyes against the late afternoon Sun, looked out over the pioneer village. Eos Chasma Town resembled dozens of other little Martian communities: housing units, shops, agricultural domes, a shuttle landing strip, a surface transport depot. The town's industry lay below the surface in a network of tunnels. Every now and then Brenna felt a tremor as the automated mining equipment tore loose new pockets of ore far beneath her feet. Minerals meant economic survival for Eos Town and much of Mars Colony. The machines never stopped.

The human work force, though, was on short shifts today because of the holidays. Local citizens thronged the village recreation center and the narrow streets. Brenna and Derek had spent several pleasant hours mingling with them and watching the friendly competitions staged for the event. Colony Days. Thirtieth anniversary! This was a special celebration for all Mars' dwellers. There had been athletic contests, land vehicle races, and prizes for the workers who sorted ore samples the fastest. The entertainment was easy-going, amicable, light-years away from the pressures and problems of Brenna's normal existence. For a while, she had almost forgotten her worries.

She adjusted the breather mask to a more comfortable position and glanced at the cliffs ringing the town. Terraform Division's oxygen-generation towers loomed above the canyon. Like the mining operations, terraforming never ceased. Yet there wasn't much noticeable change in Mars' thin atmosphere. That was expected. It would take far more than thirty years to soften the environment. Humans were newcomers to this rugged world. At present, no one could leave a building or a life-support dome without first putting on protective gear. Brenna had learned that when she was a kid, just as every Martian colonist had.

Derek finally straightened and scrambled up the slope to join Brenna. "Look," he said, holding out a chunk of rock. Brenna brushed auburn curls out of her eyes and peered at the specimen. Derek pointed to the glint of poor-grade pyrite. "Fool's gold." His breather mask muffled his voice, but his amused disdain was obvious. Derek tossed the worthless piece of slag onto the tailings, a long pitch, but nothing that would win him prizes in the village's contests. "I'm glad to see they're maintaining the standards my father set up. The inspectors are right on the job, not letting through junk like pyrite. Only top-quality stuff in *this* town's shipments," Derek said with pride. "Not like Earth. Back there, they're still killing themselves over cheaper trifles than that."

Brenna suppressed a sigh. When her private train car had arrived at the local depot four days ago, she had looked forward to a carefree interlude. Precious time spent with Derek, in one of his family's company towns. The people here, Derek promised, would respect his privacy and Brenna's. It sounded like a perfect chance to forget the outside world. And for the most part, these four days *had* been idyllic.

But occasionally Derek would make a remark that raked invisible claws through Brenna's nerves. Like that crack about Earth's decadence. She shared his scorn of their birthplace, to a degree. Derek's prejudices were far stronger, though, and as time went on he was getting more vocal about them. Inevitable. Hibernation Stasis Ship Corporation put its recruits through an intensive indoctrination program. They wanted their future interstellar colonists—such as Captain Derek Whitcomb—to be weaned completely away from any loyalty to Earth. If Derek was an example, the corporation was succeeding admirably.

No, there was nothing new in Derek's attitudes; the source of friction came from within Brenna. The pressures of the upcoming manned test flight were riding her, no matter how hard she tried to put them out of her mind.

2

Breakthrough Unlimited—her company, co-owned with her cousin Morgan McKelvey. The Saunder and McKelvey fortunes were legendary. It cost a fortune to keep Breakthrough Unlimited going, though. Problem two: Their Terran Worlds Council charter would be up for renewal in a few months, and some of the committee members had let it be known they were pretty impatient to see some results, after five years of FTL spacecraft experiments. Problem three: Staff members, leaving Breakthrough Unlimited to take employment with other companies. Like the T.W.C. committee, they were discouraged or impatient or losing their nerve. After all, Breakthrough Unlimited's record was a messy one. The dangers were past calculating. One mistake, one tiny flaw, and . . .

Dammit! Why couldn't she forget?

Warily, Brenna glanced sidelong at Derek, remembering against her will. Three years ago. Breakthrough Unlimited's first attempt to shatter the light-speed barrier. Prototype I. A radical design, a first for humanity. Other species, such as the Vahnaj, which mankind had barely begun to know, had FTL, out there in the galaxy. But not *Homo sapiens*. Not yet.

Three years ago Morgan's parents had been at the controls of Prototype I, hoping to join that special club of star travelers. Somewhere along the line, there had been a mistake, a fatal one. In helpless horror, Brenna had seen the ship blow to pieces, killing her aunt, uncle, and their third pilot. Derek had been with her and Morgan then, part of the Breakthrough Unlimited team, a hero of Space Fleet, recently attached to Brenna's company as liaison officer. He had shared Brenna's and Morgan's grief.

Team of three. They had been playmates, had grown up together. The Whitcombs were one of the wealthy families who moved in the same social circles as the famous Saunders and McKelveys. Brenna's other cousin, Stuart Saunder, was too old to join in their games, except to play bully. But Derek was the same age as Brenna and Morgan. They had formed a bond, Morgan and Derek as best friends, Brenna and Derek as lovers, in their late teens. The space brats, growing to maturity on Earth, Mars, Goddard Colony, and half a dozen other natural and artificial worlds. Learning to handle spaceships, all of them qualifying as top pilots. Unbeatable. A solid triad.

3

Until that moment three years ago when tragedy struck.

More had died in the explosion than Morgan's parents and Navigator Cesare Loezzi. Something had died in Derek. He had quit Breakthrough Unlimited shortly afterward. The love he had for Brenna, his friendship with Morgan—those remained. But he was an outsider now, going a different way, devoting himself to another pathway to the stars.

Even if the test eight days from now was a total success, Brenna knew that she would never be able to go back to that earlier happiness. She and Derek could recapture the former closeness only for a tiny space of time, on such stolen vacations as this.

A workman heading along the path west of the tailings saw the young couple and waved. "Happy Colony Days, Whitcomb! You, too, Saunder!"

Derek returned the greeting. Less enthusiastically, Brenna did also. She waited until the miner was out of their hearing, then asked, "Does everyone in this town know who I am?"

"What?" Above his mask, Derek's turquoise-blue eyes widened with surprise. "Of course. How could they not know Brenna Saunder? You're famous. Hey! I told you —quit worrying about that. My father built this town. The people are dead-on loyal. No one will blab to the newshunters. The only one who knows where we are is Morgan, and it'll stay that way until we come out of hiding."

"At least the ComLink reporters won't dig for us," Brenna agreed grudgingly. "It's a relief having a family monopoly in the news business. Saunder Enterprises usually runs the entire communications show on Mars. But Colony Days is bringing in TeleCom and all the gypsy gossip columnists. And with you and me expected to put in an appearance at the President's gala in the capital tomorrow . . ."

"Face it, my love. That's the price of fame." Laugh lines crinkled the skin around the sides of Derek's breather mask. "We're both celebrities. The interviewers pant to get an interview with a Saunder, a McKelvey, or a Whitcomb. Confess! Deep down, you enjoy the adulation. It goes right in tune with our space pilots' egos!"

Brenna glowered at him, and Derek softened his teasing

4

with an affectionate hug. She gave up, chuckling. "I suppose so. I want the fame on *my* terms, though. When I'm doing the PR routine, I'm Captain Showmanship. Sure. But . . ."

She felt a trifle desperate, unable to pin down the emotion precisely. Half-formed fears rattled in her thoughts. Not now. It was too soon. But time was ticking away. Morgan would take the controls of the Prototype in eight days. Eight days! To immortality—or to a repeat of the last disaster? No! She couldn't face it, or the reporters. Not yet. Not *yet* . . .

Derek pulled at her gently. Brenna fell into step at his side. Then, as they climbed the hill toward Derek's home, they moved apart, watching their footing. There were no stairs or escalators or other effete luxuries to ease their way across the rubble-strewn slope. Brenna kept up with Derek's pace, sometimes moving ahead. It never occurred to her to ask for his help in making her way over the treacherous ground. He would have been astonished if she had.

The manual air lock of the cliffside housing units opened onto a spartan hall. Derek's private quarters were at the far left end. Despite his father's role in founding the town and Derek's rank with Hiber-Ship Corporation, he received no special privileges. The room was cozy but very small, as plain and no-nonsense as every other dwelling in the canyon.

They took off their protective gear, stowing it in the appropriate cabinets. Then Brenna switched on the vid, wanting to catch some newscasts. Derek headed for the food dispenser. "What would you like for supper?" he asked politely.

Brenna shrugged as she watched a series of scenes of Colony Days celebrations and documentaries about the growth of Mars' human settlements. "I don't care," she said absently. "Something light."

"Again?" Derek didn't hide his concern. "Your appetite's awful. I thought getting some fresh air and watching the contests this afternoon would make you hungry."

Brenna felt as if she were walking a tightrope, and the rope was swaying. "Did you?" she said with deceptive calm. Derek's hands poised on the food dispenser controls. He gave Brenna his full attention, very much on his

5

guard as she continued. "You've been working that theory hard ever since I got here. The lovely romantic tryst. Splendid isolation. Beautiful scenery. Escape to a temporary hideaway among the honest mining folk. Oh, and we mustn't forget the sex. Lots of that. Erotica in the wilderness. Playground of the slumming rich kids. I'm sick of it!"

Derek raked a hand through his fair hair and beard. He abandoned any attempt to program supper for them and propped himself against the wall, long arms dangling, his tall, athletic frame bent in a spine-abusing slump. "You didn't have to come," he said, very softly.

There had been an undercurrent running through their time together these past four days. Fighting her own inner worries, Brenna had pretended the telltale signs weren't there. Now she couldn't ignore them any longer. Not only her tension filled the room. Something was eating at Derek, *had* been eating at him all along.

"No, I didn't have to come," Brenna said. "But I did. I'm not very good at turning down your invitations. I never have been. And you know it," she finished with a flare of resentment.

That tempting invitation: "I've got a few days' leave, Brenna. What say we get away from it all? Eos Chasma Town. You know the place. You and me. That privacy you adore. No big crowds. Hey, we need some R and R, love, if we're going to be on display at the President's bash. Bren? Please? Meet me there?"

Sweet memories, happier times, came with those words. They had been irresistible. Brenna blushed when she recalled how quickly she had jumped at the chance. She should have thought it over, at least discussed it with Morgan before she agreed. She hadn't. She had dumped everything in Morgan's lap and given him no advance warning that she was going to pull a juvenile stunt like this.

Guilt twisted at her. Before Derek's invitation, Brenna and Morgan had planned a complete schedule for the Breakthrough Unlimited test pilots. Everyone was supposed to do a certain amount of PR work. Pose in the spotlight. Rake in the publicity—and the potential investors. How they needed those! As Derek said, pilots *did* enjoy the applause. But there was a limit, and this Colony

6

Days festival was going to be a social ordeal. Brenna owed it to her cousin and to Breakthrough Unlimited to get in there with the rest and butter up the fat cats. Part of the team.

Yet Derek had snapped his fingers, and she had run away. Morgan had swallowed his annoyance. "Okay. I'll hold the fort. But try to be back at least in time for the President's party, huh? Your father and Aunt Dian expect you to be there. So do I." He hadn't quite called her a shirker, but close.

Brenna had noticed the deepening crease between her cousin's eyebrows when she had left Saunder Estates to come out to Eos Chasma. That worry line was a permanent part of Morgan's craggy face now, evidence of his own fears about Breakthrough Unlimited. Morgan's parents had died in the first test; he was going to pilot Prototype II.

And she had had the gall to leave him holding the bag during a major fund-raising opportunity! There had been no recriminations. No rumbling basso voice telling Brenna to grow up and quit jumping whenever Derek said "frog." She wished Morgan *had* chewed her out!

"Brenna?"

She came out of her dark musings, staring at Derek curiously.

"I'm glad you came," he said simply. Sometimes that tone of voice could melt her resolve. This time it was canceled out by the hovering tension.

"Okay. You're glad. So am I. But that doesn't change the rest of it. Why? Why have you been leaning over backward to . . . to avoid the subject?" Brenna demanded.

"The subject?" Derek took a deep breath and pushed himself away from the wall, walking toward Brenna. "Breakthrough Unlimited versus Hiber-Ship Corporation? *That* subject? Faster-than-light drive versus cryogenic stasis and the Isakson photon ramjet starcraft."

In a nutshell. Rival theories on the best way to get out of the Solar System. Once Derek had believed in FTL and Breakthrough Unlimited. Now he believed in cryogenic stasis, a sleep cubicle, and a crawling, asteroid-sized Colony ship that would take seventy-five years to reach the Kruger 60 planetary region.

Derek and twenty-five hundred other colonists, signing

7

up for a trip that demanded they sleep for decades. Frozen. Unaware.

But FTL—Breakthrough Unlimited's graviton spin resonance drive—would reach out to the stars in months, *weeks*.

If all went well on the upcoming test . . .

Derek caressed Brenna's face. "I'm sorry I was so obvious," he said with charming frankness. He didn't deny he had been putting on a performance the past four days. "I wanted things to be perfect for us for as long as possible. Things don't always work out right, do they?"

Brenna knew every nuance of that handsome face. She knew what Derek was planning when that blond head cocked, that strong body drew itself up to its full height.

She toyed with the emblem on his lapel. A Hiber-Ship insignia button. Derek was part of their piloting team, one of the experts they would need to take the colonists down to the planet when they reached their destination. Since he had left Breakthrough Unlimited, though, most of his piloting had been done jockeying between public appearances on Earth and in the colonies, recruiting volunteers for the great cryogenic stasis ship. Derek was good at that, particularly at convincing nubile and healthy women to become future colonists on an uninhabited world.

"The vacation *has* been perfect," Brenna said. "Almost." Derek took her hands in his as she added, "I wish we could have more times together like this. But with our mismatched schedules, that's so damned difficult."

Derek nodded. "And from now on I'm afraid we'll have even less time together."

"Less?" She managed a shaky laugh, nonplused at the statement.

"That's why I wanted this holiday for us. I . . . I needed a special time and place so I could tell you." There was a long aching pause, then Derek murmured, "And I hate to, because once I've said it, it's done. The program's complete and the engines have fired."

Beneath Brenna's boots, the floor trembled. Blasting going on, down in the mines. The queasy sensation radiated from the soles of her feet up to her belly. "What are you talking about? Tell me what? Listen, I meant it when I said I'm glad I came. These days on leave—God! How I needed them! Morgan and I knew the crew needed some

8

rest, but we did, too. Three months we've been shuttling back and forth from Mars to FTL Station. If the gang didn't get a break . . . and Colony Days was the perfect reason . . ."

She was babbling, trying to avoid the fathomless darkness lying under that tightrope.

Derek's eyes impaled her, choking off the flow of unimportant words. "I've been assigned to full-time ferry duty and ship liaison, Bren," he said with obvious pain. He had no qualms about the new job, of course. That was a promotion, a heady one. His reluctance turned entirely on what his work would mean to their relationship. "I'll be in charge of taking the final supply shipments out to *New Earth Seeker*'s orbit, near Jupiter. Everything's in the last stages now. No more recruitment tours. The lists are nearly full. Yan Bolotin and the other Hiber-Ship board members will make the announcement next week for the general public. The computers are ready; star charts the Vahnaj Ambassador gave us, on the boards." He closed his eyes momentarily, steeling himself, then said, "We leave next March."

Leave!

He wasn't just talking about leaving Brenna. *New Earth Seeker,* her cryogenic stasis cubicles full of sleeping passengers, would leave the Solar System forever. Derek intended to be aboard. He meant it. It was really going to happen.

There was another subterranean rumble, far below. Brenna barely felt the quake.

"You've been saving *this?*" Her voice was a whisper. She cleared her throat several times, trying to put some force into her building outrage. "You *knew* this when you invited me here. This whole thing was a damned manipulative . . ."

"No! Bren, I *told* you why. Dammit, this isn't easy." Derek's eyes glistened. He wasn't shamming his upset.

Neither was Brenna. She wiped furiously at her lashes, fighting the shock that threatened to erupt in tears. "You mean it. You . . ."

"I never lied to you, Bren. You knew when I signed with Hiber-Ship that this is the way it would be."

Brenna pulled away from him. She wanted to put the words back into limbo.

9

Intellectually, she *had* known. Hiber-Ship's statement of purpose: a Colony stasis craft. Destination: the Kruger 60 star system. The Vahnaj Ambassador had cleared the route with his government, back in his alien star empire. Everything was set.

Derek was part of that dream. But it *wasn't* a dream. Suddenly it was real.

This was indeed the last time they would have any leisure for themselves, any genuine solitude, a space to enjoy each other and ignore the universe outside.

She shook her head more and more violently, on the verge of lashing out blindly. Derek caught her wrists, pinning her. Brenna was strong; months of test-pilot physical training had honed her into a human machine. She could have taken Derek off balance, even though he was taller and heavier. He didn't press his luck, content to hold her until the wave of fury ebbed.

"Never easy, is it?" Brenna cried, biting her lip. "Was it easy to walk out on me and Morgan three years ago?"

"Stop it! That's not fair, and you know it. We've discussed this a thousand times, Bren. There's no point in it." The pleading note crept back into Derek's manner. "I weighed the theories, and I found the graviton spin resonance drive wanting. That's all there is to it, Bren. Hiber-Ship will work. It's been tested and proven. I'm going to the stars."

"In a frozen box . . ."

He didn't bother to refute her. They had had *that* argument over and over, too, hotly debating the merits of FTL and slow travel to other suns.

"Running again." Brenna spit the accusation.

"Would you rather I kept hitting my head against a wall? That's what you and Morgan are doing. Dammit, Bren, how many people have to be killed before you see that FTL ship is a total wipeout? It's *never* going to be successful! Breakthrough Unlimited! That's a joke. The only things it breaks are the lives of its crew . . ." The bitterness and grief poured out of him. He had loved Morgan's parents, too, had mourned them as much as Brenna and Morgan had when they died in Prototype I.

But after he had mourned, he quit. Bailed out, leaving Brenna and Morgan to pick up the pieces of their shattered confidence and trudge back into the fray.

"What do you care?" Derek said with sudden anger. "Just spend a little more money, patch together another damned test ship, staff her with another bunch of suicide-prone volunteers. The hell with the risks! Think of the glory! Well, I had a taste of that glory, Bren, and it's rotten!"

He had been wrapped up in what he was saying and had let go of her wrists. Brenna wrenched free, swinging. She caught herself when the blow was centimeters away from his face. They stood there, confronting one another, Brenna's hand frozen in mid-air. Derek made no attempt to duck. If she chose to strike, he would take the blow squarely. She wanted to carry through, to make him wince, to hurt him as he was hurting her.

And she wanted to embrace him and hold him so tightly he would never be able to get away.

Money. Did Derek *really* think the solution was that simple, even for Brenna Saunder and Morgan McKelvey? Didn't he realize the enormous sums Breakthrough Unlimited was gobbling? No, he probably didn't. Derek Whitcomb's private fortune was invested in Hiber-Ship Corporation. The supplies his wealth was buying were going into the holds of *New Earth Seeker*—supplies to support a new colony, seventy-five years from now.

Did he know about the *others* who had defected from Breakthrough Unlimited during the past three years? Derek's desertion to Hiber-Ship Corporation had hurt Brenna and Morgan the most—but there had been techs and vital staff people who had also left the company, people who had cost momentum as well as funds, and those funds were becoming tighter and tighter with every passing month without a prove-out on the FTL ship.

"Pride," Derek accused her. "Face up to it, Brenna. That's behind everything—you, Morgan, Mariette Saunder, Kevin McKelvey. You got used to running the show when your father broke the Vahnaj code years ago. Todd Saunder, the man who taught us how to talk to the alien race out there! It was wonderful. But why the hell does the rest of your family have to kill itself trying to equal what he's done? Let him have his glory. You *live*, Brenna . . ." His face crumpled, and suddenly he was framing her head in his long fingers, tenderly saying, "Oh,

11

Brenna. No! Can't you see? Can't you really see? Give it up before it kills you."

"Pride ? Is that what you think? What would you know about it? Or about loyalty or guts . . ."

Low blow. Unfair.

Or was it? When he was a young officer with Space Fleet, Derek had never been one to back off from hazard. He had taken desperate risks, capturing hijackers, clearing drifting hulks out of the commercial lanes. And when he had been with Breakthrough Unlimited, his courage had been right up there with Brenna and the rest—until the Prototype exploded.

"Which is better, Derek? Risking everything because of pride, or a certain faith that you *have* the right answer? Or abandoning me and humanity . . ."

"Hiber-Ship isn't abandoning. Earth and the colonies will go their merry way without us. We're going to make a better life out there. Spirit of Humanity, Brenna! See that! Please! *See it!*"

Brenna had spoken of faith, but she had meant "trust." She didn't share Derek's religious convictions. When a cataclysmic wave of disasters had nearly wiped out human civilization during their parents' generation, the old religions, like every other human institution, had undergone tremendous change. The old patterns no longer gave solace. New ones rose out of the chaos. The Spirit of Humanity movement combined traditional beliefs in a benign, if remote, deity with a fierce confidence in *Homo sapiens* as a species. Derek and those like him sincerely believed that humanity would endure, that some transcendent, immortal spirit of humanity itself would sustain them through any crisis. The tenets of the creed seemed muddled to Brenna, but many of her colleagues and friends had accepted the faith completely. She couldn't deny the Spirit of Humanity power. Yet she wanted to fight it. It gave Derek such maddening, stubborn assurance in his cause! He had always been stubborn. He didn't need spiritual aid in that regard!

"I *don't* see it. I never will. All I see is you," Brenna said bluntly. "And that you refuse to believe in what Morgan and I are doing. Now, or three years ago."

"This conversation never goes anywhere, does it? I

12

wanted . . . Brenna, you've *got* to see! I want you to come with me."

She flung herself away from him. Brenna couldn't get far in the tiny room, but she put as much furniture between herself and Derek as she could, appalled by the new invitation he was extending.

"Go into a cryogenic cubicle? You're crazy!" Reflexively, Brenna hugged her arms about herself, shuddering.

Derek's hand was out, encouraging her to move around the barriers. "It works. It's proven."

"It's disgusting!"

Slowly, Derek's hand dropped to his side. He stood there, helpless, shaking his head, unable to deal with her attitude. It was apparent that Brenna's loathing of cryogenic stasis was as alien to Derek as his lack of trust in Breakthrough Unlimited was to her.

If he knew . . . if he suspected some of the problems, he would use that knowledge as ammunition. Brenna had resisted the advance. The doubts were there, though. How much did she know? What if . . . what if Hiber-Ship Corporation *was* the right way? Funding wouldn't be her financial burden, then. People wouldn't die in Hiber-Ship's project unless the cryogenic stasis cubicles failed; the long trips they had taken with volunteers had proved the cubicles would hold up.

No. Derek mustn't know her true doubts.

Did *he* have any? Was there any way she could get through to him? Now, before he shipped out?

One look at his eyes told her how futile that hope was.

Two stubborn people. Pride. Philosophy. Questions of courage. Vectors dividing, veering away from each other.

Derek detected the weakness in her resolve. He coaxed her by saying, "Brenna, don't let us fight. We can't. Whatever happens, we can't end up like this. Hate the Hiber-Ship. But don't hate me."

Brenna heard herself moaning with emotional anguish. "I . . . I couldn't hate you." *I didn't hate you, even when you abandoned me and my dreams.* "But I *do* hate Hiber-Ship."

The words and pain and accusations and counteraccusations fell together in Brenna's mind. Unless she gave in, Derek was leaving her. He would get a few days here and there, between his ferry-shuttle runs out to *New Earth*

Seeker. But damned few of those. In effect, this was the beginning of their final good-bye. It had been coming for three years. And she had refused to admit it was reality.

"I love you," Derek said.

Nothing more. Nothing more was necessary. He was twisting the knife in her heart, but at least he was with her.

"I know," Brenna said in a faint whisper. "I love you. And never the twain shall remain together. That's it, isn't it?"

"I guess so," he admitted. A sad smile curved his mouth. "We had four days, Bren. Good ones. Let's make them last as long as possible. I've got a flight the day after tomorrow . . ."

His new duties, taking him away from her already.

". . . and you've got an FTL test program to run," Derek reminded her. He said that casually, not knowing the nightmares and smothered fears it conjured in Brenna's mind.

Carefully, she composed her expression. *Don't let him know. Don't let him hit you when you're vulnerable. If you give in, you'll lose yourself.* Brenna reminded herself of the most abhorrent possibility—failure. Failure to outlast Derek. Never mind the price in pain. There was integrity.

But . . . hang on. As he said, it's the last day. Make it a good one.

If we can.

While we can.

✿✿✿✿✿✿✿✿✿

CHAPTER TWO

Pavonis City

THAT hadn't been the end of their quarreling. The fight had flared up and cooled down several times more, each of them dragging forth the same arguments and recriminations, rehashing the points until they were both weary. When Derek had finally suggested they go to bed, Brenna exploded anew, seeing the invitation as one more sample of Derek's tendency to manipulate her emotions. With great difficulty, they had backed off from the conflict and settled down for an uneasy few hours of rest. Neither of them slept much. By morning they had more or less kissed and made up, agreeing to a truce.

"I wish we could skip this trip into the capital," Brenna grumbled as they packed their travel kits.

"I don't have an option," Derek said. "Unlike you and Morgan, I don't own the company I work for."

Brenna started to tell him what he could do with that company and his loyalty to cryogenic stasis and slower-than-light star travel. Then she bit her lip as she remembered the truce. Her anger turned inward, roiling her stomach. Brenna shut her pack with a savage jerk. "I've already dumped a double load of PR socializing on Morgan because I came here. He's expecting me. So are my parents. Come on. We'll miss the train."

"Ought to take a shuttle," Derek growled sourly. "It'd be faster. You and your cloak-and-dagger dodges. Just because of a few offworlder gypsy news hunters . . . all right! I'm ready. Let's go."

Derek followed her out, pausing to set his housing unit's computers on standby. Everyday procedure. Brenna had done the same thing when she left her residence at Saunder Estates:Mars. Of course, Saunder Estates' computerized home-monitoring systems were a lot more sophisticated than the ones found in a pioneer town, but the

15

principle was the same. The room would be kept clean and safely locked until its owner returned.

But when *would* Captain Derek Whitcomb return to Eos Chasma Town again? Not soon. Ever since he had signed on with Hiber-Ship Corporation, he'd been an infrequent drop-in at this mining village his father had built. And now . . .

"Departure date's been set, Brenna. We leave next March. I don't know how often we can be together. This is it."

Brenna slammed a mental door, trying to shut out the haunting echo of Derek's announcement. She channeled her dismay and tension into action and hurried out of the apartment and down the slope to the depot at a reckless pace. As they descended the hill, Derek called a warning occasionally. But he was too wise to get physical and try to stop her by force. Several times Brenna almost fell, skittering on the loose stones. By the time they reached the depot and climbed inside the train, she was sweating badly behind her breather mask. Safe inside the train car's life-support system, Brenna peeled out of the mask and her parka, getting comfortable for the ride. Derek did the same, saying nothing.

Other people were already aboard. Brenna recognized the insignia of Terraform Division on their uniforms. These men and women must be part of the oxygen-generation supervisory crew posted to Eos Town. Obviously they were eager to get to Pavonis City and join the big celebration at Mars' capital. Unlike the miners and their families, the Terraform workers usually served short rotations. For many of them, Pavonis City was their home base. Most of the passengers were watching the individual vid screens placed in various seating sections of the train car. The scenes showed the President's gala and other festivities at Pavonis City, adding to the travelers' impatience.

In a few minutes, the car glided away from Eos Chasma. Adapted mass driver propulsion meant there was almost no jolting and a minimal sense of motion. As they started the journey, Brenna watched the monitor screen in front of her. The frame was divided, part of it a relay showing the Colony Days events, the left side of the screen tracking the train's progress on a small insert map. At the moment, the train was rushing through a subterranean section

16

of track, an extension of the elaborate mining network surrounding Eos Chasma. But within twenty kilometers they were climbing, running along on the surface.

The train slowed to a stop at Coprates Junction and picked up more passengers at the depot there. A short wait, while the new arrivals settled in and allowances were made for anyone who had reached the depot late. Then the car angled northwestward again. Some of the Coprates Junction boarders were Terraform Division workers, too. They and the group from Eos Town were well acquainted. The holiday travelers bunched up in the front half of the car, starting an impromptu celebration. Brenna saw sooth-ants and stimulants being passed from hand to hand. Laughter filled the train. She envied the merrymakers, wishing she could get into the spirit of Colony Days. But how could she? With the test just a week away, and now this news Derek had handed to her—impossible!

Brenna drummed her fingers on the edge of the readout monitor. As she reached to increase the data feed rate, Derek's hand closed over hers. They waged silent war for control. Then Brenna looked at him, meeting his eyes squarely. She hadn't been aware she was holding her breath, but all of a sudden she exhaled deeply, sinking back into her acceleration-adjusted seat.

"That's better," Derek said softly. His expression glowed with love. He raised Brenna's hand to his lips. She had to smile. Derek's old-fashioned gallantries had always been one of his most charming points. But when he kissed her hand, his beard and mustache tickled her skin. He understood her reaction, unoffended. "Relax. Colony Days. Happy times. Affirmative?"

"With what happened last evening still on my mind?" Brenna exclaimed. She jerked her hand out of his grasp. In the seats ahead, people were whooping and singing, carrying out the happy mood Derek had suggested. Brenna *wanted* to belong to the crowd. *And* she wanted to jump to her feet and scream at the happy passengers to shut up and let her worry in peace.

Mixed-up emotions! Brenna Saunder, expert test pilot and ace agonizer!

And she was continuing to take out her tension and frustration on Derek. Why not? He had helped cause a major portion of her fear. No, that wasn't really true. She had been an emotional mess *before* she came to meet him at Eos Chasma. With rueful self-honesty, Brenna admitted that Derek had just added to a pile of worry she had been nursing for weeks. She peeked at him calculatingly. Derek's smile was gone. He held his tongue, waiting. Brenna forced a weak giggle. "Huh! I know what you had in mind. You were expecting compliments on your technique, weren't you? Well, it was superb. Superb! Isn't that what all your fans tell you, hotshot?"

"You've got me confused with Morgan. He's the one with the playboy reputation. There's only one woman I'm interested in, and you know it very well," Derek said. He was smiling again, that wonderful smile that disarmed opponents and made women stare in fascination. Brenna had fallen in love with that smile, and with Derek, when they were gawky adolescents, finding out about sex and each other simultaneously. Between then and now, they had taken other lovers. But eventually they had come back to the first relationship. The public thought theirs was a perfect match. Brenna Foix Saunder, youngest female member of the famous Saunder clan. Captain Derek Whitcomb, one-time hero of Space Fleet, part of the Breakthrough Unlimited FTL test-pilot team, briefly, and now the most glamorous recruit of Hiber-Ship Corporation. The vid columnists called them "hot copy" and featured them as often as they could. Brenna and Derek, young, attractive, living dangerously at the very frontiers of science and the future. Those newshunters provided just one more stress on their relationship, a relationship that was already under enormous pressures.

Brenna glanced at the readouts again. The train's schedule showed no further stops between here and Pavonis City. They were building up speed, careening along the rim of Valles Marineris. ETA in the capital, twenty minutes, allowing for deceleration.

Derek seemed encouraged by Brenna's teasing words a few moments ago. He risked a joke. "It really isn't a compliment, you know, your fidgeting like that after our idyllic getaway for two. I thought you'd be pleasantly fatigued, at the least."

"My jitters have nothing to do with sex, and you know it." Brenna eyed the readouts again, squirming. "Plus this

18

train ride. Yes, I know, it was my idea. But I just don't like being a mere passenger."

He could have taken that as a term out of space pilots' jargon, a sly reference to the civilians sharing the train car with them. Instead, Derek chose the earthier interpretation. "Oh, you do like to be in control, my love. I've noticed that. Often. Every time we . . ."

"Put that on standby," Brenna snapped.

"Why? You were the one talking about technique in bed a moment ago." Derek tugged at his beard. "Don't be so damned sensitive. Besides, who's going to object to my lewd and lascivious tongue here? No one heard me. And if they did, they wouldn't care, not with the popular vid comedians telling riper ones than that every hour on the entertainment channels." To prove what he had said, Derek nodded toward the front of the car. As far as the other passengers were concerned, the tall blond man and the slender, pretty redhead in the last seats didn't exist. Nobody paid Derek or Brenna the slightest bit of attention. "You wanted to travel incognito. You've got it."

"They don't recognize you when you're out of your Hiber-Ship uniform," Brenna said. She meant to lead from that into another teasing dig. Then the mini-display on the individual monitor screen zoomed in on the President's gala in the capital. An unseen newscaster was describing the events at the Pavonis City Rotunda while the cameras showed the dignitaries gathered there. Brenna saw important people from Earth, Goddard Colony, Lunar Base, and other communities throughout the Solar System. There were several high-ranking Terran Worlds Council members as well as their rivals from Protectors of Earth. A number of well-known actors and sports figures were present. And the Saunders were very much in evidence, of course. Brenna's father and mother were shown chatting with a powerful politician from the Jovian satellite colonies. The newscaster's voice-over described them as "Todd Saunder, the famous sponsor of Project Search and president of ComLink, and his wife, the eminent xenolinguist, Dr. Dian Foix . . ."

To Brenna's irritation, her cousin Stuart was also on the scene. Stuart rarely left his palatial mansions on Earth, not even for a celebration as big as this one. Brenna suspected that Stuart's putting in an appearance at Colony

Days meant some sort of feud was starting up between him and his mother—again. When it came to choosing sides between Stuart and her aunt Carissa, Brenna wanted out. Both of them were bad news to the rest of the family.

Brenna's other cousin, Morgan McKelvey, towered above most of the other guests at the President's party. Typically, Morgan was posing for the cameras and garnering publicity for Breakthrough Unlimited. *Doing my job,* Brenna thought with a twinge of remorse. But it wasn't too painful for Morgan. Some of the most beautiful women on Mars were hanging on his arm, competing for his eye.

At the edge of the video frame, President Grieske and Ambassador Quol-Bez of the Vahnaj planets were talking earnestly. The cameras discreetly stayed back, not trying to capture the audio. It was possible the Martian Council President and the alien were discussing top-secret diplomatic matters. The Ambassador's translator and a gaggle of Terran Worlds Council aides were hovering close, though, trying to overhear the conversation.

Suddenly, Stuart Saunder cut in front of the lens, blocking the technicians' view of the President and the Ambassador. Brenna's cousin from Earth acted as if he were unaware he was upstaging everyone. Brenna wasn't fooled. Stuart was working hard on his professional hedonist performance, and attracting an audience. She hoped those at the gala weren't fooled, either, and didn't assume Stuart was an example of what the rest of the Saunders were like.

Derek had noticed Brenna's interest in the vid display. "You overdo this shy-little-rich-girl routine, Bren. For example," Derek waved at the screen, "even if you don't count Stuart—and who does?—nobody else in your family is hiding from the limelight. Look at Morgan. That showoff! Count 'em. One, two, three women waving around their hormones and doing their best to get him to their beds after the gala. So what if half his playboy act was dreamed up by the media? It works. Morgan treats it as free advertising. He's right." Derek sensed Brenna's growing annoyance and dropped that topic. "No sale? So? What shall we do for the remainder of the journey? Watch the scenery?"

The suggestion was intended to make her smile. It succeeded. The idea was ridiculous. They had both flown over this terrain countless times in shuttles and ridden these tracks in their private train cars and company vehicles. The view was as familiar as the inside of their homes. Yet it *was* striking. The train sped on frictionless wings, climbing into the Tharsis Mountains. High speed reduced objects close to the car's sides to a blur of reds, tans, and yellowish brown. But more distant landmarks appeared to move by slowly: craters, hills, ravines—an awesome vista. Mars was a world mankind had barely begun to tame. Compared with some of the settlements, life in Eos Chasma was easy. Precipitous cliffs overhung the kilometers-deep gorge to the south. Valles Marineris was a rip in the planet, a canyon so huge that no one could absorb its dimensions from the surface. Only an aerial view captured the ancient rift, a gouge longer than some continents on Earth were wide.

Today, the view was clear and the train was using the surface route. Sometimes dust storms completely obscured the surface, driving the colonists and their vehicles underground. There were alternate tracks along most of the transport system. Computers controlled the operation, constantly sampling the conditions ahead, picking the quickest and safest course.

Brenna could see for tens of kilometers, to the horizon. Now and then she spotted traces of a prospecting community or a mining town. Always, the towns were close to the transport depots—the pioneers' lifelines to the older and better-supplied cities in the Tharsis Mountains and Syrtis Major, in the eastern hemisphere. Medical emergencies, life-support-system breakdowns, an unexpected economic setback—anything could put those little settlements in deep trouble. They weren't *quite* as vulnerable to sudden catastrophe as man-made settlements in space, but very nearly so. During the thirty years humans had lived on Mars, there had been plenty of tragedy. The colonists accepted the dangers. You didn't ship out and sign on with the mining expeditions and explorer groups unless you had the spirit to take whatever Mars might hand you. The unbreathable air, the thin, rocky soil, existence bought at a high price—this could be a hostile world. But it was also a starkly beautiful one, offering a challenge the pioneers relished. Brenna's parents and Morgan's had been part of that breed. So had Derek's.

21

Brenna divided her focus, watching the passing Marscape and the vid monitor. Other guests were joining the President and Ambassador Quol-Bez. Chairman Hong Ling-Quang of Protectors of Earth, here as a representative of the home planet, elbowed for position against Terran Worlds Councilman Ames, an old friend of Brenna's father. Politics. They both wanted to be seen shaking hands with Quol-Bez, to show their constituents, via the media, that they were on close terms with the alien from beyond Pluto. In spite of his six years in the Solar System, the Vahnaj Ambassador was still an exotic and intriguing figure to humans—the only alien any human had ever met face to face, though mankind had been in contact with his species for more than thirty years by faster-than-light radio signals.

In retrospect, it seemed incredible that humanity had once been terrified by the "threat" of the Vahnaj. They had feared that the extraterrestrials, with their far more advanced galactic civilization, would invade and destroy Earth. Mars hadn't been colonized yet, and Goddard and Lunar Base were barely established. Man *ought* to have been farther along the road to exploring the Solar System by then. But natural disasters and a series of terrible wars in the early years of the Twenty-first Century had almost made *Homo sapiens* extinct before humans established the first contact with the Vahnaj stellar empire. Brenna's father had achieved that link when he communicated with a Vahnaj robot messenger in 2040. Brenna's generation thought of that period as a dark age, when people gibbered about "Vahnaj invaders who will enslave us all!" When humanity finally met Ambassador Quol-Bez, more than thirty years later, how foolish those fears seemed!

"Look at them swarming around Quol-Bez," Brenna said scornfully. "As if they think he'll throw future trade contracts their way."

"He may," Derek said. Brenna darted a sharp glance at him as he added, "Quol-Bez has the authority to negotiate with us. He worked out the agreement with Hibernation Stasis Ship Corporation and gave us our choice of trans-Solar System colony worlds."

Brenna's smoldering anger flared. "You mean he put in a call to his government back home, and they picked

22

out a bunch of rocks they weren't interested in, anyway, and told Hiber-Ship Corporation it could colonize them."

Derek took a deep breath. He didn't back away from the subject. "Any race with their capabilities in interstellar travel and communications *can* give and take at will, Bren, and you know it. I think it was generous of them to select those planetfalls for our ship and guarantee that neither they nor any other species out there will claim them before *New Earth Seeker* arrives."

New Earth Seeker would arrive—at the world the Vahnaj had deigned to reserve for them—after a human lifetime. And Derek would be aboard her. Brenna couldn't accept that fact, even yet. A knife was twisting and cutting her emotions, and she couldn't defend herself from the pain.

The Vahnaj. Instant communications across the light-years. When her father had examined the Vahnaj robot messenger vehicle, he had learned it contained an FTL com system. Any tampering would have disintegrated the unit, but Todd Saunder had taken control and prevented Earth's governments and the military from trying to get into the communicator's guts. As a result, for thirty-four years humans and Vahnaj had been in regular contact, up to and including the time Ambassador Quol-Bez's ship had entered the Solar System. A faster-than-light ship. FTL radio. All the wonderful devices Brenna and her team so desperately yearned for! But the Vahnaj wouldn't share those devices with *Homo sapiens*. They had co-operated with Hiber-Ship Corporation, though. Ambassador Quol-Bez had patiently explained that cryogenic stasis and the Isakson photon ramjet starcraft that would carry Derek and the other sleeping colonists to the Kruger 60 star system were *human* inventions. Fine! That meant the Vahnaj would be delighted to encourage them, to map out near-star neighborhoods for Hiber-Ship's convenience, "reservations" for the primitive humans to crawl out to.

But they *wouldn't* lift a finger to help Breakthrough Unlimited acquire faster-than-light speeds. Aliens in the manger. Vahnaj logic decreed that mankind must "invent" FTL drive for itself. No helping hands from outside.

Brenna liked Quol-Bez. She saw the alien Ambassador frequently, because he moved in the same lofty social circles as her parents. The Vahnaj regarded Todd Saunder as an all-important human, the man who had found their robot messenger. Quol-Bez and Brenna's father were fast friends.

But Brenna also resented the alien. Hiber-Ship Corporation's *New Earth Seeker* was nearing completion. Departure date set. Maps on board—thanks to the Vahnaj! Crew list filling up fast with those willing to ride at sub-light speeds to a barren world an alien race had chosen for them. Meanwhile, Breakthrough Unlimited dealt with unknowns, its people dying in the explosion of the first Prototype, the terrible risks of the upcoming test creating tensions that were battering Brenna and the others. FTL travel. The key to reaching the stars in weeks, not in decades or centuries. And likable, smiling Ambassador Quol-Bez rubbed elbows with politicians, bowed, and spoke with sweet reasonableness. But he wouldn't help Todd Saunder's daughter and nephew find that key to the universe.

Don't let the primitives escape from the reservation too fast?

"We just left the Ophir region," Derek was saying. "On the Trithonium curve now. The last leg. There's Saunder Estates, coming up." A kilometer away, down an arm of the canyon rim, Brenna saw her home. Three secluded mansions—her parents', Morgan's, and hers—protected by Saunder Enterprises security forces. Close to Pavonis City, yet far enough away to offer privacy and a magnificent view of Valles Marineris from the terraces and windows of the Estates. Luxurious dwellings, for Mars. "Wishing we'd spent the last few days there?" Derek asked gently.

Brenna's mood softened. He understood. He could be so damned infuriating. Then he would probe her emotions and touch just the right note. How could they be so far apart on so many things, yet share this rapport? "No. I'm glad we were alone," Brenna said.

Despite what you told me. Despite the new fears you dumped on top of the unbearable load I'm already carrying. Being with you is vital. All the more so because you're going to leave me ... maybe forever.

His hand stole across the divider between their seats. Brenna hesitated for a fraction of a second, then reached out, their fingers interlacing. Breakthrough Unlimited and Hiber-Ship Corporation. Brenna Saunder and Derek Whitcomb. Enemies. Rivals. Philosophical opposites. And lovers.

Deceleration mode was beginning, that heavy, seat-of-the-pants sensation every pilot recognized. Outside the windows, the scene changed. Saunder Estates was special, but there were other expensive dwellings near Mars' administrative capital. The closer they came to Pavonis City, the more an imitation-Earth life style was evident. More life-support domes covering entire areas. Lots of surface and subterranean transport depots. Outlying suburbs of Pavonis City were tied to the capital by train and skimmer monorail. There were only a few mines in this area. Pavonis City was a pulse point, a computer center for the planet. Her citizens followed the same safety rules colonists in the isolated regions of Mars did, but they could do so in comparative comfort. In another fifty years, Pavonis City might be indistinguishable from most middle-sized nerve centers back on the home world.

Brenna took her travel kit out of the luggage holder. Derek had already slung his over one shoulder. When the car stopped, they moved down the aisle toward the forward doors. The other passengers had stampeded out before the P.A.'s debark message began. "We are arriving at Pavonis City Station West One-Ten, Gate Twelve. Please exit by the forward access . . ." When Brenna and Derek reached the door, most of the Terraform Division workers were on the platform beyond. A noisy holiday crowd thronged the station as the on-going Colony Days celebration spilled over from the upper levels of the city.

". . . thank you for traveling with Saunder Enterprises Transport Company," the computerized P.A. crooned. Absently, Brenna cataloged the recorded voice as translator-splitter model eighteen. Brenna owned considerable stock in that family industry, as well as in SE Transport Co. Funds flowed into the coffers every time someone rode this train. She appreciated the revenue more than she ever had. Money. A lot of it. Breakthrough Unlimited's payroll and experimental spacecraft gobbled up enormous sums.

". . . station temperature is twenty-five. The time is 2135 hours, West Central Martian Time . . ."

As Brenna and Derek walked down the exit ramp, two

25

Terraform workers whispered excitedly, "Do you know who *they* are?"

"Brenna Saunder! The real Brenna Saunder, right there in the car with us all the way! I'd heard they were at Eos Town, but I didn't see them get on board. She's taller than I expected, and younger."

"Did you see that feature about them on Ife Enegu's program last week? Derek Whitcomb. Ooh, isn't he a satisfier?"

"Sure is! I'd sign up to sleep on *his* ship any time!"

Brenna plowed into the mob, fighting her way through. Derek struggled to keep up with her. His long arms and legs were a handicap in congestion like this. "Stop it!" he yelled, grabbing Brenna's arm. "You'll knock someone down!"

"They identified us, dammit. You said nobody would blab." Brenna looked around anxiously, expecting to see a gypsy media crew closing in on them. But no one seemed to have picked up on the two women's comments. Brenna continued to worm her way through the crush, heading for the outer platform. Once they were in the clear, Derek made up for lost time, matching her gait.

Brenna grimaced, pointing at the station's wall. Holomode pictures three meters tall advertised "Mankind's Greatest Adventure!" In a heroic pose, Derek Whitcomb and several other attractive Hiber-Ship volunteers loomed above the platform. The ad copy screamed, "It's Not Too Late! You Too Can Join Hiber-Ship Corporation! Ride *New Earth Seeker* To The Stars! Cryogenic Statis Is Proven! Tame New Worlds! The Future Can Be Yours! Contact Hiber-Ship Corporation in Pavonis City or Syrtis Major Base for Details!"

"Glamour boy," Brenna said with bitterness. "I'm surprised they didn't tear your clothes off the moment they saw you, you sexy satisfier, you . . ."

"Don't be a burned-out circuit, Bren. Nothing like that happens."

"But Hiber-Ship sure does display you like a prize stud," Brenna retorted.

"They could have pounced on you just as fast. You're a celebrity, too," he said in his own defense. "The reigning Saunder princess."

"Don't call me that!"

The original "Saunder princess" had been Brenna's aunt Mariette. She and Morgan's father had founded Breakthrough Unlimited, and died in Prototype I. Mari Saunder —Brenna remembered her as a middle-aged but still lovely woman with raven hair and pale blue eyes. But the Saunder princess was dead. Long live the new princess, Brenna Foix Saunder—if she didn't make the same fatal mistakes her predecessor had.

Derek muttered something that might have been an apology. By the time they got to the service elevators, Brenna relented enough to grant him a slight smile.

Yuri Nicholaiev and one of Hiber-Ship's lieutenants, Lilika Chionis, were waiting for them. They had put corporate rivalry aside, for the present. As Brenna and Derek rushed into the foyer, their aides sealed the security doors behind them and Yuri tumbled the programming. If the gypsy news hunters were on Brenna's trail, the tactic would delay them, at least for a while. The four climbed into one of the elevators and started the long ride up through the mountain's interior. Derek peeled out of his travel coverall, with Lilika's assistance. "Whew!" he said. "That was a melee and a half down there on the platform. I'm surprised the enforcement officers aren't breaking it up."

"Not during Colony Days, Captain Whitcomb," Yuri said. He was holding Brenna's kit while she discarded her outer clothes. Yuri's eyes widened with approval when he saw the rainbow-patterned formal jumper she wore. Derek straightened his uniform. Lilika Chionis brushed a bit of lint off the officer's insignia on his shoulder. Yuri went on to explain, "They won't stop the celebrations unless there's mayhem."

"It's close to that, if you ask me."

Brenna watched the levels ticking off as they climbed five kilometers up Tharsis Ridge. Readouts showed they were passing some of the residential and commercial stories at express speed. Brenna gulped at a painful lump that extended into both her ears. Doctors could cure free-fall and Coriolis problems and compensate for gravity with a few pills. But for this age-old difficulty of altitude adjustment, they still advised patients to swallow a few times. So much for modern medicine! The elevator cab moved along vertical, angling, and horizontal tracks, rising steadily. Brenna kept swallowing and used the gleaming wall as a mirror to check her appearance before they arrived at the gala. She combed her short auburn curls with her fingers. "Has anybody figured out our arrival point yet?"

"No. Morgan arranged everything," Yuri answered her. "I do not think he even told your parents where you were."

"That's so, Captain. The secret was well kept." Lilika Chionis chimed in. Her attitude implied that the Russian's word alone wasn't good enough.

Yuri eyed the woman belligerently. "Morgan told the vid columnists that you and Captain Whitcomb would be arriving in your private craft at the northwest V.I.P. station. They have sent their camera crews down there. Some of them have been at Gate Two since the gala started."

"Gate Two? Not Gate One?" Derek feigned wounded pride. "Our celebrity status must be slipping, Bren."

Unfortunately, Yuri didn't take that as sarcasm. "Not at all, Captain. Morgan said that using Gate One would be ostentatious."

Derek grinned at him, and Yuri belatedly realized he had been set up. His square Slavic face stiffened. Lilika Chionis had the grace not to smirk.

"Do you have the update?" Brenna asked hastily.

Still visibly sulking, Yuri nodded and aligned his mini-memory terminal alongside Brenna's. Their wrist units began the transfer of information. Brenna's unit absorbed personal business data, the latest fine-tuning on the Breakthrough Unlimited test schedule, and whatever other material Morgan and George Li and the ramrods knew she would need after five days of being out of touch. Later, when she had some leisure, Brenna would play back the data on the miniaturized terminal so that she would be fully briefed when she arrived at the shuttle hangar tomorrow.

From the corner of her eye, Brenna studied Lilika Chionis. Like Yuri and Brenna, the pretty Greek lieutenant and Derek were swapping information on their mini-memory terminals. Brenna wondered if that data included things like notes on a voting proxy, which Morgan might have had to use during Brenna's absence. Hiber-Ship Corporation, though, was organized far differently from Breakthrough Unlimited. Derek and Lilika were employees of their company, not co-owners. Lilika was Derek's crewmate. They were cogs in a massive machine—biological cogs, intended to fit genetically and produce a second generation of colonists on a distant, as yet uninhabited planet. Brenna didn't know if Derek had ever been sexually involved with Lilika or with any other woman of Hiber-Ship's crew. She had made it a point not to ask. Years ago, she and Derek had agreed not to let jealousy enter their relationship. Yet she couldn't pretend people like Lilika Chionis didn't exist—especially after Derek's announcement last evening. Lilika and hundreds of other women volunteers would be sleeping in their icy cubicles when *New Earth Seeker* was launched next March. The male-female ratio on the colony ship was lopsided. More biological planning. If all went as planned, the passengers would awake from cryogenic stasis when *New Earth Seeker* established orbit around the planet the Vahnaj had reserved for them. They would shuttle down to the surface and restart human civilization there, several women taking the part of Eves to each of the ship's genetically approved Adams. One of those Adams would be Derek Whitcomb.

The data transfer was complete. Brenna massaged her wrist nervously. "We saw you guys on the vid," she told Yuri, "these past few days. Looked like everybody got a good chance to show off."

Except me. I was hiding. Letting you and Morgan and the rest do my dirty work . . .

Yuri didn't seem resentful. "Indeed! It became boring after some time. Rue Polk and Joe Habich doing interviews on Tuesday, Tumaini and his wife and children being domestic for the reporters on Wednesday, Hector and Adele on Thursday. Shoje and I have been handling PR with Morgan the past two days. Shoje Nagata said he was going to stuff several particular newscasters in the shuttle's fuel tanks when we take off tomorrow, just to get even."

Lilika giggled. "I'll bet Hector strutted his stuff, though," Derek said. "He and Tumaini are old hands at test-pilot PR."

"*Nyet*. Not this time," Yuri corrected him. "Mrs. Beno and Tumaini's children were there, which . . . uh . . . caused problems. And Hector met a certain woman he knew when he and I were in Space Fleet. He and she disappeared soon afterward," Yuri said, reddening slightly.

That was a familiar report. Brenna shook her head.

"Well, Hector's sex life is publicity of sorts, too. Poor Carmelita. I'll bet she never even opened her mouth when Hector dropped out for some fun-on-the-side. Hector's lucky she doesn't have Aluna Beno's temper . . ."

The service elevator stopped. As the four emerged and started across the hall toward the executive elevators, a gypsy newshunter suddenly jumped out from behind a corner, running, his camera pendant ready. Yuri hit the overload set on his wrist mini-terminal. Breakthrough Unlimited's equipment was designed to work at considerable distances. The power output in the little terminal easily blitzed the reporter's audio link with his superiors. The man yelped and jerked the tiny receiver out of his ear. Yuri swung in behind him, seeming eager to help. Instead, he shoved the man into the service elevator. Lilika hesitated. Hiber-Ship Corporation wasn't usually so rough with gypsy newshunters. But when Derek nodded, Lilika moved in at the reporter's side. "Is there a problem, sir?" she asked with apparent concern. "Let's check that feedback reading." Before the man could stop her, Lilika detached his camera pendant and held it out of his reach.

Yuri grinned from ear to ear. He waved as the doors slid shut on the newshunter's irate protests. For a change, Lilika and Yuri were allies, and the roving reporter had lost his gossip item.

When the cab descended, Brenna smiled. "Thanks, Derek. Lilika wouldn't have done that if you hadn't given the okay."

Derek shrugged. "That pushy character deserved it. I'm surprised Yuri didn't knock him cold, strictly as a favor to you."

"Standby on that."

They went on to the executive elevator banks. Brenna's palm print identification opened the doors for them, and they began a second rapid ascent through the administrative levels of Pavonis City. Displays on the cab's vid screen pictured a Mars-wide party going on around the planet, both day and night sides. Officially, there were four more days of festival. But this was the big one, the President's gala. The nearly million permanent and transient inhabitants of Mars were making the most of it.

Brenna touched the tiny ruby com-jewel she wore at her throat, then spoke. "We're almost up to the rotunda.

Yuri and Chionis just dusted a cretin newshunter at the crossover point. Is it all clear there?"

Her com-jewel earrings fed back her cousin's basso voice. "Right now it is. But you'd better hurry," Morgan warned. "The enemy is getting trickier. You've got two minutes. Hear me, partner?"

"We'll make it."

The executive elevators moved even faster than the service cabs, and Brenna was gulping frantically by the time they reached the top. The capital city lay below them, level upon level burrowed into the Martian bedrock, drawing water from wells drilled far into the crust or brought in from the asteroids. This was Mars Colony's highest inhabited point.

Brenna led the way through the life-support and food-supply tunnels. Robot waiters conveyed empty trays and drinking glasses in one direction and moved fresh snacks and full bottles toward the rotunda. The tunnels were cluttered and noisy, but there were no newshunters here, nor were any likely to be. This was *not* the V.I.P. entrance! Derek hurried in Brenna's wake. He spoke into his collar insignia com button, a stylish masculine version of the com-jewels Brenna wore. "Shelley? Chionis gave me the update. Liftoff at 0600. Got it. I should have recuperated from this damned soiree by then. Affirmative and underline."

Using the small personal communicators was a gamble when they were this close to the newshunter networks. But the devices were shielded. Even though this event would draw gossip collectors from the Kirkwood Asteroid Satellites and elsewhere, some newshunters using super scanners, Brenna thought it would be too late for anyone to intercept them. The gauntlet was nearly run. There was only one more identity plate between the two pilots and the rotunda.

Derek opened the door, pressing his palm against the screen. He still held his top-security clearance, a rating he had had since he joined Space Fleet—and while he had been part of Breakthrough Unlimited. The computers recognized him at once, permitting him and Brenna to pass through.

As the doors whispered shut, Brenna blinked owlishly. They had stepped from brightly lit service tunnels into a dim, plushly carpeted hall. Her eyes were still adapting to the sudden change when Morgan loped down the corridor

31

from the rotunda. He greeted them enthusiastically, sweeping an arm around Brenna's waist and lifting her into a bearhug while he pummeled Derek with his free hand.

"Fun and for-ni-ca-tion!" Morgan said with a laugh, imitating the most popular current vid entertainer. "I knew you'd be late. Knew it when you set up this romantic getaway. I trust you enjoyed yourselves out there in the badlands? You'd better have, after all I went through covering up for you . . ."

"See?" Derek said, spreading a hand to show his innocence. "Here's where I learned all those lewd and lascivious terms—from this redheaded monster."

Morgan scowled at the epithet. His hair was sandy blond, not red. And though he was a big man, he was no "monster." He had inherited his father's ruggedly attractive features. Morgan and Derek exchanged a few more friendly verbal jabs. Then Derek carried his and Brenna's travel kits to the nearby check-in alcove. Government employees and Saunder Enterprises Security maintained a storage service there for the convenience of the President's guests.

The moment Derek was out of hearing, Morgan dropped the vid-comedy cracks. "Are you all right?" he asked Brenna. He had set her back on her feet, and began gently rubbing the nape of her neck. Brenna knew he could feel the tension knotting her muscles.

"Derek's leaving," she blurted. "That's what this little tryst was all about. Damn him. He waited until yesterday to tell me. Morgan, the Hiber-Ship's actually going to go. They're launching next March. And Derek . . ."

"I know." Brenna gazed up into her cousin's gray eyes. Morgan's sympathy and strength enveloped her. "I found out a couple of days ago, while you were gone. I'm sorry. We knew they meant business, Brenna. There's a way to stop them, though."

This was the private side of Morgan, the side the public rarely saw. Not the playboy, the wealthy scion of the Saunder-McKelvey clan. Morgan Saunder McKelvey, ace test pilot, co-owner of Breakthrough Unlimited, capable businessman, an expert at reading Brenna's anguish as well as her joys.

The worries and fears were there, buzzing in the back of Brenna's mind. But now another element shoved

32

at them. New confidence. Morgan, reminding her of what would happen when they succeeded.

"Prototype II," Brenna whispered. Derek was chatting with some of the check-in employees, and she seized the opportunity, conspiring with Morgan. "We'll break the light-speed barrier."

Morgan's smile lit up the dim hall. "You and me, partner. Eight more days. And then we've got manned FTL flight. Hiber-Ship will be obsolete. They can convert her into a satellite and leave her in solar orbit. Keep remembering that, Brenna."

He shared her doubts. His parents had died in Prototype I. But Morgan wasn't going to let her drift off the track. They had each other. They *had* to win. There was no other possibility. Morgan wouldn't allow it!

"Derek will . . ." Brenna didn't put the wish into words, afraid she might jinx it.

Derek will come home then. To us. To me. His pride will be hurt. He backed the wrong spaceflight program. But that won't matter. We'll be together again.

And Breakthrough Unlimited will start a new era for mankind—opening the way to the stars.

CHAPTER THREE

✖✖✖✖✖✖✖✖

Reunion

BRENNA hugged Morgan, her gratitude pouring out into physical expression. "Thanks," she murmured. "God, but I needed help."

"So did I," Morgan said. Brenna blinked, taken aback, as Morgan went on. "It's not easy, carrying the whole load for both of us. Never fear. The sum is greater than the parts, as Dad used to say . . ."

It wasn't exactly an accusation, but it put everything in perspective for Brenna. She felt as if she had been given a new spine and looked back on her self-pity with embarrassment.

They *did* help each other. Morgan put matters into focus, telling her to keep her eye on the target. That wasn't easy to do when Derek was around, and especially when he was dropping news like *that* on her.

On course again. The problems under control. They were going to pull off a successful test. Okay!

Morgan saw Derek walking toward them and obligingly adopted his former, joking stance. He posed, arms akimbo, inviting attack. Derek threw a mock punch at the taller man's midriff. Then they wrist-wrestled for a second, laughing. The scene was a replay of a thousand earlier roughhouses. The men were too mature to push the routine past momentary horseplay now, yet the scuffle took Brenna's thoughts back fifteen years—Derek and Morgan brawling like lion cubs, and she egging them on, or as often as not diving into the scramble herself. The space brats. Prankish juvenile conspirators, sometimes outwitting the adults in their lives, sometimes ganging up to tweak Stuart Saunder's nose. Brenna's older cousin had always tried to join in their games—and dominate them. But Stuart had never succeeded. She, Morgan, and Derek had been like siblings united against the universe, pals and loving competitors.

It was no longer a game, though. The race was serious, and they were all trying to win it. The prize would be the greatest one in human history.

Not even Derek's defection to Hiber-Ship Corporation had lessened the affection between him and Morgan. They jostled one another boisterously and then abandoned the make-believe contest, slapping each other on the back. Morgan flung his long arms around his friend and Brenna. "Enough of this time-wasting." He pushed them ahead of him, up the ramp leading to the rotunda. They went along without any real struggle as he chanted, "March! March! Perform! Perform!"

"His brain's fused a circuit," Brenna said with a chuckle.

"Undoubtedly," Derek agreed. "Either that or it's rampant hormones out of control. I told him all that womanizing would catch up with him . . ."

"Insults won't save you," Morgan said.

Brenna and Derek took turns teasing him. "Didn't he ask you for an intro to that cute little sergeant dispatcher on the Mars-Luna shuttle?" Brenna inquired, shamming a frown.

"Right. He's insatiable," Derek replied, keeping the gibe going. "We saw you on the vid, Morgan, half buried in beautiful women. How do you keep track of them all? Jutta Lefferts, Pauline Bigalow, Cecily What's-her-name . . ."

"Newkirk," Brenna supplied. She simpered, mimicking the Commissioner of Martian Agriculture. "Cecily's a bit overage for you, isn't she, Morgan? Oh, well. Give the old girl a thrill . . ."

As they mounted the ramp, the dim hallway lighting gradually was replaced by ever-brighter panels. The shift gave Brenna plenty of time to get ready for the full daylight filling the bubble-domed rotunda at the end of the incline.

"He's got to be taking eroticism enhancers," Derek was saying. "That's the only way he could possibly cope with so many demands on his virility."

That, too, was an old byplay between the men. Morgan reacted with a disdainful sneer. "I don't need those. Nothing impure is going to interfere with my natural gifts, dust-brain. You're thinking about Stuart, not *this* prime specimen."

"The man with something for every woman, correct? What about Chin Jui-Sao? We haven't noticed you tumbling for her."

Morgan's face twisted with outrage. "Quol-Bez's translator? You're kidding. She's off-limits."

"You got along okay with the last translator they assigned to the Vahnaj Ambassador," Brenna reminded him. "Maybe that's why they replaced her. You distracted her so much she couldn't keep her mind on her job."

A trifle primly, Morgan responded. "I don't think it's politic to speculate about Sao's private life. For all we know, she and Quol-Bez have a thing going."

Derek stared in disbelief. "Her gray-skinned boss? Come on! There are limits to interstellar amity."

"And how," Brenna muttered. "I like Quol-Bez, but he gives me the shivers."

"That's atavism," Derek said, quoting from the diplomatic information tapes they had all read. "Instinctual. Probably caused by different evolutionary patterns. After all, Quol-Bez's species *did* evolve light-years away from Earth. Everyone gets the shivers around him now and then.

35

He does around us, too. Mere side effect. But it may mean Sao's wasting her time if she's got hormones for him."

"Tell her that, why don't you?" Morgan suggested archly as they emerged into the rotunda. "And now you're going to pay for this ribbing session, my friends."

The instant they came into view, people flocked around them, forming reception lines. The cordon of enforcement troops and security guards kept the gypsy newshunters away from the party. But there were a lot of petty officials and minor guests who were eager to meet the famous young couple. Morgan put himself on the inside of the human sandwich, forcing Brenna and Derek to shake the outstretched hands and reply to the effusive welcomes. He moved at a sadistic snail's pace, working his way across the enormous room.

"Captain Whitcomb! We met at the Polar Territorial Ratification dinner last year. Surely you remember . . ."

"So delightful to see you, Brenna, my dear. What a wonderful jumper! It must be straight from Earth's best designer . . . !"

"Vice Premier On Thuong De wanted me to give you his regards . . ."

"Do speak to your father, won't you? I have this business proposition for Saunder Enterprises to consider . . ."

Brenna shook hands until her fingers started to cramp. Her face froze in an inane smile. Morgan called this stroking-the-sycophants, a duty Saunders were expected to endure. The only family member who enjoyed these sessions was Aunt Carissa—not a model Brenna wanted to emulate, even to get free publicity for Breakthrough Unlimited!

Phrases and etiquette and rituals developed on another planet, centuries earlier. Words spoken at the courts of kings and prime ministers and presidents of Earth. Those words had probably held as little sincerity as most of these did. None of the earlier rituals could have taken place in a more splendid setting, though. Pavonis City's capitol rotunda perched on a saddle ridge in the Tharsis Mountains. The dome crowned the hemispheric and diplomatic center of Mars. From this lofty vantage point, sightseers could peer down at the outlying domed farms and the mining communities on the lower slopes. To the east, the Valles Marineris rift was faintly visible behind a late afternoon dust cloud. On either side of the rotunda two volcanic peaks loomed, Pavonis Mons to the south and Ascraeus to the north. In the northwest, the rim of Nix Olympus filled the dark sky. That incredible crater was larger in area than many of Earth's nations and five times taller than Earth's highest mountain. It was a far more appropriate home for mythological gods than its puny Terran namesake had ever been. Instead, Nix Olympus was dotted with scientific observation posts and exploratory mining digs.

The last time Brenna had been in this rotunda, the Legislature was in session. Now the voting desks and computers had been removed to make way for dozens of entertainment islands containing comfortable seats, refreshment bars, and mini-arenas reserved for dancing and theatricals. Service robots roamed about, dispensing food and liquids. Music and color played over the scene. Audio balance systems sorted out hundreds of conversations, dampening the confusion. Thin Martian sunlight streamed in the life-support dome. The light reflected off expensive clothes, gilt-powdered hair, sequin-accented faces, and fortunes in synthetic gems. These people, who normally wore plain jumpers or pants and tunics and who worked hard to turn a barren world into a habitable one, had dressed in their gaudiest for the occasion.

Morgan finally took pity and led Brenna and Derek toward the President's entertainment island. Several quiet men and women followed them at a discreet distance, as they had ever since Brenna and Derek had entered the rotunda. The shadows, Saunder Enterprises' private police —trying to blend in with the crowd. SE Security was always around wherever a Saunder or a McKelvey went, unless the family member made a special effort to ditch them, as Brenna had this past week. Now that she was back in Pavonis City, the SE guards resumed their duties. Brenna was their charge, whether she wanted to be or not. So was Morgan.

The President's entertainment island was in the center of the rotunda. A light curtain, as well as a detachment of Martian civil enforcement troops, marked off that island from the others. The transparent, glowing blue barricade was an audio baffle, shutting out excess noises. But it also acted as an effective wall to keep out lesser society. When Brenna and the two men passed through the light curtain, those hangers-on stayed outside, gazing wistfully at the

37

high rankers beyond the line. The Saunder Enterprises guards took up positions with the enforcement troopers, helping maintain the President's elite sanctuary.

Brenna had expected to see her parents or President Grieske first, but someone else was waiting to greet her. Stuart Saunder and his retinue of toadies stood directly in Brenna's path. He had obviously seen her and Morgan and Derek approaching the island. Brenna's older cousin lifted his glass. "Ah! There you are. I've been waiting to see your shining faces for days."

"And been drinking the whole time, too, no doubt," Brenna replied sweetly. She started to move by him, but Stuart caught her arm, his fingers digging in. Usually, she ignored his boorish behavior. This time she stiffened and wrenched free in one swift motion, her hand coming up for a chopping blow of retaliation. It wasn't a bluff, and Stuart knew it. His bony, pasty-white face sagged with astonishment. He backed away from Brenna hastily. His toadies were at a loss. They were hired to keep Stuart out of fracases or placate the law if he insisted on causing trouble. Their orders didn't cover this situation—Stuart menaced by another Saunder.

He drained the glass he was clutching. Liquor helped him regain his composure. "Really! How crude, Brenna, my dear."

"Be grateful it wasn't me you tried to push," Morgan said, very amused. "Brenna's too gentle."

Stuart darted a wary glance at his muscular cousin, and his unhealthy pallor turned still whiter. He then concentrated his irritation on Derek, seeking revenge. "I'm surprised, Derek. I thought you were one of those he-man, back-to-nature lunatics—scratching out civilization on a godforsaken rock. Why didn't you leap to defend her wounded honor, if I'm such an offense to good manners?"

"Oh, you are," Derek said blandly. "But she hardly needs my help to deal with someone of your caliber." His handsome face set with icy contempt, and Morgan threw him a thumbs-up in appreciation of the retort.

Stuart Saunder was six years older than Brenna and Morgan, but dissipated living, especially illicit chemical stimulants, had aged him severely. He appeared at least twenty years their senior. His once-likable features were roughening and turning ugly. Not all of that was due to

drugs and exotic sex practices. Much was caused by a rotten personal attitude, mirrored in Stuart's haunted eyes.
"What a brave bunch you are. Favorites of the media,
aren't you?" He raised his empty glass in a mocking toast.
"We who are about to watch you kill yourselves or freeze
yourselves salute you, and wish you bon voyage—to wherever it is you think you're going."

For a split second, all Brenna's dread rose to the surface of her mind once more. No, she *wasn't* going to let
Stuart know he had hurt her and stirred up fresh anguish!
She laughed at him, and Stuart rocked back on his heels
unsteadily, surprised by her response. "Go sober up," Brenna said in a condescending tone. "You're pitiful. Can't your
keepers manage you at least for Colony Days?"

"At least I know enough to—" Stuart broke off abruptly,
seeing Brenna's mother coming toward them.

"Didn't I tell you to dry up and cool off?" Dian Foix
Saunder scolded her nephew from Earth. She might have
been addressing a ten-year-old, one she was putting up with
solely for the sake of family harmony. Stuart subsided into
a pout, demanding a refill from one of his toadies' bottles.
He contented himself with sour mutterings as Dian turned
to her daughter and Derek. " 'Bout time you got here.
You're not as late as I figured you'd be. Huh! It's okay,
Derek. I know this hiding-out nonsense wasn't your idea.
Tryin' to get hold of you was impossible!"

"Now, now, Aunt Di," Morgan said soothingly. "I told
you, it was a lovers' secret." Derek jabbed an elbow in his
ribs, and Morgan grunted hammily. Then he straightened
up. "Uh-oh! Get your salutes ready, kids. Here comes
Fred."

Mars' President Fred Grieske honored the new arrivals
by greeting them personally. "So happy you could come,
children . . ." Brenna dutifully pecked his cheek, and Derek
shook the portly man's hand. "We'd hoped you could join
us for Colony Days. This is the big ceremony, too! We see
so little of you these times. Always rushing off somewhere!
This younger generation! Come along and say hello to
everyone."

To Brenna's relief, Stuart didn't include himself in that
invitation. One of the guests, an ambitious actress, had
attached herself to Stuart, distracting him from the rest of
the party. He stayed with her while Grieske escorted the

39

others toward the chairs and tiers of couches near the holo-mode theater.

Meeting these guests was pleasantly low-key, not the favor-seeking reception line Brenna had suffered through in the outer rotunda. She was on a first-name basis with many of those in the President's group, had known a lot of them since she was a little girl. Brenna moved easily among them, asking about matters that concerned them, touching hands, smiling, beginning to relax.

Todd Saunder was in a political discussion with Protectors of Earth Chairman Hong Ling-Kuang and Terran Worlds Councilman Ames. Those power competitors were doing some subtle jabbing and one-upping, with Brenna's father trying to act as the peacemaker. When Dian caught his eye, he hurriedly excused himself and rushed to embrace Brenna. "You look great, kitten! Doing okay? Derek, it's good to see you, son. To tell you the truth, I was beginning to worry you wouldn't make it here. Seems like forever since we last got together." Brenna was surprised to see that her father's eyes were misty with sentiment.

"Three months; long enough," Dian said. She winked at Brenna. "That *was* a long inspection tour your dad and I took. Maybe because we were inspectin' the wrong things." Todd's blush told his wife to save that for later. He reminded Brenna of herself, warning Derek to cut out the lewd and lascivious remarks.

Friends and acquaintances crowded around them, chatting, exchanging news. There was a reasonable mix of older and younger generations, but this was the be-nice-to-one's-elders stage of the gala. Junior diplomatic aides and promising new legislators and government personnel—most of them Brenna's age—listened politely to President Grieske, Todd and Dian Saunder, Councilman Ames, and the other older attendees. Brenna had expected a heavy dose of remember-when, and she got it. This was one of the reasons she had begged off going to the whole ten days' worth of Colony Days celebrations. The Breakthrough Unlimited team had agreed wholeheartedly, setting up a schedule so that no one had to put up with more than twenty-four hours of this type of socializing.

Surreptitiously, while the conversations buzzed around her, Brenna studied her parents. She wasn't sure what she was looking for. Three months wasn't forever, true, but that had indeed been a long inspection tour Todd and Dian had undertaken, and they weren't kids any more. Brenna searched anxiously for signs of strain or friction, finding none. Her parents had never been estranged. Yet there *had* been times, through the years, when their individual careers took them off on very different tracks, separating them for long periods. Dr. Dian Foix was an eminent scholar, sought after by the diplomats concerned about Earth's interstellar relations with the Vahnaj planets. Brenna's mother was also deeply involved with a medical foundation, which took up a lot of her leisure. Todd Saunder's ComLink network would run itself, but he was afraid of going stale and kept poking his nose into the business he had built from nothing. Judging by Dian's crack, though, that tour of the network's satellites had been more of a second honeymoon than a business trip. Well, they certainly deserved it.

Unlike Brenna's cousin Stuart, Todd and Dian appeared to be turning the clock back. Brenna's parents looked the way people in their mid-forties used to look, at the turn of the Twenty-first Century. That was typical, though, these days, for people who were in their sixties. Humanity was learning to take its greatly lengthened life span for granted.

A few laugh lines were in evidence around Dian's dark eyes. But her velvety brown skin was almost as firm as Brenna's lighter colored one. There was no gray yet in her short-cropped Negroid hair. Her expression was as pert as always; her figure was still terrific, too. Brenna hoped she would weather the years half as well.

Todd was putting on a little weight, looking the stereotype of the successful corporation executive, which he was. Recent cosmetic surgery had pared his jowls, the only thing he had been vain about. He had also quit dyeing those dramatic white streaks in his brown hair. That hadn't been vanity, however. He had been trying to cover up a telltale genetic trait he had inherited from his mother, Jael Hartman Saunder.

Jael. The family skeleton who wouldn't stay in the closet. Some people cursed her name, even in these modern times. Others were rehashing her deeds and defending her, saying history had judged her too harshly. A generation ago Jael Saunder had nearly destroyed Earth. Her son Todd had made the first contact with an intelligent extraterrestrial

41

species—the Vahnaj. And Jael's xenophobia had combined with political ambition for her older son and triggered a civil war between Earth and Goddard Colony. In addition, she had killed thousands of people entrusted to Saunder Enterprises' cryogenic facility at Earth's South Pole. It had taken a long time for the surviving family members to live down that scandal. Todd Saunder had emerged from the debacle as a hero. His brother, Patrick, had martyred himself, stopping Jael's treachery, and that had helped his widow and posthumous son regain the trust of the populace. Yet there had been strong movements against the Saunder family's quasi-nation, cries that the huge financial empire had to be broken up. Only Jael's daughter, Mariette Saunder, who had been a major supporter of the Goddard space station, had come out of the mess fairly whole. It was ancient history to Brenna, but not to her parents and Stuart's mother. When Brenna had been a child, her father refused to speak about Jael Hartman Saunder. She had heard about his dead brother and about the other victims of her grandmother's ambition and lust for power, but very little about her infamous, legendary ancestor. Now, after thirty-four years, Todd Saunder was finally letting those white streaks show in his hair. That striking effect had been Jael Saunder's visual trademark, as Brenna had seen in numerous three-dimensional images. The trademark had been missing from the family since Jael's death, but her son was reinstating it. Perhaps time had enhanced memories of Jael Saunder's better qualities and buried the tragedies caused by her enormous pride.

Derek had been paying his respects to the Vahnaj Ambassador when several of Hiber-Ship Corporation's political allies closed in on the pilot. They were courteous about it, but they soon commandeered Derek and led him off to meet some of their friends. The group put their heads together, discussing business.

Dian watched this and glowered. "You'd better not try that, girl."

Brenna winced. "Dian, I'm not a child. And of course I wouldn't do that. Morgan and I don't conduct business during a gala. But Derek has to jump. The military mind. He never got over the regulations they drilled into him when he was in Space Fleet."

"Rude," Dian muttered, still fuming over Derek's cronies.

"Your co-pilots Yuri and Hector Obregón and Tumaini Beno are all ex-Space Fleet, just like Derek. But *they* didn't huddle in corners and rehash battle maneuvers."

Brenna gave up. "Probably not. But we're Breakthrough Unlimited and Derek's part of Hiber-Ship Corporation. Listen, Dian, I'm going over and say hello to Quol-Bez and Sao."

The alien Ambassador and his human liaison-translator, Chin Jui-Sao, had been talking softly in Vahnaj when Brenna neared them. They politely stopped and turned to face her. Quol-Bez extended a three-fingered hand, swirling his silvery floor-length tunic and loose vest as he did so. Brenna took his hand and peered up into his gray face. She had to crane her neck to look at him, even though she was of greater than average height. Quol-Bez was ten centimeters taller than Morgan, who was a big man. Chin Jui-Sao wasn't right at the Ambassador's elbow, as she often was during his discussions with other diplomats. After all, Brenna was a *Saunder*. Since Todd Saunder and Dian had first established communications with the Vahnaj planets, the alien species regarded the name "Saunder" as a talisman—their main link with *Homo sapiens*. Gradually, other humans had entered that network through the years. But the Vahnaj continued to honor Todd Saunder, as did humanity. When the Vahnaj had finally sent a representative to serve as Ambassador in that backwater Solar System where Todd Saunder lived, Quol-Bez had arrived with a pre-programmed attitude that he was a "kin-friend" to everyone in Todd's family.

"I give you hello, Brenna. I hope you are in good health." Quol-Bez went through the polite forms, since this was a state occasion. His voice was raspy and high-pitched, incongruous, issuing from that gangling, Lutrinoid body. The Vahnaj had evolved from an otterlike species, as *Homo sapiens* had evolved from the primates.

"Yes, thank you, Quol-Bez. I am well," Brenna said, abiding by the same courteous formula. "I return your hello, with good wishes. *Ni haoma*, Chin Jui-Sao?" In the six months Sao had been assigned as Quol-Bez's translator, Brenna hadn't come to know her intimately. But she traded a few Pinyin phrases when they met, and they were cordial with each other.

"Most well, Brenna Foix Saunder. It is gracious of you

to inquire. We, the Ambassador and I, had been speaking of you and Morgan Saunder McKelvey just moments ago," Sao said breathlessly. She sounded as if she had rehearsed that statement. "Many of the guests had noted your absence from the gala. They were concerned for you."

Brenna was puzzled. "I'm sorry to hear that. Why on Earth . . . why would they be concerned? And what about Morgan? He's been here most of the week."

Quol-Bez's broad head waggled atop his snaky neck. That made his sideburns flutter. Six years hadn't lessened his fascination for Earthmen. Most styles came and departed, but "Quol-Bez fashion" lingered. A lot of Terran males affected long tunics and had grown sideburns in imitation of the Vahnaj Ambassador. Human facial hair, though, lacked the silky allure of Quol-Bez's adornment. For one thing, few humans could make their sideburns fluff up and flatten to suit their mood. Right now, Quol-Bez's earlocks were flattened, indicating tension. "Brenna, Chin Jui-Sao speaks ac-cu-rate-ly. Your fellow beings are worried." His labored pronunciation was more evidence of his underlying edginess. Quol-Bez spoke many Terran languages well. Chin Jui-Sao's function was as an interpreter of customs and idiomatic expressions, not as a full-time translator. When the Vahnaj lapsed into these slow speech patterns, it wasn't because he didn't know his hosts' tongue. According to Brenna's father, Quol-Bez sometimes used the tactic as a stalling method during diplomatic sessions. But that didn't seem to be the case at present. "You must ap-pre-ci-ate. You and Morgan are risk tak-ers. The method of tra-vel you pro-pose is very new. There are many who con-sider this . . . urr . . . *nesanle* . . ."

Brenna eyed him with suspicion. Her mother was a linguist, the ultimate human expert on the Vahnaj language, and Brenna had picked up quite a bit of Vahnaj without much effort. She could trill her "r's" and put a rising tone on her "n's" and speak nasally, just as Quol-Bez was doing. The shield of an alien language was no good between Quol-Bez and a Saunder.

"Dangerous," Sao supplied, relieving her employer of an embarrassing problem. Chin Jui-Sao was one of Dian's star pupils. But she sounded like a malfunctioning robot, all inflection wiped out of her voice.

"Dangerous. Yes. Agreed," Quol-Bez said. The Ambassador's lips pulled back, revealing small, pointed teeth. Humans had learned that about the Vahnaj years ago, from the Vahnaj robot messenger Todd Saunder had contacted: The Vahnaj, like many human cultures, showed friendliness with a smile. The Ambassador *was* friendly, but his teeth were alarmingly sharp. So were his comments, despite the smoke screen.

"You and Morgan are risk takers . . ."

"He means, Cuz, that you shouldn't pour yourself into that shiny steel bomb you and Morg call a graviton spin resonance faster-than-light ship," a hateful voice cut in. Stuart, the actress hanging on his arm, had butted in without an apology. He was also, to Brenna's surprise, acting a lot more sober than he had been.

"I know what Quol-Bez meant, Stuart," Brenna said, turning her back on him. "Ambassador, most humans don't travel as much as Morgan and I do, admittedly. But they do take frequent interplanetary space trips, from Earth to Mars or the satellites. Why, even Stuart manages to drag himself out of his Caribbean hole now and then, simply to honor Mars Colony Days. That's so arrogantly noble of you, Stuart. But I refuse to applaud," Brenna finished, glancing over her shoulder and dimpling at him.

Stuart acknowledged the hit with a shrug. He wasn't here by choice. His mother had pressured him into being her stand-in at the celebration. Both Stuart and Carissa Saunder hated space travel with a passion. Brenna wondered what form of blackmail Carissa had applied to force her rebellious son to cooperate *this* time. Some of the past methods had been nasty, on the edge of illegal. Stuart was obviously going through hell. Mars was a frontier world. There were no decadence-palaces here, few sex companions for hire, not many EEG distorters, or the kinds of drugs Stuart depended on. If he hadn't brought his toys with him, he was going to be in exceedingly poor shape when he returned to Earth. The actress who had leeched onto him would be, too, probably!

Brenna pretended Stuart wasn't there and spoke to the Ambassador. "Of course graviton spin resonance is regarded as a theory, and a dangerous one, by a lot of people. But Breakthrough Unlimited has run numerous unmanned tests, quite successful ones. Hiber-Ship Corporation, too, is taking risks. They've perfected cryogenic stasis, working from my grandfather's original patents. But there *were* failures of the cryogenics system in my parents' time. All the successful revivals since then haven't entirely convinced some people, you know. As far as they're concerned, Hiber-Ship is just as much a gamble as faster-than-light experimentation."

"But with bigger political guns backing Hiber-Ship," Stuart pointed out. Now and then he came up with an astute comment, touching a nerve. This was one of those times.

"We don't *need* politics," Brenna said huffily. "Breakthrough Unlimited is independent. It's a Saunder Enterprises division, entirely family-owned—"

"You need permission from Terran Worlds Council and Space Fleet to run your tests in that section of space you're using," Stuart said, stepping on the heels of her words. He was making her squirm, but there was something deeper and very unpleasant in his intent. Brenna couldn't figure out what it was, and wasn't sure she wanted to.

"We have that franchise, and we've run all the preliminary tests. This talk of danger is exaggerated."

Chin Jui-Sao whispered and Quol-Bez cocked his head, bending down to hear the Chinese woman. His large black eyes glistened behind protective contact lenses. The Vahnaj home star emitted less ultraviolet than Earth's Sun. Even at Mars' orbit, Quol-Bez needed shielding to guard his vision. That veneer of human manners and boyish, accented human speech never completely hid his origins. Humans copied his clothes and hair and powdered their faces to a gray pallor in flattering imitation of the alien. But they remained human. And he was Vahnaj. Brenna shivered involuntarily. Derek called that atavism and half-buried instinct. It happened, unpredictably. Brenna used to be apologetic about the reaction. She wasn't any more. Most humans shivered occasionally when they were in Quol-Bez's presence. What was more interesting was the fact that he shivered, too, just as instinctually troubled by their beings as they were by his. What set off that shudder? Electromagnetic forces? Some forgotten scent ability in both species? Scientists speculated but hadn't come up with definitive answers. It remained one more intriguing mystery in this on-going adventure of cross-species discovery.

Quol-Bez nodded to whatever Chin Jui-Sao had told

him, then straightened to his impressive height. "You re-a-lize that your kin-parents are most dis-turbed about this ex-per-i-ment. I be-lieve Todd should be helped, if this is not against custom . . ."

Stuart was smirking. Brenna forcibly stopped herself from hitting him. He was bad enough. Worse was Quol-Bez's presuming on his cross-species friendship with Todd Saunder and dropping none-too-subtle hints to Todd's daughter. That was partially Todd's fault, and Dian's. They knew Brenna and Morgan weren't children and were fully responsible for their own lives. Yet they tended to fuss and worry and nag. Maybe one's elders were bound to do that. It must have happened throughout history, the older generation constantly cautioning the younger: "Don't wander too far from the cave . . . don't go sailing across the ocean to unknown lands . . . don't go experimenting with newfangled faster-than-light spaceships . . ."

Brenna could almost hear her father confiding to Quol-Bez: "The Vahnaj have been star-traveling for a long time, my friend, but it's terrifyingly new for us. Progress, sure. We've got to have that. But kids always want to rush in too fast. I'd be worried no matter who was riding those FTL ships. This is my little girl, though, and my nephew. I love them both, and I'm worried sick about them. I wish they'd let someone else try it. They're so damned stubborn. If only I knew how to talk them out of it. Lord knows I've tried!"

She couldn't hear Quol-Bez's response, in her imagina-tion. Most likely the Ambassador had reassured his friend, as elders did when the "kids" were taking foolish chances.

"Any interplanetary—or interstellar—travel can be risky," Brenna said. "It's all a matter of perspective as to *how* dangerous it is."

"Per-spec-tive! This is quite . . . urr . . . per-cep-tive of you!" A peculiar bubbling growl rattled behind Quol-Bez's pointed teeth. His attempt to make a pun in an alien tongue amused him inordinately. "And your fellow beings have a limited per-cep-tion and per-spec-tive, mmm?" The Vahnaj grew solemn. "But per-haps there is reason for worry, never-the-less?"

Old suspicions filled Brenna's thoughts. *Who* was worried? Just maybe it was the Vahnaj, Quol-Bez's government back there on his home worlds, forty or more light-years from Earth. Quol-Bez was a diplomat, their mouth-piece, and he was obligated to follow the party line, as it were. Friend or not, he might be assigned to look out, first, for his own species' interests. And what were they? What if one item was a monopoly on faster-than-light travel and contact with a backward species like *Homo sapiens?* That contact was strictly one-way, at present. One Vahnaj Ambassador sent to Earth. A trade agreement, which the humans couldn't benefit from yet. No exchange Ambassador to Vahnaj yet, either, because humanity wasn't *capable* of sending a representative to the stars within that human's useful lifetime. If they used cryogenic stasis —as Hiber-Ship Corporation planned to do—the present governments of Earth and Mars might be completely changed by the time the human Ambassador arrived in the Vahnaj stellar empire. In seventy-five years of the Twenty-first Century, whole nations had been swept away, man-made and natural disasters had rearranged the face of old Earth, and entire human colonies had sprung into being on Mars and in space. Even if that hypothetical human ambassador made the journey, it could be a futile one.

But . . . if Breakthrough Unlimited achieved FTL, the Vahnaj star systems were a mere step away from the Sun. And so was free trade with other species out there in the galaxy. The Earth-Vahnaj treaty the Terran Worlds Council had worked out specified there would, if possible, be trade between their two peoples someday. What if, for undisclosed reasons, the Vahnaj wanted to control and guide that future trade to suit themselves, keep it an exclusive deal?

Brenna had weighed these possibilities a thousand times in the past. Now her suspicions coalesced, stimulated by the upcoming FTL test. Morgan would put Prototype II through its paces. And then . . .

Quol-Bez would have to contact his government for new instructions! Because humanity would no longer be controllable. It would be free to roam the stars at will, an equal of the Vahnaj and the other intelligent beings out there!

The Ambassador was studying her. So was Stuart, his aging features, a parody of his dead father's face, taut with curiosity. It occurred to Brenna that Stuart might be trying to read her mind. She almost laughed, then sobered. Perhaps Quol-Bez *could* do just that. No one knew. The Vahnaj Ambassador doled out information about his species stingily, as if he might be penalized for revealing too much to *Homo sapiens*.

Brenna tried to put a lid on her thoughts. Let the Vahnaj read her, if he could! It would give Quol-Bez a chance to prepare for the big change in diplomatic relations between their two species. Poor Ambassador Quol-Bez! Soon, no more special status. Once Breakthrough Unlimited established interstellar travel on a regular basis, there would be *many* Vahnaj visiting Earth. The alien species would become commonplace. More importantly, humans would become commonplace on the Vahnaj worlds, too.

"My parents worry needlessly," Brenna said. "There's nothing to—"

A musical tone interrupted her. Cue lights flashed in the holo-mode theaters in the center of each entertainment island. Incoming messages. Terran Worlds Council's coordination of calendars and clocks throughout the Solar System paid off to fit Colony Days. The computers had figured out an optimum time, when Mars would be in the best position to receive congratulatory messages from Earth's most populous and powerful areas, as well as from other colonies. The President's gala had been scheduled accordingly. The festival had been underway for days, would continue for days to come. But this was the highlight of the anniversary, the big show.

Quol-Bez bowed, his skinny fingers brushing Brenna's. "We must go to our seats. But I hope we may speak further, after the messages have been received."

What did he want to speak about? More hinting that she and Morgan ought not to fly test ships that might break the light-speed barrier? Digging to find out how close the humans were to achieving FTL spaceflight? But the Ambassador would know that, from his contacts on the Terran Worlds Council and with Space Fleet. What was Quol-Bez up to? She would never find out if she didn't agree to that further discussion.

"I look forward to continuing our conversation, yes," Brenna said politely. Chin Jui-Sao's eyes narrowed. The translator was on guard, smelling a rat. Brenna nodded to her, very bland; butter wouldn't melt in her mouth.

President Grieske's aides were rounding up the guests, courteously herding them toward the holo-mode theater. They escorted Quol-Bez and the translator to seats of honor. Brenna would be sitting in the front row, too, in a ringside chair. The Saunders were V.I.P.s as much as the Ambassador and the Martian President. Brenna was glad to see, though, that some protocol expert had seated Stuart at the far end of the row, as far away from Brenna and Morgan and Brenna's parents as he could be and still be part of the President's elite section.

As she followed the usher and took her chair, Brenna mulled over her last exchange with Quol-Bez, nursing a wild hope. Further discussion. That could go two ways. Quol-Bez might be probing to see what she was up to and what she knew, but she could do the same thing. Just possibly, Quol-Bez might let something slip—a precious clue about the Vahnaj technique of faster-than-light space travel, for instance, some detail she and Morgan could add to the design of Prototype II and the fleet of starships that would come in its wake. Five unmanned vehicles equipped with graviton spin resonance drive had made a successful jump to FTL. But perhaps there was an even better method, one that was easier, less fuel-expensive.

And there was the communications lag. When Morgan pushed the Prototype through the barrier, he would lose contact with them. The Vahnaj had FTL radio, but humans didn't—yet—thanks to Brenna's father and his protective attitude toward the alien robot messenger. The messenger was sitting in Terran Worlds Council's HQ at Goddard Colony, tamperproof and beyond the reach of Breakthrough Unlimited. FTL radio—one more thing Breakthrough Unlimited was going to have to discover on its own, if the Vahnaj had their way.

All things in good time!

They *would* succeed. She had to hang onto that. Push the financial worries, the risks of failure, aside. Vahnaj superiority be damned! Colony Days was a showcase. But a much bigger one was coming up. Breakthrough Unlimited would shatter the old barriers—light-speed, and the wall of space that set the Vahnaj apart, and *Homo sapiens* out in a backwater of the galaxy.

CHAPTER FOUR

⊗⊗⊗⊗⊗⊗⊗⊗

Past Triumph and Grief

ROBOT servants wheeled along the tiers of seats, passing out fresh drinks and food to those who requested them. Lights dimmed slowly within the theaters on every entertainment island, blocking the late afternoon sunlight. Hidden mechanisms raised or lowered individual seats, staggering the rows so that shorter viewers could see easily over the taller spectators. The four transparent sides of the holo-mode cubes became opaque, setting the stage. Projections from other planets and colonies would be appearing within the frames.

Coming in late, Derek plopped down into the chair beside Brenna. "How were you able to tear yourself away from your old Space Fleet buddies?" Brenna asked sweetly. He rewarded her with a pained grimace. "Dian said you were rude, talking business during the gala."

"I know. She cornered me when I was on my way over here." Derek grinned like a naughty boy caught in mischief. "It wasn't exactly my idea. Hiber-Ship's sponsors expect me to cozy up to the big money." He felt a sudden chill in the air as Brenna reacted to that reminder of a future that would tear them apart from each other. Derek hurriedly covered his gaffe. "And what were *you* doing, might I ask? I saw you with Quol-Bez, and Stuart needling you. If you weren't digging at the Ambassador for FTL travel hints, I don't recognize the gambit . . ."

Brenna paid flattering attention to the empty holo-mode cube. "You don't recognize it," she said grumpily.

"And you lie beautifully, my love. Unconvincingly, but beautifully."

An overture began and Brenna gratefully put a finger to her lips, shushing him. In the rotunda, and in other community nerve centers all over Mars, the people waited. Then, within the darkened holo-mode theater cube in front

51

of Brenna, five figures seemed to appear. One moment the interior was blank. In the next instant, lifelike images stood there. They moved and breathed and looked as if they could step right out of the cube and sit among the audience. Yet each of these five was on Earth. Each was sitting in a separate studio, surrounded by five separate broadcast crews. The magic of Saunder Enterprises' ComLink—and that of a few friendly competitors like Nakamura and Associates' TeleCom—had brought these people together and beamed their images across space to the neighboring world.

Spectators around the four sides of the holo-mode saw those images facing their way. Four sets of the same illusions. There was no shadow or overlap. Brenna couldn't see the audience on the opposite side of the theater, nor could she see those other three simultaneous projections. The holo-mode was a triumph of the art, an art developed by a grandfather Brenna had never known, "the inventive genius," as the media called him, Ward Saunder.

A professional vidcaster's voice-over started the program. "Citizens of Mars and the outer colonies and the Venusian satellites, this signal is coming to you by courtesy of SE ComLink and TeleCom. Today we are proud to present a special communication in honor of Mars Colony Days. A distinguished delegation of Earth's leaders is on hand here to convey the good wishes of all humanity to the pioneers of the fourth planet. We will hear first from . . ."

Introductions flowed, all the pat phrases. The dignitaries waiting to step into the spotlight looked as if they were standing side by side. In actuality they were as far from each other as Pavonis City was from Syrtis Major. The leaders bowed individually as the announcer read off their names. These particular people had been selected by their fellow politicians to speak for Earth on this broadcast. Not everyone *could* speak. There simply wouldn't be enough time. Too many chiefs of Earth governments, like politicians everywhere, tended to use an opportunity like this to push their pet projects. As a result, they had chosen a few of the most popular and least controversial figures from among their ranks. Each of these leaders was retired from politics or about to retire. They would be safe, have no axes to grind, the others hoped.

Jaco Dacosta of the Brazilian and Middle Atlantic Nations. Prime Minister Hidari of the Trans-Pacific Alliance. Premier Sigrid Rasmussen of the Democracies of Northern Europe. Harith Kiamil of the African tribes making up the Affiliation of the Rift countries. And President Emeritus of Protectors of Earth's Supreme Assembly, Carissa Duryea Saunder, Todd Saunder's sister-in-law and Brenna's aunt.

The four less important dignitaries looked expectantly at Carissa in a masterpiece of stage management. They were looking at cue spots, not at her. The effect, though, was respectful deference to the group's most honored member.

Carissa took a half-step forward and spoke. "President Grieske, members of the Governing Body, and all the brave citizens of Mars—on behalf of the peoples of Earth, we send you congratulations on this thirtieth anniversary of Colony Day. The commemoration of that pioneer ship's initial touchdown, April 20, 2045, will live forever in the annals of human history . . ."

Brenna was glad the semi-darkness surrounding the theater hid her expression from the other spectators. Derek picked up her emotions, however. He leaned toward her and whispered, "You're letting her bother you—again."

"God! Just look at her!" Brenna moaned. "Acting like she's the dowager empress of the whole damned human species."

Brenna's aunt beamed at her unseen audience. Her fellow leaders politely seconded the platitudes she was spouting. Carissa Saunder blushed with becoming modesty. Her costly, fashionable clothes, her soft ash-blonde hair arranged in the latest style, her elegant gestures—everything fitted the role: the martyr's widow. Patrick Saunder's sacrifice in stopping Jael Hartman Saunder's crimes had turned public fury into worship of the fallen hero. "Poor" Carissa was left to carry on Patrick's unfinished work and bear his posthumous son. She had devoted herself to the part ever since, clutching her widow's weeds, never remarrying, until she was now an aging, well-preserved, tragic madonna.

Smiling, always smiling, Carissa went on. "Earth sends you her fondest hopes for a prosperous and peaceful future, a future we will all share, a future Fairchild and Dabrowski and those who have gone before gave so much to bring into being." Thin ice. Fairchild's Peace was a "golden age" that had followed the Crisis of 2041—Jael Saunder's treachery and the hysteria surrounding Todd

Saunder's contact with the Vahnaj star empire. But now a few grumbles were starting among certain political factions on the home world. There were those who complained that the twenty-five years of Irene Fairchild's Peace, led by her Third Millennium Movement party, had really been stagnation. Carissa Saunder was one of Fairchild's protégées, one who had worked with the elder stateswoman to hang onto that long period of slow growth—and no wars. Possibly no other retired world leader could get away with what Carissa was saying. She was trading on her public image, and on her power as a Saunder.

". . . we salute Mars Colony. On this glorious occasion, we pray to the Spirit of Humanity that . . ."

That *voice!* Brenna slithered down in her seat, cringing. Media columnists described her aunt's voice as "sweet." Carissa's son, Stuart, made that into an insult—"Sweet Mother Carissa." But audiences doted on the sound. Carissa's voice was sham little-girl demure, vulnerable, trembling on the edge of tears even when she was smiling. Brenna loathed it.

Mercifully, from Brenna's point of view, Carissa kept her speech short. There were other delegates eager to take their place in the spotlight. They, too, were brief in their remarks, though it was plain they would have liked to turn the congratulatory messages into a political forum.

After the first five world leaders had their say, the holo-mode image blinked and five more appeared. They offered their predictable wishes for a continued progress. Five more. Five more. Running through the schedule quickly, precisely on time. Not only Earth's leaders were shown. Messages from other colonies were arriving now. Governor Ma Jiang of Goddard Colony and Luna expressed regrets that he could not attend the gala personally, but sent congratulations. General Norris Joslyn, commandant of Kirkwood Gap Space Fleet Base, relayed formal hopes for a successful future. Administrators Gabrielle Krowa, Matsumoto, and Gokhale of Kirkwood, Jovian satellites, and Venus outposts added their felicitations.

"Congratulations . . ."

"Many years . . ."

"May Mars Colony endure as long as human civilization exists . . ."

"Our children in space, we wish you well . . ."

And, occasionally, from Earth, a poignant note: "Do not forget us, you adventurous pioneers. You are still part of us, and we of you."

There was a flood of messages, but only the most important received show time in the holo-mode theater. When those were completed, ComLink engineers shifted to a recap of past events, explaining how and why Colony Days had come to be.

Images ticked off in tenths of seconds. Some scenes were crude, some were you-are-there sharp and vivid. There was no pretense, in most instances, that the viewers were seeing these things happening live, however. This was history condensed, a swift run-through, but not too fast for this fifth media-raised generation to absorb.

Scene: Goddard Habitat. Early in the year 2043. The great space station wheeled against the black void. In the distance, Earth's Moon was a silvery crescent pinned on eternal night. Earth lay "below," a lovely blue and brown globe, cloud-chased.

Close-ups on one of Goddard's orbiting construction shacks. An explorer ship was tethered to the drydock, ready for launch. Cameras zoomed, focusing on the loading bay. Ceremonies. People parking shuttle craft and gathering at the open port. Grinning faces, peering out of spacesuit helmet visors. There were clumsy handshakes, hampered by pressure gloves. This crew was dressed for deep space. Cheers sounded tinnily through the audio systems.

Then the focus shifted, drawing back, encompassing the dock and the surrounding emptiness for the historic moment. The explorer ship eased away. Incandescent fire lit up her tail, old-fashioned fusion engines kicking her away from Earth orbit, slinging her out onto her months-long journey to Mars.

Time telescoped, through the magic of the holo-mode pictures. A succession of scenes flashed by. Brenna's attention divided between the familiar images and the expressions on the audience's face. President Grieske was nodding, appearing very moved. He had been a young man aboard that explorer craft, and was seeing his own life replayed. Dian sat between Morgan and Todd. Now and then one of the three would point out something in the theater and make a comment to the others. Brenna saw their lips move, but couldn't hear what they said. Ambassador Quol-Bez seemed absorbed in the holo-mode's re-creation of recent human history, the scenes reflecting in miniature off his contact lenses.

Within the cube, the explorer reached her destination. The dusty red planet hung beneath the orbiting spacecraft. The broadcaster's voice-over explained all the careful prelanding, mapmaking procedures and other preparations. This big ship was a single-stage vehicle, a special craft. She could make planetfall and would serve as a warehouse for the pioneers. Other explorer craft were coming in her wake. Humans were here to stay. The bays opened and the big ship dropped a series of robot scouts, readying for the big event.

Interior shots. Scenes of the famous crew.

First Pilot Noah Olmsted. (He had died in a sub-orbital crash eight years ago, when his Mars supply ferry came in too low and too fast. There was a large monument dedicated to him at windswept Amazonis Planitia Spaceport.)

Geologist Zahra Kisongo. (She was presently the head of Chryse Scientific Research Installation. No doubt she was watching herself now on another holo-mode cube, on the opposite side of Mars.)

Historian Fred Grieske. (He sat a few meters from Brenna, being teased by his fellow legislators. They told him how much younger and handsomer he had looked back then, before he had decided to go into politics.)

Navigations Specialist Yan Bolotin. (Now a member of Terran Worlds Council and a high-ranking sponsor of Hiber-Ship Corporation—still doing his part to help humanity colonize the universe.)

Second Pilot Mariette Saunder. (A tall, lovely, dark-haired woman with eyes like pale blue fire and a smile that trapped one's soul. Dead. Killed in Breakthrough Unlimited's first catastrophic attempt to shatter the light-speed barrier.)

Expedition Commander Kevin McKelvey. (The block off which Morgan had been chipped. Those craggy McKelvey features had been passed on nearly intact. Morgan's father, like his son, was a big man, tousled sandy-blond hair, a cocksure grin. Dead. He had died with Mari Saunder and expert navigator Cesare Loezzi in that FTL Prototype ship three years ago.)

56

Within the holo-mode cube, Kevin McKelvey was giving Pilot Olmsted the go-ahead. "Take her down! Mars, here we come!"

Involuntarily, Brenna searched the shadows cloaking the audience. Todd Saunder's head was bowed. He huddled in his seat as if shaken by a powerful blow. Dian was comforting her husband, her arm around his shoulder. Their heads touched. Brenna longed to join them.

Oh, God, it hurts, doesn't it, Dad? We were so proud of them, so terribly proud. We loved them. And every time we see Aunt Mari and Uncle Kevin, it's like a laser burn ripping at us . . .

They hadn't needed the holo-mode to remind them of the past. Todd glanced at his nephew, his expression distraught. Kevin and Morgan. Father and son. So much alike. That resemblance was a solace, and a sad reminder of what they had lost.

Most of the audience wasn't interested in the myriad program checks and redundant operations pilots had to go through during such a flight, so the record skipped over those. But when the sphere of Mars loomed in the ship's lenses, the musical theme swelled anew.

Robot scouts had been dropped ahead of the shuttle to check the chosen touchdown site. Their signal beamed back: all clear. Preliminary work completed, the robots tilted their cameras up to capture the manned ship's final descent. The audience saw the landing as it would have looked to someone standing on Mars, though there had been nobody there, merely robots, on the historic date.

Mars. Barren. Alone for billions of years.

Now retro rockets, manufactured on another world, kicked up the dust that only the Martian wind and unmanned vehicles had ever touched. The sound of powerful thrusters broke the momentary silence, rushing out of the holo-mode cube and engulfing the audience. Gently, Goddard's Mars Probe I settled onto the rocky soil of the fourth planet.

There were scenes of the crew surveying, confirming exterior conditions, and checking each other's suit integrity. Then the hatch dropped open, forming a ramp. The watching robot scouts tightened focus to be sure of recording this moment for posterity—human posterity—and for alien species like the Vahnaj, which mankind had just begun to speak to across the light-years.

By mutual decision, the six crewmen stepped onto Mars together. Their names entered the history tapes side by side. Cameras relayed the once-in-a-lifetime moment to the anxious stay-at-homes waiting more than seventy-five million kilometers away.

Mankind, taking its first really gigantic step along its pathway to the stars.

Long overdue, as Mariette Saunder had often griped. Without the insane wars and economic collapses and plagues, humans should have made manned landings on Mars in the Twentieth Century and not had to wait until the mid-Twenty-first Century to fulfill that destiny! But at last, it *had* happened! A manned landing, the start of what was going to be a thriving Martian Colony.

Kevin McKelvey spoke to Earth. "We have touchdown. All personnel safe. We are on the surface, will begin initial exploration immediately. Our position is one hundred and thirty-five degrees west, eleven degrees three minutes north. Landing was at 0830, GMT. In the name of *Homo sapiens,* we claim this planet . . ."

A spontaneous shout rose from the audience. They were sophisticated but not immune to the thrill of this memorial. "Colony Day! Colony Day! 2045! Touchdown! Mars is *ours . . . !*"

Glasses clinked together. Laughter and cheers mingled. Many guests stood up, too exhilarated to remain in their seats. All around the domed room, people gave themselves over to holiday enthusiasm.

Brenna was one of the few who sat through the final wrap-up. The holo-mode show ended on a high note. The newscaster recapped the program, adding the good wishes of the media staffers who had participated in this impressive airing. But Brenna didn't see or hear any of that. Her mind was locked on the earlier scenes, on those people whose names had gone into the histories forever.

Leif Ericsson . . . Columbus . . . Magellan . . . Cook . . . Byrd . . . Armstrong . . . McKelvey . . . and Saunder . . .

The Saunders were making a lot of entries in the historical ledgers in this century. First Ward Saunder, who had invented so many things the modern world now depended on. Jael Hartman Saunder, who had earned her own sort of immortality, for all of her evil actions. Patrick Saunder, who'd saved the home world from destroying itself and stopped a civil war between Earth and Goddard Colony. Todd Saunder, Brenna's father, the man who had reached out and touched the stars and introduced humanity to the Vahnaj. That *was* immortality indeed, and damned hard to live up to if you were part of the next generation of Saunders and McKelveys!

But what of the failures? What of the would-be immortals who had never made it, who had died attempting to reach the unknown? Their names were lost. It was worse than never having lived at all, to have lived and failed. What about Mariette Saunder and Kevin McKelvey? History would remember them as members of the first Mars Colony ship, true. But Mari and Kevin had wanted to be remembered for something more vital—for giving faster-than-light drive to mankind. They had failed. Their only chance for immortality, regarding FTL, depended on their niece and son's carrying through and Breakthrough Unlimited's succeeding.

And if it didn't . . .

The threat of failure was a terrible nightmare, lurking in the back of Brenna's consciousness no matter what else was taking place. Couldn't she ever shake it?

Yes, she could! By being there when Morgan took the ride, watching him win, canceling out the defeat her aunt and uncle had taken—a defeat that had cost them their lives.

Sudden death. A possibility. Always there. Test pilots lived with it. Failure, though, was the ultimate disaster in more ways than one.

A hand touched her face, very gently. Derek was bending over her, his expression deeply concerned.

"Bren? You all right?"

She blinked several times, orienting herself. Colony Days. The rotunda. The holo-mode show.

"Yes, fine. I was just . . . somewhere else."

"I saw that. A million parsecs away." Brenna trembled, and Derek cuddled her hands against his chest, chafing her skin until it began to warm. After a few minutes, he helped her to her feet, his arm supporting her. She didn't shake it off, appreciating his closeness. The nightmare was

59

receding a little, going back into its dark cubbyhole in her brain. "It was that damned holo-mode program, wasn't it?" Derek guessed. "It hit a nerve. Those cretins at ComLink shouldn't have . . ."

"No, I'm glad they did. How could they celebrate Colony Days without . . ."

"It was damned insensitive, nevertheless. Didn't you have any warning of what they were going to show?"

"We'd seen the tape before, or versions of it," Brenna said. She glanced along the tier of seats, seeing her parents standing side by side, talking softly. Brenna wended her way toward them, Derek's arm still around her and supporting her. When they drew close to the older couple, Brenna saw that her father's eyes were swollen, though now dry. He must have been crying, there in the semi-darkness, watching the show. Brenna reached out to him.

"No, it's okay, kitten," Todd Saunder said, looking somewhat embarrassed at his display of emotion.

Derek repeated his comments about ComLink's insensitivity. Dian shook her hand as she watched her husband anxiously. "There's a bit more to it than that. Nostalgia getting out of hand, you might say."

Brenna's father peered up at the rotunda dome. His voice shook. "Years and years ago. Hadn't thought about it until . . . until now. The old place at Saunderhome, that night we broke the news about the Vahnaj robot messenger, Dian. Remember?" Dian was nodding, sighing. Clearly she wished he wouldn't open his old wounds in this way. "Watching the holo-mode images of my father . . . he'd been dead for years by then, kids," Todd explained to Brenna and Derek. Like Dian, they nodded politely, not sure how to cheer up the older man and bring him out of his sad mood. "The old place had a dome, too, a much smaller one, of course. I kept thinking about that night, and about all the good people I knew then who are . . . Roy and Beth and Ed and Mikhail . . ."

"They're preserved cryogenically," Dian reminded him. "And someday the doctors will revive them. The technique's perfected now, not like it was when—" She broke off, not wanting to bring up any more thoughts of the past. "Come on. Let's get you a drink and talk to some old friends, huh?"

Dian led him away slowly, heading toward a knot of

older guests several meters from the holo-mode theater. She obviously meant to distract him with conversation and the living presence of friends he *hadn't* lost to time and death. Brenna watched him go, then allowed Derek to work the same trick on her. She went along willingly. The show was over. Guests were gathering in many little groups, usually along generational lines. Near Brenna and Derek dance music was flowing from the overhead audio systems —a fast, drumming rhythm. The younger guests were drawn to it as if by a magnet. The sound baffles confined the raucous music, so that others who wanted to talk nearby wouldn't be disturbed.

"Come on, you two!" Morgan shouted to his cousin and Derek. In moments Brenna was swept up in the gaiety, her worries about her father scattering as laughing companions surrounded her. Intense lighting played over their faces and pulsed with the music. Brenna linked arms with the other women and they circled, running, kicking, and bowing in unison. Their clothes flew in the breeze they were creating.

The melody ended its first phase and changed, and the women stooped, their hands still linked. The men leaped over them, shaping an inner circle. This part of the dance was much more athletic, a challenge stunt. When the men galloped around the circle, it was a test of stamina—who could run the fastest without losing his balance? Mars' gravity seemed feeble to these children of Earth. The men jumped high into the air, soaring. Any of their leaps would have won prizes on the home world, but not here.

The music shifted to a third rhythm. The circles joined, became one, then broke apart into couples. Brenna locked her hands behind Derek's neck. His hands were tight against her waist as they danced and sprang into the air in wild, paired jumps, panting and laughing uproariously. Each couple tried to outdo the rest. Then the twosomes combined. Brenna and Jutta Lefferts faced one another, as did Morgan and Derek. Brenna took a tight grip on the men's shoulders as the four of them began to spin. "Now!" Morgan cued. He grinned mischievously at Derek. The men braced themselves, anchoring the women, turning around and around in an ever-smaller, faster-moving circle. Brenna's feet raised from the floor. Jutta, too, was going with the centrifugal force. Both women tilted, pointing their toes away from the circle, becoming flying dolls riding a spinning top. Jutta's long dark hair streamed away from the spin angle like a comet's tail. Brenna's short curls clung in sweaty tendrils to her face and throat.

The other dancers dropped out, standing on the sidelines, clapping and cheering Morgan's team. Brenna sucked in air breathlessly, exulting in the dizzy sensations. Morgan's face was very flushed. Derek's eyes shone like a sunlit Earth sky.

The music rose to a crescendo, then gradually softened, slowing. Morgan and Derek timed their movements precisely to match the tune, gently lowering the women back to their feet as the spin came to a stop. At the last instant, both men dropped to their knees and took their partners' hands, copying a quaint pose from bygone days. The final notes died in a bell-like, music-box coda.

"Winners! The winners!" someone yelled, and a chorus took up the chant.

Brenna wiped her forehead, giggling. Jutta was starting to hiccup. Too much excitement! Morgan would have pounded her on the back as a cure, but Jutta waved him off. "Next turn!" the spectators cried.

Morgan turned the offer down. "No chance! That was the main performance. The floor's all yours now—amateurs!"

The four of them walked away arm in arm, laughing. Brenna admired Jutta Lefferts, hiccups and all. It took a spunky woman to keep up with Morgan's pranks, and Jutta had done extremely well. She was a good sport, which some of Morgan's other love interests hadn't been.

"We're getting pretty good at this," Derek said. "We ought to start an entertainment schedule on the vid circuits. I thought I'd be out of practice since . . . how long ago was it when we danced together? Last fall? At Saunderhome?"

"It must be at least that long," Morgan agreed.

"Oh?" Jutta raised an eyebrow. "And just who were you dancing with *then?*"

"Nobody who needs concern you, m'dear," Morgan said hammily, curling a non-existent mustache. That led to a hilarious pantomime between him and Derek, with Derek offering to shed some of his abundant facial hair so that Morgan wouldn't have to fake his mustache-twirling. Morgan amused himself more than he did anyone else, though all of them were chuckling before the mime was done. "I'm as winded as a first-time free faller. Come on. Let's get something to drink."

The rotunda's efficient life-support systems hadn't been able to keep up with their exertions. All of them were sweating, and their color was very high. They sauntered away from the dance arena, and Morgan hailed a service robot. He passed out tumblers of alcohol soothants to the women and Derek, took a large glass of citrus drink for himself. They stood sipping their refreshments, cooling down. Less energetic dances went on, and elsewhere pockets of conversation buzzed. Brenna's foursome wandered close to the one where her parents and President Grieske were. Quol-Bez and Sao and other dignitaries were on the fringes of an on-going discussion. Someone had mentioned the scheduled awards ceremony on Earth next month, at Protectors of Earth's Supreme Assembly. Ambassador Quol-Bez and Todd Saunder were supposed to be honored then, in memory of the first contact between humans and Vahnaj. But the event might be postponed because of an outbreak of the neo-anthrax plague bacillus. Conversation turned to the past, to the wars which had originally bred that mutant plague, with the older people launching into personal horror stories of "I remember when."

"It all seems so damned dumb," Brenna muttered. "What could have possessed Earth's leaders back then, letting loose a wild contagion like that? Surely they could have guessed the scheme would backfire."

According to the records, though, the warlords *hadn't* believed that would happen, not until it was too late. Neo-anthrax and neo-smallpox, among other deadly leftovers, reminded mankind of past folly. Artificial plagues, lab-manufactured, had been weapons during the infamous Death Years and the Chaos that reigned from 2012 through 2030. The wars were over, the quarrels that triggered them now sounding incredibly petty. The plagues, however, refused to return to the labs. Contagion lurked in unsuspected hot spots, exploding every now and again. Even today, after decades of peace, Earth's health officials had to quarantine huge areas whenever one of the terrible epidemics erupted anew. It was beginning to seem as if humanity would never be quite free of that nightmare out of its past.

"And we're still paying for those mad experiments," Derek said bitterly. His mother had been one of the victims during the neo-anthrax outbreak in the late Fifties. "They'll probably be rooting out plague into the 2200s, at this rate. Those maniacs permanently wrecked the planet."

His Hiber-Ship Corporation indoctrination was showing. The stasis-ship volunteers were trained in primitive world survival and to respect ecosystems. Few of the volunteers had any patience for runaway technology turned to evil purposes. That intensive preparatory course, combined with Derek's family tragedy, had made him prone to lump all Earth's population together: There were the sane ones, who got out and colonized elsewhere, and there were the blind ones, who remained bogged down in Earth's decadence.

Brenna gently laid a hand on his arm.

"You mustn't blame them all," Todd said. "Billions of decent people fought those plague experiments during the wars, and that took courage. Right now they're reclaiming the poisoned lands. We just have to give them time. Earth will come back. You can rely on it."

On the other side of the small group, Stuart Saunder edged closer, trying to hear. The actress was some distance away, being pampered by Stuart's flunkies. It was obvious she had arranged a liaison with the wealthy Earth-based Saunder scion for later in the evening. For now, however, Stuart seemed more interested in this discussion, which puzzled Brenna.

"Microorganisms need not be laboratory-bred to cause harm," Chin Jui-Sao was saying. "Even the most beneficial intestinal bacteria can be deadly, under the wrong conditions. All life forms must be treated with cautious respect."

Derek nodded. "The Spirit of Humanity put an amen to that, Sao."

Some of the listeners eyed Quol-Bez. No doubt they were remembering the conditions under which the Vahnaj Ambassador had come to the Solar System. From the moment Todd Saunder had begun communicating with the Vahnaj, thirty-four years ago, Earth's scientists had strong reservations about face-to-face meetings between the two species. Their worry was a valid one, and not related to the xenophobic hysteria that had seized so many humans during that era—though the scientists' questions inevitably added to some people's fear of extraterrestrials. Because of those complicated questions, it had taken years to work out a treaty so that a Vahnaj Ambassador would be allowed to come to Todd Saunder's home world.

Question: Cross-species contagion—could it occur?

Answer: *Yes!*

The Vahnaj, though, had a further answer. They were an old civilization. They had been exploring their section of the galaxy for many generations, and they had dealt with this thorny problem before, on other worlds. They had found a workable solution.

Their Ambassador would, for the first part of his stay among humans, be a willing guinea pig. Quol-Bez would be available for any tests Earth's scientists wished to subject him to. He would enter quarantine. For Earth's additional protection, Ambassador Quol-Bez would bring with him samples of other Vahnaj micro-life, for Earth's scientists to play with. Also, Quol-Bez's own symbiote bacteria and antibodies, those microorganisms necessary for his existence, would be attenuated by Vahnaj medicine prior to his departure from his planet. He would be rendered as harmless as possible to humans—even at the risk of weakening his own biological defense systems. Certainly no offer could be more generous. Under those terms, if an accident occurred during the quarantine period and Vahnaj microorganisms should escape Earth's testing areas, the threat to human life would still be minimal. The Vahnaj backed up their scientific reassurances with documentation relayed across the light-years to Todd Saunder and to the rest of mankind. Eventually, they convinced the skeptics.

Earth's leaders continued to worry, though. What if the Vahnaj Ambassador were infected by *Earth's* microorganisms? If his biological defenses had been weakened, he would be especially vulnerable. He might die. Vahnaj was far ahead of Earth in technology—and in space-war capability. Might she not, in that case, take revenge for her Ambassador?

The Vahnaj were a trifle insulted by that query. They replied that they were a *civilized* species. They fully understood the risks, and they accepted them. They would sign a treaty to guarantee, among other things, that their Ambassador was expendable. Diplomacy. The nature of cross-species meetings. And worth the gamble, to the Vahnaj. They hoped their treaty of good faith would pay off in centuries to come, when *Homo sapiens* would be a full trading partner in the Vahnaj sphere of influence.

If their Ambassador survived, *if* the two species were compatible, then Vahnaj and Earth would take further steps and enlarge the treaty. Those steps would also depend, of course, on how quickly Earth's culture expanded into the galaxy on its own. The trade agreement might be in effect in scant years, once humans discovered their own method of faster-than-light travel. *If* they did. Otherwise, most treaty terms would remain inactive, or nearly so.

The treaty was signed, and Todd Saunder's ComLink network and other media sold the package to humanity. And as the terms were understood, mankind began to look on the soon-to-arrive Vahnaj Ambassador in a different light. The Vahnaj were sending him to an alien Solar System with cool calculation. Quol-Bez might die, victim of an Earth virus. That was what a diplomat got paid for—to be a sacrificial goat, if necessary. When Quol-Bez reached Earth, after those years of tortuous negotiations, and entered quarantine, humanity came to know him through interviews on remote vid cameras. This tall, skinny, funny-faced otterlike creature with a child's voice and pointy teeth was the "alien invader" so many had feared? Quol-Bez had seemed more like a noble peacemaker, walking willingly into possible death if it would help advance the cause of interstellar relations between his people and Earth's.

Quol-Bez didn't die. He survived the quarantine. And human volunteers survived exposure to the Vahnaj microorganisms Quol-Bez had brought for the scientists to test. Vahnaj and human blood, laden with new antibodies, provided sera. A major step. The two species *could* coexist.

Now came the next steps, including travel to Vahnaj. That might not be as "easy" as conquering xenophobia and the danger of cross-species contagion had been!

The conversational topic was changing. People were complimenting Brenna's father on the holo-mode broadcasts. "Whole thing went off great, Todd," Fred Grieske said. "Your people outdid themselves this time."

"And didn't Carissa look simply charming?"

Brenna didn't see who had said that. But Dian commented *sotto voce,* right in Brenna's ear. "She ought to.

66

Her beauty experts work hard enough to keep 'Rissa eternally forty."

A few other people had heard her, too. Deputy Commissioner Pecora rushed into the awkward silence. "Best holo-mode technique ever, Todd . . ."

Todd Saunder was still a trifle pale. The emotional upheaval of seeing his dead sister and brother-in-law recreated in the images hadn't completely subsided. But he smiled his thanks. "Glad you liked it. ComLink tries to do right by the customers. Communications is our lifeblood, has been since before Goddard and the Lunar Base were founded. Why, in the last century my father was working on updating old-fashioned comsats. Imagine the primitive methods we had to use back then—wires and ground-anchored towers! All that just to send messages from one spot to another on a single planet . . ."

"An improvement over tom-toms and semaphores, you must admit, Uncle Todd," Stuart suddenly put in. "But still centuries behind what the *really* advanced species are using, hmm? Like that heavily protected Vahnaj radio our Ambassador and the treaty makers use. Makes our systems look pathetic by comparison. Still, we *are* making progress, eh?"

People around him didn't know how to respond to his sarcastic comments. Brenna found herself studying Quol-Bez intently, looking for signs that he was displeased or startled. For one of the few times in her life, she applauded Stuart, though silently. Her cousin had pinched the Vahnaj Ambassador's toes and reminded the smug souls who backed Hiber-Ship Corporation that they were trading their hopes of a future as star lords for a mess of pottage the aliens were throwing their way.

The FTL radio that had ridden to the Solar System in a Vahnaj robot was a mere symbol. A symbol that sooner or later mankind was going to grab for itself!

His expression sardonic, Stuart Saunder raised his glass —he nearly always had a glass in his hand! "Here's to progress!"

✪✪✪✪✪✪✪✪✪

CHAPTER FIVE

Quarrels—Friendly and Otherwise

IN varying degrees of approval, others joined Stuart's toast. When they were done, President Grieske jumped in. "Yes, progress, but with constant setbacks, I fear. Such as that new economic cutthroat competition between Alamshah and Nakamura Kaisya . . . very bad! I do hope it won't involve any other of our interplanetary suppliers." He turned to Terran Worlds Councilman Ames. "Is the T.W.C. going to get in on the arbitration?"

"T.W.C. has not been invited to participate in the discussions," Chairman Hong Ling-Kuang of Protectors of Earth replied huffily. "It is strictly a one-planet matter."

"Not if the Progressive Expansionist Coalition has its way," Ames said with a superior smile. "They've been pressuring some of our Space Fleet contractors, and that *will* involve other planets."

"Gentlemen, gentlemen," Grieske pleaded, "my apologies for bringing this up. I wasn't aware tempers were so touchy on the subject. It's because we're quite divorced from Earth's politics out here. Except for our friends and Space Fleet personnel who travel back to the home world frequently. Isn't that right, Todd? You don't think this competition will spread, do you? Not to step on your toes, but we need Nakamura's TeleCom network and Alamshah's transport connections almost as much as we do Saunder Enterprises." The President laughed and patted Todd's arm to show he wasn't taking his own suggestions at all seriously.

Todd returned the smile. "I wouldn't be overly concerned, no. They'll solve it, eventually. I found out years ago that there are no simple answers. But there *are* answers. The trick is to find them. And they will. Rely on it."

Brenna and her mother and Morgan exchanged amused glances. No simple answers. Yet Todd Saunder had built his life's work on the belief that answers could always be found—*somewhere*. If he hadn't thought that, he never would have sponsored Project Search. Earth might never have made contact with Quol-Bez's species. Todd Saunder was proof that tough questions yielded if one were persistent enough.

"Politics and religion," Stuart chimed in again. Brenna listened warily. Where was he going and what was he scheming? "Dreadful mix. You have no idea what it can be like on Earth. You think you have a lot of Space Fleet troopers and personal bodyguards here?" He made a rude noise, dismissing Mars' finest officers and the private police who kept order. "Ambassador Quol-Bez and his charming translator could tell you what *real* personal risk is all about. In some cities back there, you can't *move* without a full contingent of armed soldiers to protect you from the mobs."

Unexpectedly, Chin Jui-Sao agreed, her soft voice troubled. "This is so, unfortunately. There are, for example, surprisingly large remnants of the Earth First Party to be found in some areas. The Ambassador has been unpleasantly harassed by these fanatics, many times. They seem to be fighting the philosophical battles of decades ago, still fearful of a Vahnaj invasion." The guests around her chuckled at this absurdity, shaking their heads in pity.

"They don't realize their entire premise is passé," Stuart added. "Fear of the unknown, the analysts call it. But how can that be?" He waved a graceful, well-manicured hand at Quol-Bez. "Is our esteemed Vahnaj Ambassador an 'unknown'? Ridiculous! Still, we can't disclaim those misguided fools completely. They *are* part of our human society, like it or not, with their crazy ideas and reactionary terrors."

Brenna had been listening with growing attention, amazed at how much she wanted to second her cousin. Suddenly she exclaimed, "That's right. They're humans, every one of them. Tell us, Quol-Bez, did the Vahnaj go through this same sort of madness in your early history? You know—hot spots left over from past nuclear wars, mutant viruses, head-in-the-sand factions afraid of anything new or different, fanatics quoting garbled religious or scientific passages to prove that there are things man should never try to do. How long *does* it take a species to get past this awkward stage of development?" Her adrenaline was pumping. She noticed Stuart gloating, reveling in the rare experience of being backed up by another member of the Saunder clan. Brenna had the bit in her teeth, plowing ahead. "How long? Centuries? Millennia? What's the prognosis for backward people like us?"

She was acutely aware of the faces in the gathering crowd around her. Councilman Ames of T.W.C. and Chairman Hong of P.O.E. were both inordinately interested in what answers Quol-Bez might give to Brenna's impertinent questions. Others showed a mix of idle curiosity, barely veiled chauvinistic pride in human endeavor that resented Vahnaj power, and some apprehension that Brenna had mortally offended the being from the stars. President Grieske spoke for that group when he said in dismay, "You exaggerate the situation, my dear. Those things you mention are just temporary aberrations, hardly typical of normal human activities . . ."

"Maybe they're growing pains," Stuart said.

The words prodded Brenna, made her still more reckless. She confronted Quol-Bez. "Any hints—from the advanced race to the uncouth savages?"

"You're out of line, girl," Dian warned.

Quol-Bez raised a three-fingered hand, quieting the stir of whispers running through the group. "It is wel-come, Dr. Foix. We do not require protocols among kin-friends of Todd Saunder. Such con-ver-sa-tions are . . . urr . . . *tha-shei-dul* . . ."

Dian opened her mouth, but it was her pupil Sao who explained the Vahnaj phrase for the benefit of the rest. " 'Off the record.' 'Just among close acquaintances.' " She stared angrily at Brenna as she spoke, plainly challenging Brenna's right to be the Ambassador's "kin-friend" when she was assaulting the alien verbally in this manner.

Morgan moved close to Brenna, gripping her shoulder and shaking her lightly. "Cool off," he urged softly. She ignored him.

Quol-Bez's high, raspy voice was amiable. "We of the Vahnaj worlds have indeed suf-fered war-fare among ourselves, and with other species, I am ashamed to ad-mit, in our less ci-vi-lized centuries, as you have guessed. We, too, em-ployed bio-weapons. We have known dif-fer-ences of phil-o-so-phy. But we sur-vived. Obviously." The alien's

70

pointed teeth showed. He seemed to be enjoying himself in some mysterious way.

"Muddling through, just as we've been doing, eh?" Stuart put in. He was taking the trouble to be charming. He didn't do that often, but when he chose to, he was good at it. "Just have to make our mistakes and take our lumps. Wars, plagues, all the floundering around. Pity. For instance, we can barely haul ourselves out of planetary orbit, yet . . ."

"We'll go a hell of a lot farther than that," Brenna said firmly.

A soft, beloved voice murmured, "Or die trying." Derek. He looked morose. He didn't avoid Brenna's answering glare. Truce or not, he had meant that soft comment for her and Morgan, meant them to hear it.

"Breakthrough Unlimited is going to conquer the light-speed barrier," Brenna insisted, her chin held high.

"That is possible," Quol-Bez said in his condescending, irritatingly smug way. "There are cer-tain se-quences of tech-no-log-i-cal development for any intelligent species."

"But are we following the right one?" Brenna prodded. "That's what Stuart means about floundering. We're working in the dark, trying to read between the lines of the Vahnaj historical tapes you've loaned us. And damned skimpy peeks you've given us, too."

Morgan broke in, his annoyance now showing. "Don't expect the Ambassador to do our work for us. You know his diplomatic mission won't allow him to clue us in on the things you're talking about." He met Quol-Bez's calm gaze, a hint of a smile playing on Morgan's face. It was as if the two of them shared some special knowledge they weren't letting Brenna in on. She toyed with the urge to kick Morgan's shins. Whose side was he on, anyway!

Dian tugged at her husband's sleeve, but Todd Saunder was engrossed in what was going on. Her face taut with exasperation, Dian simply walked away. Brenna had seen that happen at other times. Her mother refused to hang around during a squabble, saying she had done enough of that when she was younger. Unless there was an urgent reason for her to get involved, she wouldn't. A rhetorical argument certainly didn't qualify as "urgent."

"My kin-friend Brenna, permit me to cor-rect you: *Homo sapiens* is not a sav-age species. It is not primitive.

71

It *is* aggressive. But all species which develop in these manners, es-pe-ci-al-ly those which leave the origin world, must be aggressive."

"But we always have to find our own way." Heads swiveled toward Derek. The guests listened respectfully to the famous former Space Fleet pilot. Brenna read their thoughts. Derek had experience with all forms of spaceflight, including Breakthrough Unlimited's craft. Expert opinion. He spoke and they paid attention—even if his judgment about Breakthrough Unlimited and the right way to reach the stars was wrong! "The Isakson modified photon propulsion system is something we've developed ourselves during the past twenty years. So is cryogenic stasis, which we owe to Todd Saunder's father. Those two independent discoveries enable us to build a sub-light-speed starship and leave the Solar System. No help needed from the Vahnaj or from any other species outside our own patterns of orderly progress."

"There's a faster way," Brenna retorted, now that he had breached the truce. "Graviton spin resonance drive will give us FTL, and *that* comes out of our own technology, too!"

"*If* it works," Derek shot back. "Space Fleet dropped their experiments before Breakthrough Unlimited adopted the theory. That seems to say they doubted its feasibility even then. Affirmative, Councilman Ames?"

The Terran Worlds Councilman's face was an unreadable mask. He refused to rise to the bait. But Stuart didn't. He said, "Oh, come on, Derek. We all know why T.W.C. turned the process over to a civilian outfit like Saunder Enterprises. Politics! They're afraid of stepping on the Vahnajes' toes. Their precious treaty, you know. Hiber-Ship's frozen coffin of a starship doesn't really concern them. Ah! But they get nervous about faster-than-light travel. Of course, we have that constant reminder, don't we? The Ambassador's little spaceship, with its Vahnaj FTL drive, parked out there in orbit beyond the asteroid belt. Hmm? Isn't that like dangling bait in front of us? Look but don't touch!"

"Whatever the military's reasons," Brenna said, "they gave up on graviton spin resonance too soon, and we'll prove it." Derek gulped down the remainder of his drink. Morgan was glowering at Brenna as she continued. "You're

72

right. The Vahnaj starship *is* bait, Stuart. It's been sitting out there, guarded by Space Fleet for six years, just in case Quol-Bez decides to use it for a quick trip back to his home worlds. But he never takes the trip. Why won't he lend the ship to us for a while, then? We'd know how to make good use of it . . ."

That had been a test pilot's fantasy for six years, ever since the bare-bones facts about the alien ship had been revealed. An FTL drive! In the Solar System! A Vahnaj ship, diplomatically off-limits. But oh, how tempting! Nearly everyone in Breakthrough Unlimited and the other various FTL experimental groups in the same race with them dreamed of "borrowing" Quol-Bez's ship and learning its secrets. So what if there was hell to pay with the politicos afterward? It would be a *fait accompli*. The Vahnaj bragged they hadn't waged war against any other species in centuries. Were they about to start now, over an incident like that? Probably they would slap Earth's wrists, figuratively, and accept the reality. And humanity would have faster-than-light travel, while being spared the risks, the expense, the deaths . . .

However, there *was* a small impediment. Space Fleet. A crack cordon making sure no humans, particularly no civilians, ever got close to the ship.

"Maybe that ship's there to keep us humble," Brenna speculated. "To keep us from getting uppity."

"Dammit! Stop it! You, too, Stuart! You're egging her on!" Todd Saunder roared.

Brenna was taken aback. So was everyone else, including Stuart. Brenna was flabbergasted by *that*. Stuart would never have reacted to his mother that way. But for all the frictions within the family's branches, he still respected his uncle. A lifetime of her father's stern admonitions rang through Brenna's head:

We're Saunders. And a Saunder is the best. We've got power, wealth, and honor. We have to live up to those things.

Noblesse oblige. A foolish, weak-minded notion, to Stuart, normally. But this time he obeyed Todd's rules, mumbling apologies.

Todd Saunder's credo—graciousness to friend and foe, acknowledgment of one's debts to society in exchange for privileges enjoyed. For Brenna's father, those debts in-

73

cluded his mother's crimes and never forgetting his dead siblings. And sometimes, in his caring about old debts, he overlooked the fact that the new generation felt no obligation for those debts. Across the buzz of voices, Morgan and Brenna caught each other's eyes and were united. Morgan's annoyance with Brenna's earlier pushiness vanished in a heartbeat. Those debts had burdened their parents, as the old plagues left scars on the previous generation. *This* generation of Saunders and McKelveys had their own lives to live, their own dreams and goals, and no emotional debts from the past, except those that they allowed their elders to pile on them.

Brenna didn't intend to carry those debts. Courtesy, yes. Guilt, no. Not for crimes she had never committed and events that had happened before she and Morgan were born.

Quol-Bez broke through the whispering confusion. "My friend Todd, you must not be disturbed. I do not object. Sin-cere-ly! Brenna and I talked of these things earlier. I in-vited this discussion."

Todd looked at his daughter, frowning. Brenna squared her shoulders as Quol-Bez peered down at her, seeking confirmation. "That's so, Dad. After all, it's understandable. The Ambassador knows how important these theories of faster-than-light travel are to Morgan and me." Derek edged away from her, his face a storm cloud. Defiantly, Brenna went on. "As Stuart hinted, in a lot of ways the Ambassador's ship *could* be construed as psychological 'bait.' Not that anyone has any serious intention of 'kidnapping' the ship!" she hastened to assure the listeners. As far as logic went, she meant that. Emotionally, she nursed reservations. If only . . . ! Chin Jui-Sao was translating the nuances of Brenna's statements for Quol-Bez as Brenna continued. "And we're not the *only* ones interested, come to that. There are several other FTL projects in competition with us right now."

For the first time in this whole conversation, Terran Worlds Councilman Ames's serene confidence cracked a trifle. He looked distinctly uneasy, as if he wished Brenna hadn't brought that matter to everyone's attention. Brenna found this amusing. None of the other faster-than-light projects had the remotest chance of success. Surely Ames

74

knew it. Only Breakthrough Unlimited's graviton spin resonance drive could do the job.

Derek had ordered another alcoholic drink from a passing service robot. His courage bolstered, he cut in abruptly. "What Brenna would really like you to do, Quol-Bez, is tell the rest of those FTL experimenters to give up—and throw their investment capital in with Breakthrough Unlimited. Collect all the pellet fuel in one tank, you might say."

Morgan had tried to shut Brenna up when she was needling Quol-Bez and pushing the limits of courtesy. But now that Derek had spilled the bag, Morgan was solidly on Brenna's team. "You bastard," he growled at his lifelong friend. Morgan's lopsided, rueful smile made the words a fond epithet rather than an insult.

Derek tipped an imaginary cap to him in ironic salute. "Just thought I'd save us all some time. You and Brenna *do* tend to beat around the bush an awful lot."

"How droll!" Stuart sneered. "Aren't you supposed to be on the opposing side, Whitcomb? Does Hiber-Ship know you're playing cutesy games with the enemy? Going to bed with one of them, too . . ."

A few listeners began squirming uncomfortably at Stuart's lack of taste. Brenna was used to it. She felt oddly relieved that he was falling into his normal bad habits. She had been operating without any charts for a few minutes a while ago, when she had found her only ally in the room to be Stuart. Brenna and Stuart Saunder, taking on the Vahnaj Ambassador together! She began to wonder if his drink had been spiked with something exceptionally potent. She could count the times in her life she and Stuart had joined forces—*this* time. It wasn't likely to happen again soon, if ever!

What had Stuart gotten out of the debate? He had seemed to enjoy it while it was going on. Speculating on Stuart's motives was a dead-end hobby, though. Not even Stuart knew what was going on in his burned-out brain cells.

President Grieske and Brenna's father kept trying to apologize to Quol-Bez, despite the Ambassador's reassurances that he wasn't offended in the slightest. He smiled at them in tolerant amusement and brushed aside their efforts. Seeing that, Brenna began to seethe. Quol-Bez had been an excellent choice for this diplomatic mission. He had adapted wonderfully well to human culture and customs. Perhaps too well. Right now he was copying the all-too-familiar patterns of Brenna's elders—patronizing the "kids," and making allowances for their brashness and foolishness.

"We don't need anyone to give us the answers on a platinum plate," Brenna said loudly. Chatter died away. People looked at her warily, waiting to see if the argument was going to start anew. "Morgan and I know we've got the FTL race won."

"That is quite possible," Quol-Bez said very quietly.

Dance music was playing, people were laughing and talking elsewhere in the rotunda, a constant ambiance of sound that the audio baffles couldn't completely dampen. But for Brenna, there was sudden, total silence. She and Morgan and Derek and Quol-Bez were quite alone. Despite her bragging, the alien had shot the floor out from under her. Dangling that bait—again—this time hinting at a glimpse into the future, foreknowledge that Brenna desperately wanted to possess.

The Ambassador sensed that burning need to know and elaborated on his shocking statement. "Un-ques-tion-ably, in time, *Homo sapiens* will achieve faster-than-light space travel. Unless your species succumbs to a self-generated or natural catastrophe, like a nova, which your Spirit of Humanity I hope will pre-vent, such a stage of in-ven-tion must come to you." The patronizing tone was gone. Quol-Bez was speaking as one being to another who was almost his equal.

Almost.

But not quite.

"Then what?" Brenna demanded, hungering for that insight of what lay ahead. The financial worries, the nightmare fear of failure, crowded in on her, making her breathless. Quol-Bez could wipe out the uncertainties with a few words, if he chose to. "How fast can we develop *after* we achieve FTL?" Brenna demanded. "Trade within the Solar System? We've already got that. FTL will just speed up the process. What about outside the Solar System? Will the Vahnaj welcome Earth as a full trading partner? And what about the other species in the near-galactic neighborhood? Will they welcome us, too?"

Morgan broke in, rebuking her once more. "Brenna, you know you're asking Quol-Bez questions that are out of line."

Quol-Bez silenced him with a gesture. He was smiling at Morgan, that peculiar, superior smile that so irked Brenna. But Morgan wasn't bothered by it. He nodded, exuding friendship. There seemed to be a tacit conversation going on between them. Brenna had noticed that happening at other family gatherings Quol-Bez had attended in the past. Even more than Brenna's father, Morgan appeared to fall into an easy, one-on-one exchange with the Ambassador with no effort whatsoever. Brenna both envied the talent and resented it. Morgan's smile was becoming as smug as the alien's.

Then Quol-Bez's stare shifted to Brenna. The dark eyes bored at her and she shivered, recalling the articles about possible telepathic abilities among the Vahnaj.

"I could not pre-dict what you wish to know," Quol-Bez said at last.

Brenna sighed. She had been holding her breath, and felt giddy. She drew herself up and refused to accept that reply. "Could not? Or will not?"

"All the things you ask of me would require a lengthy consultation with my government before I could answer. I am sorry." The unspoken additional regret lay under the words. With the Vahnaj FTL radio, such communications might be lengthy, but they would be almost instantaneous. Quol-Bez was saying that he knew in advance his government would instruct him to clam up and tell Brenna nothing. "I am sorry," Quol-Bez repeated. "I beg you to understand."

Five years out of the quarantine period, and he had been Todd Saunder's friend, via communications devices, long before then, and on casual social terms with the Saunder family ever since. Yet in many ways Brenna knew so little about Quol-Bez. His sad black eyes seemed to say, "Please do not demand what I cannot give you. I am bound by rules I dare not break. I am a diplomat, a servant of my government. Am I to risk betraying my people, revealing something they might not wish revealed just yet, to please the daughter of my kin-friend Todd Saunder?"

77

Brenna felt cornered and chagrined. How had she gotten into this mess? By opening her big mouth at the wrong time! What was the matter with her? Beyond the obvious —nerves rubbed raw because of the upcoming Prototype test. She never gave in to such brash impulses this way, not in a friendly gathering like this! The difference, at this gala, was Stuart. Brenna narrowed her eyes, studying her dissipated cousin. Stuart was blatant in his enjoyment of the fracas. He had relished setting Brenna at Quol-Bez's throat, and now he was snickering over her discomfiture— from a safe distance. He remembered her temper from countless childhood arguments.

Then Quol-Bez's eyes sparkled, and he turned again to Brenna. "I am told there is a par-ti-cu-lar human idiomatic expression. I would like to offer it to you, Brenna: 'May the best team win.'"

"That's us," she said lightly, returning his smile.

"Your kin-people spoke the same." Quol-Bez's reference to Mariette Saunder and Kevin McKelvey shook Brenna's composure. "They, too, were very brave. They wished to ad-vance your species, as you do. I regret that I did not know them longer. I ad-mired them very much. Your kin-aunt often said that she wished to build the faster-than-light ship without any out-side as-sistance . . ."

Todd Saunder suddenly broke in, speaking with great emotion. "That was Mari, and Kevin. They always wanted to go it alone. She was furious when I first contacted your Vahnaj messenger beacon years ago, Quol-Bez. Do you know why? Because *she* wanted to be the one to find *you* —to go beyond our star system. Eventually, she got used to the idea of meeting the Vahnaj halfway. Mariette real-ized it doesn't make any difference. The important thing is that Vahnaj and *Homo sapiens* coexist in peace, and that *humans* are living in peace with each other, finally!"

Brenna took her lumps, sheepishly saying, "Dad's right. So Aunt Mari learned. It takes patience. We have to learn that, sometimes. We *are*. *I* am. I'm sorry if I came on too strong earlier. I guess I got the forest mixed up with the trees and became too . . . aggressive. Wasn't that the word you used to describe us . . ."

"Sav-ages?" Quol-Bez finished for her. His wide face split in a sly and remarkably human grin. He might patronize her now and then, but it was almost impossible to stay mad at such a likable being as this.

Brenna held out her hand, and Quol-Bez's long fingers wrapped around hers. Morgan clapped his big paws around the handshake, sealing it, looking relieved that the too-hot discussion was over.

Then, without warning, two men rushed out of the surrounding crowd. They moved in separate directions, knocking guests out of their way and screaming unintelligibly.

Pandemonium erupted. Men and women cried out in alarm, bewildered.

There was a flash of light, a reflection off something polished. A plasticene dagger. The weapon was swinging up in an arc, ready for a murderous blow, and Brenna noticed that the second man had a knife, too.

She saw everything in slow motion, her long-honed test pilot's physical training going into top gear. This invasion was too astonishing for rational thought to cope with. She fell back on instincts, reflexes taking over, moving her arms and legs for her.

Brenna lunged in front of Quol-Bez and her father, dropping into a defensive crouch, hands poised to chop or parry. She was at a free-fall gym session, or felt as if she were. Chin Jui-Sao also had acted at once to protect the Ambassador with her own body. Together the young women formed a wall.

But neither woman was alone. There were uniformed Space Fleet personnel and diplomatic corps guards everywhere, forming a second defense line to shield Quol-Bez. Brenna hadn't seen where they had come from. They could have materialized out of nowhere.

The would-be assassins weren't attacking Quol-Bez, though, as everyone had automatically assumed. They were running *past* Quol-Bez and his protectors, still yelling. Brenna could just about make out what they were saying: "Traitor!"

She thrust out her foot in the path of one. The man hit her boot while he was running full-tilt, gasped, and stumbled, losing his balance. Derek and half a dozen Space Fleet and enforcement guards piled on him instantly, knocking him to the floor and wrestling with him.

Morgan and other guards stopped the second attacker,

spread-eagling the thrashing, wild-eyed screamer. Brenna stepped out from the cordon of protection around Quol-Bez, staring dazedly, absorbing what she saw. Both men wore civilian clothes marked with P.O.E. diplomats' patches. She couldn't recall seeing or meeting either of them during any of the earlier conversations. Who were they? And how had they smuggled weapons past the enforcement police shielding the President's entertainment island? And who were they accusing of treachery?

Derek chopped at one assassin's wrist, using vicious Space Fleet survival tactics. The helpless captive's hand opened and the transparent knife clattered to the floor. The police disarmed the other man, taking the knives.

The frenzied men kept on fighting, like contestants in Earth's controlled-violence arenas, not aware their struggle was useless. The one Morgan was sitting on turned a look of glittering hatred on his would-have-been victim: Terran Worlds Councilman Ames. "You traitor! You sold us out! You son of a bitch. You . . . *Spacer!* Long live Protectors of Earth . . . !"

"They are Earth First fanatics!" Chin Jui-Sao exclaimed in horror. *"Wei shenme?"*

Guards seized the men by the hair, dragging their heads back roughly and examining their eyes. "No hyperendors, General, but they might be on illicit accelerators." This was Mars Colony, and President Fred Grieske was the ranking authority. Yet the Space Fleet troops deferred to the would-be assassins' target, Terran Worlds Councilman Ames. Ames waved his hand negligently, giving control back to his host. Grieske seized that power, jerking his thumb. The soldiers and police fastened the captives' arms behind their backs and hauled them to their feet. "Come on, you . . . get them to Security. Keep the media out!"

Dian had rushed back into the circle the moment the danger began. She stood beside Todd, deeply concerned, not accepting his claims that he hadn't been hurt or even at risk. Quol-Bez, too, was surrounded by people anxious for his welfare; he kept assuring them he was all right. Everyone watched in morbid fascination as the soldiers hustled the prisoners past the light curtain and across the rotunda and out of sight.

Morgan, Derek, and Brenna stood close together. Brenna's heart had been thumping loudly, but was settling down fast. She thanked years of rigorous physical training that she had been ready for this unexpected crisis. Think-quick-or-die was the motto out in space. She and Morgan and Derek were reacting, and getting their nerves steady once more, just as well as the professional soldiers were, energy-charged, but not at all panicky, as a few of the civilians were. Some of the police and troops paused to thank them for their help in apprehending the fanatics.

Protectors of Earth's Chairman Hong Ling-Kuang had hurried over to where Councilman Ames stood, and he was now talking earnestly to the black man. Ames was stony-faced, listening to his political rival. The Chairman swore he had never seen the potential threat. Pieces of the puzzle fell into place for Brenna. The assassins had been part of Chairman Hong's entourage. *That* was how they had gotten invitations to this gala. It might explain, too, in part, how they had successfully brought weapons into the rotunda. Metal arms would have been detected at once. But many stylish ornaments and personal communications jewels were made of plasticene. A plasticene knife could be deadly, though. Councilman Ames had been very lucky.

Little wonder the P.O.E. Chairman was repeating again and again that he had had no idea those men were Earth First adherents, that they had passed rigid personnel checks but had never revealed their secret political fanaticism. It might even be true. On the surface, though, the situation looked very suspicious. Chairman Hong had lost face, unintentionally insulted President Grieske and the Vahnaj Ambassador, and, worst of all, been put in a painful position because of his organization's well-known rivalry with Terran Worlds Council. Sao wrinkled her nose at him, scornful, for the Chairman was almost blubbering apologies. The implications of offworld conspiracies disgusted the other onlookers, too.

"Did you hear what they called the Councilman? Spacer! My God, are they still spouting that sort of hatred down there on Earth?"

"They ought to put all of them in cryogenic cages . . ."

"Outrageous! The Vahnaj *will* think we're barbarians . . ."

"It's those crazies from Earth, not us. They're not *Colonists* . . ."

For several minutes, there was chaos. Grieske's aides circulated through the crowd, assuring the guests everything was okay. It took a lot of talking to convince them. Such crimes were virtually unknown on Mars. There would be a thorough investigation, and punishment would be meted out. Chairman Hong Ling-Kuang left the rotunda arm in arm with Ames, still jabbering, aides following like dust on a badlands wind. People watched them go, muttering, the gossip spreading.

"Politics," Brenna said in revulsion. "Damned politics. Even at the gala."

Derek rubbed the back of her neck. "Forget it. They're out of the way now, and they didn't hurt anyone."

"Thanks to you two. You'll probably get some medals . . ."

Derek and Morgan grinned and punched each other lightly on the biceps. "That and fifty credit units might get us a good meal somewhere," Morgan said.

President Grieske was giving orders, hurrying the schedule forward to cover up the unexpected crisis. "Start the fireworks. *Now.* Take people's minds off this dreadful interruption . . ."

It was evening, not full night, but on Mars that meant the sky was already black outside the bubble dome. Interior lighting had compensated so well that not many participants had noticed the passing time. When the fireworks display was announced they looked upward, excitement rising. As patriotic melodies filled the rotunda, the first spectacular color bursts exploded against the transparent dome.

"Ah! Look . . . !"

"Another! There!"

"Three at once!"

"*Four!* One for each of the Tharsis volcanoes. Wonderful colors!"

The show was a good one, one of the best Brenna had ever seen. The President's strategy paid off. Not everyone forgot what had happened earlier, but all were content to enjoy the anniversary fireworks.

Brenna was a girl again, remembering a smaller display under a much smaller life-support dome. Pavonis City had been new then. Their parents had brought her and Morgan to watch the tenth-anniversary Colony Days show—twenty years ago this night. The pleasure, the dazzling lights, the childlike wonder, came back to her. Jutta and Brenna vied to see who could spot the best fire bursts. Derek and

Morgan did the same. No ancient pyrotechnics could match this. These were holo-mode images, pure, flawless, without any heat or danger. No one risked explosion by touching off tricky fuses. No spent cinders from real skyrockets fell on the audience. The deafening roars that used to accompany such shows had been replaced by music, by popular request. The only other sounds were cries of delight.

As the final, breathtaking fireworks exploded, the Colony Anthem played. Under the spangled canopy, with a sky full of real stars beyond the dome, the people sang. Some voices were off-key. Others were blurred by stimulants or soothants or emotions. Stronger ones carried them. Rank was forgotten. Assembly members and secretaries and Space Fleet soldiers stood side by side. Permanent residents and transients who spent but part of the year on Mars saluted the planet together. The lyrics were trite, written by a sentimental amateur poet to commemorate the first anniversary of Mars Colony's founding. But emotion canceled out critical judgment. At the last chorus, their voices shook the dome:

"Across the darkest sea of all to claim this barren
    world;
Her rocks and rifts now ours to tame—Earth's
    banners are unfurled!
Olympus! On to Chryse's plains! Our Colony is she!
We'll make of Mars a better Earth, a Mars forever
    free!"

Tumultuous applause followed, and those who had headgear flung it in the air. Quol-Bez stood at courteous attention throughout, respecting his hosts' ritual. Chin Jui-Sao, like many others, was cheering herself hoarse, abandoning her normal decorum. The ceremony acted as a catharsis, washing away remnants of confusion and bad feelings the assassination attempt had caused. After all, no one had been hurt! And Councilman Ames and Chairman Hong would no doubt settle their differences—politicians always did, somehow. What did those crazy Earth First fanatics have to do with anything? This was the high point of Colony Days!

The fireworks display and the anthem weren't the closing events, but they put the cap on the evening, a bit sooner than President Grieske had planned. As the lights came back up, there was a lot of milling around. Dance music started once more. Vid dramas and live performances were scheduled for the little theaters on each entertainment island. Some went to get good seats. Others resumed their dancing. Most stood around chatting.

For some guests, it was time to leave. There were other, less public parties planned elsewhere. One of those would be at Saunder Estates, adjacent to President Grieske's summer residence, near Valles Marineris. Quol-Bez had other duty calls to make, and he and Sao and the diplomatic contingent escorting them bade good-bye, for the moment, to Brenna's parents and the President and numerous other dignitaries. They would all meet later, at one of the estates. Quol-Bez's embassy on Mars was in the same general area, east of Pavonis City, as Saunder Estates, making a later rendezvous at the private party quite easy for him.

"Time for us to go, too," Todd Saunder said when Quol-Bez had left. "It's been a great show, Fred. Event of the year. We'll see you at the Estates—about eleven or so?"

There were the obligatory pleas to stay a bit longer, courteously declined. President Grieske included Brenna and her young friends in the invitation. Brenna shrank from the idea, as did Derek and the others. A quiet party full of a lot of old Colonists! They would sit around complaining that this wasn't like the good old days and talk about people and places which meant nothing to Brenna's generation. Brenna and her friends turned down the President's urgings as politely as they could.

Todd Saunder lingered, asking his daughter, "You're not stopping by the Estates at all tonight, kitten, you and Derek?"

"Probably not, Dad. We've both got flights tomorrow. I've already booked the SE suite at Amazonis Spaceport. I imagine Morgan will be staying over, though I don't know how much time he'll spend at the party." Brenna nodded to Jutta Lefferts, who was talking with some acquaintances a few meters away.

"Well . . . then . . . we'll see you," her father said awkwardly. Brenna kissed him and Dian, but Todd was still reluctant to leave. Only when Dian insisted did he turn toward the light curtain with an irritable "Nag, nag! All *right!*" When they stepped away from the entertainment island, half a dozen Saunder Enterprises private police, in mufti, closed in around the older couple. After what had happened, security would be tight. There were many visitors from Earth here on Mars for Colony Days. The SE guards were taking no chances. Brenna knew that from now on, her longing for privacy would be futile. She and Derek would only be left alone once they were safely locked in the suite at the spaceport. She hadn't known about Derek's new plans when she had reserved that suite. And there had been a while, last night, when she had considered canceling their final night together before their ships launched. When she looked at Derek, though, she realized she would never have forgiven herself if she had. Each moment was going to be infinitely precious—and achingly rare in the future.

Morgan was staring after the departing older couple. "What's bothering Uncle Todd? I didn't think those crazies had upset him that much."

"No, it wasn't that," Brenna said. "It was the Mars landing holo-mode." She was mildly surprised that Morgan hadn't noticed the program's effect on her father. "You're looking more and more like Uncle Kevin. It broke Dad up. Didn't you see?"

"No, I guess I didn't. Maybe I *should* grow a mustache. That might lessen the resemblance . . ."

"At least it would act as a barricade to keep you from putting your foot in your mouth," Derek joshed.

"That's what *I* need," Brenna said, grimacing. "That got totally out of hand. I feel like an ass. Damn! Morgan and I have quizzed Quol-Bez plenty of times when he visited Saunder Estates here or Saunderhome back on Earth. But this time, with Stuart needling me . . . where the hell *is* he, now that he caused so much trouble?"

Derek jerked a thumb over his shoulder. "He left as soon as the excitement with the assassins started. No hero, he."

"Not unless he can find a sucker like me to do his dirty work," Brenna said. "It's probably just as well. This way the gossipers will get to talk about him and Aunt Carissa." She nodded to a group of well-known rumor mongers nearby. "Sometimes they're as bad as newshunters. One of them was hinting to me earlier, trying to find out if Stuart and Carissa are 'officially' feuding again or not."

Morgan guffawed. "Hardly likely! Not after the price he paid the *last* time. Messy, messy! A mistress with a kid she could prove was Stuart's. Stuart almost went along with her, too, before Carissa decided she didn't want a daughter-in-law *yet*. Little signature here, grease a judge's palm there, and no more mistress. Stuart kisses Auntie Carissa's hand, and she admits him back into his promised inheritance." His amusement faded. "The biggest price got paid by those poor little clones Carissa brewed up when she was trying to bring Stuart back into the fold."

"Shh!" Brenna warned.

"It worked," Morgan said, shaking his head. "Threaten him with cloned copies of her late, martyred husband. 'Tell me, Stuart, dear—who would have the better legal claim to being the *true* inheritor of Patrick Saunder, you or these children with Patrick's genetic structure?'"

"That was an atrocity," Derek said, discreetly lowering his voice. "What's she going to do with those babies? The whole thing was pretty damned shady, in legal terms. Cloning people is forbidden . . ."

"But it's done," Brenna said with a shrug. "If you can pay for it, and 'Rissa can."

"Clones! The concept's repellent. Not even a surrogate birth!"

Brenna rolled her eyes, fearing one of Derek's hobby-horses would come riding into the conversation. She and Morgan, like a lot of other kids of wealthy parents, were surrogate-born. The practice was fairly common among the upper classes, and, unlike Carissa Saunder's clandestine cloning adventure, surrogate births were quite legal. The fertilized ovum, lab-nurtured from the real parents' genetic material, was planted in a hired gestator. The woman was paid well for her nine months' efforts of carrying the tiny parasite. The child wasn't hers at all, simply renting space in her womb, so that older or low-fertility-problem women, or women with important careers, such as Dr. Dian Foix and Mariette Saunder, wouldn't be slowed down in the process of creating their families.

Common practice, for the elite; but Derek, and many other people, disliked it. His own mother had borne him, and he had always been touchy on the subject when he, Brenna, and Morgan were playmates years ago. Since he had signed on with Hiber-Ship Corporation and undergone its intense colonization training, he had become even more prejudiced. Brenna acknowledged Hiber-Ship Corporation had a point with its "roughing-it" indoctrination. There would be few modern conveniences on a frontier, never-been-explored alien planet. No special privileges like surrogate births. The pioneers would *have* to revert to the "basic" method of enlarging their colony. It wasn't Brenna's cup of stimulant, but she appreciated Derek's attitude.

"Cloning is repellent," he said again. "Not the kids. The people who cloned them."

"Agreed, but the tactic worked for Carissa. Held those babies over Stuart's head, and he sure shaped up fast. 'Rissa's got him jumping through hoops again, like one of her damned pet dogs."

"She's fine. Stuart's back in her good graces and planning how he'll spend his inheritance," Morgan said, his face flushing with anger. "And nobody gives a damn about those five babies copied out of Patrick Saunder's genes."

"Four," Brenna corrected him. The men looked at her, and Brenna nodded. "Dian told me that one of them died last month, never had been viable. Probably a couple of the others will die before they're pubescent, too. They're retardates, simply riddled with defective DNA. Cloning isn't *quite* the perfected art Aunt 'Rissa's scientists claimed it was. Listen, this is totally depressing. Let's talk about something else. Morgan, I told Dad you'd be dropping in at Saunder Estates tonight, even if I wasn't going to. Did I foul up your plans?"

Morgan's grin was wolfish. "Nope! Jutta and I will stay and chat with the old folks for a while, just to be polite. Then we intend to duck out and cross over the gorge to my estate. Picture it. That magnificent view from my balcony window. The lonely wind whistling down Valles Marineris. Some imported wine. A late-night snack. Some erotic holo-modes. A little appropriate mood music . . ."

"And all the 'lewd and lascivious' appetites you can handle," Derek said.

"Hey! This new dog knows some very interesting old tricks, friend," Morgan boasted. "My ladies never complain."

"Neither does mine . . ."

"What about tomorrow's launch?" Brenna demanded.

Morgan tapped his wrist mini-terminal. "Window's not

till 1800. Pre-launch chores are yours. Yuri will make sure you don't fall asleep over the computer. I'll show up in time for the PR show, never fear." Morgan touched his tiny collar com, talking to an unseen Saunder Enterprises security officer. "This is McKelvey. Please have my escort waiting. Assemblywoman Lefferts and I will be leaving the President's party immediately."

Brenna looked at Derek and read agreement in his face. The gala would be over, as far as they were concerned, when Morgan left. Time for a quiet departure. No one was likely to miss them now. The celebration would go on quite well without them. Brenna spoke into her jeweled pendant. "Captain Saunder and Captain Whitcomb will be heading out, too. We'll take the skimmer to Amazonis. I'd appreciate the usual backup guards. Thank you."

Morgan and Jutta were going east, using the main elevators to the train station. Derek muttered a few questions as he and Brenna started off toward the opposite side of the rotunda, Saunder Enterprises police dogging their heels. "Skimmer?" Derek said disbelievingly.

"Trust me. You'll like it."

Jumbled bits of conversation, laughter, and scraps of music floated out of each entertainment island they walked past. The areas now resembled real islands, isolated spots of light and activity beneath an arching life-support cover. The upper part of the dome was dark, the fireworks holo-mode stored away until next year.

As Brenna and Derek descended the ramp to the lower hall, a lone gypsy newshunter saw them. The man had been running toward the V.I.P. exit farther along the curving corridor, possibly hoping to intercept Morgan and Jutta. When he saw Brenna, he slammed to a halt. The guards closed in on him and commandeered his communicators and camera pendant. Was this the same over-eager type who had run afoul of Yuri this afternoon? Brenna couldn't be certain in the dim light. She almost felt sorry for the man, whomever he sold his scoops to. But not sorry enough to let him spoil her plans.

A guard detained the newshunter while the rest trooped along the hall. Thick silicate carpeting squeaked under their boots. They took the dogleg exit off Ramp Eighteen. That wasn't used much—which was Brenna's reason for choosing it. They met no one else as they jogged right, then left, then right again to reach the short-run elevators, which took them directly to the skimmer platforms. These, too, were deserted, so early in the evening. Brenna ordered three skimmers, one each for the guard groups and one for herself and Derek.

A disembodied robot dispatcher replied, "Your vehicles will be here from storage in ninety seconds. Please stand by."

Brenna tapped her foot impatiently. Ninety seconds was ridiculous! But this was a comparatively antiquated method of transport, the very first built on Mars Colony. Finally, the platform hatch *whooshed* open. The skimmers sat at the rail curb, left wing doors standing open. The guards fanned out, quickly checking all three vehicles. In Brenna's lifetime, no Saunder Enterprises security officer had ever found a bomb or other harmful device during one of these checks. Brenna considered the whole thing a nuisance, but her father and Carissa were adamant, repeating dire warnings and saying no one could be too careful. Brenna tolerated the delay with ill grace. Then they climbed aboard, letting the guards take the front and rear skimmers. In moments, the programming was on the screens and they were sailing away from the station.

The frictionless-drive, two-person cars swayed along the monorail. A series of air-lock irises opened and closed rapidly, stepping the three skimmers down through the atmospheres. The lead skimmer was opening up some distance, and Brenna couldn't see its running lights when her vehicle emerged out of the last air lock. The phosphorescent retaining banks bracketed them for several kilometers as the skimmers climbed a mountain shoulder. Then they were clear of the city, and night surrounded them. Brenna dimmed her car's lights so that she could see the view better.

Much of Pavonis City was out of sight, carved into the ridge, of course. But as the skimmers traversed the volcanic slopes above, Brenna and Derek could look down on agricultural stations and recreation domes. The rotunda was the biggest of the latter, though, strictly speaking, it wasn't usually a recreation area. The life-support bubble was an enormous blister, with many lights shining inside. They could just make out tiny figures moving around the floor.

Then even that sign of the capital was gone. Only the faint gleam from the skimmer's programmer screen remained, and Brenna masked that. Stars frosted the bowl of the sky. A broad, fuzzy band, the Milky Way, crossed the zenith and bisected the southern horizon, silhouetting some of Mars' rugged terrain. Except for the escort skimmers, there was no other man-made light in view. From this point on, any signs of human habitation would be rare—a few Terraform Division monitoring stations near Nix Olympus, an occasional shuttle beacon, or an isolated mining community's dome. During the journey to Amazonis Planitia Spaceport, they would be in utter darkness. A dust storm, like the bad one in '72, could shut down skimmer tracks. It was dangerous to use these little cars in the teeth of the fierce Martian winds. But this season, the air was almost still. The skimmer drifted eerily through black silence.

Brenna and Derek cuddled together in the double seat. It was more than a thousand kilometers to Amazonis Spaceport, and skimmer travel was leisurely. A two-hour ride lay ahead of them. "We could have cut the trip time to nothing on a train," Derek said, "or taken one of your SE shuttles. Or I could have checked a spare Hiber-Ship craft out for the night . . ."

"What's your hurry, hotshot?" Brenna leaned back, staring up at the night sky. It was like looking into infinity. She could fall—upward—forever into that starry void. The thought didn't frighten her at all. "What I'd really enjoy would be a low-level skid-plane flight, the way we would travel if we were on Earth. But Terraform Division's got some distance to go yet."

"Fifty years, at least, before the air's thick enough to support non-rocket flight," Derek agreed. "This will have to do for now." The skimmer rounded a curve along Nix Olympus's flank. Brenna moved with the skimmer, clinging closer to Derek. Laughter rumbled in his chest, and he stretched out beside her. Their arms folded about each other. "I was right to trust you, my love," he said. "I *do* like this. It's a marvelous idea."

"Of course! I'm a Saunder. Genes prove out. I came supplied with an extra amount of brains."

"Among other things."

They rode through the night, unhurried. The skimmer's insulation shut out the world but let in the starlight. Very shortly, though, neither of the passengers was watching the stars. They left the driving to the programmer as the little car glided onward into the Martian highlands and toward Amazonis Planitia Spaceport.

CHAPTER SIX

⊗⊗⊗⊗⊗⊗⊗⊗

Reach for the Stars

DEREK had already left when the suite's monitor screen waked Brenna at 0600. She peered blearily around the hotel bedroom, then focused on the terminal and forced her mind to function. There was a handwritten note propped against the screen, as usual. Handwriting was a dying art. But Derek's Hiber-Ship teachers trained their volunteers in that skill. It would be a useful tool, they believed, for rebuilding human society on the Kruger 60 worlds. Being a Saunder, Brenna had enjoyed the benefits of an expensive education, including how to read handwriting, even a scrawl like Derek's. She read the small square of disposa-fiche. "I love you. Good luck to you and Morgan. Take care, both of you. I'll see you again as soon as I can. D."

As soon as he could. And next March . . . never again.

Brenna and Derek had learned, long ago in their busy schedules, not to say good-bye face to face. They had hit on the note as a substitute. But this one hurt, reminding her of so much left unsaid, and of the lonely future.

She reread the brief message several times and worked her way through the morning routine—a sonic scrub, a snack from the food alcove, packing her travel kit with two weeks' worth of work clothes. Finally, she folded the note lovingly and sealed it in the pocket of her onepiecer.

Brenna sat down in front of the terminal, weighing several uncomfortable options. Then she cued the screen. "Saunder Estates. See if either of my parents is awake yet."

Dian was. Her image came on the monitor almost at once. "Hi, girl," she said brightly. "You look like morning doesn't agree with you. Never did, huh?"

Without preamble, Brenna asked, "Are you and Dad coming to the test next week?"

Her mother's face froze. "Did you ask your father that? Well, don't."

Brenna cocked her head, propping it up with her fist, gazing glumly at the woman on the vid. "I didn't ask him. But I was hoping . . ."

"No," Dian said, her tone hard and flat. "We've been through this. Drop it."

"Nothing's going to go wrong!" Brenna exclaimed in exasperation. "We've got it licked. The experts say so, the unmanned tests say so."

"Mari and Kevin thought that, too. They're dead. Your father was there when their ship went nova." The vid image brought out harsh shadows in Dian's features which Brenna hadn't noticed in the past. Her mother *was* beginning to show a few of her sixty-three years, under stress. "Dammit, girl, can't you understand?" Dian's mouth trembled. She was fighting emotion, but not winning. "Neither of us could take it if . . . all right, maybe it won't. I pray to God nothing *will* go wrong. Call it superstition. We'd go crazy, sitting up there at your FTL Station while you and Morgan and the others fly out to where nobody living has been . . ."

"Nobody *human*. We'll change that."

Dian underlined and amended her earlier words. "I hope and pray to God that you do. But we simply can't watch you try it. It'd be unbearable. It'd kill your father and me if . . ."

There was a heavy silence, the image dancing a little. Bad connection. Someone at ComLink would get kicked for that. Letting the boss's daughter and wife see a shoddy signal on the call terminal! Maintenance heads would roll.

Very softly, Brenna asked, "Would you take it better if I were going aboard Hiber-Ship and frozen in cryogenic stasis? I'd be leaving the Solar System for the rest of your lives. You'd never see me again."

"You'd be alive, with Derek," Dian said, unshakable. "We'd know that. We could imagine you waking up, living, having kids, even if we were long dead. That's different."

"Okay." Brenna felt as if she had handed over some irreplaceable part of her being and was watching it slowly bleed dry. "Where . . . where *will* you be?"

Dian glanced away, checking something on a business calendar. "I'm en route for Earth tomorrow. Linguists' conference in Brasilia, remember? Your father's staying here. A little business, a little vacation . . ."

"Then he'll be close when we . . ." Brenna didn't finish. She had heard herself sounding like a foolish, hopeful child. Why did it matter so much? Even if her father watched the test from FTL Station, he would be thousands of kilometers from the actual site. Here on Mars, he'd just get the results on a slightly delayed basis. Of course, if he wouldn't be watching, some aide would have to deliver the news.

And yet, it made a big difference. Derek wouldn't be at FTL Station. Neither would her parents. All three had been there, back in '72, when Mariette and Kevin and Cesare had made the first manned flight attempt. Two months after that, Derek had signed on with Hiber-Ship Corporation, making a major philosophical statement about his future, beginning the separation between him and Brenna. And Brenna's father and mother had refused to come to any future tests. They barely asked how things were going. They didn't want to know, emotionally. They avoided the subject of Breakthrough Unlimited as much as possible. Widening gaps. And Brenna didn't know how to pull all of them back together.

"Well, I guess I'd better let you go," Brenna said slowly, unwillingly. "Give Dad a kiss for me. Have a safe trip to Earth . . ."

"*You* have a safe trip, too, girl, you and Morgan." It was as close as the older woman could skirt to the dangerous topic. Dian's dark eyes penetrated the distance and the medium, sending aching maternal concern and love. "Bye."

Brenna gazed at the darkened screen for a long while.

Seven days and counting. Last leg of the big test. Events were certainly off to a wonderful start! All the old pressures she had accumulated through the months of preparation for this critical test—and some big new ones, including family problems.

Finally, she roused herself out of her gloom. She didn't

have time to sit around and wallow in self-pity. There was too much to do.

Two Saunder Enterprises guards came to attention as Brenna exited from the private suite. They followed her down the slide stairs to the Spaceport Inn's lobby. Other pilots and travelers were there, dozing, reading, or waiting for rides out to their ships. Brenna sympathized with her fellow early risers and ignored the few with weird biorhythms who insisted on being cheerful. She was fully awake now, her mind on click-click status, but damned if she would greet the Martian dawn with a grin, as they were doing!

The SE private sub-surface shuttle train was at the lower-lobby platform, as ordered. The single-car vehicle carried Brenna directly from the inn to Saunder Enterprises' facility at the west edge of the spaceport. It was a very short trip. Thanks to Mariette Saunder's close involvement with the Mars landing and first settlement, Saunder Enterprises had been the first leaser when Amazonis Planitia Spacecraft was being built, and had a prime location.

Brenna debarked and headed for the Breakthrough Unlimited section. She passed the main office along the way, glancing in to see if anything was going on there yet. Flight Controller George Li and his assistants were busy already. A few media personnel, yawning, had showed up. The public relations show wouldn't begin until 1030 hours, local zone time. A small group was watching the vid, where the news was all about the unprecedented assassination attempt yesterday. ". . . Martian Civil Enforcement, with the full cooperation of Protectors of Earth and Terran Worlds Council's Space Fleet, is investigating the shocking attempt on Councilman Ames's life. Early indications are that this was a premeditated action on the part of a fanatic fringe of the now-defunct Earth First Party, which recently infiltrated several highly placed delegations of Earth's governing bodies. There is no evidence that Chairman Hong had any knowledge of this clandestine group or that his aides were in any way involved with the . . ."

So that was going to be the official story. Brenna imagined a lot of wheeling and dealing behind the scenes. Quite possibly the leaders of Protectors of Earth *didn't* realize various fanatics were still operating on the home planet and murderously intent on stopping Terran Worlds Council's eclipse of P.O.E. in Solar System affairs. But if so, it made Chairman Hong and his fellow rulers seem woefully naive.

Was this better than open warfare? Mankind at peace with itself, for an impressively long period. Earth, Mars, and the satellites coexisting without conflict. Instead of civil war, though, there were factions, economic undercover operations, and cat's-paw fanatics who could be planted in crucial positions and even try to kill individual power figures among their opponents. Maybe the frequently heard comment at last night's gala was valid—Mars and the outside-Earth colonies ought to cut loose and go their separate ways and leave Earth for the stay-at-homes.

When Brenna reached Flight Operations, she found some of the support crew watching that same newscast. They shook their heads, echoing her sour opinions of the whole affair. Many of Breakthrough Unlimited's pilots and team members were Earth-born and were forced, for business reasons, to make trips back "home" several times a year. But their attitudes were colonial, outward-oriented, as Brenna's were.

Yuri Nicholaiev, Rue Polk, Hector Obregón, and the younger pilots had checked in and were busy getting into harness. Morgan and Tumaini Beno would be the last to arrive, according to the time-off schedule. Brenna found an empty terminal screen and got to work with the others. They had had three months' intensive preparation for the all-important upcoming test, and two weeks of badly needed R & R. The vacation had put everyone in fine shape. The excitement was regenerating, crackling like electricity through the flight operations room. Jokes and gear-up chatter made the preparations go smoothly, rather than distracting them.

Pulling together. Organizing for the Big One, the one they had been in training for all this time.

Delayed-time messages came in from the advance team, which was already out at FTL Station, warming things up for the rest. The flight team and George Li's coordinators put everything in the hopper. Fuel requisitions, necessary food and water, and spare parts. For FTL Station, it was an unusually small supply order. No more three-month sessions! After the successful run, the lengthy test prelims would be no more!

Brenna absorbed all the accumulated data and combined

it with the update Yuri Nicholaiev had swapped with her mini-terminal until she could recite everything without hesitation. She was synchronizing programs with Yuri, Rue, and Hector. When Tumaini and Morgan got there, the Prototype, Chase craft, and backup pilots went into a huddle, doing a hasty talk-through of routines they all knew forward and backward.

There was one brief interruption during Brenna's vector plot check. The vid was usually turned to the news channels, to pick up the constant babble about Colony Days and the scandal at the gala. However at 0930 the spaceport's observation channel showed a liftoff from Amazonis's northwest quadrant, and Brenna watched the silvery needle ride its plume of exhaust up into the dark sky. The view was long-range, but she didn't need to read the insignia or the ident printout at the bottom of the screen. That was Hiber-Ship Corporation's Mars-Deimos shuttle. It would be taking Derek, Lilika Chionis, and a number of other corporation crew people up to Hiber-Ship's transshipment post near Mars' outer moon. They would rendezvous there with their fleet of ferries and pick up Earth-manufactured pharmaceuticals and shipments of animal-breeding stock. The six-ship convoy would then take the precious cargo on to near-Jovian orbit, where Hiber-Ship's *New Earth Seeker* was being built and provisioned for her decades-long trip out into the universe.

A moment of fire, a muffled roar, barely heard through Mars' thin atmosphere, and the shuttle was out of sight. Derek was on his way. But only on a supply trip. *New Earth Seeker* wouldn't launch on her journey until early next spring. Derek would be returning, this time.

Brenna became aware that Yuri was watching her, looking worried. She shook off her melancholy. "I'm okay. Full attention." Yuri's gaze was disturbingly intent. Not doubting. But understanding more than Brenna might have wished him to. She felt guilty, then relieved when he finally turned away.

Morgan arrived shortly after that, and Tumaini Beno a half hour later, barely in time to get ready for the PR show. The Affiliation of the Rift expatriate was miffed when he found out Morgan had checked in first. Apparently they had had some private bet going, and Tumaini had lost. He flung a few choice Mwera curses, and Morgan

96

laughed and retaliated with the same in other languages, including a Vahnaj epithet or two.

George Li poked his head in the pilots' room. "On stage, everybody. The newshunters are here. Publicity hour!"

Among themselves, the pilots had pithier names for this sort of display: "Dashing and Daring Bastards Show." "Glamorous Idiots Revue." "Smile for the Cretins, You Fuckers . . ." They donned their tunics and precisely tailored pants and polished boots and made sure the Breakthrough Unlimited patches on their shoulders and breasts showed prominently, then paraded into the small theater near the main office. Hector's and Tumaini's wives and kids were there. That was part of the show. They were the only married members of the pilots' team, since Rue had broken up with her husband a couple of years before. And the kids were cute, always good for a lot of human-interest copy for the media newshunters.

The vid session came first. Brenna and Morgan posed by themselves and with other pilots and George Li, Tumaini and his little nuclear family, Hector Obregón with his, women and children standing by their men. Carmelita's smile was shy, Aluna Beno's was hard, and she placed her hands firmly on her sons' shoulders, as if she and Tumaini were in competition for the boys' loyalty.

Then the various flight teams posed. Morgan, Tumaini, and Rue—the lucky ones chosen to fly Prototype II. They had won the coin toss, in other words. Brenna and Yuri Nicholaiev would fly Chase One. Hector and Shoje Nagata would be backup, in Chase Two. They smiled on cue, but with some of their envy of the Prototype II team showing. Adele Zyto and Joe Habich wouldn't be at the test-flight area at all. When the main shuttle took off later today, they would be aboard the second section's shuttle, heading out on a different vector. It would take the second shuttle, a converted Chase ship stripped for speed, considerable time to get to the "completed hop" point. Adele and Joe had been through all the preliminaries in advance, in order to make the long trip out to the asteroids. An emergency crew was already out there on Breakthrough Unlimited's small satellite. Backup med staffers and com techs, mostly. During the series of unmanned tests, there had been little need for those people—just for someone to fetch the unmanned FTL test vehicles if they had refused to obey programmed commands and reverse course. They hadn't. Five times the lonely "completed-hop"-point pilots had sat out there, waiting uselessly for a drone vehicle. This time, they hoped they wouldn't be needed, either. A successful test! Nobody wanted to be put out of a job worse than those standby crews heading for distant orbit.

It griped Brenna that the reporters didn't understand the importance of their mission. But that was typical. The pilots expected it, and gnashed their teeth a bit.

Morgan and Tumaini and Rue didn't lord it over them. But there was no mistaking their joy.

Brenna wanted to tell Adele and Joe and Shoje, the youngest members of the pilot team, that as bad as it was to be on the outside looking in, it was worse when you were fully qualified—as she and Yuri and Hector all were —yet had lost the flip of a coin to your fellow pilots. Equally qualified, but second in line.

Somebody had to be second. That was the way it was. Fate. Bad luck.

There would be other faster-than-light flights, sure. But there would be only one successful *first* one, ever!

The photos and posing were the easy part. Then came the interviews. ComLink's Ife Enegu was a pet media person, one of Saunder Enterprises' hired hands, though a very well-paid and famous one. Others, like Charlie Dahl of Nakamura and Associates' TeleCom and independents such as Navarro and Pickard and Reilly, were sharper, looking for chinks in Breakthrough Unlimited's armor.

"Is it true Dr. de Groote's computers expressed some concern over the hull strength . . . ?"

"Is it true you have secret access to Vahnaj FTL techniques through your connections with T.W.C.'s diplomatic negotiators . . . ?"

"Isn't this the same propulsion system which Space Fleet dropped in '69 because of unsurmountable power problems . . . ?"

The questions were ones that had been answered many times, and some were deliberately obtuse or outrageous, designed to chew up footage—so that the newshunters' vid teams could feature their reporters on screen.

Brenna took over part of the question-fielding. That job went with the glamour. "Graviton spin resonance is a working theory, people. It's been thoroughly tested. If you'll check your releases, which George Li handed out earlier, you'll see the entire record." Morgan and Yuri were cueing diagrams and charts on the wall screen terminal behind Brenna, pointing out significant aspects as she and George Li traded the lecture back and forth.

"Here you see the field barrier specs. Resonance field is developed and interchanges energy between electromagnetic and gravitational spin fields," Brenna explained. Morgan's big hands made swooping motions. He was grinning, amused at the repetitive program. Brenna half expected him to make a crack about taking this show on the vid-entertainment circles, they were becoming so expert at it after five years—three under the present Breakthrough Unlimited team. Yuri traced the critical layer in the outer hull as Brenna added, "The barrier field lies here, creating a thin near-singularity on a momentary basis . . ."

George Li spoke up. "There will be no speed gain in the physical frame. But graviton spin resonance field, fully engaged, results in a 'hop' of length dependent on the amplitude of the pulse and of duration determined by frequency . . ."

Many of the media types were looking slightly glazed. But the holo-mode dutifully took it all in. It sounded impressive to laymen, and to those knowledgeable in celestial flight mechanics, the solid theory made a very good case for Breakthrough Unlimited.

Yuri's slight accent lent a colorful touch as he continued the explanation. "The ship will move along a ballistic trajectory determined by initial velocity, local gravitational fields, and 'interhop' timing. Ordinary high-efficiency spacecraft engines—such as those used by our Chase ships and most Space Fleet ships—will maneuver Prototype II and set direction. When the field is turned on, pseudo speed will develop . . ."

"And it's worked perfectly five times now, with unmanned test craft," Brenna finished. "On a single jump, we can send an unmanned graviton spin resonance equipped vehicle to Jovian orbit in four minutes . . . or considerably less, people. Calculate that with current top-speed flight specs!"

George stressed, "We have run thirty-six general equipment tests and eighteen unmanned tests over the past three years, including those five successful unmanned flights quite recently. We are ready."

"But there *were* some failures, weren't there?" Charlie Dahl of TeleCom persisted.

"One failure," Morgan said, with heavy emphasis. "Ask the experimental programmers. They'll tell you that's nominal, Charlie."

"But aren't you worried that . . ."

"What about the other faster-than-light projects?" several reporters demanded. No one heard the rest of Dahl's query.

"We don't consider them serious competition," Rue Polk stated boldly.

Tumaini Beno's black face split in a cheery smile. "Indeed! The experts agree, too. Hosi No Miti Kaisya's matter-antimatter attempts have, shall we say, not been exactly fruitful." Dahl and the other TeleCom staffers scowled at that accurate reference. Hosi No Miti Kaisya was, of course, Nakamura and Associates, their employer. Tumaini Beno went on. "And Exo-Trans' tachyon employment has had a long succession of failures. Their theory is okay, but under present levels of propulsion technology, that form of FTL simply is not practical. It would be better applied to achieving sub-space radio capability, such as the Vahnaj and more advanced galactic civilizations currently enjoy . . ."

"Yes," Yuri said, "and when *we* achieve faster-than-light travel, we will *need* sub-space communications more than ever."

The junior pilots were fidgeting, unable to contribute too much at this stage. They knew who ranked, and they didn't. But they presented a united front with the others. The pilots, all friendly rivals when it came to in-flight glory, were allies against outsiders. And newshunters, even the ones on their side, qualified as outsiders. Passengers. Stowaways. Non-contribs, in pilots' slang.

"LeFevre Société's photon bypass . . ."

"Theory. Only theory," George Li insisted. "They don't even have a working model. No, people, graviton spin resonance is *It*. In about a week from now, everyone will know it. As for Terran Worlds Council's Space Fleet's 'letting' a civilian outfit take over the project—well, people, we all know about appropriations and intergroup politics. Ours is not to question why. We just produce."

Morgan summed it all up: "And you can bet that when we *do* produce a working faster-than-light ship, the military will be right there to pick our brains. Bigger and better propulsion systems to catch asteroid hijackers farther and farther out from the Sun, huh? You might say we're doing our bit for everyone—for the commercial trader who hopes to do business on a regular basis with the Vahnaj and other species, for the Space Fleet, and for the ordinary citizen, who can spend his future vacations on some *really* exotic worlds, light-years from Mars!"

There were a few more requests for pictures. Pilots, support crew, in different combinations. Brenna, Rue Polk, and Adele Zyto posed together, because there was still a reactionary element, on Earth, which was fascinated by the idea of women test pilots even though women had been flying at equal risk with their male counterparts for a century and a half. Brenna's red head was next to Rue's blond one, with Adele's sleek dark hair framing the other side of the threesome. Brenna made sure, too, that Adele and Nagata and Joe Habich got heavy coverage. They were juniors now. Someday they would be on the main line. They were the future. She treated them as her protégés.

The onerous PR chore out of the way, the pilots and support crew who were taking the first shuttle up to FTL Station headed for Suitup. The mood grew edgy, despite the jokes. It didn't matter that they had been through hundreds of flights. Safety regs were in full effect. That was how people stayed alive. Every step was checked, double-checked, and triple-checked. Life packs. Emergency procedure rehearsals, the works. Spaceflight wasn't yet boring. Even civilians had to go through this routine on an interplanetary trip or a ride from planet to station.

Boarding. Launch. Right on time at 1800.

Brenna had first solo-piloted a spacecraft when she was fifteen. But each takeoff remained a fresh, exhilarating experience. The noise, the shuddering of the beautiful machine around her, the pressure of the extra gees—it all added up. This was when she and Morgan and every other pilot really started to come alive.

Their view monitors split the scenes, showing scans in all directions from the ascending ship. A launch from Mars was distinctly different in "feel" from one out of Earth's deep gravity well or a satellite's tiny one. Mars had a much lower density than Earth, but it *was* a planet, one on which Brenna now spent a great deal of her time. She watched the red, rocky terrain fall away. The rapidly shifting perspective filled the screens. Horizons stretched and began to curve as the rocket climbed, adding its thrust to Mars' rotational velocity. Amazonis Planitia shrank. Beacons marking the hangars and the spaceport's upper structures dwindled and were lost in the Marscape.

As the ship's track angled ever more steeply, Tharsis Montes' shield volcanoes swam by below, looking very tiny, as they had to Earth's first unmanned Mariner vehicles scanning from Mars orbit. The awesome craters seemed little more than pockmarks on the ancient world's face.

Then they were passing that continent-wide rift—the Valles Marineris.

The living map appeared to turn as the spacecraft pierced the tenuous Martian atmosphere. At the surface, Terraform Division was making some progress in enriching that air. Out here, it had never been worth considering and soon was high vacuum.

Gravity and acceleration balanced. Free fall. Safety webbing held the crew and passengers in their couches. Programs were on automatic, but Yuri and Rue Polk had the backup controls for this flight, ready to go to manual if necessary.

At this altitude, only the navigational scanners could pick out any signs of human habitation down on the planet. Infrared outlined patches of Mars' changing ecology —genetic manipulation of Earth life forms, plants which would break down soil and rocks and release their own by-products and materials trapped in Mars' elements for thousands of millennia. It was a start. In a hundred years or so, humans would walk on Mars' surface without need of special life-support equipment. And pilots could fly non-rocket craft through Mars' air. They would tame Mars and make it a sister Earth.

Vector launch point. Everyone checked safety gear. Mars wouldn't slingshot them, as Hiber-Ship would be helped into launch out of the Solar System by Jupiter's enormous gravitational field. But the smaller planet gave them some help. There was no sense wasting fuel—yet! They would gulp fuel like spendthrifts during the upcoming test.

Mars faded with startling rapidity. Zoom screens had

102

already located an irregular orbiting lump off to port—Deimos. Brenna couldn't see Hiber-Ship's ferry warehouse, of course. She knew Derek was there, but there was little cross-system communications, beyond necessary navigational talk between their different computers. In a few seconds, Mars' outer moon was beyond the remote lenses' reach, and they were on the way.

The vidcasters described this sort of voyage as "rocketing up from Mars." To an Earth-bound point of view, it was. To a space traveler's eyes, however, the shuttle was moving from one minute spot to another on an infinity-wide grid. Technically, there *was* no "up" or "down" out here. Yet from Earth's plane, the ship appeared to move northward, toward the galactic pole. Ambassador Quol-Bez had sometimes noted that, to the Vahnaj, *Earth* was "northward" from the Vahnaj home world. Now that he lived among humans, Quol-Bez abided by their star maps and spoke in their terms. When in Rome . . . And on those maps the Vahnaj Ambassador's closely guarded faster-than-light vehicle was parked "below" the Solar System, in Lower Quadrant Sector Eleven of Space Fleet's charts. Breakthrough Unlimited's test-run area, franchised to them for their exclusive use, was in Upper Quadrant Sector Five, well out of the orbital paths of any major bodies or space traffic. Prototype II would need plenty of elbow room when it made its leap to FTL.

Brenna envisioned citizens on Earth watching some of Breakthrough Unlimited's publicity material right about now. They would see a model of planets whirling around a ludicrously undersized Sun. On the model, Breakthrough Unlimited's high ecliptic FTL Station would loom very large, looking "down" on the busy microcosm of the Sun's family: Venus, Earth, Mars, the asteroids, Jupiter, and so on. In actuality, there was nothing to see, from FTL Station *or* from the shuttle heading "up" toward that Station. The shuttle was racing through tens of thousands of kilometers, surrounded by nothingness. Earth was a faint light showing only on the navigational screens. Mars was a shrinking disk. Venus and Mercury were washed out by the Sun's golden presence. Jupiter was a yellowish blob at five o'clock aft, as the quaint old-time expression went. There was little else but space junk, and not much of that, since now they were out of traffic vectors. Their destination,

FTL Station, was much too small and too far away for the scanners to detect it as anything but a com signal yet.

Emptiness. And nothing between Brenna and that but the ship's triple hull. People like her aunt Carissa loathed spacing and never left Earth's sanctuary because of their fear. That reaction was more alien than Quol-Bez was, to Brenna. She had loved spacing ever since her first ride, as a baby, in her father's private shuttle. All of gravity's restraints and narrow planetary horizons swept away. Complete freedom. How could anyone *not* love it?

Brenna cupped her hands symbolically, drawing that wonderful, limitless void to herself. She glanced around. Yuri was smiling at her, comprehending and sharing the emotion. Morgan, too, had noticed Brenna's gesture. His gray eyes shone. He copied Brenna's action, closing his hands into big fists.

"Seven more days, and we'll own the whole damned universe," he said.

Or die in a fireball . . .

No! Brenna would *not* let the stresses break out of the dark part of her mind.

But she knew they were going to. The only thing she could try to do was control them, tamp them down, make that tension work for her instead of against her, if possible.

The trip to FTL Station chewed up most of a twenty-four-hour Earth-type day. Along the way, the calendars rolled up.

Day Six, and counting.

Ahead lay a long, busy schedule. There were delays built in, necessary ones Brenna would have to suffer through. No skipping them. George Li and the med staffers and everyone else insisted the delays were essential to the pre-planned program. They had to do this right. For history's sake, if not for the pilots' impatience.

And not only the pilots were impatient. They would all be chewing the equipment, before the final moment clicked into the timers.

Deceleration began at 1545. People had been napping in the shuttle or catching up on their homework en route. Gradually, those who were sleeping awoke. Those who had been running computers finished their programs. Everyone checked gear, fidgeting, wanting to dock at the Station and get started.

Yuri and Rue followed the rules, though. They stepped the shuttle's speed down by exact stages, slowly bringing her into FTL Station's orbit and maneuvering alongside with vernier thrusters.

Breakthrough Unlimited's FTL Station was a home away from home. It had grown from an ungainly cluster of interconnected life-support pods to a large artificial habitat able to house more than a hundred people. For nearly a year after that first failed Prototype, the survivors hadn't done much but rehash the accident, finding the mistakes. When they had decided what had gone wrong, they had gone back to work, and part of the new plan called for beefing up FTL Station to provide better flight support. They had fulfilled the goal, and then some.

The shuttle warped in close, and boarding tunnels attached. Brenna felt proud of that slick efficiency showing in all operations. FTL Station was no competition for a gigantic facility like Goddard or Kirkwood, of course. But it served Breakthrough Unlimited very well. Like all manmade constructs in high vacuum, it looked strange to those unused to free fall. There were bulbous projections, thousands of antenna feelers and dishes bristling from every angle, and tunnels snaking between the free-floating sections. It was lovely to a Spacer, though.

Interim reports were coming in from the second section shuttle, now well on its way out to the little satellite at the "completed hop" point. Right on schedule. They would arrive in time to set up and be ready, as observers if nothing else, when the test began and Morgan and the first team took the Prototype through the light-speed barrier and jumped out to the backup satellite—and beyond! Adele Zyto and Joe Habich were far enough along their journey now so that a communications lag was beginning to show up, long pauses interrupting each exchange while the voices and images crossed the lengthening distance between FTL Station and the second section shuttle.

At FTL Station, the first team and the Chase ship pilots went into intense simulator refresher courses. The Chase pilots were like understudies, supporting the stars but inwardly half hoping that they would get a chance to step on stage themselves and handle the main ship. No such luck! Morgan, Tumaini, and Rue were in peak condition, primed for the big event.

Day Five.

The pool newshunters arrived and settled in for the buildup and the test. ComLink sent Ife Enegu herself. She was Goddard-raised and thoroughly at home in a space habitat like this. TeleCom sent lesser rankers. The gypsy newshunters weren't a problem here. They couldn't afford the passage to high ecliptic. TeleCom and some of the independent pool reporters were mildly abrasive, but that was part of the pilots' fitness preparation. It kept them alert.

Day Four, and counting. Nerves already taut drew still tighter as the day of the test loomed.

Dr. Helen Ives, chief of FTL Station's medical department, put the pilots through their paces, showing no mercy. She and her assistants did this for the pilots' own sakes. Med Staff had to certify that each test pilot was in top form, or he or she wouldn't take the ride—even if that person flunked was Brenna or Morgan, the co-owners of Breakthrough Unlimited. The possibility of rejection gave everyone nightmares. But at least medications were available to cure those. The pilots wondered if they could will themselves into A-One clearances. If desire alone could do it, they would.

"Close your eyes. Open your mouth wide, Rue . . ."

"Tumaini, touch the calibrator with your fingertips . . ."

"Make a fist, McKelvey. You, too, Saunder . . ."

"Hector, step up on the gravity treader . . ."

"Run in place, Yuri . . ."

"Inhale! Exhale, Shoje . . ."

The psych tests were worse, pushing the pilots' tempers to the edges.

"Why did you react to that question with such hostility . . . ?"

"Do you often notice these sensations when you're under stress . . . ?"

"What are you thinking about when you look at this sketch . . . ?"

Day Three, and counting.

Another media session was on the schedule. Smile and look confident.

There was a dichotomy to the entire relationship between Breakthrough Unlimited's pilots and the working media.

On one hand, the pilots looked down on these camera-toting questioners as outsiders, not part of the exclusive breed to which they themselves belonged. Yet there wasn't any pilot, privacy-seeking Brenna Saunder or shy Yuri Nicholaiev not excepted, who wasn't actually aware of the power media wielded. That was adulation, at the other end of those inane questions and constant demands to pose for holo-mode recordings. And it was future wealth and fame. The pilots wanted both, when they were honest enough to admit that to one another. The exclusive club status *and* the fame could only be achieved *if* these news-hunters spread their names and images throughout the Solar System.

"What are your personal feelings as you prepare for this historic event?"

"We're ready." It didn't matter who had said that. As it happened, it was Morgan, first pilot for Prototype II.

"Does it worry you at all that the first attempt, three years ago, failed?"

The question no one should ask. Bad luck. Bad form.

"We'd be fools if we didn't take that previous test into account," Tumaini Beno responded. "But this is a new design. All the bugs are out now."

They radiated confidence, soaking up the occasional covetous or envious glance from the newshunters and their support crew.

Day Two. The reporters were out of their hair. But that didn't seem to help. Now the last push was coming up, and the time every pilot dreaded most—the go-or-no-go decisions from the people paid to oversee their physical, mental, and emotional well-being.

The pilots went through rigorous final-stage simulation testing. They rode exact mock-ups of Test and Chase craft. Time after time Brenna and the others went through their paces, as they had been doing now, in some cases, for nearly five years. Readouts duplicated those they would see during the actual run. At random points, the program fed in flaws, testing the pilots' reflexes. Emergency situation. Think fast! Counter! Power loss. Meteor impact. Life-support-systems failure. Think! React! Build brain pathway alternates. Speed up the natural processes to their limits. No time must be wasted if that one-in-ten-million impossibility occurred and they had to *use* these training procedures.

Some of the psych staffers had debated whether there was such a thing as too much emergency stress training. Boredom might set in. Majority overruled them. Safety regs would apply. Full testing schedule. Blood and urine samples. Lung capacity. Stamina. Neural exchange potentials. Emotional profiles. The pilots were honed and checked as their machines were honed and checked.

No one flunked. The backup pilots, who had gone through all the testing agonies, tried not to look too disappointed. Next time, they insisted, *they* would be the ones taking the ride.

Dr. Ives induced one long, final, dream-laden sleep session to get rid of lingering unconscious foul-ups that might spoil concentration.

Day One. The waiting, the testing, the anticipation, were over.

There was a brief bon voyage celebration in FTL Station's main control room. Out at the hangars, visible on remote scans, the support crews' parties were going on, too. Reporters horned in, grabbing a few last opportunities to rub elbows with these elite people. From now on, they would be watching—as would the support crew and backup pilots—from a distance, out of the real action.

"We're ready on our relays," Ife Enegu, spokeswoman for the media pool, said. "Right through on our satellite feeds to Mars and Earth."

Brenna grinned. "Just be sure to get our names spelled right in the printouts, huh? Big, fat letters." That was good for a tension-releasing round of laughter. There was a short, noisy argument about how each participant wanted to be listed in the annals. A joke. The media already had complete bios on everyone, including George Li and Dr. Helen Ives and the other non-pilot team members. The names would be spelled right. The important thing was the date, and the newshunters already had that noted. April 28, 2075, would rank right up there with July 20, 1969.

The pilots started their adventure, heading for Suitup, good wishes ringing in their ears.

Programs, rolling.

The med staffers' dream therapy had worked. They felt

the supreme confidence they needed, not cocky, but keenly alert. Brenna was acutely conscious of every sensation—the soft spacesuit inner liner, the cool rush of bottled air over the cilia in her nostrils, the way the light gleamed on the ready room's walls, and a sweet aftertaste from the non-alcoholic syntha wine she had drunk during the celebration in Main Control.

Computers checked the human support crews' work. Cleared for departure. The pilots cycled the air locks and rode the mini-skidder over to the hangars. Brenna barely noticed the shifts in gravity as they left the skids and climbed aboard their ships. The days of hyperendors, gravity compensation medications, and super-nutriments had done a splendid job, fine-tuning biology.

The prep tests took another hour and a half, just to be sure. Maintenance craft flitted around the three test ships —Prototype II and Chase One and Chase Two. Plug-ins. Making sure observation stations and drone camera deployments were secure. Morgan, Tumaini, and Rue were busy in Prototype II. Brenna and Yuri Nicholaiev, in Chase One, and Hector Obregón and Shoje Nagata in Chase Two, had their own extremely heavy schedules to complete before launch.

Waiting. The simulator rooms all over again, the tension growing. This was different, though. No drill. No more drills at all! After today, there would be little need for simulator training, except for the flood of new recruit pilots they'd get.

Remote monitors showed the three ships floating in space within the hangar. Chase One and Two appeared to be copies of Prototype II. Right now, antenna and thruster ports were open on all three ships. That would change, once the test point was reached. By modern standards, these ships looked weird—sleek and spheroid and capable of buttoning up totally so that nothing interrupted the hull. There had never been a ship quite like Prototype II, not even its ill-fated predecessor.

"Central, George Li, Flight Control. Five minutes . . ."

"We read you, Control." That came through on three channels—Morgan's, then Brenna's, then Hector's.

"All circuits go."

"We copy, George. We are go. Beginning recording sequence," Yuri noted.

Tumaini and Nagata repeated that. Rue Polk added, "All on-board observation systems are green . . ."

"Confirm, Prototype II."

"Power systems are green," Tumaini said. "We are ready, little sisters."

Time ticked away. George Li was saying, "Twenty seconds. Bring us a souvenir from Jupiter's orbit."

Morgan's grin lit up the screens, even from behind his protective helmet faceplate. "Will do! Will do!" His enthusiasm overrode the distortions of the audio. Brenna returned his smile, staring into the screen linking her with the main ship. She held up a thumb.

"Here we go. Follow my lead, Brenna, Hector . . . !"

Zero. Programs aligned. Thrusters fired simultaneously. The three ships eased out of the hangar, dropping clear. Brenna's hands were everywhere as she monitored the computers and screens. She and Yuri voice-cued and absorbed, as the other pilots were doing.

They "fell" a kilometer from FTL Station before they fired their big engines. This was an incredible kick in the pants, an exciting one. They left the Station like meteors outward bound from the Sun, accelerating.

Programs rippled across the screens. The computers did most of the work. But Brenna and the others weren't passengers by a long shot.

Economy didn't matter. This was what they had been saving the fuel for. The three ships were open wide—on conventional power systems—rushing to reach test-point start.

Dr. Ives and an emergency medical team had ridden out ahead of them and were already on station. The rescue squad wasn't allowed to get too close to the test-run area, because of the unknown energies involved in graviton spin resonance drive. If the worst happened and Prototype II *and* the Chase ships were disabled, someone had to be within rescue distance. Brenna smiled at the thought, her newfound assurance buoying her. No rescue teams would be needed, either here or at the "completed hop" point out beyond the asteroids!

Signals fed back to FTL Station, data for George Li, audio and computer compatible beams compressing, carrying the information on to Mars from there.

110

"Hope we're bombing through," Brenna commented in a rare moment when she had the leisure to chat. Yuri's expression, on the monitor, was quizzical. She couldn't see him directly; he was behind a safety bulkhead on the other side of the cockpit. "Dian will chew me out if she doesn't get a full copy for Saunder Enterprises' archives," Brenna explained. The thought caused a pang. Dian was halfway to Earth by now, heading in the opposite direction, running away from her daughter's historic journey to the edge of new frontiers.

Suddenly Morgan's face appeared beside Yuri's on the screen. "I heard that. So will Aunt Dian, when the signal catches up with her."

"Then let's give her and Dad a good show . . ."

"Two minutes to 'hop' point."

They had gone through this many times before, when unmanned FTL vehicles had rushed toward this point and "disappeared" when the graviton spin resonance field engaged. On the last few tests, Breakthrough Unlimited had saved money by not posting anyone out at the second section "completed hop" point—where Adele Zyto and Joe Habich and the standby emergency medical and rescue personnel were waiting right now. It seemed as if the standby teams had rehearsed enough to be ready for *this* test, and it was cheaper to send someone out to fetch the unmanned probe in case it didn't function properly and return. But today, humans would be aboard the FTL ship, a full-sized craft, not a scaled-down test model. Graviton spin resonance would hurtle them forward at fourteen times the speed of light, retracing the unmanned test vehicles' infinity-ripping path. Jumping to Jovian orbit in minutes, not days!

The three ships were on ballistic courses. Chase One and Two stood off thirty kilometers, sending out their close-up drone cameras. They would all hit peak acceleration, for civilian-available ships. The only spacecraft that could surpass them in the Solar System were a few military vehicles and Quol-Bez's Vahnaj ship.

Images of Quol-Bez's gray face flashed in Brenna's mind. That didn't distract her but became part of her focus. The Vahnaj. A highly intelligent alien species, star rovers, far ahead of *Homo sapiens* in technology.

111

For now. And now that was going to change.

Trajectories set. Computers marking off the seconds. Three ships plunging through the void. Nothing in their way for millions and millions of kilometers.

"Stress high nominal," Hector said. "All systems steady . . ."

They were too far out from FTL Station now. Chase One and Two assumed backup monitoring because the signals from George Li would take precious fractions of seconds to travel to them, even at the speed of light.

"Prototype II is now shutting her ports," Yuri added. "All antennae are fully retracted. Signal drop is as expected. We are receiving adequately."

"We're at the top of the gauge," Brenna said. As fast as she could push her ship.

But not as fast as Morgan could go!

Jealousy and affectionate pride warred within her. If it couldn't be Brenna Saunder, let it be Morgan McKelvey. All in the family. Yet . . .

If only that damned coin had fallen the other way!

Readings jumped astonishingly as Morgan engaged the graviton spin resonance drive. His ship was about to become a 4000-metric-ton missile, ripping the fabric of space-time. The barrier field between the hulls was shimmering.

A last image, Morgan, raising his hands, cradling an unseen treasure. Holding all of space within his grasp.

Brenna swallowed a painful lump stuck in her throat. Morgan or her. It didn't matter. *We're Saunders. And Saunders are the best!*

"Take her, Morgan, out to the stars!"

Morgan's image vanished. A flood of computer data continued to pour in from Prototype II. The human eye couldn't take it all in, but the comps told Brenna what she needed to know.

Audio, scratchy. But coming through. Graviton spin field amplitude, soaring. Drag coefficient within acceptable range. Pseudo-speed point . . .

"Chase One and Two, we are go for pseudo-speed hop." Rue Polk. Tests had shown her clear soprano penetrated the audio interference better than a man's voice would.

On Brenna's screen, Rue's announcement showed a vertical graph line. Power off the scale. "Optimum resonance in twenty seconds," Brenna whispered.

"Normal time: 1704," Yuri said. "Ten seconds to pulse."

Morgan would be saying the same thing to Prototype II's recorders.

Monitor graphs were green smears. Readouts refused to believe the incoming data. Not possible. Not in space as mankind had traveled it, until now.

Time hit zero.

The stars. Waiting . . .

The screens!

The vertical lines that had lanced upward were falling, tearing up into jagged, ugly squiggles. Static crashed in Brenna's headphones. Green bled to red, all across the boards. Alarms shrieked, jolting nerve endings raw.

Not Rue's voice, this time. Morgan's. Roaring frantically.

"Mayday! Field instability! Overload! We have overload and hull collapse! We are losing life-support . . . !"

Tumaini Beno was yelling in Mwera, his African heritage overriding his impeccable English, stark evidence of the disaster seizing him and his fellow pilots.

A high-pitched scream pierced Brenna's brain through her audio receivers. "Fire!" Morgan was crying. "We have fire! God! Hang on, Rue! I'm here! I'll get you out . . . Tumaini! Watch out . . . !"

The Affiliation of the Rift native came back to basic com language, shouting desperately, "Mayday! Chase ships —Mayday!"

Explosion! Somewhere off to Brenna's left, thirty kilometers away, the gallant effort was over before it ever began. The beautiful Prototype was being burned, a sleet of radiation pouring out of her and over the Chase craft paralleling her course. Hard stuff, but already gone.

The fire was still raging inside Prototype II.

The explosion had decelerated her and thrown her off vector, adding to the stresses the crew must be suffering. Brenna knew she would have to get there fast. Without conscious thought, she was reprogramming, her propulsion systems adjusting to fit. Retro thrusters fired and vernier thrusters altered her track, trying to match the hurt Prototype's radically distorted course and come alongside it.

Sixty kilometers away, Hector Obregón held his position, hating it, but following the rules. Chase Two stands by.

Chase One goes in to help until the emergency medical team can get there.

A dissipating fireball, snuffing out in vacuum, boiled away from Prototype II. And in the middle of that holocaust Morgan and Rue Polk and Tumaini Beno were fighting for their lives.

CHAPTER SEVEN

ထထထထထထထ

Condition: Critical

THEY had rehearsed this countless times, never expecting to need it. Never wanting to. But the training paid off. Brenna was part of the machine, moving on automatic.

"Breakthrough Unlimited, FTL Station, we have a problem," Yuri said with deceptive calm. A tremble in the words betrayed him. "Internal fire and explosion aboard Prototype II. No faster-than-light jump made. Repeat: No FTL. We are en route to assist. Stand by, Med Staff . . ."

George Li's slightly delayed signal was reaching them. It wasn't aimed at the Chase ships, however. "Coordinate, Breakthrough Unlimited Mars HQ. Impound and duplicate all incoming data at once. Full emergency schedule is now in effect. Pull all memories. Feed data directly. We will try to recover the spacecraft for examination . . ."

Recover the wrecked spacecraft. Standard operating procedure in cases like this . . .

Failure!

And far more important, what about the crew? Could they recover *them*?

Three years ago, replaying, a living nightmare. Mariette, Kevin, and Third Pilot Cesare Loezzi. Primed for what they believed would be a successful faster-than-light jump, and then . . . failure.

There had been nothing to pick up then, no spacecraft worth salvaging, just mountains of recorded data to show where three good people had died with terrifying suddenness. They and their ship were debris, part of Sol's perpetually orbiting veil of galactic dust.

Brenna was piling it on, risking collision in her frantic desire to get alongside the wounded Prototype.

There had been no further communication since those last cries for help. Bio systems *were* getting through. So were internal recording data. They told a grim story. Safety systems faltering. Two-thirds of the power plant open to space. If anyone was alive, he would have to be in the forward emergency sections, now sealed off, the readings said, though badly damaged.

The emergency medical vehicle was moving in slowly. But the pre-test safety regulations put it badly out of position. The craft simply lacked the capability of the Chase ships. Brenna cursed the penny-pinching that had put them in this bind. Her people on Prototype II needed help *now!* But it would be an hour, at least, before Dr. Helen Ives and her staffers would be close enough to do any good!

As she drew near, Brenna saw with relief that Prototype II wasn't tumbling. None of them needed any additional problems during this rescue attempt!

The fireball was gone now. Only gaseous residue hovered around the wreck's orbit. Maybe, Brenna hoped, with the fire out, the worst was over for Prototype II. Any moment, Morgan would come back on the com, cursing his failure, making plans for the next run-through.

But the ominous communications silence continued.

Brenna's screens were eyeballing the damage. Hull compression, Morgan had said. Bad. It showed. The once-sleek faster-than-light spacecraft looked as if a giant had kicked her, then scorched her in a star's heat. Sensors probed, checking Prototype II's integrity. Some air leakage, but she hadn't lost all her life-support yet. And the crew was wearing full suits as a safety precaution.

Brenna brought Chase One in fifty meters to starboard. Radiation detectors complained, but the readings weren't fatal. She shut off the annoying sound. The lights continued nagging at her, anyway.

"We're full-suited, too," Yuri said, pointing out the obvious. Like Brenna's, his deep concern for the other pilots overrode the rules. "We can take five hours at this radiation level."

With fading hope, Brenna tried the com. "Prototype II?

Do you read? This is Chase One. We are ready to launch emergency rescue sled."

"N . . . no." The protest was pathetically faint. Brenna punched gain to the top. At first she couldn't identify the hoarse whisper. Then she made out Tumaini's accent as he gasped, "Stay out. Fire . . . radiation."

"We see that. We're coming to help," Brenna replied stubbornly.

Tumaini Beno coughed, a sound that dug knives into Brenna's lungs. "Don't come . . . don't come aboard. Get a tow on us . . ."

"Forget it! We'll pick up the damned ship later!"

"Incoming," Yuri cut in. He fed the voice to Brenna's headphones.

Dr. Helen Ives's distinctive pronunciation rattled, harsh with the surgeon's keyed-up emotion. "Chase One! We're getting the biomed readings. Don't wait on us. Repeat: Don't wait! We'll set up a rendezvous. Get them out of there and into Emergency Pod Carriers as fast as you can!"

That was all the okay Brenna needed. She had intended to move ahead, but the doctor's urgings acted as a spur. Yuri was on the com, trying to get a further response out of Tumaini. "What about the others? Tumaini?" There was no answer. Brenna suspected the Rift pilot had fainted.

"Let's go!"

The Russian already had his safety webbing off and the compartment bulkhead open. He and Brenna pulled themselves aft to the equipment bay at flank speed. They bumped into each other at first, awkward in their haste, ignoring all the free-fall movement tricks they had known since they were kids. Then, without a word, Brenna and Yuri regained control. Years of training made them concentrate. They went on into the bay smoothly, acting in unison. Brenna started the air-lock cycling while Yuri unshipped the rescue sled. She hit the trigger too hard, momentarily sending herself spinning in the opposite direction. Brenna swore, steadying down expertly. Yuri hooked a Carrier to the tow bar. Brenna hated the spacesuit's gloves, though they were vital. The things made her clumsy. She forced the connectors of two more Emergency Pod Carriers onto the bar, then shoved off against the wall, sailing up over Yuri, steering herself with a hand on his shoulder. Brenna dropped into the forward sled seat and locked the

116

safety strap, disengaging the tether that had held her to the equipment bay's guide rails.

Yuri fired thrusters and they scooted out of the bay, heading to the other ship. "We're free of Chase, Hector," Brenna said, as much for the recorders as for her fellow pilot. Her own biomed readings, and Yuri's, including their exposure to residual radiation, would be showing on Chase Two's monitors. Hector and Shoje would be keeping an eye on them, in case they started getting into serious trouble during the rescue operation. Brenna knew her breathing and heart rates were elevated. How could they *not* be?

Tension knotted her gut as they slowed and drew close to Prototype II. A blackened cavity loomed large in the sled's lights. Part of the metal near the graviton spin resonance power plant was peeled back, splitting both strong hulls. A comet's tail of junk danced around the rupture, orbiting with the wrecked ship. Smears left by smoke and fire stained the once-shiny ship.

"Gear down," Yuri warned. He decelerated sooner than Brenna would have, but that was a wise precaution. They wouldn't do the injured any good if they piled up. Radiation counters were grumbling on the sled's small screens. Neither of them paid any attention to the alarms.

Brenna fired the anchoring tether. They used the cable as a safety line and towed the Pod Carriers with them, making their way across the Prototype II.

"Can't use the rear access," Brenna announced. She turned her head, letting her helmet's cameras record the extent of the disaster. Most of the drones they had sent out had been fried when the graviton drive blew. These shots and the long-range ones from the Chase ships would be the first post-disaster scenes George Li and the support team would receive. And all such data were essential if they were going to figure out what went wrong. "Generator blasted open both hulls. We're heading forward now."

She and Yuri crept the length of the ship, laying out parasite lines from the anchor cable and setting self-riveting posts as they went along one hull. An ordinary ship would be studded with convenient cable holds and tie bars. Prototype II had none. She had been buttoned up for FTL flight. Robbed of power and wrecked, she could not even help her rescuers reach her forward air lock.

Imagination? The hull seemed hot to the touch, even

through Brenna's multilayered gloves and suiting. Readings said the internal fire was extinguished. Surely the outer skin wasn't *that* hot, not in vacuum and near absolute zero. Heat exchanges would leach out the energy fast.

There was another kind of heat, though, unfelt, but a deadly threat.

Time. Five lives at stake—hers and Yuri's and the three injured crewmen. They were racing against wounds and radiation-exposure limits.

Automatic systems activated the lock hatch, but the mechanism resisted. Obviously it, too, had been damaged. Brenna murmured a prayer. After agonizing suspense, the thick seal finally opened. She and Yuri crowded into the air lock, dragging the deflated Pods with them. There was a heart-stopping moment when it appeared that the outer lock wouldn't *close*. If it didn't . . . Brenna and Yuri would be okay, safe inside their spacesuits. But without air-lock integrity they didn't dare open the inner door. They would kill their helpless friends by explosive decompression as the remaining ship's atmosphere rushed into space. It took twenty long seconds for the circuitry to do its job, another ten before the controls came on, feebly, telling them the air lock was tight once more.

Yuri's expression was morose. "We have to make it in one trip—get them all out now."

"Agreed. We can't rely on those doors," Brenna said. "We'll probably have to blow the damned things off."

The inner lock, too, gave trouble. Once opened, it stayed that way. What was left of its readout panel flashed FAILED. More than ever, there were no options. Nothing at all keeping the crew from instant death.

Pockets of smoke were sucked out into the air lock as that door opened. Brenna tried to wave the stuff away. It merely separated into smaller spherical clouds, obstructing her field of view. She and Yuri made their way through the shambles, swimming past junk and dirty mist.

The three individual cockpits had ceased to exist. Dividing bulkheads had been blasted to pieces. Through the smoke clouds, Brenna saw the flight couches had been wrenched out of their moorings and twisted around the stanchions. The stress tests hadn't done *that* to the equipment! Power overloads had melted the panels and some of the circuitry, proof of tremendous heat feedback. Residue

118

coated everything. The walls dripped. Whole sections of duraperm alloy had disintegrated in the thermal storm. If the fire had done that to plating, what had happened to the crew's protective spacesuits? Shattered monitors and broken fairings were embedded in the black excrescence on the walls.

Brenna knew the specs. She gazed at the ruin, appalled, imagining the gees and the temperatures involved.

Within the crumpled garbage that had been the cockpits were the three bodies. They drifted in free fall, now and then jerking spasmodically and moaning when particles of floating debris touched them. Their helmets, suiting, and gloves had been destroyed, as had the ship. The new and radical systems on board Prototype II had made hash of normal heat and impact-resistant materials. The protective gear had been a weapon turned against its wearers. Plexi and silicate were melted into skin, and the pilots' skins were sloughing off in hideous blackening patches. It was difficult to tell who was who at a quick, horrified glance—Morgan and Rue were as dark as Tumaini.

Brenna and Yuri scissored their legs, moving expertly. They had been through somewhat similar crises in emergency mock-up training. Their first-aid training had to pay off now. They examined without touching, talking to the distant backup crew and to Dr. Helen Ives's med team, acting as their eyes. Yuri applied the biomed scan from the kit they had brought with them—the original sensors had been lost when the suits and helmets burned. According to those scans, Tumaini Beno was the least hurt of the three, and he was in critical condition.

"Extreme caution," Dr. Ives warned. She was interpreting the data they were sending her, feeding back an expert opinion. "We'll be there as quick as we can . . . have to get them some airways. Not you. Don't try it. Too risky. Get them into the Pods and out of there."

"We copy, Dr. Ives. Will do." Brenna wondered if that was she, talking so coldly. She sounded like a robot! It was the only way to keep her personal emotions out of this. She couldn't acknowledge that the biggest form, so terribly burned, thrashing in agony, was Morgan; and the others, equally in pain, were good friends.

She was two people. One was stricken with angry grief, fighting nausea and tears. The other person was functioning as part of a highly trained team and performing gruesome tasks.

Vital signs very low on McKelvey and Polk. Slightly better on Beno. Indications of internal injuries and fractures. Severe fluid losses. Polk's pupils uneven. McKelvey's eyes too badly involved to check.

Brenna and Yuri inflated the Carriers and blew away clinging smoke with negative pressure systems. They moved Tumaini first. Triage. He had the best chance. Free fall helped enormously. They paused until he had quit reacting to his pain and was momentarily quiescent, then guided the floating pilot into the expanding bubble. Stera-gel surrounded him, seeping through every rent in his suit and helmet, coating the seared flesh. Breathing apparatus provided more negative pressure around his face, waldo arms and tiny jets holding the thing in place without touching Beno. That was as much as Brenna and the Russian could do to help him. The surgeon would have to insert a better airway, if Tumaini survived until Dr. Ives reached him.

Morgan was next. His large body and inertia gave them some trouble. Awful gargling sounds emerged from swollen lips. His entire face was a massive oozing blister, dotted with bits of fried plexi. As they gingerly steered his twisting form into a Pod Carrier, Brenna whispered, "It's us, Morgan. Take it easy. We'll get you out of here. Calm down . . ."

How to tell a man who was suffering the tortures of the damned to "calm down" and make matters easier for his rescuers? Burns! Every human's worst fear!

Rue gave them the least trouble of all. She was barely moving now, and Brenna knew that was not a good sign. The once-lovely blonde was hairless and cooked within her own hide, unresponsive even as they gently pushed her inside the third Pod.

Tumaini was rousing, fighting his lifesaving prison. As Yuri strung the loaded Pods together, Brenna hovered beside Beno's carrier, talking through the Pod's intercom. "Tumaini? It's okay. We've got you. Relax. Going to tow you back to Chase One . . ."

Distorted mumbling. "Bad . . . bad . . . fire. Can't get loose . . . bulkhead's giving way . . . overload! Have to . . . have to get out! Morgan? Morgan, help! Rue!" His eyes focused on Brenna for a split second, faint recognition dawning.

"Brenna . . . ?" The breathing apparatus forced air over his burned skin around mouth and nose—necessary, but hurting him. Tumaini gasped and cried hoarsely. "Morgan . . . Morgan got Rue out of that . . . oh, God! She hit the bulkhead so hard. Her neck . . . I think . . . he pulled me out, too . . ." The pitiful voice faltered, faded away in labored breathing.

Shoje's paging frequency chirped in Brenna's headphones. "Data feed shut down on board, Brenna. The book says to locate and remove on-board recorder if possible . . ."

The book. What they were supposed to do, in the event of the never-could-happen disaster. Mustn't lose the data. They had to find out what to correct, so that the next time . . .

The *next* time!

Brenna refused to give in to her bitter heartache. Time blurred. She was doing all the right things without conscious thought. She and Yuri sealed the Pods, putting the bubbles on self-contained life-support. That was necessary before they took their comrades out to the sled, because they *would* have to blow the air-lock doors to get free of Prototype II. The outrush of released ship's atmosphere made the carriers bob, even though Brenna and Yuri had anchored them well before firing the door bolts. The steragel cushioned the wounded crew members, fortunately.

They left beacons on the battered hulk, homing signals for the salvage crew that would be coming out to get her.

No way for a proud lady to end her voyage to the stars . . .

Carefully, Brenna and Yuri made their way over to Chase One, Yuri handling the sled while Brenna floated on a tether and kept the three Carriers from jouncing too much in action-reaction movements. Once they were inside the equipment bay, they tied the Carriers fast. Yuri hurried forward, taking the controls. Their computer-calculated rendezvous point with Dr. Ives's med team was on the boards, but no pilot quite trusted the programs to do the job as well as a human could. Brenna felt the thrusters firing, altering their vector once again. Hector and Shoje would be following them, leaving Prototype II behind and running escort for Chase One, just in case something *else* went wrong while they were on their way to meet Dr. Ives.

"Slow and steady," Brenna cautioned everyone. Not

needed. They were all very much aware that acceleration stress might add to the victims' pain and detract from their chances for life. Yuri and Hector built the Chase ships' speed with skill.

At this closing range, communications lag was minimal. Dr. Ives was hurrying to meet them, her medical announcements preceding her. "Brenna? We've got the latest biomed data you fed us. Rough. Not good. But you know that. Once my team's aboard Chase One, set vector for Mars orbit, the Wyoma Lee Foix Space Hospital. Do *not* head for FTL Station. We can't begin to treat them there. We simply haven't enough equipment."

Brenna was badly shaken. FTL Station had a modern sickbay, one of the best available. But now Helen Ives was saying it wasn't good enough, not for Morgan, Tumaini, and Rue. Mars was far away. Too far? Could Morgan and the others hang on till Chase One reached the W.L.F. Space Hospital orbiting the red planet?

That was debatable. But Dr. Ives was tops in emergency space medicine. In her judgment, there was no alternative.

"Okay," Brenna said, her resolve becoming durasteel. "We'll get them there."

The pilots conferred, busier than they had ever been. Yuri and Hector, like Tumaini, had the benefit of Space Fleet backgrounds. They went on "war footing," as if the Chase ships were under attack. In a sense, they were—by impending death for the three Prototype pilots. Brenna and Shoje were civilians, but moved in step with their comrades.

Vectors, closing. The emergency medical craft was piloted by one of the older team members. But she had trained with Kevin McKelvey and Olmsted and knew her stuff. The flight paths lined up delicately. Sleds shuttled back and forth between the emergency vehicle and Chase One, transferring the med staffers. FTL Station was falling farther behind them every second. Reserve fuel packages were transferred from the emergency vehicle to Chase One and Two as well, setting them up for the long ride to Mars. As soon as the transfers were completed, the emergency craft headed home for FTL Station. Chase One and Two plotted fresh vectors, two silvery spaceships darting side by side through the void at hair-raising speed. There was no sensation of speed at all, though. Those were the laws of physics.

122

The medics took over. Brenna's and Yuri's emergency training had carried their friends this far. But now they needed much more than any layman could give. The doctor and her aides were manipulating arcane tools by remote controls within the three Pods, using knives and tubes to bypass seared lips and throats and to force air directly into the injured lungs of the pilots. Brenna retreated toward the cockpit, feeling helpless. By the time she reached her seat and took up part of the piloting from Yuri, Dr. Ives was talking urgently over the com. "For God's sake, get us to the hospital. Time is critical. They're all losing ground fast."

Flight Director George Li contacted them. "Brenna, we've sent word ahead. Wyoma Lee Foix Space Hospital will be on standby, waiting for you. You're cleared straight in ..."

A rogue signal, illegally boosted, overrode George's information. A new face supplanted Li's on Brenna's screen. "Hello? Are you receiving me out there? This is Dahl. We understand from the news pool feed that there's been some kind of problem on the superspeed test. How about some details, Saunder? Is McKelvey involved? Who's—"

Brenna's drawn-taut patience snapped. "Goddammit, Charlie! Get off this frequency! This is a life-and-death emergency!"

Charlie Dahl. TeleCom. Nakamura and Associates. That outfit had been a rival of the Saunders since Brenna's father was a young man. And they were still rivals, in a minor way, always nipping at Saunder Enterprises' heels and gloating whenever a Saunder flopped. This was a flop, and Charlie Dahl was like a shark in an Earth ocean, sniffing blood. Nakamura and Associates had their own faster-than-light project, a matter-antimatter experiment —still pretty much on the drawing boards but with a good theoretical chance of working out someday, if someone didn't beat them to it!

Helen Ives was cutting in, repeating the same things Brenna had said and stressing her medical credentials, ordering the callous newshunter to butt out. She was less profane than Brenna and had less effect.

"You can't tell *me* to get off the free air—or space!" Dahl's techs were using excessive power, blasting George

123

Li's incoming messages. "Just because your family owns half the Solar System, you don't have any right to—"

"If you interfere and cause a fatal delay, Charlie, I'll personally fly you over Nix Olympus and drop you into the crater!" Brenna thundered at him.

"TeleCom will take this to Protectors of Earth, Saunder! There's freedom of the—"

"You fornicating cretin! George, pull the plug on him." The flight director, unable to get through, had been listening. At that command, he used more power than Tele-Com's, drawing on the greater resources of Saunder Enterprises. Dahl's voice choked off in mid-syllable, as if he had been strangled. For a few moments, there was blessed silence. Then more messages, legitimate ones, started pouring in. Updates from FTL Station and Breakthrough Unlimited's HQ on Mars were now closing the communications gap between the Chase ships and the planet. New programming was feeding the ships' computers. Fuel expenditures were predicted.

There were outgoing messages, too. Dr. Ives was conferring with her colleagues aboard the Space Hospital, saving time they would need when they arrived.

Brenna let Yuri handle the calls meant for their ship. She was still relishing Charlie Dahl's consternation with vicious triumph. That pompous TeleCom bastard! Well, he wouldn't cut in on them again. SE techs would take care of that. Dahl's broadcast center would need hours to repair the feedback it had dumped on him. That was one advantage—among many—of being Todd Saunder's daughter! Blitzing a rival's signal, especially this time, had felt damned good.

Of course, there would be hell to pay later. No doubt Dahl's company would lodge a noisy legal protest with P.O.E. That might cost Saunder Enterprises at least a day's income in fines. Well worth it.

If it came to a hearing, she would admit what she had done without shame. She had run roughshod over another corporation's com network franchise—another quasi-nation company, as Saunder Enterprises and ComLink were branches of the Saunder quasi-nation. That was a bit different from faking out gypsy newshunters, which was a shady but winked-at practice.

But, dammit, this *had* been an emergency! Even Protectors of Earth's stodgy courts should understand that. And if not, Brenna didn't care. She cared about those three people in the Pod Carriers.

She flicked on the screen showing the emergency equipment bay, not wanting to see what was going on but compelled to look in. Dr. Ives's team had peeled away part of the ruined helmets and spacesuits to let stera-gel and other medications get to the terrible burns. Rue's face and Morgan's were awful. Morgan's entire head was a bleeding lump, no discernible features, no eyebrows, no hair.

He'll hate that. Women love to run their hands through his curly mane. I guess it'll be a while before he and Jutta sneak off to his estate for some lewd and lascivious pleasure. Or maybe he'd rather go back with Pauline. Or that dispatcher with Space Fleet, the one Morgan was asking Derek about at the gala. So many beautiful women! And he keeps them all coming back for more! Overgrown playboy! Morgan Saunder McKelvey, ideal of every would-be free and sexy, healthy human male . . .

Suppressed tears hurt Brenna's eyes. She was holding reality off and pretending things were as they had been. Confronting reality meant reliving the earlier FTL ship's tragedy—and that was unbearable.

Bio readouts flashed on one of the screens as Dr. Ives sent fresh data to Space Hospital. Life signs ominous, downturning. Tumaini barely holding his own. Morgan failing badly. Rue in the worst shape of all.

Time was the enemy, standing between the mercy-run Chase ship and the hospital orbiting Mars. Brenna gobbled hyperendors and CV levelers. All the pilots were doing that by now. They had never expected to make this long a flight. Those special medications weren't supposed to be used for these purposes, but those handling the controls needed the boost.

Breakthrough Unlimited's regular shuttles made the FTL Station-to-Mars run in seven hours if they were stripped and heedless of fuel consumption. Heading Sunward added a lot of velocity. The Chase ships were not only carrying light passenger loads, they were full-fueled, taking a direct ballistic course, and they had a much more powerful propulsion plant than the shuttles. They used the extra push. Gauge readings dropped. But the ETA was shortening steadily, too. Five hours and thirty-five minutes, and shrinking. Deceleration time was already on the boards. There was nothing much they could juggle there. Brenna considered the options, then fed reserve retro fuel into the programs and increased Chase One's speed a trifle more. She saw Yuri's expression and was grateful. No protests. No remarks about how she was gambling. All the other pilots were willing to gamble with her. They knew that if any problems surfaced along the way now, they would be in trouble, with no power to spare.

Again that vid-drama schematic of the Solar System formed in Brenna's mind's eye. She saw their tiny ships arcing "down" through space. They weren't the Prototype, racing to shatter the light-speed barrier. But they were very fast, cutting corners, missiles aimed at Mars.

The radically altered course and program kept them all busy. Brenna was glad of that. The hyperactivity couldn't cancel out her intense worry, but it forced her to fix her attention mostly on hardware. She filled her thoughts with update figures and revised schedules. This was what she had prepared for ever since falling in love with space travel. Sudden catastrophe was a part of that career, a threat you could never quite outrun. No pilot allowed it to take over his or her emotions, though, not for long. That alone could be deadly.

Grimly, Brenna checked the screens, watched the chronometer readings. Elapsed time. ETA. Four hours . . .

Three . . .

Two and a half . . .

Two . . .

The messages continued to flood in. Saunder Enterprises HQ sifted out the chaff, sending through only the important ones. One of those came from Dian's ship. She was nearing Earth, for the linguistics conference. It would take her days to return to Mars. But she was doing just that, from the instant she had received the terrible news. She was cracking the whip, too, via ComLink. Dian wasn't a physician, but she had established the Wyoma Lee Foix Medical Foundation as a memorial to her grandmother, a heroine of the Death Years and the Chaos. The late Dr. Foix had never enjoyed the luxury of a real hospital. She had done most of her lifesaving on the war-torn streets of Chicago, in the region that was slated to become one of the United Ghetto States. She would have been amazed and proud to know a modern social services and medical facility now bore her name. The W.L.F. Medical Foundation had numerous branches on Earth, Mars, and the satellites, and one of the very best, specializing in space accidents, was the hospital in Martian orbit.

"Brenna, our salvage crews are standing off near Prototype II," George Li reported. "We'll monitor until she cools down."

Sensible. No need for them to rush in and risk their lives.

An extremely personal message came through Saunder Enterprises' discreet relay system. A familiar voice, shockingly agitated. Derek. The message was received on a delayed basis and recorded, with George Li's replies. Hiber-Ship's convoy was six days anti-Sunward from Mars, but the words were very clear. "Breakthrough? Do you read? Hiber-Ship Ferry One-Seven. Spirit of Humanity, we just got the news here. What *happened*? Who's hurt? Brenna? Let me talk to Brenna. Is she . . . ?"

George Li answered him, soothing. He spelled out details, and Brenna heard and saw Derek's relief when he learned Brenna wasn't among the injured. She saw, too, his face draining of blood when he heard about Morgan and the other pilots.

"I'm returning. Over and out."

How well Brenna knew that tone! Loved it, sometimes raged against it. Derek in his absolutely dead-set mode. When he was going against her wishes, she could fight all she wanted to and it wouldn't do any good—not when he adopted that icy manner. His mind was made up. His sudden decision affected her deeply. Yan Bolotin and the Hiber-Ship board members would seethe when they found out their popular captain, the selected leader of *New Earth Seeker,* was disobeying orders. They wanted the supplies he was ferrying out at Jovian orbit, at the interstellar ship. Instead, Derek Whitcomb was detouring. Brenna could tell them to save their breath and not bother yelling at him. He would refuse to listen. Morgan McKelvey was his friend, and he knew how this failure would hit Brenna as well. So he was coming home to Mars, to be with them. It was the next best thing to having him alongside her in the cockpit.

Other messages. Someone getting hold of Aluna Beno, arranging for transportation up to the hospital so she could be there with her badly injured husband. Brenna remembered Aluna's pinched face during the PR sessions. Had Aluna Beno anticipated disaster for Tumaini? Would she blame Tumaini's fellow pilots for what had happened? That was a meeting Brenna wasn't looking forward to.

Messages from high-ranking people just receiving the news, reacting with horror, conveying their sympathy and concern. Aunt Carissa, saying all the right things. Zahra Kisongo, sounding very distressed. Governor Ma Jiang of Goddard. President Grieske. Councilman Ames. Chairman Hong. Ambassador Quol-Bez and Chin Jui-Sao, seeming sincerely upset.

"Brenna," Yuri said, waking her out of job-tending on the control panel. "Incoming message. It's your father."

Todd Saunder's square face was lined and haggard. He raked his nails through his hair. "Brenna? Thank God I got hold of you. Some idiot didn't notify me until just now. Didn't want to interrupt a meeting. Can you imagine? Morgan—what about Morgan?"

In less than an hour, the Chase ships would be at the orbiting hospital. There was no signal lag at all. Brenna replied at once. "Morgan's alive, Dad. So are the others. There's not much else I can tell you yet. It's up to the doctors . . ."

He wasn't listening any more. He had made his decision, talking to someone off screen. ". . . dump the meeting! Elaine can take over. Ali, call the spaceport."

Brenna tried to talk sense to him. "Dad, they won't let us be with Morgan. Not at first. He'll be in the burn ward, quarantined to prevent infection . . ."

The screen was empty. An apologetic Saunder Enterprises aide came on and covered up for his boss's abrupt departure. "It's okay," Brenna said wearily. "I got the message. Breakthrough Unlimited Chase One, out."

At five hundred kilometers the hospital's traffic department locked into the incoming ships' systems. No one remarked on the nearly empty fuel reserves. These wouldn't be the first spacecraft to arrive at W.L.F. Hospital running on hope, bearing mangled victims of a disaster. Traffic drew the high-speed ships directly into the docks. There was nothing for Brenna or her fellow pilots to do at this point except stay out of the medics' way.

They watched helplessly as Dr. Ives and staffers from the orbiting hospital hustled the Pods into Emergency. Saunder Enterprises personnel were on guard in the corridors, to keep the curious out of Brenna's hair. One more fringe benefit of being the daughter of the hospital's sponsor! A courteous hospital liaison officer suggested the pilots would be more comfortable waiting up in the lounge. Out of their element, suddenly bereft of tasks to keep minds and hands occupied, they went along without an argument. The hospital was a wheel-shaped space station, with free-fall conditions at the hub and an artificial, two-thirds Earth gravity beyond the outer rim. That was supposed to aid both patients—in free-fall ICU wards—and visitors newly arrived from Mars or Earth. It wasn't good news, however, for space pilots who had just made a breakneck plunge from high ecliptic orbit, gobbling anti-stress medications en route. The drugs were beginning to wear off.

They sprawled in the lounge chairs. A few passersby eyed them, but the SE guards made them stay their distance. All the Breakthrough Unlimited pilots were famous, recognized on sight because of their appearances on the vid. Little wonder the civilians watched them in fascination.

Brenna lost track of time. She remembered, dimly, that there had been a message from Adele Zyto and Joe Habich, now plodding their way back from the distant completed hop point. Brenna wished she had some good news to send back to her fellow pilots. After an hour and a half, Hector Obregón volunteered to go down to see if the medics had anything to report. When he returned, the others looked at him hopefully, but Obregón shook his head. "Maybe soon, they said." He fussed with his mustaches a moment, then dug into his flight-suit pocket. "The overload record. I picked it up while I was down there. Do we want to look at it?"

Yuri cracked his knuckles loudly. "Sorry. I suppose we should," he added with great reluctance. "That is the drill, is it not? We must find out what happened."

Brenna pointed to an available playback monitor, and they gathered around it to watch the last minutes of Prototype II's tragic flight. The first scenes were especially poignant. Their friends were putting Prototype II through

129

her paces, coaxing the graviton spin resonance drive toward peak function. Morgan's craggy, good-natured face split in a grin, and he winked at the recording lenses as if he, Rue Polk, and Tumaini Beno were putting on a show.

Then the screen turned an impossible fiery golden color. Morgan was yelling, "Mayday! Field instability . . ."

Everything occurred in fractions of seconds. Explosion. A wave of awesome fire, generated by forces outside current knowledge. Energies discharging as heat. Fragments of equipment hitting the lens. A brief, sickening glimpse of Rue Polk thrown out of her couch like a doll, smashing into a bulkhead amid the thickest flames while the explosions still raged. Tumaini, slumped over his controls, and Morgan dragging him bodily, flailing in free fall and violent deceleration stresses. Then Morgan plunging into the inferno to get Rue out of danger—even though it was already too late! The onlookers watched in numb shock, seeing suits disintegrating in those strange energy waves; helmets, searing skin, covering beloved, familiar faces. Morgan was ablaze, screaming in wordless pain, carrying Rue forward. The automatic systems were damping the fire, but not in time. The three of them were tossed about wildly. Morgan McKelvey—nearly two meters tall and weighing more than ninety kilograms, an impressive mass even in free fall—was being battered! Losing his grasp on Rue Polk, his head swallowed in the lingering flames.

Their bodies sagged, tongues of flame snuffing out, the victims not caring. Merciless, the cameras rolled on. Electronic recording gear could take much more heat than the human body. An erratic stream of data tracked below the grisly images of the charred pilots, spelling out the disaster Brenna and her comrades had witnessed.

"My God, no . . . !"

Todd Saunder was standing behind the pilots. He had obviously walked into the lounge while the tape was running, a gaggle of aides accompanying him. The older man had seen part of the terrible record. Too much. Brenna moved toward her father as he started to crumple. Yuri Nicholaiev, Hector Obregón, and the aides caught him hastily, helping him to a nearby chair. Brenna forgot her tough test-pilot pose and knelt in front of her father, clasping his hands tightly. He didn't seem aware of her presence. She had never seen him look so beaten and old.

"Dad . . . ?"

"They're all going to die," he said in a trancelike way, staring into nothing. "Everyone. My father, my mother, Pat, Mari, Kevin . . . not Morgan, too!"

His daughter and his aides and the pilots tried to encourage him. One aide ran to fetch a medic who might administer a sedative to the distraught older man. Brenna kept murmuring to him, not getting through.

". . . never did recover Ward's body after that plane crash. And I watched Pat and Mother die. Couldn't do a damned thing to stop them from killing each other. I thought nothing could hurt that bad. But then Mari died, and so did Kevin. Never recovered their bodies, either. They . . . they had so many good years left. They shouldn't have died. My kid sister, and that lovable bear of a man . . . and Mari . . . Mari wasn't even as old as Jael was when . . . when . . . everyone in this accursed family is doomed to die before reaching his parents' age."

"You haven't," Brenna reminded him as gently as she could. There was finally a flicker of recognition in his dark blue eyes. He focused on her with difficulty. "You're older than my grandmother was," Brenna said, "or than your father was when he was killed. Remember? You told me about . . ."

"And I don't want to be the sole exception to the rule. I *won't* be!" He suddenly swept Brenna into his arms, holding her in a painfully tight embrace. After an endless moment, Todd Saunder gave his daughter space to breathe, but he didn't let go. "If . . . if you go on this way, kitten, you'll die . . . die just like Mari did in that damned faster-than-light ship!" He choked on his grief, sobbing. "So young! You're so young, kitten. Younger than they were . . . and they're all dead. *All* of them! The people I loved so much! You're going to die before I will. You and Morgan. Both dead."

131

☙☙☙☙☙☙☙☙

CHAPTER EIGHT

Picking Up the Pieces

BRENNA continued to reassure him. It didn't work, though her father gradually came back from that dark, haunted place where he had been. He was enough in control to refuse drugs when the aide returned with some medics. Brenna glanced up and saw Dr. Helen Ives and another physician standing beside Todd Saunder, frowning, assessing his condition. Behind them, Brenna saw other new arrivals to the lounge—the hospital's liaison officer, escorting Aluna Beno. Tumaini's wife seemed clad in ice, distant from everyone, but in a quite different way than Todd Saunder had been moments before.

"Brenna," Dr. Ives said, "this is Dr. Stefan Dybas, chief of Emergency Services here."

"Are they stabilized?" Brenna asked bluntly, too tired to be sociable.

Dr. Dybas had been trying to smile. He gave it up. "Uh . . . shall we go into a conference room? It's pretty public out here."

Herded along, apprehensions growing, they adjourned as he had suggested and settled into a nearby closed area. The hospital liaison stayed. So did one of Todd Saunder's aides. They offered to fetch caffeine or soothants, especially pampering Todd and Mrs. Beno. Both of them refused, sitting tensely, waiting. Brenna's father was like a man dreading a blow; Aluna Beno, an unsmiling black statue. None of the pilots sat down. They leaned on the bulkhead, challenging the doctors with their eyes, deliberately stony-faced. Bad news was coming, and they were pulling their ranks together, comrades against danger.

Helen Ives took the lead. "Aluna, Tumaini's coming along nicely. We think with some luck, he's going to make it. He took some radiation, of course, and he's got some severe burns, especially on his legs. But we've debrided the wound areas, and he's responding very well to the allografts and anti-infection therapy ..."

Dr. Dybas nodded encouragingly. He caught Helen's subtle hint and didn't approach Aluna Beno. Tumaini's wife took the good news with no change of expression whatsoever. Brenna wondered what was going through the woman's mind.

There was a pained silence. Yuri found his courage first. "What about the others?"

This time, Dr. Dybas took the burden off Helen's shoulders. "I'm sorry to have to tell you that Miss Polk died a short while ago."

Brenna groaned, her vision blurring. Grief stunned her. She imagined Joe Habich learning this terrible news. Joe and Rue had been very close these past few months. More than anything else, he would somehow feel responsible and guilty, because he had been at the first completed-hop point, helpless and out of touch. Telling him there was nothing he could have done, even if he had been right at the test point, wasn't likely to provide much solace.

The doctor waited a few moments until the first wave of sorrow had passed. "I'm afraid she never had a real chance," he then said solemnly. "Her lungs were completely involved, and . . . there was irreversible spinal column damage as well, plus the burns." He hesitated, eyeing Todd Saunder. "McKelvey's in bad shape, but he's hanging on. His condition is extremely critical. We can't make any firm prognosis at this time."

"Morgan's incredibly strong," Dr. Ives put in hastily. "That's the key. If he can resist infection for the next few crucial days, we can help him a great deal more with some of our new treatments. We've already ordered his DNA tissue samples shipped from the Cryogenic Enclave branch on Mars."

Todd Saunder flinched, and for a split second Brenna wanted to attack the older woman. Dr. Ives meant well. But this was the wrong time to remind Todd of anything connected with the Enclave. The original cryogenic Enclave had been a Saunder Enterprises franchise at Earth's South Pole—and Jael Saunder had used her power over thousands of stasis-frozen confinees there to murder for money and political power. The old family scandal. It never went away, not even now, when the doctors planned to use cryogenically preserved tissue to save Morgan's life.

"Dad?" Brenna managed to attract his attention and lift him out of a private hell. "Dad, we all donated tissue specimens to the . . . the cryo storage banks on Mars. For medical emergencies. They can regenerate or synthesize replacement tissue from those models. Right, Helen?"

Dr. Ives agreed at once, attempting to put a hopeful tone into the discussion. "Right! We've really got some super methods to deal with cases like this."

Cases like this. Morgan McKelvey, at the edge of death.

"Skin grafts," Todd Saunder said weakly, his voice a hoarse croak.

The medics looked at him with pity. Dr. Dybas shook his head. "No, I'm afraid that's not possible. With Tumaini Beno, we *can* graft and use tissue from other sources to do the trick until his own systems take over." Aluna Beno showed her first glimmerings of interest in what was being said. Patiently, Dybas explained, "McKelvey hasn't enough original tissue left. None, in fact. Interior problems, too. To be quite frank, his lungs are nearly gone. We have to duplicate his DNA patterns fast and replace lung tissue and skin with synthetic mimics. With any kind of help from the patient, we can pull him through. This is a tried and tested technique, Mr. Saunder. We've used it for decades and saved a lot of people who would otherwise have died in more primitive times. Syntha skin and syntha pleura aren't as good as the real thing, of course. There's very little incorporation of nerve endings at all, though some capillary acceptance. Well, that's medicalese. I won't bore you with it. Nothing for you to concern yourself about, sir."

Brenna was two people again—the tough, by-the-book pilot, accepting the gamble and the risks of the game as the go-to-glory price. The rest of her felt sick.

Morgan. Alive but trapped forever inside an artificial skin. She had seen documentaries on this lifesaving method during the first-aid courses she had taken. It was true. Burn victims *did* live because of this miracle invention. Live? A skin that looked as if it came from a mannequin, with touchy heat and cold sensitivity and nil tactile qualities. There would be muscle atrophy, constant danger of infection . . . what else? She didn't want to know. The doctors weren't giving them the full story yet. That was merciful. Morgan's survival wasn't assured, and there was no point in being cruel, spelling out what his future would be like—until they were sure he *had* a future.

"Look," Dr. Ives was saying, "there's not a lot any of you can do here right now. Your husband's under sedation, Aluna, as much as we dare give him. I don't think it's wise for you to try to see him at present. And Morgan's in a coma. So . . ."

The liaison officer spoke up. "We've arranged quarters for everyone, in the visitors' area. If there's anything we can do to make you more comfortable, let us know." He was eager to please. It wasn't often this branch of Wyoma Lee Foix Space Hospital had the chance to host its sponsor's husband and daughter and assorted entourages.

Brenna cleared her throat. The effort hurt. An enormous, sharp lump was stuck there—unshed tears for Rue and Morgan and Tumaini. "We . . . we have to make arrangements . . ."

"For Miss Polk, of course," the liaison officer said sympathetically. "Lieutenant Polk's . . . uh . . . final-request specs are on file with Breakthrough Unlimited." He waved at one of the aides who had accompanied Todd Saunder to the hospital. "Your man Evanow is coordinating with me. Everything will be set up the way Lieutenant Polk would have wished."

Helen Ives's mother-henning instincts were coming to the fore. The pilots were no longer in training for a major flight, but she tried to shoo them away to the visitors' quarters for some rest. They all fended her off, refusing, and after a bit of arguing, she departed in disgust. Other hospital staffers were helping Brenna's father and Aluna Beno, nursemaiding the shocked and stricken family and friends. Brenna entrusted her father to his aides and the others and detained Evanow in the conference room. Before Aluna left, Brenna tried to express her regrets. Tumaini's wife rounded on her with a fierce glare. "I do not wish to talk to you, Saunder. To *any* of you!" Mrs. Beno's icy fury took in all of her husband's comrades. Then, without another word, she stalked out, letting a hospital staffer show her to the room that had been reserved for her.

"She never was . . ." Hector began, then caught a warning glance from Brenna and shut up.

Brenna beckoned to Evanow and hastily ran through some of the PR info he would need. ComLink and Tele-Com and the independents would be besieging the hospital for updates. Evanow had his work cut out for him. Brenna was glad the man had plenty of experience with Breakthrough Unlimited and her father's branch of Saunder Enterprises. He was a colonist, too, so the free-fall and partial-gravity conditions aboard the hospital weren't likely to trouble him. ". . . and one last thing," Brenna said as Evanow was completing the entries on his mini-memory wrist terminal. "I want Charlie Dahl out of touch. Lock him on the other side of the door. Let that bastard freeze his balls off before he gets another scrap of news from any of us." Evanow looked as if he would rather enjoy that assignment. The abrasive TeleCom reporter had stepped on other toes besides Brenna's. "Feed tidbits to whoever's Charlie's worst rival at TeleCom. Got it?" Evanow nodded and left.

Brenna wondered for a moment if her fellow pilots would think she was being vindictive. Nagata answered that. "We should do much worse to him. He caused a delay. He may have killed . . ."

"No," Brenna said hastily, not wanting to hear more, superstition flaring. *If it's spoken, it might come true!* "No, Dahl's interference wasn't critical. But he shouldn't have butted in. He's been riding too high too long, and it's time someone took him down. This will teach him a lesson."

Nagata sought someone to blame for the disaster. "None of it should have happened. All our unmanned tests were perfect."

Brenna was tempted to remind him that he, Joe Habich, and Adele Zyto were the "kids" of the project. They had been with Breakthrough Unlimited only for eighteen months and hadn't participated in several of those unmanned tests Shoje referred to. This wasn't the time to emphasize how green they were, though, in the project's terms. They all *did* have a good, solid background in commercial spaceflight. None of them was an amateur.

"If we only knew what fouled up . . ."

"The Vahnaj could tell us," Hector chimed in. "But

136

they're not going to. Quol-Bez is a nice guy, sure, but his government? They care nothing for us humans."

"Why should they?" Nagata responded bitterly. "They already *have* FTL drive."

Hector nodded. "That's right. FTL spaceships like the Ambassador's and FTL radio to boot."

"Lording it over us," Shoje Nagata mumbled, nursing his anger. "Laughing at us squatting here in our backyard. They will give Hiber-Ship everything it asks for, but not us."

"Knock it off," Brenna warned.

Guards posted outside the door and now and then a passing hospital staffer heard the loud voices in the conference room and peered in curiously. This was no place for a pilots' bullshit session! But Brenna was losing control, couldn't shut them up.

"Somebody ought to take that Vahnaj ship and pick her guts apart . . ."

"Yeah! If we'd done that before now, maybe this wouldn't have . . ."

Yuri Nicholaiev tried to break in. "Durák! We do not know that yet. We do not even have all the data . . ."

"What the hell do you know about it, Nicholaiev? You can always go back to Space Fleet if the going gets too rough at Breakthrough . . ."

The Russian clenched his fists. Hector stepped between him and Nagata hastily, before either of them could start swinging. Yuri and the younger pilot glared at each other, plainly struggling to keep their tempers.

Brenna jumped into the momentary silence. "Shut off this fuel flow right now! You're not thinking straight."

Yuri nodded. "That is so," Hector said. "We can talk this over later, when we are calmer. There is a lot we must find out first."

"We know the Vahnaj still can step all over us in interstellar space," Shoje retorted. "Maybe you'd like to go back to Space Fleet, too? Or better yet, sign up with Hiber-Ship and get to the stars *that* way . . ."

"That's *enough!*" Brenna had to yell to make the order effective. It worked. Civilian heads turned. All the pilots finally became conscious of where they were and who was listening to them. Some semblance of discipline returned, the rebellion fading from their faces. Brenna sighed. "All right. We each have things to do. Nagata, you're in charge of refueling and refitting our ships. Arrange for someone from Breakthrough Unlimited on Mars to ferry Chase One and Two back to FTL Station. Okay? Yuri, you work with Evanow. Have him send additional PR staffers up here, if necessary. It looks as if we'll be here for a while. Dad and I will be, for sure. Evanow can handle media releases—unless someone else here wants to go on camera and be all smiles for the public?" Their glum expressions mirrored Brenna's. There were no volunteers. "Hector, you coordinate with George Li and Adele and Joe. Keep them abreast of what's happening. I'll help you as much as I can, but my dad's going to fill up a lot of my hours until further notice. Mmm, someone ought to stay with Aluna Beno, I guess . . ."

Again, there were no volunteers. Tumaini's wife had ruffled too many feathers among her husband's fellow pilots. Finally Hector squared his shoulders. "I'll call Carmelita. She'll come and hold Aluna's hand. Carmelita can leave the kids at the spaceport's child-care hostel." That would be rough on Carmelita Obregón. But Tumaini's wife was likely to tolerate her presence much better than she would any of her husband's crewmates. Mutual negative admiration. Aluna Beno regarded them all as maniacs who had lured her husband into a near-fatal disaster, and they regarded her as someone who never should have been a pilot's wife.

Agreed on their assignments, they split up. Rue's death was an open wound none of them could forget. They would have to force themselves not to dwell on that, or they'd come unglued. Brenna hoped keeping busy would do the trick.

"They'll make it," Dr. Ives said. She was standing at Brenna's side. "So will you. Come on. Log some sack time. It's going to be days before this all sorts itself out."

Dr. Ives hadn't exaggerated. Worse, there was no routine, nothing Brenna could rely on. Time schedules and normal work procedures were totally wiped out. Everything went on standby, and they all muddled along.

Yuri asked Brenna to check out Evanow's work. The man was an expert, but this was a delicate situation. He didn't want to consult his nominal boss, Todd Saunder, nor did Brenna want him to bother her father at this time. Evanow's releases were usually just fine, the right note of tragic courage and hope, combined with the regular medical bulletins—all of which sounded impressive and said very little. Brenna rubber-stamped the results and told the PR people to take care of it. She supposed that eventually she would have to take a greater interest in this aspect of Breakthrough Unlimited. PR was Morgan's specialty. But Morgan wouldn't be able to take that load off her shoulders for quite a while.

Todd Saunder woke up at irregular intervals and prowled the lounge and corridors like a caged, graying tiger. He was a bit more communicative than he had been, but not by much. When his aides brought him food, he ate it. When Brenna spoke to him, he answered her, saying no more than he had to—a man rationing words. Dr. Ives didn't have any better luck. On a rare respite from her duties with the ICU team, she explained that the requested cryogenically preserved DNA samples had arrived and the hospital's labs were growing syntha skin and synthapleural tissue, gradually introducing these into Morgan's body. Some of the syntha skin wouldn't "take," but they hoped most of it would and then extend its coverage. The human skin was the body's largest organ, absolutely necessary for life. Since Morgan had none of his own left, replacement was his only hope. Todd Saunder listened without comment, then returned to watching his nephew on the remote monitor. That was a form of punishment, for him or for anyone else who loved Morgan.

Brenna was little better off than her father. Sleep wouldn't come. She roamed the hospital at odd hours, usually ending up where her father had spent so much time —looking at the monitor screens. She used ComLink to try to contact Derek, but apparently he was maintaining silence, possibly to refuse his employers' irate calls.

Hours crept by, became a full day, then two full days. Dr. Ives reported that Tumaini was making great progress. By the third day, when he was fully conscious and breathing on his own, the medics took a chance and gave him mild pain drugs. Tumaini was coping well with the antiradiation therapy and fighting off infection. And he was beginning to bitch. That was the most favorable sign of all. His fellow pilots took turns at the visitors' screen when the doctors gave permission for short conversations with

139

the patient. Tumaini was still in isolation, of course, but he could talk to them and see them on the two-way com. Brenna and the others traded gripes with him, joking to take his mind off his hurts. Aluna Beno made a point of not being in the room when they were. She scheduled her visits separately.

The medics were so elated with Tumaini Beno's condition that they made plans to transfer the FTL pilot to a Mars-side hospital by early the following week, if he continued improving at the present rate. In a planetary gravity he would have fewer problems during rehabilitation. Tumaini looked forward to the prospect, no matter how painful the actual transfer might be. Anything to get out of the stera-gel fishbowl, as he put it!

Nobody said anything about moving Morgan out of the free-fall burn ward or about possible future rehabilitation therapy for him. "Let's wait and see," Dr. Ives temporized.

Inevitably, Tumaini asked about his crewmates. At first Brenna lied to him, afraid the truth would cause a relapse. But he wasn't fooled. Nor was he too surprised when they told him what had happened. He had anticipated Rue's death while the accident was taking place, knowing how brutally she'd been hurled into the walls. Through burn-puffed lips, Tumaini said, "The Spirit of Humanity will receive her soul and give her eternal peace."

The others seconded him, even those who didn't share Tumaini's strong religious faith. Rue—and Joe Habich—had. Brenna was grateful for that. She hoped that had been some solace to Rue during her last horrible moments of consciousness, and that the same faith would comfort Joe, the man who had loved her. Rue's will—they had all made them out, just in case—stipulated that she be buried in space. The ceremony would be held in the hospital's meditation hall the following day. Tumaini wanted to attend the service, but that was out of the question. Dr. Ives agreed to set up a monitor between the hall and ICU, even though some of her colleagues disapproved of that much stress on their patient.

They told Tumaini about Morgan. He was silent for a long while, his eyes closed. Then his beliefs sustained him again. He would pray for his badly hurt friend. Soon Tumaini was the one doing the encouraging, trying to cheer up the other pilots by recounting anecdotes to underline just how tough Morgan McKelvey was. Brenna smiled for the first time in days. That crazy Rift Affiliation optimist! He made *her* believe, too. Morgan McKelvey, done for? Not damned likely! Not with friends like Tumaini Beno rooting for his recovery!

As the fifth day rolled up on the chronometers, a group of mourners gathered in the meditation hall. Todd Saunder, very much more himself now, joined the others. Carmelita Obregón and Aluna Beno stood side by side, though Aluna still wouldn't be in the same part of the room as the pilots, even at a funeral. She was going through the expected social forms, but that was it.

Pilot Rue Polk had no living relatives, and her separation from her ex-husband hadn't been amicable, so no one had pressured him to attend this service. There were just Rue's fellow pilots, Dr. Ives and some sympathetic med staffers, and various Saunder Enterprises aides. No newshunters.

Joe Habich and Adele Zyto had arrived at the hospital just hours before. What everyone had hoped would be a reunion for a victory celebration was now a reunion to say good-bye to their dead comrade. Joe was bearing up well under his grief, but the strain showed on him, as it did on all of them.

As the senior ranking pilot with Breakthrough Unlimited, it was Brenna's job to deliver the eulogy. She had offered the privilege to Joe Habich, but he'd declined. He wasn't sure he could handle that ordeal. The pilots stood at parade rest, though none was now with Space Fleet. Brenna hoped she would do this right. She hadn't had to after the previous FTL failure. Her father and older contemporaries of Mariette Saunder, Kevin McKelvey, and Cesare Loezzi had said the necessary things then.

The memorial service was carried by ComLink and TeleCom to a large, curious audience on Earth, Mars, and the satellites. Brenna kept the words simple. Rue Polk had been a gutsy, no-nonsense woman who admired straight dealing. Brenna reminded the audience of that, in euphemistic terms. She told them the rest of Rue Polk's story as well, not the obituary stuff, but what made Rue Polk's life important.

"She believed in what she was doing. Rue Polk knew how to dream, and to make those dreams into reality. She taught her friends to trust in those dreams, too. She was there to encourage us whenever we doubted. She came to Breakthrough Unlimited after a highly distinguished career as a Terran Worlds Council shuttle pilot. She remained loyal to the goals of T.W.C.—peace and prosperity for all the worlds humans inhabit, now and in the future. For Rue Polk, those goals led straight to the stars. She wanted to be part of the team that took the first giant leap outward into the galaxy. And she *was* part of that team—a vital, irreplaceable part. Our lives all are richer for knowing Rue. And her spirit lives on in the work we have to do. That's the highest accolade we can give her—that she's a permanent member of our crew. Rue Polk will never die. She believed that a human being lives on, after death, in the Spirit of Humanity, and in the memories of her friends. She *is* remembered, with respect and with love. Go in peace, Rue."

One by one, the pilots stepped forward to lay their tokens on the sealed capsule bearing Rue's corpse. Breakthrough Unlimited always stressed its civilian background. This ritual, though, had been around a long time. They gave Rue the Prototype II test-flight patches they had worn so proudly, to go with her into eternal darkness. The starburst emblems nestled together, looking too fresh and new to be part of an awful failure. The pilots stepped back, heads high. Per Rue's request, there was no music. Instead, there was a profound silence, a space for private thoughts. Then a small sighing noise caused the capsule to drop through the jettison lock. Exterior scan screens showed the coffin riding its mini-jets, leaving the hospital. Eventually, the capsule would assume orbit around Mars.

"Good-bye, Rue," Brenna whispered, the others echoing her. Despite the brave words, it hurt, deeply, to think that Rue wouldn't see the final triumph—the triumph that *had* to come, someday.

A few more words were spoken in praise of the dead woman. Nothing fancy. It wasn't a wake, but Brenna and her fellow pilots had to remain until everyone had a chance to express regrets. Brenna's father held her hands for so long that Brenna grew uneasy. She feared another breakdown. But Todd Saunder was past that stage. He finally left, as did everyone else but the Breakthrough Unlimited crews.

They held an impromptu decision-session in an anteroom. The ceremony seemed to put everything in focus for the pilots, after days of aimlessly marking time.

"We . . . I do not think there is much I can do here," Hector Obregón said. "The visitors' quarters are limited. I would do more good if I went back to FTL Station. I do not like this idleness." Joe Habich, Nagata, and Zyto looked tempted by that thought. Brenna nodded. Joe, especially, shouldn't be allowed to brood. And the junior pilots would get rusty if they didn't get back to work soon.

But there was an unhappy kicker to Hector's suggestion. "You know we'll have to put FTL Station on skeleton operations, at least temporarily." The others looked as if they would argue, until Brenna nodded. "I don't like it any better than you do, but we've got to face facts. It's going to be weeks, at best, before we know what fouled up. We can't even begin to correct the flaws till then. And whether anyone believes it or not, we Saunders do not have an inexhaustible supply of funds." They dropped their eyes, chagrined by the reminder. Morgan and Brenna were so much a part of the team, it was sometimes easy to forget they were also scions of a quasi-nation, and the sole source of Breakthrough Unlimited's financing. "Okay. I'll keep everybody on the payroll as long as I possibly can. Once Salvage completes the job and brings Prototype II in, we'll have to pull our people back to Mars, except for Maintenance. Yeah, sure, that cuts flight time. But that's the way it is."

Hector shrugged. "That seems wise."

"We'll go with Hector," Nagata said, speaking for the three junior pilots. "Don't worry, Brenna. We'll assist on salvage and pick up every molecule. We won't miss anything. *Then* we can do a good analysis." Now that he had selected his assignment—and knew he would be flying spacecraft regularly for a while—Nagata, as well as Joe and Adele, was eager to get to it.

"I, too, feel useless here," Yuri said. "I will go to Mars Base. I can set up things for George Li and the support teams. And I will coordinate with Dr. Ives and your mother's staff. Everything must be ready when they transport Tumaini and Morgan planetside."

The others eyed him guiltily. Scut work. Necessary, but not very exciting.

143

Nicholaiev mistook their expressions for pity. "I do not mind," he said with some heat. Then he added with a tolerant smile at the younger pilots, "This goes with the crowds ripping your clothes off and all the I-was-there contracts with the media."

That touched off a round of laughter. "Anybody torn *your* clothes off, Zyto?" "No!" "If they do, let me know, sweetie. You *or* Brenna—I want to be there to watch!" "Shut up, hormone-crazy . . . !"

They finally settled down. "It sounds good," Brenna said. "I have to stay here. The old family ties and all that. You guys take off. Hector, does Carmelita need a ride back to Mars?"

Obregón was scornful. "Nah. She has a seat on the next regular hospital shuttle going planetside." He paused. "Aluna's going with her." Tumaini was still in ICU. It seemed cold-blooded for his wife to be leaving already, even if the doctors said he was going to make it. But no one had any urge to quiz Aluna Beno about her actions.

Yuri raised another question, though. "Brenna? Do we have a long-range plan?"

That one had a thin hull. Brenna didn't want to consider it yet. She hid her uncertainties, playing enthusiastic team leader. "Let's just pick up the pieces. First things first. Then we talk. Okay? Okay!"

They huddled and linked hands briefly, recapturing some of their old spirit. The others went to pick up their gear and arrange for transportation. Brenna checked in at her father's room to see how he was doing—better—then tried to restore some kind of steady routine for herself.

What *was* routine in this confused situation? She couldn't hang around ICU all the time. Gloomy discussions with the doctors weren't good for her morale. There were a few things that needed doing, however, and she had been putting them off too long already. Breakthrough Unlimited's business and Brenna Saunder's personal correspondence and financial affairs. She cued her com screen and started talking to the Saunder Enterprises staffers working for her interests at Mars HQ.

Correspondence to clear up, first on the agenda. The condolences were still coming in. Brenna asked her personal secretary to deal with all except those from close friends of the family. The latter were a strange mixture.

There was a tearful vid tape from Freda Appel, Morgan's surrogate mother. Most women who had performed that function for pay had little further interest in the family they had worked for, once the "job" was done. Freda was different. For twenty-seven years she had sent Morgan birthday greetings and followed his career with pride, as if he were her own son, not the artificially conceived child of Mariette Saunder and Kevin McKelvey which she had merely carried for nine months. She had mourned his parents' deaths as she now worried over Morgan's injuries.

Another tape was from Dian, who was en route to Mars. She spoke briskly. Her face showed tension, though. "We're running ahead of schedule. I offered some bonuses. Worked, too. Should be at the hospital about 0900 Thursday. I passed the word to some of the doctors up there. They've got to get some decent food and vitamins into your father, girl. He looks terrible! I'm paying for service at Wyoma Lee Foix Foundation, and by damn I mean to get it. You take care of yourself, hear? *You* don't look so hot, either."

There was a special, diplomatic-clearance tape from Quol-Bez. Chin Jui-Sao was with him, nervously flexing her hands again and again and avoiding direct eye contact with the lens. The Vahnaj Ambassador's sideburns drooped with sorrow and his broad, flat nostrils flared with each breath. Body language showed how much he cared, this being from another star system, this *friend*.

"I am . . . am most distressed, Brenna. This is such a ter-ri-ble thing. Morgan has my sin-cere hopes for quick healing." Sao whispered to him, and Quol-Bez amended his words. *"Our* sin-cere hopes. We wish to help. But we do not perceive how this is poss-i-ble. Only human physicians are proper-ly trained to minister to your species. I could con-tri-bute nothing. This is my shame. Please, if I may speak to your father in the future, I will offer what I may. We wish very much to visit Morgan, when he is able to accept visitors."

Brenna had to wake herself out of a momentary depression. "Of course." She spoke too softly. The audio didn't register. "Tash, tell them yes, of course." The secretary made notes and Brenna added, "They've sent a lot of messages, one every day. I appreciate it. Let them know, if you see them . . ."

The next private tape had originated on Earth, at Saunderhome. Stuart basked in the Caribbean sunshine, beaming at the camera. His behavior at the gala and the way he had left the scene so hurriedly the moment any real peril threatened roused Brenna's animosity anew. What the hell did Stuart want? She almost cut off the tape, then resigned herself to sit back and watch. "Hello, there! Just landed and got the dreadful news. Sweet Mother Carissa is all atwitter, as you can imagine. Gibbering about how dangerous spaceflight is, as if she knew!" Stuart spoke casually, out of his "vast experience" as a seasoned traveler. As far as Brenna knew, his trip to the Martian Colony Days gala had been his first journey away from Earth's near-neighborhood in at least a year. Stuart waved his hand airily. "Doesn't understand a damned thing about what's going on—how important your work is, Cuz. Well, *I* do." His manner grew serious, for a few seconds. "Believe it or not, Brenna, that's so. This business with Morg —too bad!" He lifted his glass. "Here's to a speedy recovery for the big kid. I'd have called sooner, but just couldn't get the time clear."

Brenna gazed daggers at the dissipation-marked face and mousy hair and colorless eyes. Stuart wasn't dumb. And he could even act with style and grace, though he hadn't bothered, recently—not since Carissa had crushed his brief attempt to break the apron strings and run away with his mistress and child. Her illicit cloning of her late husband's genes had stopped that cold. Defeated, but not reconciled, the man seethed with hatred, radiating resentment. That much anger, and that much wealth and power, in one package! Brenna was sure this message tape was something manipulative, part of some convoluted scheme no one but Stuart could fathom.

"They tell me Sweet Mother Carissa beat me to sending our sympathy, we Earth-based Saunders. As usual. One-upping me. Never even mentioned it to me. Rude of her, wasn't it? But I'll get her for it. I found a way to pay her back, and curdle her milk in the bargain. No need to thank me. Just a friendly cousinly helping hand, you might say. Thanks to me, Morg will no doubt be kicking sand in my face again in no time. Well, I have to get back to serious matters . . . hey! Come here, gorgeous." A pretty young woman with a vacuous expression came into the camera frame. She wasn't the same hanger-on who had been following Stuart around at the gala. He changed his hired sexual partners as often as he changed his clothes. Now, after pawing the woman's breasts, he ordered her to fetch him a fresh drink. As she walked away, Stuart, licking his lips, rose and followed her. After a moment, an anonymous Saunder Enterprises employee at Saunderhome signed off the message in his master's absence.

Brenna wondered what Stuart had meant about a "cousinly helping hand." It didn't take her long to find out, via ComLink. Stuart hadn't tried to conceal this slap at his mother. He had transferred some of his impressive financial petty cash over to Dian's medical foundation, to be used for Morgan McKelvey's cure. Brenna whistled at the amount Stuart had tossed away. The gesture looked magnanimous, but she wasn't fooled. It was an astute move on Stuart's part. Instead of squandering his allowance on women, drugs, and gambling, he had made a donation to a family charity for the sake of his cousin. Carissa wouldn't be able to chew him out for *that!* And he would get marvelous publicity from it, too—*his* idea, not *hers*. The media would make much of the fact. Brenna sighed and dismissed the internecine warfare. Carissa and Stuart's battles didn't concern her or Morgan. But they *could* use the money Stuart had thrown their way!

She turned to the staggering accumulation of Breakthrough Unlimited business. The staff had handled a lot, but there was still plenty to be dealt with. She would have to use her proxy and pull strings to her and Morgan's mutual benefit, if possible. She and Morgan had each inherited large fortunes. Each generation of Saunders built on the previous one's thrift and investments. It had begun with Ward Saunder's patents, which Jael Hartman Saunder had pyramided into the wealth and power of a quasi-nation. After her death there had been a public outcry, demanding some of that vast financial empire be broken up; if *one* Saunder had been corrupted, might not others be? But Todd had been a hero. So had his martyred brother. And Mariette Saunder had been on the winning side in that family struggle. In time, the hatred had faded somewhat, and the Saunders—and their wealth—had survived. Actually, there had been little Protectors of Earth could legally do to tear down the empire Jael had built. She might have been murderously ambitious, but she had also been the acknowledged mistress of her era when it came to wheeling and dealing. Once the family had weathered the scandal, they had done very well. Carissa Duryea Saunder and Stuart were among the richest families on Earth. Todd Saunder had diversified ComLink wisely, providing plenty of profits for Dian's endowment of W.L.F. Foundation and setting up a lucrative income for Brenna. Morgan McKelvey rode a similarly luxuriously appointed gravy train. His parents had bought asteroid mining stock before the big strikes came in. In addition, when they had died, their shares of Goddard Power Satellites went to Morgan. So Brenna Foix Saunder and Morgan Saunder McKelvey had been born with a full set of platinum spoons in their mouths. Under ordinary circumstances, they would never be pressed for funds.

Ordinary circumstances? These weren't. The FTL ship had a huge appetite, whether or not any tests were going on, whether there was success or failure. And without success, everything went out, nothing came in. Breakthrough Unlimited's payroll was loaded with highly skilled, expensive talent. And now there would be massive medical bills. Tumaini would be a long time recovering, and he had a family to help care for, financially. The doctors had tried hard to save Rue, and they were entitled to payment for their noble efforts. Nobody was putting a recovery date on Morgan. At the very least, Brenna was looking at costly round-the-clock med staffers and rehabilitation therapists for months.

Her secretary's image flashed on one side of the screen, a row of figures on the other. "Okay on this one, Tash," Brenna said, lightly touching the surface and picking a stock option. "Put this one off, at least until July. Assign Noelle. She can be soothing as all hell. Besides, I think she's got hormones for that guy. Did you get the update on the pilots' schedules? Good. Work with Yuri when he gets down there. This one . . . mmm . . . let's wait on it, too. I don't want to touch any of Morgan's mining capital. We're going to need every ounce of that. Check with SE Industrial Division and SE United Asteroid Mining Inc. See how many more mass driver ore carriers they can turn out for us in the next fiscal year. The more we send Sunward and the more we sell on Mars and Earth, the better.

Okay on this one . . . contact Miller. I need some legal brains . . ."

"Your aunt suggested . . ."

"I'll bet! Eli? That unctuous non-contrib doesn't meddle with *my* money! I do not want her pet lawyer sniffing around my affairs. Flatter her and tell her no, thanks, but we've got a contract with Miller and that's that."

"It'll be done, Brenna," the secretary promised.

"All set for Dian's arrival here at the hospital? The way her timing looks now, she'll just about match orbits with us when she and my father will have to turn around and head back to Earth. Dad's due at the Protectors of Earth Supreme Assembly awards session later in June."

"Oh, that's been postponed," Tash said. "Sorry, didn't I get an update to you? More neo-anthrax. P.O.E. has put off the ceremony until August."

Brenna programmed her own entries to agree with that changed calendar. "Okay. Makes sense. Let's keep our own people out of the quarantine-closed areas until P.O.E. gives the all-clear. The delay will take some pressure off my father, anyway. He needs to rest up before he has to rub elbows with all those Earth politicians . . ."

The upcoming awards ceremony was a hokey one, a performance put on for Protectors of Earth's global constituency. The excuse was a commemoration of first contact between Vahnaj and Earth and of Ambassador Quol-Bez's arrival on Earth. Now, particularly after the outrageous attack on Terran Worlds Councilman Ames, P.O.E. would need to polish its tarnished prestige and show the alien that the fanatics had nothing to do with legitimate Earth interests. Protectors of Earth wanted desperately to join the big guys, out there, in the galaxy. Honoring Quol-Bez and his "kin-friend" Todd Saunder was a good way to do it. They staged this display every year, making speeches about Todd Saunder's wonderful contributions to humanity —when some of those same elderly speechmakers had once been bitter opponents of Brenna's father, during the Crisis of 2041! They would drape posthumous awards on Ward Saunder, too, and Todd would accept them all with thanks. Brenna could recite the phrases by heart. ". . . Ward Saunder, that inventive genius, and to you, his son, who carried his quest on into the future . . ." ". . . thank you, and if my father had lived to witness these great events, I know

149

he would thank you, too." The ceremonies were very formal, very impressive, and very boring. Brenna's father hated them and would have ducked out, gladly, if he could have found an excuse. Brenna suspected Quol-Bez was equally bored by them, but presumably he was paid to be bored, among other things.

Brenna was glad they had postponed the awards session for another reason, a very private one. Neo-anthrax. Even if all precautions were taken, she didn't want her father anywhere near an outbreak of that stuff, or any other pandemic. One of the family secrets was Todd Saunder's phobia about pandemics. He had been traumatized by the biological warfare outbreaks when he was a kid, even though no one close to him had died as a result, as Derek's mother had. Brenna and her mother had seen the ComLink executive reduced to shivering helplessness, racked by nightmares, by a near-approach of one of the old plagues. Todd Saunder wasn't going Earthside until the current outbreak was bottled up and stomped, not if his wife and daughter had anything to say about it!

Her thoughts drifted to the other honoree at the ceremony—Quol-Bez. He symbolized so much, to so many different humans, like the officials at Protectors of Earth, afraid they were losing their hold on Earth's colonies, and like Terran Worlds Council, which sought to take over P.O.E.'s old influence, in the name of those same colonies. Brenna liked Quol-Bez a lot. And he had proved a steadfast friend of the family indeed during this awful ordeal. An alien, a Vahnaj, *and* a friend of the family. But she wanted to meet *other* aliens, the representatives of those tantalizing names in the Vahnaj cultural tapes—species named Whimed, Trannon, Ulisor . . . Yet . . . Earth was stuck in its own backyard.

"Let's take care of the rest of this stuff later, Tash," Brenna said, and the screen cleared. In place of her secretary and financial reports, a standard vid newscast appeared. ". . . Polk's funeral ceremony was carried on the network and will be available for rebroadcast. Update from Space Hospital, Mars: Dr. Stefan Dybas, chief surgeon, Emergency, says that Breakthrough Unlimited Pilot Morgan Saunder McKelvey, son of Goddard Colony's former governor, Kevin McKelvey, and Mariette Saunder, is still in critical condition. Pilot Tumaini Beno, one-time

Space Fleet cruiser commander, is progressing and is now listed in stable condition. He will probably be moved to W.L.F. Mars Hospital later this week. On the labor front, the strike of the United Krill Fisheries employees against Southern Pacific and Antarctic Territories has gone to the bargaining table, and negotiators predict that . . ."

Brenna muted the sound, staring at the reporter's image but not seeing her.

The stats. All neatly summed up. Breakthrough Unlimited's Prototype II test. Results: one dead, one in critical condition, one progressing but a long way from home.

How much was achieving FTL going to cost? Not in money—as a Saunder, she assumed there would always be more of that coming, from somewhere. But lives couldn't be replaced. Even if one believed in the Spirit of Humanity or another religious philosophy, that still meant that when a person died, he or she was removed from the present plane of existence, perhaps forever. Each person was unique. Cloning experiments, such as those Carissa's illegal labs had pulled off, proved there was no guarantee of producing exact copies by *that* technique. Those five pitiful little offshoots of Patrick Saunder's genes varied noticeably. Environment, in utero and after birth, nutrition, education, and countless other qualities all acted on a human being. There had been only one Mariette Saunder. One Kevin McKelvey. One Cesare Loezzi. One Rue Polk. One Morgan McKelvey . . .

No! She would *not* add Morgan to that list. She had to believe, as Morgan would have if the situation had been reversed. It *could* have been. The luck of the toss had determined that Morgan would command Prototype II, not Brenna.

Okay. The gamble. That was what set them apart from everyone else. The magnificent wager with Death. The trick was to maintain control. A spacecraft was just a machine. The human pilot was what mattered. Ride her right out to the edge, and bring her back safe. Death was always there, millimeters away. You couldn't make any mistakes, or he would bring everything crashing down around you.

They had made a mistake. A bad one. Somewhere along the line, they had miscalculated *Twice*. Four people were

151

dead. Two were still suffering from the blow Death had dealt them. A near-miss? Or . . .

"Brenna?"

A shock went through her, a totally pleasant sensation. She had almost forgotten how that felt. Brenna thrust the chair back and spun around. Derek stood in the doorway of her quarters. He was still wearing his spacesuit. The seals were ripped open carelessly, now that he was within the hospital's life-support. He had ditched his helmet, probably left it in Arrivals, at the hub.

He looked like a man who had broken every speed record and regulation on the books—those communications silences, for one! This was a man who needed a shower, a shave, and twelve hours of uninterrupted sleep.

He looked wonderful.

CHAPTER NINE

❈❈❈❈❈❈❈❈

Prognosis

BRENNA didn't remember moving toward him. But she was suddenly there, holding him close and forgetting the outside world. For many minutes, neither of them spoke. There was no need. Brenna was content simply to *be*. Oddly, sexuality wasn't part of her feelings. This was far more basic, an emotional nourishment she hadn't known she wanted so desperately, until now. Derek's presence gave her back lost hope, regenerated badly depleted energy. She was startled by the power of her response to him. This reunion was affecting her much more than any previous one with Derek.

Like father, like daughter. I'm getting older. I can't take these events and bounce back as well as I used to . . .

Distantly, as if it had happened not to her but to someone else, Brenna recalled the scene in FTL Station during the first Prototype's test three years ago. That was before Derek had joined Hiber-Ship Corporation. He had been there as an observer, a friend, when disaster struck.

152

Stunned, Brenna, Derek, and Morgan had seen the readings, the explosion—Brenna and Morgan from Chase ships, Derek from the satellite. When the cousins had returned to FTL Station, they had cast aside, for a brief period, the constraints of their profession and clung to each other like children. They were playmates again, suddenly confronted with overwhelming grief. They smothered that breakdown in emotion as quickly as possible, hiding their pain. Defenses went up. The space pilots' unwritten code.

Never let Death know he scored a direct hit.

In retrospect, Brenna felt cheated. She ached for what they had endured when they all bottled up that hurt. In private, later, she'd wept. She knew that Morgan and Derek had, too, mourning Mari, Kevin, and Cesare. They didn't speak of it, not to each other nor to anyone else. They said all the things expected of them, while the cameras stared ruthlessly: "Those who died would have wanted it this way." How many times in human history had that been said, as agonized survivors crawled out of the wreckage of their emotions? How many other pilots went through that sham of composed faces, dry eyes, in public? Was it a hero mythos? Whatever it was, it was a prison. Chin up! Carry the look of eagles! Brave sadness, but no tears. Never any tears.

But now she was crying, guilt and anger pouring from her eyes. Derek held her, and she could feel him shuddering. He was weeping, too. For once they had privacy. Nobody would see them releasing their pain in this way. The tears helped enormously. Brenna had been embarrassed when her father had been so crushed by Morgan's accident. How dare she be so cold-blooded and stand in judgment of him? She recoiled from that moment, disliking herself and the stupid code that made her behave in such a way.

Finally, they were able to release one another and even smile a bit. Derek peeled out of his spacesuit, with Brenna's help. He rubbed his face with his knuckles, reddening the skin. Brenna laughed softly. The sound surprised her. She hadn't laughed since before the accident. "I'll bet you and the ship are both out of fuel. Whatever it is that cats drag in, you look like it."

Derek laughed, too, bone-weariness making his voice raspy. "I suppose I do. I can't imagine why." He dropped

153

heavily onto the bed, sitting in a slump, his hands dangling across his long legs. "It's nothing compared with what I'll look like after Yan and the other board members get through with me. You're right; I drained the ferry, getting here. Piled it on and decelerated like hell."

"Hotshot," Brenna said fondly. She touched his cheek, tracing the dark lines under his turquoise-blue eyes. "If they give you any trouble, I'll sic Saunder Enterprises on them. Carissa's got some money in their stock . . ." She gazed at him, abandoning the attempts at humor. "I don't have any words to tell you what your being here means. I love you for coming back."

Derek drew her hand to his lips. "How could I *not* come back?" Then he grimaced. "I stopped by ICU on my way up here to the visitors' quarters. Spirit of Humanity! I'd expected it to be bad, but . . . God! Tumaini seems to be coming out of it okay. But Morgan . . . !"

Brenna sat beside him. They leaned together, not embracing, though their heads touched lightly. Brenna knew she should tell Derek to get into the refresher and shower and log some sleep time. He was wasted with fatigue. Yet she was reluctant to move or to break the silent rapport they were sharing.

They both sensed a third person in the room. Brenna stiffened, peering at the door. Dr. Ives was standing there, waiting on the threshold. Helen forced one of the shakiest smiles Brenna had ever seen, and apprehension roiled the pilot's viscera. Brenna half rose. "Morgan? He isn't . . . ?"

"No, he's alive. Relax. Both of you." Just the same, there was a defeated note in the words. Without an invitation, Dr. Ives dragged the room's chair along its track, swiveled it to face Brenna and Derek, and flopped herself onto the cushions. Brenna was about to explode when the older woman began to explain. "As a matter of fact, we now see every indication that he's going to stay alive."

"Ha! Okay! I *knew* it!" Brenna shouted. Derek was on his feet, hugging Brenna and dancing her around. They kissed and laughed and exulted, Brenna exclaiming happily, "I knew it, I knew it! Nobody can beat a Saunder or a Mc-Kelvey for long!"

Slowly, her elation faded. Dr. Ives wasn't joining in. "What is it? You said he was going to be all right."

"I said he was likely to stay alive. That's not the same

154

thing." The space medicine specialist looked quietly angry at someone or something Brenna couldn't see. "You'd better sit down. Stefan and I have gone over this with the burn rehabilitation team, trying to make it come out more hopeful. We can't. At least the syntha skin and pleural substitute are working fairly well now. He's losing less, every day. We were afraid these injuries would be too severe for anyone to overcome. But, as you say, never underestimate a McKelvey. No doubt Dybas's staff will get a fantastic medical presentation out of his case for their next all-planets trauma conference. They literally performed miracles for Morgan. Of course, his stamina helped, even while he was unconscious. He's the worst burn case they ever tackled, with such extensive exterior *and* interior wounds." Helen Ives paused, then finished with a soft "Damn."

An ominous atmosphere filled the small cabin. Derek frowned. "Obviously there's more. What is it?"

"He's coming to," Dr. Ives said. "That's not an unmixed blessing. It means he's getting stronger. It'll also mean he'll become aware of what nerve endings he has left and how badly his lungs are affected. In other words, he'll start to feel what happened to him." Her voice trailed off, and another painful silence fell.

"Doctor, I'm tired," Derek said harshly. "You wouldn't believe how tired. I've broken so many rules to get here that I've lost count of them. I'm in trouble with my employers—I don't yet know how much. I'm seeing Brenna torn to pieces with worry. And I'm worried sick, too. I should be a gentleman and wait for you to deliver your news at your own chosen speed. But I refuse. Dammit, quit circling us! What *has* happened to Morgan? We're not fools. We can see him in ICU. He's not the first friend I've had to pray for through a crisis. We know he's going to have a rough road. If you don't give us some answers right now, I'm going to shake them loose—from somebody!"

Brenna was amazed. She had never heard Derek forget his chivalry this way before, certainly not with an older woman. He knew Dr. Ives almost as well as Brenna did, and he respected her. But no patience was endless, including Derek Whitcomb's.

"How *much* praying are you prepared to do, this time? Very well. Straight." Helen Ives cued the terminal, calling up a view from ICU. They saw Morgan in the stera-gel tank. He was moving restlessly, pathetic twitches, like an infant with no control over its limbs and no strength at all. A medic in infection-proof clothing floated beside the tank, operating waldos to apply medication inside the box. Brenna wanted to shove that figure aside and break open the tank. Morgan was hurting. Couldn't they see that? Why didn't they help him? She knew why, intellectually. That didn't shut off the empathy. The new syntha skin looked very strange, as the medics had warned it would. It wasn't oozing or blackened or blistered with ruined spacesuit pieces, as Morgan's flesh had been right after the explosion and fire. But it wasn't human skin. The color wasn't quite right, and it was much too tight, almost inflexible. Brenna knew from reading first-aid literature that the tautness had something to do with reducing formation of scar tissue. It also reduced the humanness—by appearance—of the burn victim within that replacement skin.

Helen Ives's expression betrayed her deep personal involvement with her patient. But her voice was toneless, like an old-fashioned computer. She ticked off points on her fingers as she spoke. "One: He's lost the effective use of his hands and fingers. When he's stronger, we'll implant myoelectric prosthesis tendons and bones under the new skin. They'll work well. But touch sensation will be almost nil, I'm afraid. Modern medicine has its limits.

"Two: His throat and larynx are hopelessly scarred. He's also lost the nerve endings in his lips, tongue, and nose. Again, we can effect substitutes nearly as good as the originals. But he won't have much sense of taste or smell. And he'll have to learn how to speak all over again. He *will* have a voice, once he gets onto the tricks of using an artificial larynx and how to move his tongue and lips even though he can't feel them . . . plus the problem with his lungs. That's a major one. It will last for months. We don't know if the synthetic pleural materials will ever adequately take over for what he's lost. We're hoping to bring him back to sixty percent or so of what he had in breathing capability. But of course his body was adapted for one hundred percent. He hasn't got that any more. Never will have."

By now, Derek had taken Dr. Ives's earlier advice. He was sitting down. Brenna braced herself against the com

156

terminal desk, staring at her cousin's figure on the screen.

Well, we asked for it. And Helen is letting us have it. All the bad news we dreaded. And worse.

"Three: His appearance will be greatly altered, even after reconstructive surgery is complete—as you can already tell. Syntha skin is saving his life. But it's only a fair substitute at best. His freedom of movement will always be severely restricted from now on. His coloring won't vary much with his mood or internal temperature, even though syntha skin accepts some capillary channels. It's a comparatively poor temperature regulator, unlike real skin. We'll have to protect him against hypo- *and* hyperthermia. The slightest infection could, frankly, cook him."

Brenna was hypnotized by the image on the screen and by Helen's brutal recital of facts.

"Four: His musculature is wrecked. The new energies produced a different kind of fire—and burn trauma— than any we've previously dealt with. Morgan will have to wear lattice casts on his arms and legs. The balance is delicate. Too much exertion, as in rehab conditioning, could exhaust him critically, even kill him. So will inactivity; he'll simply wither away. For those reasons, we want to move him Mars-side as soon as possible, even if it's risky. Zero gravity is easier on him—too easy. The longer Morgan stays in free fall, the harder it'll be for him to adjust to planetary gravity, and the greater the chances of crippling atrophy. We're going to move him in about a week, if he's up to it. That's rushing it. But we can't wait. His movement and cardiovascular functions are already deteriorating. With luck, eventually we'll be able to move him to a specially equipped mini-hospital out at his estate on Valles Marineris, where he'll feel more at home."

Helen hesitated before going on. "Five: He's been more or less neutered by the burns." Derek flinched, and Dr. Ives eyed him compassionately for a moment, then continued. "Reproductively, that doesn't much matter. He's in the cryogenic pool, like everyone else is. If Morgan wants to father children sometime in the future, he can, since his sperm are on file. As far as urogenital function goes, we're reconstructing. There's an outside possibility he'll regain some erective power, but very doubtful that he'll ever have the *strength* to engage in a sexual act. Nor, probably, the inclination."

157

Another long hesitation. Instinct warned Brenna to give up her perch on the desk. She lowered herself to the floor and sat looking up at the doctor. Helen Ives's hand was closed into a fist. She didn't bother adding a finger on the other hand or counting any more. "He's blind." Brenna opened her mouth. Nothing came out. "I assure you, he won't look hideous, and he *will* see," Dr. Ives said very gently. "When the surgeons are done, Morgan's eyes will appear pretty much as before. They'll be computerized prostheses directly linked to the visual centers of his brain. This won't give him the kind of vision he's known, but it's a useful form of sight. A great many people have been fitted with these opti-scan eyes. They're a marvel. In some ways, more versatile. Morgan will be able to detect thermal changes at considerable distances, for example."

The doctor tried to make that sound like an advantage. But her phenomenal calm was faltering. She bowed her head, clenching her fists until her knuckles whitened. She had been on this case since it began, in shattering failure. Brenna doubted the woman had enjoyed more than a few hours' sleep in each twenty-four-hour period since then.

Time ran backward. Colony Days. The gala. Morgan running down the ramp from the rotunda to greet Brenna and Derek. He would pick her up in his powerful arms and swing her around playfully, the way he had since they were kids and he started to get his full growth. Morgan and Derek would tease each other, Derek ribbing Morgan about the latest in his long string of romances. Morgan grinning and throwing back a ribald crack in return. Confident. Laughing. A sandy-haired bear. Sexy. Top pilot. Getting ready to ride Prototype II on her historic trip out to the edge of a real space and beyond . . .

Never again.

There were handicapped pilots. Brenna had close friends among that admirable club, men and women who kept on flying spacecraft, and flying well, after losing an arm or a leg or even an eye. None of them, however, had ever fought back from the terrible injuries Dr. Ives had just described. Sterility and impotence were cruel sentences for a man as vital as Morgan McKelvey; but for a pilot, the other changes were insurmountable. Skin that wouldn't bend or stretch or cope well with cold or heat. Severe muscle atrophy. Impaired voice function. Artificial hands and fingers. Blindness . . .

Too many check marks against him. Morgan McKelvey would never handle a ship's controls again. He wouldn't speak in his former voice, wouldn't see people as they actually were. He would walk with difficulty, if at all. No more dancing or those awesome low-gravity leaps. No more enjoying his strong body and the sheer delight of being alive, young, and healthy. Instead, there would be stera-gel and watchdog medical attendants, physical therapy to make his ruined muscles and bones retain a small fraction of their former abilities. As for Morgan's much-envied reputation as a lover, that was a sweet memory. Even if he could touch Jutta or Pauline or any of the dozens of other women who had shared joy with him, sensation would be missing, blocked out by syntha skin and destroyed nerve endings. Pain *and* pleasure—forever gone.

A violent sound tore Brenna out of her trance. Derek lunged at the bulkhead and slammed his fists into the wall. Instantly, both women grappled with him. Derek was strong enough to throw them off, but his wild rage evaporated as quickly as it had seized him. He didn't resist when they led him a few steps away. He gulped, fighting horror. "Oh, God! He'd rather be dead than *this!*"

"That's not so!" Brenna heard her own denial with astonishment. With odd detachment, she turned the words over in her mind, examining them. "No, Morgan would *not* rather be dead, Derek. Think about it."

Derek's fingers bit hard into her flesh as he cried, "Didn't you hear? He's been wrecked. He's not fully human any more. He'll be a cyborg of the worst kind, an artificial shell, a *thing,* trapped inside a useless body . . ."

"So you're going to give up on him. Is that it?" Brenna ignored the hurt he was inflicting. She hurt him, in return, with that accusation. Derek's eyes widened. Brenna eased away from his punishing grip, massaging her bruised upper arms. "Who the hell gave you the right to pass judgment and write Morgan off like this? He'd never do that to *you,* or to me, and you damned well know it! His body may be hurt, but what about his brain? That's the *real* Morgan. Helen?"

"No, his EEG and cerebral scans are tops. He'll do fine, even after the opti-scan prostheses are implanted."

Derek swayed a trifle, visibly struggling with himself. Brenna was furious with his lack of faith in Morgan. But she also understood part of his reaction. Slowly, he reached out to her. Brenna didn't move away. Derek caressed her shoulder and face. His eyes were as gentle as his touch. "I . . . I'm sorry. So sorry. I didn't mean to . . . didn't . . . it was just hearing it all at once . . ."

Helen Ives could have told him he had asked for it. She didn't. "It *is* a shock. But don't forget that Morgan's a hell of a fighter. He's proved it time and again, double-crossing every prediction in the medical tapes. He deserves support, if only for his courage."

"Of course," Derek murmured. His expression showed his misery. "I'm sorry," he repeated, blushing. "I guess I just went crazy for a moment. It was as if it had been me who'd been hurt. I started imagining how I'd feel when I found out . . ."

Brenna and the doctor nodded, letting him know they accepted his point of view. Hiber-Ship crew members were all prime physical and mental specimens. No weaklings need apply. Derek himself had always been disgustingly healthy. All of his co-workers—fellow colonist volunteers —were, too. He took it for granted, emotionally, that his contemporaries would always be in that league—fit, intelligent, highly trained, and self-sufficient. Quite suddenly, his best friend didn't qualify any more. The intelligence was unaltered. Everything else was affected by the gruesome aftereffects of the burns. Derek wasn't coping well with the change. A bias, one that made him squirm, but one he couldn't shake off.

Brenna's anger was gone. She hugged Derek. "I know. It's okay. We'll be okay. You'll see."

"Let me have a look at your hands," Dr. Ives ordered. Subdued, Derek obeyed. Helen probed, tapping his fingertips. "Nothing seems broken. But you'll have some impressive bruises. Blonds show off broken capillaries so well." She went into the cabin's refresher and fetched an aid kit, then deftly applied spray bandage to the scraped knuckles. "I'll take a bone and tendon scan tomorrow. But I can practically guarantee there's no real damage."

Derek's outburst had distracted Brenna from other problems. Now that he had quieted down, she remembered one of them. Worriedly, she asked, "Have you told my father yet—about Morgan?"

"I'll have to. As soon as I leave here." Helen wasn't looking forward to breaking that news. "I'll soften it as much as possible. As for you two, what you need is sleep, and a lot of it. You've been running yourselves down to the bare circuitry, and it's costing you. Do you cooperate? Or do I send for sedatives? Remember, this is a hospital, and a medic's word is law up here."

Chastened, Derek nodded. "That . . . that won't be necessary. I don't know what took over my skull earlier."

"Human decency and caring. Don't blame yourself for it." Dr. Ives tossed the kit back into the refresher, then punched *cancel* on the monitor, nodding in satisfaction when the screen blacked out. "And don't watch that any more. Morgan's the med department's responsibility for the present. Let us do the worrying. He doesn't need you to flog yourselves for his sake."

"What *does* he need from us?" Brenna asked.

"Love, when he's awake enough to know you're there. That will be sooner than you expect. His hearing's only slightly affected, thank God. He'll need your help recuperating from *emotional* trauma. There's plenty. Your support will be crucial. We'll let you know when."

After Helen had left, Brenna tried to recall what she had been doing before the doctor handed them that dismaying update. Derek. He'd just arrived at W.L.F. Space Hospital. A long, non-stop, throttles-wide-open journey. She hadn't even asked him if he'd eaten or had a room at the visitors' quarters. She did so now. Derek stared numbly. "I ought to go to ICU . . ."

"Uh-uh. You heard the doctor. She's right." Brenna interrupted herself with a huge yawn. "We *are* running down to the bare wires. Let's recoup. It's only sensible. Grab a shower and come to bed." Derek shuffled toward the refresher, moving like a robot. That was the clincher, proving Dr. Ives's case.

Brenna posted the *Disturb Only for Emergencies* panel on the ident screen outside and sealed the door. When Derek emerged from the shower, she pushed him into the narrow bunk and crawled in beside him. Ordinarily, that cozy arrangement would have led to a happy tussle and some sex. Not this time. Their passion was burned out by exhaustion, spent in grief, not sexuality. They cuddled like children afraid of monsters in the dark.

Yet Derek fought sleep. He tensed, then relaxed many times, resisting possible nightmares. Brenna held him tight and murmured. The meaningless sounds were designed to soothe her as well as Derek. Gradually, his breathing became deep and regular, broken only occasionally by a whimper. In the night screen's pale glow, Brenna studied his face, now completely open and vulnerable. *He looks like a boy, despite his beard. So does Morgan, when he's asleep. Correction: So did Morgan. We don't know what Morgan will look like after the surgeons get through with him. At least he'll have a future. He's going to live.* Finally, she gave up all thought, sinking into emptiness.

There must have been dreams. But she had no memory of them when she awoke. Brenna squinted at the timekeeper on the night screen. Nine hours! Nine hours of precious nothingness. It felt so good. Dr. Ives had been right. The grinding depression of yesterday had disappeared. Mind and body felt wonderfully restored after that enforced shutdown. Maybe she *could* cope with the mountains of problems that would lie ahead in the next weeks and months.

Brenna catnapped for another hour or so until Derek began to stir. He always woke up bright-eyed and alert, an ability Brenna sometimes resented. This time she enjoyed watching the process from the beginning. The awful fatigue had been wiped off his face. He smiled, and Brenna returned it along with a sly invitation. She was vaguely aware of a lingering soreness in her upper arms where Derek had bruised her. But that wasn't important. Much more intense sensations overrode anything so minor.

She could recall no previous time when sex had occurred so easily and quickly for them. After years of intimacy, they knew each other's moods and desires well. One moment they were gazing seductively at one another. In the next they were drowning in sexual delight, a marathon in which both of them won.

The minutes were idyllic, and too short. Brenna wanted to prolong the pleasure. Delicious aftershocks were still making her shiver as she lay beside Derek. His smile had turned into a smug, contented grin. Reluctantly, then, Brenna noticed a light winking on the screen. Messages.

162

More discreet than a human knocking on the door, but just as persistent.

The outside world was waiting. It never went away.

What had she told Yuri and the others? Pick up the pieces. Time to do that, and so much else.

With a heartfelt sigh, Brenna rolled away from Derek and stood up. He caught her hand, holding on. Brenna wanted very much to yield to that temptation. But the chance was lost. The outside world was intruding on his consciousness, too, clouding his bright eyes. Duty called Captain Derek Whitcomb.

". . . I'm in trouble with my employers. I don't yet know how much . . ."

The lovely respite was over.

They rushed through getting ready. Saunder Enterprises Security brought Derek's spare clothes kit up from his ship. Brenna showered. They gobbled breakfast and were off and running—again.

Derek finally had to break his communications silence and check in with Hiber-Ship Corporation. They knew where he was, of course. They'd been tracking him all the way, via their Space Fleet connections. Nevertheless, when he came on the com and reported, the execs screamed, long and loud. After they quit yelling, they decided to call Derek's rebellion a "compassionate leave." Many of those execs, such as Yan Bolotin, were former space pilots themselves. They understood Derek's motivations and forgave the breach of corporate discipline.

Todd Saunder welcomed Derek's presence in their circle. Brenna guessed that was in part because he had known Derek since he was a boy. It gave the illusion that another member of the family had joined their vigil. Derek provided an emotional boost that paid off in actions. Bit by bit, Todd Saunder took up his normal routine where he had dropped it so abruptly when he first heard the news.

When Morgan was conscious, Dr. Ives, true to her promise, let his loved ones into the monitoring room. The medics had been explaining the situation to Morgan for some time, strangers, taking the worst brunt of a patient's understandable anger and helpless fear. Brenna, Derek, and Todd Saunder bobbed at the safety railing outside the ICU, watching through the window. Dr. Ives had been breaking some of the news to Morgan as other doctors checked on

Morgan's bio-cerebral interface readings, alert to any indications this horrible revelation would send the patient into deep shock. The readings dipped and wavered but never dropped precipitously. The doctors seemed amazed Morgan was adjusting so well.

It was time for Morgan's family and friends to try communicating with him, if they could. Todd's voice broke. "Morgan? It's Uncle Todd. Everybody's here but Dian, and she'll be here very soon. It's going to get better. You've got the best doctors in the Solar System, son. The very best . . ."

Hastily, Derek took over the mike, sparing the old man further painful effort. "Tumaini's right next door to you, Morgan. Griping like hell, half of it in Mwera. The docs are going to give him a ride planetside tomorrow. Maybe *that* will shut him up! He'll save you a cushy room down there. We'll all be heading to Mars before you know it . . ."

Brenna noticed Derek wasn't looking through the window. He spoke cheerily but avoided the sight within ICU. His hang-up. He cared so much it hurt him, yet looking at Morgan—Morgan grossly different from what he had been —was more than Derek could take.

The doctors reported that Morgan's hearing was a little distorted. His outer ears weren't rebuilt completely. Hearing, though, was his only contact with the world. His destroyed eyes were covered with medication. Breathing apparatus protruded from a hole in his throat. The lattice casts Dr. Ives had referred to kept his arms and legs straight, and Morgan immobile. Trapped—inside his brain.

Brenna took the mike from Derek. "You heard all that? Straight stuff, partner. Helen's going to pull you out of that glorified bathtub as soon as she can. When she does, the goldbricking's over. For right now, you concentrate on getting well. I'll take care of everything until you're back on your feet."

Brenna wasn't sure Morgan had heard them. Then, with painstaking effort, he rolled his head along the stera-gel, turning slightly toward the audio monitor within his tank. He nodded, a barely detectable motion, but as plain as a shout to Brenna. He *had* heard! That feeble movement was Morgan's equivalent of a defiant yell and a thumbs-up. From where was he getting the strength? From where he always got it. A McKelvey was hard to kill! Morgan had lost consciousness while he was in excruciating pain but still a whole man. He was waking up to living hell—blind, mute, crippled, struggling for every breath of air. But he *was* struggling, not rolling over and giving up. Believing in what the doctors told him, what Brenna had promised him.

"*. . . you concentrate on getting well . . .*"

But would Morgan ever get well? Very doubtful. He would probably depend on Brenna and the medics for the rest of his life.

"*. . . I'll take care of everything . . .*"

She had promised. Somehow, she would deliver. She glanced sidelong at her father, remembering Todd Saunder's pet slogan: "There are no simple answers. But there *are* answers. The trick is to find them." She had heard that for years. Maybe it had soaked in until she really believed it. She would find the answers for Morgan, just as her father had found the Vahnaj messenger vehicle more than thirty years ago.

Visiting "hours" were over. Morgan couldn't take much wakefulness. Communication with him would be limited to minutes until he was stronger. Helen shooed them out of ICU, then stayed to chat for a while in the V.I.P. lounge before she went back to work.

"Did you hear?" Todd Saunder crowed. "Saturday! They're going to transfer Morgan planetside on Saturday. That's wonderful! I'll call Quol-Bez and let him know so he can make the arrangements."

"Quol-Bez?" Brenna asked, bewildered. "What does he have to do with it?"

"Oh, didn't I tell you? He's lending me his personal vehicle for Morgan's ambulance ride. He practically insisted. I can't refuse. It might be grounds for a diplomatic incident if I offend the Vahnaj Ambassador," Todd said with a chuckle.

"That's nice, Dad," Brenna murmured absently. Derek added his praise of the Ambassador's kind and unusual gesture.

The Ambassador's personal vehicle. That was the one Terran Worlds Council Space Fleet provided for Quol-Bez's exclusive use. It was staffed royally. Capable of tremendous speed—so the Vahnaj Ambassador wouldn't be late to any meetings with anxious Terran leaders! The spacecraft was

165

a luxury model of Space Fleet's finest. Of course, it was a "loaner," supplied for the convenience of humanity's first full-time alien visitor. The *real* Vahnaj ship remained parked semi-permanently in space. Yet, for a heart-stopping instant, Brenna had thought her father was referring to *that* spaceship. Her mouth had watered at the hope of coming in close contact with that famous faster-than-light vehicle. Just an hour's worth of examination time could tell her so much! Including where Prototype II's design had erred, perhaps. Then common sense took hold. No, Quol-Bez couldn't break his diplomatic instructions, not even for personal friendship with Todd Saunder and his kin. And it was apparent the Vahnaj government did *not* want humans roaming around in that alien ship.

"The very best," her father was saying. "Quol-Bez has already spoken to Morgan's doctors, too. He never misses a detail. Talk about his putting himself out for others . . ."

"Well, Dad, after all, he's known you longer than he has any other *Homo sapiens*," Brenna said with a smile. "You and Dian were talking to the Vahnaj long before Quol-Bez was assigned to our planets. He's at ease with you, even when he's reserved with every other human."

"Not reserved, just polite," Todd said, leading the way to the elevators for the visitors' quarters. "He's really a very warm being. You know that. Come on. I've got a megaton of calls to make."

The pace became hectic. Schedules changed hourly. Media demands for info declined only slightly, Evanow's PR staff reported. The Saunders were still very much in the minds of Earthmen and the colonists throughout the Solar System. Evanow set up a few brief in-person interviews on the vid with Brenna and her father, to satisfy the public's craving for news. In a way, that continued interest was gratifying. Evanow was SE, asking all the right questions. Exactly the sort of media exposure Brenna approved of—not the grasping and needling of the outsider newshunters.

On Monday, the regular ambulance shuttle transferred Tumaini Beno to Mars. Derek and Brenna went down to see him off, with his escort of medics. But Tumaini was barely aware of their presence. Pre-flight medications made him groggy. Brenna and Derek went to the observation port to watch the ambulance drop away on its journey to the planet. "Below," on Mars, they could see the terminator marking a new dawn over Syrtis Major. In orbit, the Sun never set. Eternal sunlight here wasn't as bright as it was near Earth, yet bright enough so that Brenna was glad the port window was tinted. The ambulance shuttle was a glimmering needle, appearing to fall, not using much thrust at all in order to give the injured passengers a gentle ride. Tumaini wasn't the only patient being transferred today. Three others were taking the ride with him—a Deimos warehouse worker who had been hurt in an industrial accident, and two United Asteroid miners who had been ferrying an ore cargo Sunward when their drive went out of control and piled them into an unmanned beacon station a scant million kilometers from Mars orbit.

During the week, surgeons performed a series of small, delicate operations on Morgan. Drs. Dybas and Ives tried to explain these procedures, in rather more detail than laymen cared to hear. It was necessary, the physicians said, to get these surgical repairs out of the way while Morgan was still in the free-fall burn unit. They were paving the way for the eventual laryngeal and optic implants as well as lessening scar tissue formations. By doing these things now, they could complete them with minimal discomfort for the patient and without resorting to overly dangerous anesthetics.

"Minimal discomfort." A cute medical term. Softer than "pain." The medics kept saying Morgan wasn't in great pain. But Brenna didn't believe it. She imagined her own body subjected to cutting, scraping, and laser-seaming, and she winced in sympathy.

Dian beat her predicted ETA to the hospital by more than twelve hours. More heavy fuel expenditures for Saunder Enterprises' accounts! When Brenna commented on that, Dian muttered that ComLink would simply have to raise its advertising rates a trifle to foot the bill. Brenna was touched by the warmth of her parents' reunion. Dian's arrival lifted Todd Saunder from hope to growing confidence, chasing away most of his depression. Brenna watched her mother admiringly. There were legends about Dian, not about this still-active black woman in her sixties, but about a skinny kid helping her grandmother care for the wounded and the dying, and about a young linguist who had cracked the Vahnaj code and taught mankind

167

how to talk to the stars. Her earlier experiences had made Dian Foix Saunder a tough customer. She didn't even blink when she saw Morgan. She spoke calmly and encouragingly to him, when he was in Recovery after surgery. And she drew Brenna, Derek, and her husband into the shelter of her assurance, too. Everyone felt more at ease now that she was there.

Quol-Bez didn't deliver his personal spacecraft to the hospital himself. Her crew of Space Fleet troopers did that, well in advance of the planned departure time, so the hospital's vehicle mechanics could convert part of the ship's cabin into a mini-ambulance. Brenna was being swept along in the arrangements, more than willing to let others handle the job. The only moment she resented came when they were boarding. Morgan had already been moved, with infinite tenderness, into the converted ambulance area of the ship, with Helen Ives and her experts caring for him. Derek and the Saunders and their aides were ushered into the main passenger compartment. Passengers, not pilots. Supercargo, in fact. Brenna wanted to go up front. So did Derek. But Derek knew better. Space Fleet kept the cockpit off-limits—no non-military personnel allowed.

The Ambassador's ship eased out of the hospital's dock so slowly, Brenna double-checked to be sure they were moving. Terrific ship! Masterful pilots! She would love to recruit them for Breakthrough Unlimited. Then she decided that, in effect, she already had—Yuri, Tumaini, and Hector were all former Space Fleet pilots. Little wonder when they had joined the FTL project that so much expertise showed in everything they did at a ship's controls.

The orbital descent was incredibly smooth, dropping through a rigidly graduated spiral, the ship prodigal with its fuel. Space Fleet could be even more spendthrift than Saunder Enterprises. Terran Worlds Council was drawing on taxes and funds not even a Saunder could tap. Steady burns. Balanced vernier thrust. No bumps. No sudden deceleration. Amazonis Planitia Spaceport was bypassed. They were going to put her down at the restricted V.I.P. strip just outside Pavonis City. Diplomatic privilege, extended to Quol-Bez's human friend Todd Saunder.

Coming back to Mars in style . . . supercargo of a crippled man, his family and best friend, and assorted employees.

168

A private sub-surface train was waiting at the strip. Boarding was very slow. Dr. Ives insisted on moving Morgan a centimeter at a time, constantly monitoring his condition. The trip down to gravity had caused him stress. Brenna and the others had taken gravity compensation medications, but Morgan was severely limited in what drugs he could handle right now.

Once aboard, it was a short ride to the W.L.F. Mars Hospital. Again they would roll into the V.I.P. area. It occurred to Brenna that she hadn't seen the surface of Mars since the night before her departure for FTL Station. She hadn't walked on Mars' rocky soil since the holiday she and Derek had spent at Eos Chasm. Had that really been only three weeks ago? She had an aberrant desire to stop the train and take an elevator to open air. Or to Mars' nearest equivalent of air. Even roaming the surface in a spacesuit would satisfy. She was suddenly sick and tired of confining walls—space stations, spaceship cockpits, the whole thing. Why? Claustrophobia? That was a death sentence for a space pilot! Then she glanced at the rear of the train car, at Morgan's Pod Carrier. Morgan was asleep now, unaware of his surroundings. But every time he awoke, for days without end, he would find himself trapped, pent up inside walls of one sort or another, including a skin that wasn't his own. Maybe Brenna's emotion had been empathy, sharing what Morgan was going to feel.

They had to walk from the V.I.P. platform into the hospital. At one point the newshunters spotted them. Saunder Enterprises Security cordoned their bosses, but they couldn't stop the shouting, the rude queries, hammering at the patient's loved ones.

"Todd! Hey, Todd Saunder! Did the Vahnaj Ambassador let you use the fancy ship because your sister-in-law's Prez Emeritus of P.O.E.?"

"Did Councilman Ames twist his arm? Didn't your daughter and McKelvey and Whitcomb save his life during the Colony Days gala?"

"Hey! Whitcomb! You quitting Hiber-Ship and joining those FTL crazies?"

"Saunder! How about the Terran Worlds Council franchise? Won't you lose your right to experiment up there in space now?"

169

"Let us see McKelvey! Is that him in that plastic coffin?"

Mercifully, the doors shut between the hall and Receiving. Brenna couldn't hear those vultures, in here. She shook with fury. Those ghouls! They would like Morgan to be dead! That would make a juicier story! One of the famous Saunder clan, killed trying to break the light-speed barrier. They could make all manner of allusions to rich people getting too bold and thinking they could buy their way into or out of anything. That would be good for weeks of "we told you so" on their sleazy vid programs. Like father, like son. Like mother, like son, too!

The one small consolation Brenna had was that one of those screeching ghouls out in the hall was Charlie Dahl. She had caught a glimpse of his hateful face when she was rushing past the line. Charlie had come down a big notch. Evanow had carried out her orders to the letter, apparently. Instead of sitting in the driver's seat and ranking with the top newscasters, Charlie was now hopping up and down with the gypsies and the third-rate stringers, trying to yell his way into a story. Good enough for him!

Derek put his arm around her, drawing Brenna farther away from the doors lest she hear some of the ghouls' nasty questions even in here. Receiving was a haven. All the faces here were friendly and concerned. Morgan had been whisked off to ICU. For a few minutes, his relatives and other caring people were at a loss. They wandered into the nearby lounge. "Why can't we see him?" Todd asked plaintively. "They said he was going to be all right."

"He will be," Dian assured him. She threaded her arm through his. "They're monitoring him. It's the shift to gravity. Bound to be a shock. He'll get used to it, though. Huh! Haven't I had to nag you often enough to take your grav medications?"

Quol-Bez was waiting there. He took Todd's hand, murmuring encouragement. Brenna recalled the Ambassador's frequent inquiries and expressions of sympathy—capped off by donating his private craft to be Morgan's ambulance. Her longstanding envy of Vahnaj superiority in FTL mingled with affection for this dependable friend of the family. And now he was here, at just the right time, to greet her father and say the right things.

". . . so ver-y strong. You must not be dis-mayed, my

170

friend." The alien's head bobbed on that snaky neck. The child's voice no longer seemed as odd as it sometimes had. Vahnaj or human, it was the reaching out, the caring, that made all the difference between intelligent, sensitive beings. In that regard, Quol-Bez was far more "human" than those ghoulish newshunters. "Yes. The phy-si-cians informed me of the ter-ri-ble nature of Morgan's injuries. No, please, my friend. I understand. Blind-ness seems very cruel to your species. But the phy-si-cians can remedy this. And you must realize that there are many methods of seeing." Brenna and the others were all listening intently. Quol-Bez was the sage, the giver of wisdom, a creature out of mythology they suddenly trusted completely. He would help them penetrate the veil covering the future, somehow. Quol-Bez nodded again, speaking softly. "Per-haps the method they will give Morgan will open doors formerly closed to him, and to the rest of your species."

CHAPTER TEN

⊗⊗⊗⊗⊗⊗⊗⊗

Partnership

DR. IVES traced the holo-mode CAT visualization, pointing out improvements in Morgan's condition. Brenna listened patiently. What she was learning might someday be applicable in the field. She had never expected emergency burn-aid techniques to be useful, either, but that course had helped save Morgan's and Tumaini's lives. Helen was a good teacher. If she hadn't made a career of space medicine, she would have had no trouble winning a chair at a top university on Earth or on Mars. Instead, she had become Saunder Enterprises' ultimate medical specialist, with her own five-person staff, the latest equipment, and one patient.

May had disappeared. June was gone, too. Brenna remembered those months dimly. A few important events interwoven with long days of worry and tedium.

One red-letter day had been Tumaini's release from the

171

hospital in mid-June. He was now an outpatient, undergoing rehabilitation therapy. However, the Rift Affiliation native spent far more time visiting Morgan and hanging around Breakthrough Unlimited's HQ at Amazonis Spaceport than he did in following doctors' orders. Aluna Beno's relationship with her husband's co-workers was still strained, despite Carmelita Obregón's efforts at peacemaking. Brenna hadn't seen Aluna for nearly a month, and she was content to leave it at that. Whatever was going on between the Benos wasn't any of her business. She just hoped it wouldn't interfere with Tumaini's recovery. Tumaini walked with a bad limp and was going to need extensive further surgery on his back. But in general, he was getting along well.

On the monitor screens Brenna saw med aides, wearing infection-proof clothing, helping Morgan off the exercise equipment in his room. That was a painful process to watch, always. Yet it was one of the few times when Morgan seemed fairly alert. Brenna wondered if his reaction had anything to do with the presence of the aides. Once a day, they suited up and entered his sterile living quarters, the only people who did so. No direct touch, of course. But maybe just being that close to other people made a difference in his morale.

Morgan was no longer at W.L.F. Hospital. Since the end of June he had been here at Saunder Estates, in a private clinic, in effect, built entirely for his comfort. Brenna and her parents had arranged for the addition, a fully equipped mini-hospital, with residential sections to house Helen Ives and her people. The theory was: Morgan would feel more "at home" *in* his home, and that would help his mental state, and, maybe, his physical condition as well.

Brenna visited him as often as she could, daily, when she was on Mars. Some family member was always at the Estates now. The peripatetic Martian Colony branch of the Saunders was more home-based than it had been in years because of Morgan's accident.

Other members of the Breakthrough Unlimited group dropped in regularly, too. But their visits were restricted, on Dr. Ives's orders. Morgan wasn't yet able to cope with much activity at all.

When Brenna and Yuri had taken trips out to FTL Station in May and several times in June, Tumaini Beno had been their "stand-in" during visiting times. The trips were necessary, if Breakthrough Unlimited was to continue. Lingering radiation in Prototype II had hampered salvage efforts badly. After a lot of nail biting and cursing and hasty conferences at the Station, Shoje Nagata had come up with the idea of pulling the hot core and leaving that in high ecliptic orbit, for the time being. The rest of the wreckage—including most of the graviton spin resonance power pack—could then be towed to Mars. Brenna congratulated the junior pilot on that idea, and Nagata had, with surprising modesty, credited Adele Zyto and Joe Habich for thinking up the plan. Whoever was responsible, it had worked. Since early July, Brenna and the team had been poring over the collected pieces of the once-beautiful FTL spacecraft, trying to figure out what had caused the barrier field to collapse so disastrously. The job was turning into a rotten mess, as they had known it would.

Dr. Ives had excused herself to answer a call on an adjacent com screen. Brenna leaned back, staring out the window at the magnificent view. Morgan's estate perched on the north rim of Valles Marineris, and the early morning sunlight was casting stark shadows into the gorges.

Brenna reviewed her own status, as she and Helen had been reviewing Morgan's. She was still handling sympathy messages, some with a new element. The media were tending to romanticize Morgan McKelvey as a "tragic hero," and a lot of women who had never known him before the accident were now interested in him, in a way Brenna considered abnormal. There were women who yearned to bear Morgan's children, via artificial insemination with his preserved sperm. Women who wanted to "give" him their eyes or skin or other organs—too uneducated to realize the donations weren't needed and wouldn't do Morgan any good, anyway. Women begging for personally inscribed holo-mode images of Morgan Saunder McKelvey the way he *used* to look. Brenna hadn't troubled Morgan with any of this strange correspondence. She hadn't troubled herself with it, either, any more than she could help, leaving that mail for a tolerant secretary to handle.

Friends and acquaintances had kept up polite inquiries and had visited Morgan, at first. That hadn't been easy for them. Even the bravest ones couldn't cope at all well with

173

what they saw when they came face to face with the patient. And Morgan had been very unresponsive, either because of his terrible injuries or because of their reactions to him. Eventually, they didn't come any more, or most of them didn't. Ambassador Quol-Bez and his translator were among the exceptions. They were quite familiar faces at Saunder Estates now. Quol-Bez seemed to be manufacturing reasons to spend time at his embassy on Mars, near the Saunder family complex, apparently so that he could continue to express kindness and concern for his kin-friend's invalid nephew. Brenna had seen more of Quol-Bez and Chin Jui-Sao in the past weeks than she had in the entire previous half year. Brenna was actually discovering a great many shared attitudes with Sao, though she had never known the Chinese woman well at all before Morgan's accident.

Personal life? A joke. Derek's bosses had put him back to work, intending to recoup what he had cost them with his detour. So he had little leisure. Brenna estimated that they had been alone less than five times since that trip down from Space Hospital. Alone? Was a "tryst" in the busy Amazonis Spaceport's cafeteria, for example, being "alone"? Their relationship was as precisely scheduled as a vid drama, and far less satisfying. Today Derek *was* at Saunder Estates, for an hour or so. Then he had to catch a flight somewhere. As usual.

Everything revolved around Morgan and his slow recuperation. Tiny victories. He had regained his voice early in May. At first he could make only awful strangling sounds, but everyone had celebrated, nevertheless. Morgan had worked like hell with the therapists, learning to control his impaired breathing and reconstructed vocal apparatus —learning to talk for the second time in his life.

He had eyesight again, too, of a sort. That had been less emotionally exciting for the family but probably more so for Morgan. Brenna wasn't sure. Morgan didn't use his new synthetic voice much. Getting a "hello" or a "thank you" out of him was sometimes a major effort. Psychological adjustment problems, Dr. Ives said. They had to give him time, she advised. Indeed! After what he had been through!

Helen Ives had finished her call and was back at the med monitor. "By September, we'll insert an additional vision booster here, on the circuit behind the left ear," she said, touching a spot on the screen. A tiny green blip appeared on the indicated neural map of Morgan's brain. "That will give him more depth perception and better color differentiation."

"He'll like that," Brenna remarked politely. "He's complained that things look flat and fuzzy with his new eyes. I mean, even *allowing* for the fact that it all resembles a computer diagram."

"Not quite that bad," Helen said, defending her discipline and the fantastic prostheses that could replace human eyesight.

Correction: "Substitute for," not "replace." Morgan could read quite well. The printed word fitted his vision fine. Diagrams were great. But scenes of places he had never been and pictures of people he had never seen registered poorly on the computerized opti-scan prostheses. Morgan couldn't pick up delicate nuances of expression. He had to rely so much on figures, numbers, and other people. That had always been true to some degree for the blind, of course. Before biosynth surgery was perfected, the blind had depended on friends or listened to transcriptions, or read coded writing through their fingertips. That last technique wouldn't work for Morgan. There was too little tactile sensation in his syntha-skin fingertips. The now-outdated Braille system would be virtually useless to him.

"We're working on it," Dr. Ives insisted. "We're going to upgrade his synthetic voice box, too. Intonation refinement, that sort of thing. I understand the implant is closely related to the very same translator-splitter device your father developed from Ward Saunder's patents. We'll match Morgan's pre-accident voice with the implant, and no one will tell the difference."

Brenna gazed at the older woman solemnly. Helen was sincere. She really believed the implant could make Morgan's voice a convincing copy of the original. That would only happen years from now, if at all. The doctors didn't hear the enormous change in voice quality. It wasn't a matter of pitch or timbre or breathiness. Some essential ingredient was gone from that beloved basso, and Brenna didn't believe any medical miracle could bring it back.

"Has Quol-Bez been here yet this morning?" Brenna asked suddenly, changing the subject.

175

"Why, yes. He and Sao visited Morgan very early. They're over at your father's estate, with Derek. Didn't he tell you?"

Mildly embarrassed, Brenna shook her head. "I haven't seen him. Got back late from the spaceport. Just stopped to see if Morgan was okay and then slept like a rock. Things have been a little jumbled at Breakthrough lately."

"You ought to take some R and R."

"I don't notice *you* taking any," Brenna shot back, smiling. "Dedication above and beyond the call of duty, huh?"

"If you feel that way, maybe I should put my staff in for raises," Helen said, leading the way toward Morgan's rooms. She was teasing, but Brenna made note of the idea. Dr. Ives and her people had earned every unit of their salaries and more, these past weeks.

At the main monitoring station, two medic aides were stowing their sterile suits in the clean lockers. Another was watching the bio scans. Two more medics were on standby. In an emergency, they would all be here in moments, since they were housed in the adjacent wing. "He did quite well on the rehab exercises, Dr. Ives," one medic reported. On the screen, they could see waldos wheeling away the treadmill and lifting bars until the next therapy session. The little fetch-and-carry robot which was always in the room with Morgan was adjusting the therma-blankets carefully on the rack that held the fabric free of Morgan's fragile skin. The robot was handy. And it eliminated the need for human attendants to be with Morgan every minute. That would have been unpleasant for the medics; Morgan's room was a large hyperbaric chamber. The high pressure helped his badly hurt lungs, but long exposure to it forced "normal" humans to go through lengthy decompression. Instead, the therapists left as soon as possible after every exercise session. Morgan's only true around-the-clock companion was the little octopus-shaped robot on wheels.

"If he's tired, I could come back later . . ."

Helen checked the scans. "No, he's okay. His breathing rate's increased almost four percent. Did I tell you he can stand without constant support now? Marvelous! Go on in. We'll let you know if he becomes fatigued."

Brenna walked past the monitoring station and into the alcove off Morgan's room. She peered through the transparent wall. Opposite the alcove another clear wall gave

176

Morgan a view of the canyon. It probably meant little to him now. Morgan used to love the view. That was why he and his father had selected this site for Saunder Estates: Mars. The splendid landscape, and conveniently close to Pavonis City. Morgan had been a teenager when Kevin McKelvey laid out the claim—a teenager with perfect eyesight and a strong physique.

Morgan was lying on his stera-gel chair-bed, listening to a ComLink broadcast. He had graduated from the tank of glop some time ago, but he still required stera-gel to guard against infection and support his syntha skin in Mars' gravity. The chair-bed appeared fairly ordinary, except for the jellylike pink substance serving as "cushions."

Brenna sat down facing the pli-wall dividing the alcove from the hyperbaric chamber. "Hello, Morgan." Audio circuits fed her voice past the wall and into the room. No one could speak to him directly. Too much infection risk.

"Brenna?" Morgan swiveled his head slowly, seeming to stare at her. "Chair—take me to the alcove wall." The chair-bed glided toward Brenna, the little robot rolling out of its path. The chair-bed reshaped itself and propped Morgan's head and upper torso at a forty-five-degree angle to put him at eye level with his visitor. It also formed a spongy pocket under his withered legs, cradling his knees. Brenna pressed her hand against a special section of the wall. The material gave like an invisible glove, shaping itself around her flesh. On the other side, Morgan reached toward her, carefully; he didn't yet trust his control over his myoelectric hands. They were as close to touching each other as was possible, but the thin veil of plasticene still separated their fingers.

Morgan was wearing a loose hospital robe this morning. That was tremendous progress! When he had first arrived on Mars, he couldn't wear any clothing at all, for fear of endangering his delicate syntha skin. Almost his first words when his voice had been restored were to complain that there was no comfortable position for him to lie in—one that wouldn't slough off the stuff. Eventually he had graduated to a glorified loincloth, when the syntha skin seemed likely to bond to his body and stay. Now he could wear a robe. When Brenna had arrived at the alcove, the waldos attached to the chair-bed had neatly folded back the blanket covering his legs, giving Morgan the illusion that he

177

had freedom of movement and the blanket was just to keep his useless feet warm.

There was a long, awkward silence. Frequent visitors here got used to that. Or they gave up. A lot of them had given up. Morgan wasn't hideously scarred. But there were *some* scars. His skin was too taut, allowing little facial expression. The surgeons had re-created his hair and eyebrows, duplicating the originals as best they could. He still tended to look like an emotionless, vid-drama "android."

"Did you have a good trip?" Morgan asked finally.

"No problems." Brenna was almost accustomed to his new voice now. The hyperbaric chamber further intensified changes in tone quality.

Another silence. Then, "When did you get in? About two?"

"Uh-huh. Yuri reminded us of the time, or I'd still be there, working on that damned oscillator. It's *got* to be the oscillator that went wrong. But . . . we can't stay there twenty-four hours a day. We'll drop."

"I watched the data feed until you shut up shop at one A.M." Morgan tilted his head slightly toward the vid screen attached to the chair-bed. The thing operated on voice command alone, if need be, so that he wouldn't have to exert his frail body.

ComLink. His lifeline to the world outside this room. His uncle's vast communications network enabled Morgan to cross continents and interplanetary space. Dramas and standard holo-mode images didn't do much for him any more. But he could hear, and he could read from the text with fewer distractions than most normally sighted people. Thanks to ComLink, he had been watching over Brenna's shoulder while she and the Breakthrough Unlimited team hunted for the probable cause of Prototype II's blowup. He had been a thousand kilometers from the hangar, but distance didn't matter.

"That was an interesting readout you got on number five graviton baffle. The peak stresses obviously hit there first," Morgan said. "The field instability links right up with the hull material flaw. It's all going to tie together."

That was practically an oration for Morgan. Brenna started with pleased surprise. "You think so? I do, too. But you're better at metallurgy analyses. Yuri agrees. George and Hector and the kids are halfway convinced the trouble's in the power plant. Even Tumaini said we could solve everything if we just 'borrowed' Quol-Bez's ship and took her engines . . ."

"Don't." That came out sharply, straining Morgan's artificial vocal cords. He fell into his staring mode, looking through her. Brenna wanted to ask what had upset him so, but was afraid to. The old wish? "Borrowing" Quol-Bez's ship and examining the Vahnaj version of faster-than-light drive? Why would *that* recurrent fantasy disturb him? Morgan, too, had played with that scenario during moments of FTL piloting frustration. "It can't be done," Morgan said. His unnatural voice was more solemn now. "Don't you realize Space Fleet would have slipped agents past the cordon to do exactly that, long before now, if it were possible? It isn't."

"They're afraid of diplomatic repercussions. But a civilian outfit . . ."

"No." Very flat, allowing no argument. "As Derek says, 'Affirmative and underline.' The Vahnaj aren't that stupid. They won't let humans steal it. They made sure we can't."

Brenna stared at him, her curiosity simmering. "How do you know? Did Quol-Bez tell you that?" There was no reply. She waited, a long time. Morgan didn't move and didn't speak. Only the labored rise and fall of his chest showed that he was alive. Those inhuman, computerized gray eyes were unblinking. "You okay?" Brenna asked anxiously.

"It's not the power plant," Morgan replied finally. The non sequitur threw her for a moment. He had dropped what they had been talking about and had gone back to discussing the problems with Prototype II, refusing to answer further questions about the Vahnaj FTL ship. That only heightened her curiosity, rather than shutting it off. "It's the oscillator," he said, with as much emphasis as he could. Was that a former test pilot's gut feeling . . . or was he somehow picking up hints from Quol-Bez? The Ambassador was with him so much nowadays. Helen Ives had commented on how well Quol-Bez and Morgan seemed to be communicating. The doctor appreciated the alien's kind interest in her patient. Brenna wondered if there was more to it than that. A growing rapport existed between Morgan and the Vahnaj Ambassador. Other people had

179

noted the subtle changes in the relationship. Echoes of past remarks rattled in Brenna's thoughts. Quol-Bez's saying there were other means of opening doors—seeing and speaking and touching—than most *Homo sapiens* realized, means Morgan now might discover. Quol-Bez's steadfast loyalty to Morgan, and Morgan's family, ever since the accident. Speculations about Vahnaj extrasensory abilities. Morgan's sensory organs, except for his ears, were radically altered and limited now. That might indeed make a difference in communication. It *did*, with other humans. Had the injuries worked the opposite effect with Quol-Bez, making it *easier* for the Vahnaj and Morgan to understand each other?

"Check the oscillator," Morgan insisted.

"Okay. Sure."

"And then what?" Brenna frowned, trying to figure out what Morgan meant. "The franchise runs out in September," he said. "What are you going to do about it?"

"I . . . I hadn't thought that far ahead yet."

"You'd better. You've got to apply for renewal or lose the option at high ecliptic orbit," Morgan reminded her.

He wasn't the first to do so. Yuri had hinted around the subject. Tumaini and Hector and the junior pilots were bringing it up with embarrassing frequency, too. It wasn't their initiative. They were fellow pilots, but not co-owners. It was Brenna's responsibility, and they were very much aware she had made no moves to do anything about it. Without a franchise on a test area in space, Breakthrough Unlimited would be in even more serious trouble than it was now, its entire future program in doubt.

Question: *Was* Breakthrough Unlimited going to continue?

Morgan was looking at her, that hard, unnerving stare that prickled the hair on her nape. The eyes were the same color they had always been, not artificial-looking at all. But the expressiveness was gone. The ingenious microcomputers filling the sockets didn't know how to duplicate subconscious human byplays, that silent language that added so much. Warmth, humor, smothered rage—missing. Not a blank stare, quite. Brenna felt she was under two inquisitors' cameras.

"Are you going to Earth?" Morgan asked. "You could combine Uncle Todd's trip to the P.O.E. awards ceremony with the franchise grants meeting at Terran Worlds Council. Quol-Bez told me Councilman Ames is chairing the meeting this year. He's pro-FTL, and he's an old buddy of Uncle Todd's. He'd be favorable to renewing the franchise."

Brenna shrugged uneasily.

"I want you to answer something."

Without hesitation, Brenna said, "Of course."

Morgan's mouth pulled back in a tiny grimace that was supposed to be a smile. The effect was grotesque. Brenna forced herself to show no reaction. "Don't agree so fast. Your dad taught you to read the fine print, just as mine did."

"Okay. If I *can* answer, I will. How's that?"

"Much better. Straight: Am I still your partner?" Morgan asked softly.

For a second, Brenna was speechless. Then she blurted, "That's the stupidest damned dumb question I've ever heard!"

"Is it? Do I still have full voting rights?"

Brenna was hurt. "I won't even dignify that with a reply."

"I wasn't sure. I needed to know. I . . . I feel locked out. I want to be back on the line. I want to take part." His voice didn't register the poignancy in the words. His syntha skin couldn't paint his inner anguish. But Brenna touched the man behind the medical miracles, her heart twisting in a knot.

Some of the monitoring equipment was winking. Alarms. Elevated pulse rate. Stressed breathing. Brenna half expected Dr. Ives and her aides to burst in and pull the plug on the conversation.

Morgan wasn't ready for that and wouldn't accept it. His intense stare shifted toward the ubiquitous cameras and bio scanners. He spoke to the unseen doctor. "Helen, if you interrupt, I'll give you a fight. Turn off those spy eyes. I'm not a museum display! Brenna and I want privacy. We have business to discuss."

Dr. Ives's voice issued from the vid screen. "If the bio scans get worse, all bets are off."

"Bargain."

The cameras' *on* lights died. It was the first time since the accident that Brenna could recall this situation. She and Morgan, alone. No medics. No co-workers. No other members of the family or friends. No eavesdroppers anywhere. "What about it?" Morgan was making an effort to control his crippled body. Bio scans showed the graphs steadying out—not in the safe range, but better. A fine tracery of newly developed blue veins throbbed visibly within his syntha skin.

Brenna took a deep breath. "As far as I'm concerned, nothing's really changed."

He grimaced again. "It's changed. But if the partnership hasn't . . ."

"You can tap into all the corporation data any time . . ."

"I already have. That's how I know you haven't made an appointment at T.W.C.'s franchise meeting. Were you waiting on my vote before proceeding?" His question gave her an out, if she wanted it. An excuse for indecision.

"I . . . I've had my uncertain days," Brenna confessed. "After what happened . . ."

"It happened," Morgan said imperturbably, the stiff mannequin's face revealing nothing. "That's the past. Are you quitting? Do the others want to quit?"

"They're gung-ho." Brenna bit her lip, considering how to express her feelings. "I'm . . . I'm experiencing a bad case of guilt, I suppose."

"You weren't flying her. I was. She blew. We'll find out why. The decision to go with the test was mutual. There's no guilt," Morgan said, the cold voice chilling her.

No guilt? Rue dead. Tumaini invalided for no one was sure how long. And Morgan . . .

"Rue was my observer pilot," Morgan said. "Tumaini's already said he wants to go along on the next big ride. He's not scared. Let me have the guilt, if that's the problem, Brenna. I don't mind. I haven't got very much else to do with my time, in here . . ." There was the faintest intonation of irony in that. Maybe he *was* learning how to manipulate the vocal apparatus more skillfully!

Brenna weighed what he had said. "Okay. Partner, we have to make the big decision. You and me. Yuri doesn't have a vote. Neither does Tumaini or anyone else. They can volunteer, but we're running the show."

"I say go." Just like that. Morgan Saunder McKelvey had given as much to Breakthrough Unlimited as any human being could and still live. He knew the terrible risks.

182

And he still was willing to shoulder that responsibility and that guilt on future pilots' behalf.

Brenna was obligated to play devil's advocate. "Maybe we're wrong. Maybe graviton spin resonance drive isn't the answer."

"It is. And you know it. Nakamura's M-AM is fifty years away, if that. Tachyon and photon bypass are theories, cruddy ones. If we're going to reach the stars in our lifetimes, it's graviton drive."

". . . in our lifetimes . . ." How much of a lifetime could Morgan expect? There would be no berth for him aboard a Hiber-Space Corporation ship, no cubicle waiting on *New Earth Seeker II* or on the stasis ships that would follow the first colonizer out to Sol's near neighbors. Morgan wasn't an able-bodied specimen any more, nor a man capable of fathering children the "natural" way. Besides, he couldn't take a long space voyage of *any* sort. The potential speed of FTL was Morgan's only hope of ever seeing the stars and worlds beyond the Solar System in *his* lifetime. Was it selfish of him to vote for going ahead with Breakthrough Unlimited, under those circumstances? Or was it selfish of Brenna to doubt and consider the possibility of abandoning the only project that could give him those hopes?

"Maybe you have private reasons for wanting out?" Morgan said.

Another form of selfishness. Derek. Hiber-Ship Corporation. A guaranteed way out to the stars—for Brenna Foix Saunder. But not for Morgan.

A new life, with Derek, starting civilization all over again on a world no human had ever set foot on. Challenge! A name in the history tapes, right alongside her father's, and Mariette's, and her grandfather Ward's—and even alongside Jael's, another Saunder woman who had been willing to push aside those she loved for causes she loved even more.

Hiber-Ship. A safe trip, but a slow one. Seventy-five to a hundred years, estimated. The figures were a weight, crushing Brenna's mind. Calendar readouts spinning—ten years, twenty-five, forty—her parents would probably be dead by then. Morgan would certainly be long dead. Any children he had sired by sperm bank or cloning would be adults, never knowing "Cousin Brenna." Sixty, seventy-five—all her contemporaries who had stayed behind would be reaching the ends of their lives, unless medicine improved dramatically beyond its present miracles in geriatrics. Meanwhile, Brenna Saunder would sail on into the future, sleeping, unaware. The lure was there. And the horror. Those imaginary passing decades hit her like tangible blows.

No!

"We can do it," she said. Then, timidly, fearfully, "Can't we?"

Make me believe, Morgan. The way you used to, when we were kids and you spun those crazy yarns . . .

"We can. I can concentrate on test analyses and stress factors more clearly than I ever have, Brenna. It *can* be done. If we believe in it."

Morgan had believed. Look at him now.

Brenna clasped her fingers around his, through the plimaterial. He could sense some pressure, if not vivid tactile impressions. And he could see the symbolic handshake—in his eyes' vid picture built of geometric shapes.

"That makes it unanimous, partner," Morgan said. He didn't try to smile. There were no mirrors in his room, but he was aware of how his appearance affected others. "I can go anywhere with you, via ComLink. I can still be useful. Don't shut me out."

"I won't."

"But *you'll* have to go to Earth for the franchise meeting. Those old codgers on the Council don't trust vid images. They want to press the flesh."

"Okay. But some of them . . ." Brenna warned, remembering the last meeting.

"You can convince them," Morgan assured her, trying to boost her confidence. After a lengthy pause, he added wistfully, "I wish I could go with you. PR's always been my job."

I wish it still was, Morgan. Oh, God, how I wish it was. And I wish there was some way I could help you.

Morgan's eyes lowered, focusing on their still-clasped —or almost—hands. "I can't feel your fingers, Brenna. Even if the wall wasn't here, I couldn't. When the medics lead me around for my exercises, I can't feel the texture of their sterile suits when they brush against my bare skin. I can't tell if the floor's hot or cold under the soles of my feet. Can't feel this hospital robe. Or the bed. Crazy, isn't it? I can measure distances down to the millimeter; little numbers print up, inside my eyes, just like I was reading a computer screen. But I can't make real *contact* with anything."

"Morgan . . ." Brenna stopped, unable to think of anything to say.

"Never mind," he said suddenly, using one of her pet phrases. "Excuse the self-pity."

"You're entitled to a few indulgences, as long as you don't overdo it."

He flexed his free hand, examining it as if he had never seen it before. He had dropped into one of those increasingly frequent phases where he seemed unaware of anyone else. Morgan had momentarily forgotten, apparently, the closeness of their hands, or that Brenna was talking to him. He turned the too-pale, too-scrawny, pitiful copy of Morgan McKelvey's hand, gazing in disapproval. "I'm so weak. So damned weak. I've got to . . . got to take more rehab exercises, if they'll let me. Get . . . get back in shape."

Not possible. He knew it, intellectually. Yet . . .

"Do that," she encouraged him. What else could she do? "But you mind Helen. Mental energy's cheap. You said you'd concentrate on that and solve those stats for us. Brains. Let me supply the legwork and brawn for the time being . . ."

"Hasn't it always been that way?" Morgan couldn't wink. The syntha skin wouldn't stretch and retract that well. But some of his former humor was there, under the artificialities.

"Listen, you're the lucky one. *I'm* the partner who has to go to Earth and jabber at all those stuffy old T.W.C. members. *And* show up at Aunt 'Rissa's obligatory after-the-P.O.E.-awards soiree. Just picture me putting up with her yappy dogs and trying not to knock out Stuart's teeth and cause a scandal."

The corners of his mouth quirked. A grin, or what passed for it. "I will. Have fun."

Brenna hammed a ferocious scowl, glad of the chance to play the goat and amuse him. He had so damned little to be amused about!

"Show them how it's done, Brenna. These new dogs know a lot of old tricks."

185

"Right!"

A hand touched her arm, making her jump. Brenna glanced around and saw Dr. Ives. "Sorry to startle you. Your time's up, Morgan. You're pushing it. Your pulse is elevated."

"It's a good elevation," he retorted, his mouth curving a bit more. That was an effort, but he obviously thought it was worth it. Morgan reluctantly withdrew his hand from the pli-material. The limb fell back limply onto the chairbed. The wheeled robot was scuttling around, assisting the waldos as they pulled the covers up over the support frame again, taking care of Morgan as they would a helpless infant. Morgan accepted the machines' ministrations without protest. "That's all right. The business conference is over. We got a lot settled, didn't we, Brenna?" She nodded vigorously, so that he would be able to pick up the movement easily with his prosthetic eyes. "You'll remember?"

"Everything," Brenna assured him.

As she turned to go, he called, "Keep in touch!"

She paused at the monitoring station, watching Morgan on the screens. The vid and audio circuits were working once more. The chair-bed had carried Morgan back to the center of the room. Lights dimmed. Helen was telling him to get some rest or she would use medication to get his pulse rate down where it belonged. Doctors and servo mechanisms were running his life—business as usual.

"He was really animated today," the medic on duty exulted. "Your visit did him a lot of good, Miss Saunder. He's a little excited, but nothing to worry about. The important thing is, he came out of his shell."

Brenna muttered something that might be taken for agreement. The medic had understated the case. Two months and more of "museum display" existence. No privacy. Physical problems compounded beyond what any human should bear. No power to do much of anything for himself. Total dependency plus severe sensory deprivation. Little wonder he had suddenly broken out of the shell! He must have been storing up this confrontation in his mind for weeks: *Am I still your partner?* Brenna reproached herself. She should have started the dialogue. But Morgan had been so damned uncommunicative. Until today.

186

Well, he had done it. The vote was taken. They were committed, for whatever that might lead to.

She strode down the corridor to the main part of Morgan's estate, crossing the great room. Morgan used to spend a lot of his at-home time in this area, enjoying the view. The room was still clean. Bar and refreshment alcove fully stocked. Furniture neatly placed. Drapes pulled to reveal the magnificent vista of the Martian rift valley. As if any moment the owner of the mansion would walk in, a beautiful woman on his arm, laughing guests in his wake, ready for a party.

Life had changed, for Morgan, and for Brenna. She had never been besieged by so many "what-ifs" and nervous-making questions. Had Morgan tricked her? There was nothing wrong with his brain cells. Those worked fine. Better than before, he insisted, without former distractions. No, he hadn't manipulated her. She had made her choice freely. Breakthrough Unlimited would go ahead. Build another ship. Train another crew. Locate the flaw and correct it—they hoped and prayed.

One more gamble, and the stakes were incredibly high —win *or* lose.

CHAPTER ELEVEN

✸✸✸✸✸✸✸✸

Action and Reaction

THERE was a spring in her step when Brenna left Morgan's estate. She mounted the connecting bridge leading to her father's residence, bypassing her own private mansion. Some guests at Saunder Estates refused to use the outer bridges. They would take the underground tunnels or the roundabout tramway which offered no view of Valles Marineris. Brenna had to admit it might be a trifle daunting for some people to peer down through the transparent floor of the bridge and realize it was a three-kilometer drop to the bottom of the gorge. It didn't bother her, however.

The shared properties of Saunder Estates: Mars had been

designed to fit into the natural terrain. Mansions and bridges complemented rather than clashed with the surrounding jumble of native rock and red dust. Lichen patches crawled along the cliffs outside the Estates' life-support domes, evidence of Terraform Division's success in nurturing flora in Mars' skimpy atmosphere. Most of the mansions' structures were underground, for energy efficiency, but here and there windows peeped out of cliff walls or afforded a view. Streams issued from deep-drill wells, spilling over the boulders, forming pools that sparkled in the morning sunlight. Some quasi-nations, with the Saunders' resources, would have built slide ramps, not walkways, to connect the three separate estates. That had always struck the Mars-based Saunders as ostentatious and silly. If Morgan had been able to leave his hyperbaric room, their opinion might have changed, and they surely would have motorized the bridges for his convenience. Since he couldn't, the bridges remained as they were, attractive ways to sightsee while getting from one side of the property to the other.

SE Security patrolled the outer grounds, driving rock-rovers, bumping over the unspoiled land. Down on the main parking lot, Brenna noted some visitors' mass driver cars amid the off-duty Security rock-rovers. Diplomatic markings on the strangers' vehicles. Terran Worlds Council. Escort for Quol-Bez, who would be taking Brenna's father to his personal launch site for their trip to Earth, probably leaving shortly after lunch.

Brenna stepped off the bridge at the garden gate and wandered through the greenhouse. The SE security guards posted there touched their caps politely. Brenna read their name badges and wished them a good day. The gardener interrupted supervising his weeder robots to say hello as she strolled along the path. Mechanical pruners and waterers continued their work without pause. Brenna wound her way through a miniature forest of deciduous trees and conifers, transplants from Earth. Outside the dome, only lichen and a few hardy molds grew in the harsh Martian climate, even this close to the equator. Inside, the climate resembled a cool spring in Beijing or New Chicago of the United Ghetto States back on the home world. If you had a life-support bubble and a good water-retrieval system, solar energy, and plenty of money, you could bring Earth to Mars, as the Saunders' designers had done here. Brenna had long thought that even her space-travel-hating aunt Carissa would feel comfortable in this garden. But they could never convince her to make the trip, not even for kinship's sake. Carissa Duryea Saunder wasn't alone in that bias. A lot of powerful leaders on Earth had never taken a space voyage. Political analysts insisted that was why Protectors of Earth was losing its power to the space-roving Terran Worlds Council, which represented *all* the human habitations in the Solar System, not merely Earth.

Another SE security guard was posted at the main door. The woman acted as if she were personally holding open the door for Brenna, when in fact servos had identified Todd Saunder's daughter and cleared her for entry when Brenna was still ten meters from the door. The portal sighed open at exactly the right time to let the least amount of controlled-humidity garden air into the living quarters.

Brenna checked the terminal in the foyer. "Where's my father?"

"In the solarium, Miss Saunder."

Each residence on the Estates was tailored to the occupant's taste. Brenna's ran to free-form art and holo-mode scenes of spaceflight and lots of cubbyholes and functional furnishings. Morgan's house—the part of it he couldn't use now—was strongly oriented toward sensual effects, with plush couches and thick carpets and erotic art. Todd Saunder's preferences were walls full of holo-modes—scenes of Earth and Mars—and chairs backdropped by illusions of watery horizons and open skies. Brenna walked through rooms where the ceilings glowed with Earthly fair-weather clouds and light blue heavens rich in oxygen. In one room, the holo-modes spun out their projections against Mars' real scenery, the Valles Marineris, showing fluffy cumulus hanging over the dark canyon rim. Someday, if humans kept working on Mars' climate, that might not be just a pretty fake. There were, of course, vid and audio devices in every corner and niche. ComLink, everywhere. This *was*, after all, the home base of the illustrious president of that corporation. Mars and Earth, tied together through technology generated from Ward Saunder's patents and his children's and grandchildren's industry.

189

The Saunders, one of Earth's—and Mars'—most powerful dynasties.

Brenna walked up the long ramp leading to the solarium. Below the balcony she saw a group of Saunder Enterprises guards and a few diplomatic staffers and some Terran Worlds Council Space Fleet troopers, standing around and snacking on food supplied by the auto dispensers. A caste system prevailed. A few guards and troopers chatted with the diplomats, but for the most part the private police and Space Fleet personnel segregated themselves. Brenna had noticed the same patterns on Goddard Colony and even at Kirkwood Gap Asteroid Station. For all the contrasts in gravity, living conditions, and space-oriented philosophies, humans seemed to carry their social habits with them, surprisingly often.

The solarium's triple temp-control locks dilated in smooth sequence as Brenna went through the well-lit passage. Each compartment was warmer and stickier than the one lower down. When she finally reached the solarium, she had adjusted to the change fairly well. The garden surrounding this estate was Earth-temperate zone. The solarium was Earth-tropic zone. There were exotic plants, pet birds, and insects to pollinate the flora. Brenna had sometimes complained about that last. In her opinion, it was carrying slice-of-Earth realism too far, especially the stinging bugs. Todd gave her a tall story about ecosystems and enjoyed lolling about on his miniature tropical beach. He and Dian spent as much time here as they could, when they were on Mars. Ambassador Quol-Bez seemed to like the solarium, too. Once, when humans had asked, he had said his home world was a warm one, and the solarium's life-support balance was very close to what he had been used to. In his embassy in Pavonis City he had had a similar one built. Terran Worlds Council had copied the design from Todd Saunder's estate, as the ultimate in flattery of his taste.

Todd's chef and her helper were setting up a brunch. There weren't a lot of servants on Mars, not even at Saunder Estates. Colony worlds generally attracted a different economic level—tech and mech and computer experts and com specialists. But there were a few, and working for a Saunder paid well. Todd Saunder employed an excellent kitchen staff, though he had to put up with his

190

wife's and daughter's teasing as a result. He wasn't a gourmet, they claimed, he just liked to eat.

Brenna's father and Ambassador Quol-Bez were watching Chef Reva set out the table while Derek and Chin Jui-Sao stayed out of the way. When Derek saw Brenna he broke off his conversation with the Chinese woman as courteously as he could and hurried across the domed room, cornering Brenna in a thicket of bamboo. They took advantage of the moment of concealment. Then Brenna chuckled, wriggled out of his smothering embrace. Derek peered up at the lush foliage. "What a romantic setting! I love this place!"

"You and Dad. I think it smells like a jungle. Just like Aunt 'Rissa's Saunderhome, Earthside." Brenna tugged at the lapels of Derek's captain's uniform, pulled his head down for another kiss.

"Please!" he protested unconvincingly. "What will the others say?"

"I doubt if they'll be shocked. If they are, I'll tell them I have to grab you while you're available, which isn't often, these days. But you're right. We shouldn't be rude." She linked her arm through his and started toward the little pool in the center of the solarium. It was difficult walking side by side, because the path was so overhung with immense leaves and vines.

Derek grew somber. "How's Morgan? He seemed awfully locked up when I stopped in earlier."

"He's much better now." Brenna smiled with satisfaction.

"Is he? That's great!" Derek appeared surprised but gratified. He studied Brenna's Cheshire-cat expression. "What's going on? Are you up to something?"

They were too close to the others now for private conversations. Brenna chose not to explain. She nodded hello to Sao and Quol-Bez and added her compliments to her father's regarding the luncheon. "Reva's outdone herself. Send-off party, huh?"

Quol-Bez was holding a bowl of minced fruit and an imported seafood delicacy. "It is most gracious, and tasteful." He glanced at Sao. " 'Send-off'?"

"A friendly, festive occasion preceding a journey by one of the attendees," Sao translated.

"Splendid. A new phrase!" The Vahnaj Ambassador balanced his carved wooden bowl on the tips of his skinny fingers, turning the container around slowly and admiring the decorations. Behind his gray head, bright flowers and palm fronds formed a curtain, contrasting with his dark clothes. He looked like a character from a vid documentary —the visiting alien anthropologist exclaiming over the craftsmanship of the natives.

Brenna moved along the table, filling her own bowl. "I hear they're going to give you another honorary degree at the upcoming Protectors of Earth ceremony, Dad," she teased. "How many will that make? Five? Six?"

Todd Saunder was eyeing a sugary confection. "As a matter of fact, it makes eight. Your mother takes fiendish delight in keeping track of the stupid things." He suddenly yielded to temptation and scooped the forbidden food onto his dish.

"I'll tell Dian," Brenna threatened.

"Impertinent brat. You do and I'll cut off your allowance."

Quol-Bez was puzzled by the amusement that caused. Chin Jui-Sao defined the archaic term "allowance" for him, after which his rattling laughter joined the rest.

"You do not wish to receive these honorary certificates of knowledge, sir?" Sao asked.

"If they meant something, I would be very pleased, my dear. But they're devices, shams. It's not *me* they're honoring. It's my father's gadgets, the inventions that make the modern world possible. The famous institutions handing out those diplomas are a lot more interested in an endowment from Saunder Enterprises than in acknowledging me as a mental wizard, truth be told."

"Dad's just cynical. Maybe that's because he never studied at a so-called institution of higher learning himself. Neither did I."

"That doesn't count, kitten," Todd said. "You space kids had a totally different upbringing, fully computerized, highly stimulated. There's no comparison with formal education the way it used to be. Of course, being at peace makes an incalculable difference. It's impossible to convey to the younger generations what society was like then." Brenna and Derek and Sao were smiling tolerantly. "Don't laugh," Todd said with mild annoyance. "You may find there are things you can learn from us old fogies and from history. Why does each generation think it's making

192

life's discoveries for the first time, ever, in human existence?" It was Quol-Bez's turn to look tolerant, sharing Todd's point of view. The elder Saunder shrugged. "As for education in general, though, I suppose the mass of humanity nearly always has been condemned to illiteracy, or its near-equivalent, unfortunately. You kids don't realize how elitist and well trained the colonial populations are . . ."

" 'Skimming off the brightest and best that Earth has to give,' " Derek quoted. The grand old man of Earth's Progressive Expansionist Coalition had turned that slogan into a popular lament. Derek recited it as a boast, as most "space kids" did. He took it as a compliment, not feeling guilty at all.

"Indeed! The colonies *have* done that." Todd Saunder shook his head. "It took a supreme effort to get a good education during the Death Years and the Chaos. Oh, you *could*, if you were lucky and had the intelligence and the desire. Dian's emphatic about that. She says kids taught themselves to read even in the United Ghetto States, when it seemed like the whole world was coming apart around them during the missile attacks. You can't keep people with *that* kind of courage and drive illiterate!"

"This is true," Chin Jui-Sao admitted. "Perhaps conditions are healthier now that the universities of Earth appreciate how easily their status may be lost by political upheaval." Quol-Bez nibbled his fish and fruit, listening politely. No doubt he had studied human history thoroughly. But he didn't seem bored. "So many institutions of learning ceased to exist in the Death Years and the Chaos and the years immediately after," Sao said. "As I recall, there were almost no major universities open in the North American Union when you were a young man, Todd Saunder."

"No, and it was the *Central* North American Union then, of course. It wasn't until Fairchild's Peace that the west coast of the continent rejoined the old sections of the Twentieth-Century nation. So many things have changed . . ." He was looking into the distance, seeing things that weren't there. "We Saunders got off very lucky, even before my father's patents started paying off for us. We had books —it's such a pity most of those are gone. And we had vid tapes. And the best all-around instructors in the world in science and politics and economics and literature. They didn't teach history. They made it."

Brenna's grandparents. Legends. Ghosts. There were times—this was one of them—when Brenna had to grit her teeth to keep from yelling that she was sick of hearing about her famous grandparents. Previous generations haunted their descendants. She and her father and Morgan lived in the shadow of those legends and had to fight to be accepted as individuals.

"Well, that was a long time ago," Todd said with embarrassment. Brenna was relieved. She had expected a "when I was a boy" reminiscence. "We adapt, if we can. That's what intelligence is—adaptation. Times change. We have to try to change with them, if we can. But some things . . ." He grew morose and set aside his unfinished food. "All our intelligence and technology and Saunder wealth—what's it doing for Morgan? He's just sinking into apathy, and we can't help him."

"That's not permanent, sir," Derek said hastily. "Why, Brenna said he was much better when she saw him."

All of them stared at her. Only Quol-Bez did not seem surprised. "Oh?" said her father. "Really? That's wonderful! I can't get anything out of him but monosyllables."

"Neither can I," Derek said. "At least he's talking to someone. That's important. Dr. Ives insisted we maintain contact with him."

"What did he talk about?" Todd wanted to know. "He's . . . he's not becoming suicidal or anything like that, is he?"

Brenna choked on a shocked laugh. "Morgan? Hardly. No, Dad, we talked about business."

Quol-Bez brightened, two pointy fang tips showing at the edges of his lower lip. Todd and Derek were bewildered.

"Business?" Derek repeated. "Surely you didn't trouble him about payrolls and stuff like that?"

"Not at all. I didn't 'trouble' him. He brought Breakthrough Unlimited up. *He* wanted to talk about it."

Sunlight, concentrated by the solarium's dome, shone through the tropical leaves and warmed faces and bodies. Overhead, birds evolved half an astronomical unit away flew from branch to branch and twittered. Yet Brenna was cold. The sensation emanated from Derek. Icy ripples added to it, sent out by her father's emotional state.

"I thought you were just marking time," Todd said, looking ill at ease.

"I was. Until Morgan was strong enough to express his viewpoint again. He did."

"And?" Derek demanded.

"And what?" Brenna retorted defiantly. "We're going ahead. I'm scheduling a trip Earthside to renew our franchise. We'll need space to conduct tests on the hull material and oscillator . . ."

"Dammit, Bren! Excuse me, Mr. Ambassador, sir . . . but what the hell's going on?" Derek cried. "In the Spirit of Humanity, you can't be serious! How the hell can you do this to Morgan?"

"Easy, son," Todd said soothingly. "I'm sure we can settle this."

"Can we?" Those turquoise-blue eyes pierced Brenna.

"It was Morgan's choice." She amazed herself, maintaining a calm exterior while her gut was churning acid. "I didn't bully him, if that's what you're implying. He's been nursing this for weeks. He's bored and frustrated and feeling cut off. He wants to get back to work. Unanimous decision by the voting members of the governing board—all two of us."

"For the——" Derek flung up his arms in exasperation, pacing around the side of the pool. "Get back to work? My God! You're insane. You're responsible for him, Brenna. Have pity! The poor guy's blind."

"He is *not* blind!" Brenna roared. Derek froze in midstride and gawked as Brenna went on. "He's not a witless infant, either—though too many people are treating him like one, just because he's been hurt. He's responsible for his own choices, and he's making them. Maybe *that's* why he won't communicate with you or Dad. He says he can talk to Quol-Bez. And he talks to *me*. So tell me what the special difference is. It just might be that he knows we'll *listen* to him, believe in him. We don't patronize him. Hell, he hates that! You ought to realize that, Derek, better than anyone."

Her father's arm went around her shoulders. Brenna was trembling. She was as taut as a guy wire, ready to strike out at an attacker. There was no one within easy reach but her father, though. And no one she really wanted to hit. It was the light-speed barrier and prejudices

195

she wanted to chop down. Abstracts. They made lousy opponents.

"Easy, kitten. Please. It's okay . . ."

Brenna almost flung the platitudes back in his concerned face. She closed her eyes, swallowing the bitter taste filling her mouth. "Sorry," she murmured. With nowhere for the rage to go, it turned back on her, sapping her. "I didn't mean to create a big scene. It's just . . . Morgan got through to me today, and I had a tiny glimpse of what he's been suffering."

Her father patted her shoulder. "Sure. We understand. I feel the same way. So does Derek."

Brenna dug her nails into her palms, then forced herself to unclench her fists. Futile. She had to stop this. She was volatile fuel, eager for a spark. So was Derek. He was wearing that handsome, graven-in-stone, stubborn mask of his. "My fault, sir. I lost my temper first. I apologize." Ever the gracious gentleman, the future colonial leader, the intrepid stasis-ship captain. Brenna wished he would drop it and slug it out with her, just once.

Quol-Bez and Sao had remained on the sidelines, very discreet. They wouldn't carry any of this tale—much to the newshunters' disgust. A family quarrel. Derek was part of the Saunder circle. They had known him as long as they had Brenna. Sao seemed terribly sad. Quol-Bez's broad face was pale in sympathy for his friend Todd Saunder and Todd's daughter and Derek.

"Let's just cool off," Todd suggested. "We need some clarification here. *I* need some. Brenna, you're serious? You really mean to continue with Breakthrough Unlimited?" Brenna didn't trust herself to answer, afraid she would trigger another explosion. She nodded, daring anyone to sound off. "But is it . . . is it possible for Morgan?" her father asked.

"I'm sure it is. And that's what Morgan wants. What *I* want. He'll handle the data breakdowns and I'll do the planet hopping and test piloting."

Derek was shaking his head, refusing to accept.

"Well," Todd Saunder said inanely. He seemed stunned.

"Dr. Ives is a very com-pe-tent phy-si-cian," Quol-Bez said suddenly.

His human friend seized on the logic. "Yes! Of course! Helen wouldn't let him attempt anything he wasn't ready

196

for, would she? He really did say he wanted to go on with
. . . with the FTL project, kitten? Well," Todd said again,
searching for words. "I guess . . . I guess if Morgan wants
it . . ."

"He does, Dad. So do I." Brenna's gaze was drawn to
Quol-Bez. She wanted to probe that alien mind and find
out what he was thinking. Did Morgan's accident duplicate similar tragedies in Vahnaj history? Had a Vahnaj
counterpart of Morgan Saunder McKelvey been horribly
crippled in a failed attempt to break the light-speed barrier? What had happened next? Had he or she survived
and courageously continued the quest? And won? Somebody in the Vahnaj star empire *had* won, eventually. Vahnaj had FTL. They had the stars.

"That's that, then," Derek said, letting out the breath
he had been holding. It wasn't a surrender. Brenna recognized the tone. He was refusing to argue any more. Waste
of energy. "All we can do is wish you both good luck."

"Rely on it! Good luck, kitten, to you and Morgan."
Brenna's father kissed her forehead. She could sense his
terror, though. This wasn't a wish for success—it was a
whispered prayer for her survival, thinly disguised.

"Wan shi ru yi," Sao chimed in, wishing good fortune.

"May the best team win," Quol-Bez said, repeating the
human phrase he had quoted at the Colony Days gala.

The forms, the semi-congratulations, hoping for a smooth
future, went on for a minute or so. Then Derek made a
show of checking his wrist mini-terminal. "I'm afraid I
have to run, sir. I'm due at Syrtis launch point at 2100."

"Must you leave?" Todd protested, quite sincerely.

"Afraid so. You'll have to be heading out for your ship,
too, in an hour or so." The Vahnaj Ambassador was giving
his human friend Todd a "lift" to Earth in his diplomatic
vehicle—a nice gesture, and a logical one, since their reasons for going to Earth were identical: to appear at the
P.O.E. awards ceremony. "Have a safe trip. I know the
speeches will be great." Derek shook hands and praised
the food and the company, then headed for the door.

Brenna excused herself and followed him through the
climate-control locks. The ramp beyond was shadowy and
cool, a bit of a shock after the solarium's tropical atmosphere. She ran to get ahead of Derek, blocking his
path. "It was *his* idea!" she repeated.

For a heartbeat, she thought he was going to push her out of the way. But he didn't. Muted lighting formed a nimbus around his pale hair, transforming him. He didn't look like a man but a wrathful demigod, judging her and finding her wanting. "Have a good trip to the franchise-renewal meeting, Earthside. While your dedicated partner . . ."

"Derek! Stop it! I didn't lie. Morgan proposed it, not me!"

"No, I don't think you *are* lying. That's worse. It'd be easier to take if I believed you were deluding yourself," Derek said. The anger was still there. There was also a hint of contempt. With great difficulty, Brenna kept herself from hitting him. "Morgan's got computers for eyes, talks in a mechanical voice, and wheels around in a chair full of stera-gel. My best friend, reduced to . . ." Derek shuddered violently. "And you're going right ahead with this insane project as if nothing happened."

"We know what happened. How could Morgan *not* know? What's he supposed to do?" Brenna's eyes stung with pent-up tears. "Turn into a vegetable? Let people pretend he never existed? If you're his friend, is that what you want for him?"

"It's because I *am* his friend that I can't take this. Dammit, why does it have to be *manned* FTL ships? Go ahead with your experiment—but for the Spirit of Humanity, why not use robots?"

"You could colonize Kruger 60's terrene planets with robots, too," Brenna said, lashing back, knowing how to hurt him.

Derek stiffened. "The Kruger 60 worlds aren't going to be colonized by machines, but by human beings . . ."

"And *we're* going to go to the stars via faster-than-light ships, not send robots to do the job for us." Brenna stood with arms akimbo, glaring at him. The same old arguments! How could she get through to that closed mind of his? "You say we're crazy-dedicated? That sounds strange, coming from a proponent of cryo stasis."

"It's a proven technique . . ."

"A journey that far out isn't. It's a gamble, just as Breakthrough Unlimited is."

Derek fought back. "Let's compare scores. FTL experiments have killed four people in your group. Twelve on

198

the military project. And Nakamura's first matter-anti-matter test took out a whole space station—what was it, twenty-five personnel? The tachyon 'ship' came to pieces in the lab. That was a first; it killed the metallurgists, but no pilots. Count a plus for Exo-Trans—*if* they don't insist on trying again. LeFevre's photon bypass is still in diagrams; if they've got any brains, it'll stay there. And what about *you*? Morgan's got a valid excuse, poor guy! But *you!* Brenna, what will it take to make you see what's going to happen?"

No more contempt. Horror and fear, her father's fear, seeing her destroyed in a fiery explosion. Derek drew her into his arms and kissed her, as if he could drive away the fear with love. The hope was a snare for Brenna, too, and she didn't want to escape it, she realized with her own form of fear—fear that she was losing her courage. "You . . . you've got some time. You could catch the next Hiber-Ship ferry," Brenna whispered. "If we could just . . ."

"Talk to Morgan. Stop this idiocy *now*," Derek begged.

The moment of intimacy shattered. Brenna pulled away. "God damn you! I will not be manipulated like that!"

He was stricken, denying it. "It wasn't . . . that wasn't what I was doing, I swear. Brenna, you can't. If we mean anything at all to each other . . . think what it will mean to Morgan when . . ."

He didn't finish. It wasn't necessary. *When someone else dies. You.*

"I know you. If you go on with this FTL project, the next time around it'll be *you* who climbs into that cockpit. Oh, God, I don't want to lose you!" Derek reached for her again, but Brenna eluded his grasp. Conscious of it or not, he *had* been manipulating her emotions!

"If you don't want to lose me, drop out of Hiber-Ship Corporation," she said bitterly.

Derek's hands fell to his sides. "I can't do that. You know I can't do that."

"Then maybe we don't mean as much to each other as we claim we do."

A second's silence lasted an eternity. Then, very softly, Derek spoke. "Maybe the problem is that we mean too damned *much* to each other."

They were being cut to pieces. This was why they had agreed to the truce. This was what happened when they broke it. No visible wounds, but they were cruelly hurting each other just the same. Derek made matters worse; he leaned forward and kissed her gently. Then he hurried away, practically running down the hall toward the sub-surface transport system. As he crossed the balcony, some of the Space Fleet troopers and SE guards stared up at him curiously. They recognized him, and one or two raised a hand and called a greeting. Derek didn't reply. He rushed on, disappearing beyond the exit doors, on his way to Syrtis Spaceport.

Brenna stood very still, quaking inwardly, fighting a pent-up flood of tears. Had she made a mistake? And if so, what *was* the mistake? Not following Derek? Not agreeing to give up everything she believed in? Or would the mistake be to tell Morgan it was no go and shut down operations on Breakthrough Unlimited?

If she yielded, she could go to the stars—with Derek.

But Morgan never would. The only way he would reach them was through the quantum jump past the light-speed barrier. That was Morgan's ticket—the only one he would ever be able to cash, *if* his ravaged body could survive until Breakthrough Unlimited achieved faster-than-light space-flight.

Brenna felt a slight shift of air pressure. Tropical scents tickled her nose. She looked toward the solarium, seeing the outer climate-control lock closing. Chin Jui-Sao had just left the room. The Chinese woman hesitated, then walked toward Brenna. "Captain Whitcomb has departed?"

"Yes." There didn't seem to be anything else to say. Brenna suspected the full story was written on her face, anyway.

To her surprise, Sao touched her hand. The contact was brief, but very sympathetic. "Forgive me if I intrude. I comprehend your dilemma. It is not always possible to communicate one's feelings. And emotion thwarts our best efforts at times." Brenna wondered if Sao had a lover. Had she faced this same "dilemma," agonizing over which choices to make?

"Derek and I have quarreled before, over the same thing, in fact."

"Morgan McKelvey is an isolated man," Chin Jui-Sao said suddenly. That made Brenna stare into those black eyes. "The Ambassador, too, is isolated," Sao added. "There

200

has been an empathy, a new understanding, between them. I am glad Morgan chose to communicate with you as well. But I do not wish him to stop communicating with the Ambassador. The situation is of help to the Ambassador as well as to Morgan McKelvey. You see, Ambassador Quol-Bez is sometimes . . . lonely." The moment she had let that word out, Sao's mouth snapped shut. She nodded politely and left the hall before Brenna could ask her any questions.

Did the comments really need further elaboration? Brenna mulled over Sao's words. It was obvious Sao felt she had broken a rule by revealing something of the Ambassador's personal motivations. But Brenna had sensed the deep compassion behind that moment of truth, for which she was grateful. Whether or not things were exactly as Sao pictured them, she had spoken about them in an effort to reassure Brenna. Until recently, Chin Jui-Sao had seemed like Quol-Bez's hanger-on, just another translator like all the rest Terran Worlds Council had assigned to assist the Vahnaj Ambassador during these past years. Faceless experts, there to help with the Vahnaj's language problems. Interchangeable people. Brenna had assumed Sao would be a transient, someone to treat with courtesy, but hardly a friend. Now there seemed more to it. This liaison expert was special, as was the being she served.

Brenna noticed a few high-ranking diplomatic aides walking along the opposite balcony, heading for the northern door to the solarium. Going to notify Quol-Bez that time was approaching for the planned departure. The Ambassador and Todd Saunder would be leaving this afternoon, from the nearby V.I.P. space strip. At least by riding in the superswift Space Fleet diplomatic ship, Brenna's father wouldn't be worn out by the journey when he reached Earth. It could make the trip in less than a week, as opposed to a week and a half for most civilian ships.

Dian would meet them at the V.I.P. strip, taking time out of her own hectic schedule. Right now the Mars branch of Wyoma Lee Foix Foundation was holding its annual convention at Chryse City. Dian wouldn't be taking the trip to Earth with her husband, though she usually accompanied him to these awards affairs. Everyone had agreed that Morgan's needs took precedence. Dian would keep tabs on her nephew while Todd was bowing and scraping and saying thank you on Earth. Brenna knew her mother would relish one bonus in staying home—she wouldn't have to attend the obligatory after-the-awards-ceremony festival at Saunderhome and put up with Carissa. The sisters-in-law weren't exactly on the best of terms.

Originally, Brenna had expected to trade off time spent with Morgan with her mother. But if she was to make the T.W.C. franchise-grant session on Earth next month, she would have to leave as soon as possible. A regular Saunder Enterprise shuttle would depart the day after tomorrow. She had a great deal to do before then, but there would always be space aboard one of those craft for a Saunder and her team members. Brenna made hasty plans. She'd return to the solarium and be sociable, joining the escort that would drive her father and the Ambassador to the V.I.P. strip. That would give her a chance to discuss schedules with Dian. Later, after Morgan had rested, she'd drop in on him again and talk to him some more. They had a lot of things to set up before Brenna headed Sunward . . .

And if she kept busy enough, she wouldn't have time to let her emotions rattle her. Discipline. That was the trick. If Morgan could teach himself to talk and see all over again, she could wait out Derek's mood without coming apart at the seams.

The hours clicked by, and it was tomorrow, and Brenna was checking in at Breakthrough Unlimited's hangar at Amazonis Spaceport. The key support-crew personnel were hard at work on the probable-cause reassembly, and all the pilots were there. When she made her announcement about going to Earth to renew the franchise, pandemonium broke out.

Yuri picked Brenna up in his arms, dancing around, his square face glowing with delight. "*Khoroshó!* Ah! *Spassíbo*, Brenna!" and in a spontaneous display he kissed her. Tumaini and Hector were laughing, the junior pilots clenching their fists, thumbs up, grinning from ear to ear. Yuri finally lowered Brenna to her feet, mumbling a lame apology for getting so carried away. He was blushing. "I am . . . it is just that . . . we were not sure you were going to . . . to go ahead."

"Neither was I," Brenna confessed. The cheers running through the cavernous hangar warmed her, and shamed her. She'd kept them all dangling in suspense. Until right now, they hadn't known if they had a future or were just marking time until she would tell them Breakthrough Unlimited was finished and they'd all have to find other jobs. Now the enthusiasm rose in a tidal wave, work on the wrecked Prototype II temporarily forgotten. There *was* a future! Three cheers for Brenna Foix Saunder! "Morgan cast the deciding vote," Brenna said. "He's the one who got me off my ass and back in gear. My partner says we go. So we go!"

Techs poured cups of stimu-caf and toasted Morgan. Some of the pilots wanted to call him right then and convey their feelings personally. Brenna assured them Morgan was aware of their loyalty. Besides, he couldn't handle too much vid correspondence—not when he was preoccupied with pinpointing the flaws they would need to correct before they built Prototype III!

Camaraderie buoyed them. Doubted dreams were solid once more. That pile of junk filling half the hangar was evidence of a fatal mistake—a ship designed to tear through the fabric of space. But it hadn't. Inexplicably, it had collapsed, failed. But now the pieces were coming together, painstakingly reconstructed and examined. They'd find the problems and solve them. Together.

"Yuri, I'll need you along on the Earth trip. Somebody's got to play PR games and tap into those back-home metallurgy experts while I do the drill with Terran Worlds Council."

Tumaini Beno spoke up. "How about taking the kids with you, Brenna? They could use the exposure. Grin for the public on Earth. Let them see 'em up close. Interviewers crawling all over them." Joe Habich, Adele, and Shoje made faces, pretending dismay. But Brenna could see the prospect pleased them. Hector Obregón and Yuri weren't quite so enchanted with the proposal, though. Brenna assumed Hector's nose was out of joint because Yuri would get the PR exposure on Earth—where there were bigger crowds and more people awed by the "glamour" of space piloting. Obregón would be stuck here on Mars while his friendly rival among the pilots was gallivanting with Earth's high society! Brenna couldn't imagine what Yuri's objections might be. Of all the FTL pilots, he was the least limelight-addicted. She was sure it wasn't jealousy of the "kids" or fear they would steal his show.

"Okay," Brenna said. "Let's get to it!"

The schedule was a whirlwind. A lot of packing. A lot of calling to arrange things on Earth in preparation. Setting up trip space on the SE shuttle. But time elapsed, and finally they were aboard—Brenna, Yuri Nicholaiev, and the three eager junior pilots. Liftoff, arcing up from Amazonis Planitia.

The Saunder Enterprises shuttle was a good workhorse. She couldn't catch up with Ambassador Quol-Bez's ship, of course, but she could match any other civilian ship in space. Best of all, the tickets were free! SE Trans Co, both planetary systems and interplanetary shuttles, was jointly owned by Brenna, her father, and Morgan. Might as well make use of the ships!

An incident at the departure lounge, an hour before, lingered in Brenna's thoughts. Tumaini Beno flaring at some innocent remark of Hector's. He'd been astonishingly edgy, ready to slug the other man. Hector had kept his temper in check, not wanting to be accused of fighting with an invalid—but smart enough not to call Tumaini that. Eventually, the group had cooled Tumaini down, and he had shaken hands and seemed chagrined at his behavior. At the time, Brenna had pegged the unusual event to Tumaini's rehab therapy. He was restive and irritable much of the time, wanting to be okayed for full duty, and knowing that was a long way off yet.

"Yuri?" The Russian was poring over a stress-data analysis paper he had been memorizing for presentation to the experts when they reached Earth. He looked up quizzically, visibly shifting mental gears. Brenna frowned. "What's eating Tumaini? It's more than his physical condition, isn't it?"

Yuri sighed and shook his head. "It's Aluna. She left him. Took the kids. She just packed up and got aboard the Alamshah shuttle early this morning. I guess she's returning to Earth permanently, from the gossip I heard. There are many opportunities there for reclamation biochemists . . ."

"Yeah. A whole planet that needs reclaiming, after what Earth's been doing to itself this past century or so," Brenna said bitterly, letting herself float against the safety webbing. She should have sensed this coming. Damn Aluna Beno! How could she do this to Tumaini? "I should have kicked her ass all over the field the first time she came to watch Tumaini fly out of Amazonis. He's been a pilot since he was seventeen, long before she met him. She can't claim his being a pilot was a surprise . . ."

Yuri cracked his knuckles. "She told Carmelita Obregón that it was his scars—seeing him at the hospital."

"I can't believe that! My God! You mean she's walking out on him—and taking his sons to Earth—because he got hurt? That's the dumbest damn reason I ever heard for deserting someone you love."

Yuri shrugged. "The relationship would not work any more. She broke it. It is very hard on Tumaini, however."

Brenna thought of her quarrel with Derek. At least that was mutual. They were both healthy. And nobody had broken the relationship completely, yet. Derek was on his way out to the asteroids for Hiber-Ship Corporation. She was heading to Earth, on Breakthrough Unlimited business. Inevitable separation, for two people highly involved with their jobs.

Aluna Beno, walking out because—she *said*—Tumaini got hurt. And she couldn't take that any more.

Derek, saying, ". . . the next time around it'll be *you* who climbs into that cockpit."

Afraid of losing her. Afraid of seeing her killed, or worse. In a way, Derek and Aluna had a lot in common. But the situation was so very different.

Wasn't it?

An aberrant, very dangerous doubt lurked far in the back of Brenna's mind. Breakthrough Unlimited. Prototype III. All the obstacles cleared. Go for test run. She was sitting where she wanted to be, at the master controls. Ready to ride her to glory.

But what if it fails . . . *again?*

Flashing images of Morgan, surrounded by a maelstrom of fire. And Morgan lying in the chair-bed, helpless, encased in a body that no longer looked like him or obeyed him.

Brenna shivered and locked the safety webbing tighter. Yuri was watching her with concern. She forced a smile, switching on her individual vid monitor. *Reports. Presentations. Have to convince the T.W.C. bunch to renew the franchise. Don't think about what comes next. Let Morgan do that. Above all, don't think about failure. Never!*

205

✪✪✪✪✪✪✪✪✪

CHAPTER TWELVE

Unknown Opponents

BRENNA leaned back and caught her breath. She needed a pause to decide what she would say next. The Terran Worlds Council members needed time to read over what she had already presented. The stuff was printing up on their vid monitors at each place around the huge table. Most of the Councilmen had come to the meeting with their tech assistants. They put their heads together with these hired experts, considering the data on Breakthrough Unlimited. Some of the material on the screens was very current, almost as new to Brenna as it was to the Councilmen—it had come in from Breakthrough Unlimited Mars HQ an hour before the meeting, relayed from Morgan. A new metallurgy stress analysis and kilometers of formulae on the oscillator. The data had impressed the Council and awed Brenna. But now . . . she couldn't figure out which way they were leaning, which way they would vote. Yes? Or no? Being impressed wasn't the same as being convinced.

Councilman Ames was sitting to her right. He wasn't bothering to mull over the data or consult with his aides. He'd skimmed the readout quickly, nodding. Then the former general leaned toward Brenna. "Quit worrying," he whispered. "They'll give you the extension."

"How can you be so sure, sir?"

"Girl, I'm always sure. And I always back the winning side," Ames said with cold humor.

That was encouraging. He always *did* back winning sides. That was how he had survived the Death Years and the Chaos and the Crisis of 2041, when Jael Saunder had tried to take over the world. Ames had backed Irene Fairchild's political party, that time, and he'd backed Todd Saunder—the ultimate winners. He had once been a rising star in Protectors of Earth Enforcement. But during the

Fairchild Peace, when the Terran Worlds Council was formed, Ames had resigned that commission and helped shape the crack military outfit that was now known as Space Fleet—in on the ground floor. While Fairchild's successors on Earth, such as Carissa Duryea Saunder, had been plodding along, proud of their founder's peace achievements but stagnating in so many other ways, Terran Worlds Council had been roaming among the colonies, dealing with the future that was already here, gaining power. Earth still led the way in population numbers. But in economics and initiative, she was losing. This meeting was an example. In theory, Terran Worlds Council represented Earth and all the colonies. But this was the first time in seven years that the annual meeting of the members had been held *on* Earth. The other six had been held on one of the colony worlds or on an artificial satellite, and *next* year's meeting would head back into space. The booming markets, the new inventions, the explosion in info technology and Twenty-second-Century thinking, were out there, not here on the home world. Earth, hanging on, and her grasp was slipping.

One proof of that was the resurgence of the fanaticism of the early Forties. Earth First Party, crawling out of its dark holes, trying to assassinate members of Terran Worlds Council. What was next? Earth was still racked by xenophobia. And her colonies, populated by pioneers who had emigrated from Earth, were now the targets of that xenophobia. The hatred of Spacers was still strong. It had existed since Goddard Colony and Lunar Base Copernicus were founded. The Spacers lived a different life, an *alien* life, and to too many residents of Earth, that made the *colonists* aliens, people to be feared.

Ames patted Brenna's hand, very elderly uncle. He was never a warm type, like Fred Grieske. But he had known Brenna's father even longer than Fred had and felt some of the same father-surrogate attitudes toward Brenna that so many of Todd Saunder's contemporaries displayed. She gritted her teeth and smiled, repressing her urge to tell him she wasn't a "girl," hadn't been for years. He remembered her that way, though—scabbed knees and missing teeth—and behaved accordingly. She was stuck with it.

One by one, the Council members looked up from the

207

vid screens. They doodled on their mini-memory wrist terminals, taking notes, and chatted with their aides. Brenna perched on the edge of her chair. Always before, when she and Morgan had reached this stage of asking for a franchise renewal, Morgan had taken over. Every year, since '72. Before then, Mariette or Kevin had handled the chore. Now there was no one left but Brenna, the last living and healthy member of Breakthrough Unlimited's family-owned corporation.

She had spoken to Morgan yesterday, on a direct line. That could be frustrating under good circumstances, because of the time lag in vid signals between Earth and Mars. Talking to Morgan, by that method, just lengthened the already daunting silences in his conversations. Even so, Brenna had suggested that perhaps he might like to join her at this meeting, via ComLink, and make the franchise-extension pitch, as he usually did. After one of those terrible silences, he had said, "No," emphatically. Then he'd explained. The Council members might be put off by his appearance and voice. Chances were far better if he stayed off stage. He had shut off the image feed of himself after that, but continued to send Brenna constant updates on the technical stuff he was researching.

Brenna gazed around the table, trying to gauge the committee. This didn't constitute the whole Terran Worlds Council, of course, just the group dealing with such things as space reservation franchises and designated interplanetary trade routes. Brenna was one applicant among many in this current session. She was expected to give the presentation—showing she had done her homework—and take their decision and leave, making room for the next hopeful applicant for a mining claim or a fuel depot license.

There were some very powerful people on this particular T.W.C. committee. A few, like Ames, Brenna was sure she could count on. Others, like Ubaldi and Mpenda and Yan Bolotin, a prime sponsor of Hiber-Ship Corporation, she wasn't at all sure of. Which way would they jump?

Bolotin was the presiding officer, and he finally called for order. "Any concluding statements, Saunder?"

Brenna waved at the vid screens. "The readouts bring you up to date on where we are. We . . . uh . . . I admit we've had a setback. But our science consultants continue to predict success. As you've seen, Morgan McKelvey is

208

coordinating the probable-cause analysis. We're certain the accident was due to mechanical problems. There's no flaw in the basic design."

To her relief, Bolotin said nothing. She had expected him to draw comparisons between Hiber-Ship's proven, though snail-slow, star-reaching method and the so far disastrous record of Breakthrough Unlimited. Whatever his personal opinion, he was being scrupulously fair, letting the others debate without him.

"These projected financing figures for your next year . . . they're pretty steep," Councilman Ubaldi said. "Are you sure you can count on those funds?" Ubaldi was one of Ames's cronies from their P.O.E. military service days, but the two men didn't always see eye to eye.

"Of course she can," Ames retorted. "She's a Saunder."

The magic name. Talisman. What had Brenna told her crew? Despite popular impressions, the Saunders were not an inexhaustible source of money. Yet Ames invoked that legend, tellingly. Many of the committee members were nodding. Brenna felt obligated to stress how solidly the young Saunders were backing the FTL project. "I already have most of the funding set aside, Councilman Ubaldi. I've reserved my next eight quarters' profits from my interest in Saunder Enterprises Trans Co."

"All of it?" Mpenda asked, taken aback. Other committeemen were equally shocked.

"Yes. Interplanetary *and* planetary income, if necessary," Brenna said. These people were well informed re SE's solvency. They knew what kind of finances Brenna was talking about. Several of them whistled, rolling their eyes. "I'll also use my dividends from ComLink and SE Industrial Division, should the need arise. There won't be any demands on Terran Worlds Council for supplementary funds." She didn't add that it probably *would* be necessary to dip into some of those reserved private sources if Breakthrough Unlimited's expenses kept climbing the way they had been. "I'm not going to touch any of Morgan's holdings for the time being, even though he's quite willing to contribute to the kitty. His medical bills . . ."

There was a hasty, sympathetic chorus around the table, assuring Brenna she didn't need to go into detail. They understood perfectly. And none of them wanted to be thought callous. Most of this meeting's business would be confidential, but the raw bones would be released to the media. The committee could envision vid columnists licking their lips hungrily, setting up grabber opening lines: "TERRAN WORLDS COUNCIL KICKS GALLANT TEST PILOT MORGAN SAUNDER MC KELVEY WHILE HE LIES GRIEVOUSLY WOUNDED . . . !" No, there would be no demand that Morgan's half of the partnership contribute equally to satisfy the committee's funding inquiries!

Suddenly, Yan Bolotin interrupted. "You have funding from another Saunder, don't you?"

Mpenda brightened, mistaking the reference. "Todd Saunder?"

"No," Brenna said, too sharply. They looked at her with surprise, and she softened the denial. "My father . . . has other investments to take care of. He's helping out so much with Morgan's hospitalization, and so forth . . ." She hoped that would satisfy them and get them off that tack.

Breakthrough Unlimited had nothing to do with Todd Saunder. Not only was the project an anathema to her father, but Brenna didn't *want* his financial assistance. Just once in her life she was going to accomplish something on her own! She and Morgan. Inherited money, yes. But now it was theirs to use as they chose, and when the graviton spin resonance ship finally worked, no one would be able to say it was proved out by "Todd Saunder's daughter" or "Mariette Saunder's son." They would have names, and reputations, all their own—no debts owed to the older generation of Saunders!

"I meant Stuart Duryea Saunder," Chairman Bolotin said, and Brenna stiffened. Derek's boss hadn't missed a thing. He had done *his* homework, too. That donation Stuart had tossed away so casually—an enormous amount —certainly did help the overall financial picture. Technically, Brenna had to admit, it *did* make Stuart an investor, of sorts, in Breakthrough Unlimited. The third member of the Saunders' new generation, though she and Morgan didn't want Stuart on their bandwagon. There was murmuring around the table, heads nodding.

"Ah! If the Earth-based branch of the Saunders is supporting the project . . ."

Brenna had been backed into a pocket. She didn't blame T.W.C. for wanting assurances. They had factions to answer to, powerful ones. There were always questions about any franchises granted. And so far they had had no publicity return on Breakthrough Unlimited's franchise except *bad* publicity.

"I don't know," Councilman Taliaferro was saying, studying the readouts once more. "There have been so many accidents . . ."

Hamaguchi jumped on his doubts, waving her arms excitedly. "Every new idea in space travel and commerce carries risks. It is imperative for the survival of human civilization that Breakthrough Unlimited make the faster-than-light achievement!" Her small fists smashed down on the table. Hamaguchi packed a lot of energy. Everyone here knew her motives weren't selfless. It wasn't that she was personally involved in Brenna's project or in the advance of human civilization; her clan, now allied with the Matsumotos of the Jovian orbit manufacturing colonies, had been, in effect, chased off Earth by the Nakamura and Associates conglomerate. *Any* rival of Nakamura's had her wholehearted support. "I will *not* approve Hosi No Miti Kaisya's faster-than-light experiments! Nakamura Kaisya is no friend of Terran Worlds Council. It must not be allowed to defeat the Saunders. Further, Taisi Quol-Bez is a friend of the Saunders. Does this not promise us that Breakthrough Unlimited has indeed discovered the true star gateway?"

"Unless the alien's playing some kind of tricky game with mankind," Ubaldi growled.

Ames made a rude noise. "You're paranoid, Vic. What would the Vahnaj have to gain by that?"

"Who knows? Maybe it's to their advantage to keep us cooped up and ignorant. We've discussed this often enough in the main sessions. What better red herring could they throw us than encouraging us to waste our time backing an FTL travel theory the Vahnaj have already tried and found out won't work?"

Brenna squirmed inwardly. Why did Ubaldi have to bring that point up now? What if he persuaded others and they started doubting, too?

"Todd Saunder's the man who first made contact with the Vahnaj," Ames reminded the Council. "His wife deciphered the aliens' language and made it possible for us to talk to them. I've met Quol-Bez a hundred times or

211

more in these past six years since he's been with us. I think you'll acknowledge I'm a fair judge of character, Vic, whether the character's human or from somewhere outside the Solar System. Quol-Bez isn't out to double-cross Todd Saunder or his daughter . . . or us."

Brenna stared at Ames hopefully. ". . . *I always back the winning side.*"

"*Hai*, Brenna, you have my vote!" Hamaguchi cried. Others supported the future of interstellar exploration, which they hoped would eventually bring profit to Earth's colonies. But age-old rivalries, nurtured on Earth, played an important part in Terran Worlds Council's decisions, too. Several members held up their hands, seconding Hamaguchi.

Ubaldi wasn't ready to give up. "Just a minute. I have some more questions. How long is this operation of yours going to take, Saunder? How about setting an outside limit, say a year?"

Brenna protested. "Councilman, we could run into an unforeseen snag."

"You usually do." Ubaldi glowered at Ames and Hamaguchi. "Others seem willing to vote to renew this franchise indefinitely. I'm not. The Fleet could use that section of space for other things. And unlike *some* people who have special status with subsidiary Saunder companies, I'm not . . ." Ames's eyes were glittering black coals. Yan Bolotin raised his gavel, ready to declare Ubaldi out of order before a scene started. But Ubaldi didn't go ahead with that innuendo about Ames's private investments. "A year. How about it? Produce an FTL breakthrough in a year, and you keep your franchise, Saunder." Ames and Hamaguchi wanted to argue the point. No one else did. It passed. Ubaldi pressed on. "Another thing: Who's piloting, now that McKelvey's kid is out of the action?"

Brenna resented that flippant phrase, but didn't let her annoyance show. "The test-flight team won't be chosen until we set up the next full-fledged run."

"You can make an educated guess, surely. You know your people. Who? Nicholaiev? Obregón? The Rift native? No, he's crippled, too, isn't he?" It was Councilman Mpenda's turn to take umbrage at Ubaldi's cavalier remarks. Mpenda, like Tumaini, was an Affiliation of the Rift "native." The older man ignored him. "I'd like to know what kind of package we're agreeing to. Hardware's one thing, but it's the men who make the difference. *You're* not going to be flying that crate, are you?"

Comprehension dawned. This man, for all his modern attitudes about Earth's need to colonize the Solar System, was a dinosaur, living in the past—a long time in the past. Brenna had often heard Ames say to her father, jokingly, that Ubaldi had been born a couple of centuries too late. The old war horse accepted the need for interstellar flight, in the abstract. But he wanted things run the old way, the "right" way, in *his* point of view.

"I'm part of the flight crew, of course," Brenna said carefully.

"Don't like the idea. You could get blown up, just like Saunder's sister did. They never should have let a woman aboard that ship in the first place. Bad policy . . ."

Brenna's jaw dropped, her anger canceled out by pitying amusement. How antiquarian he was! She pulled her thoughts together and responded as politely as she could. "Women have been handling spacecraft for more than a hundred years, sir."

"And getting killed doing it. Looks bad when a woman gets killed that way. I knew Polk's family. Thank God they didn't live to see what happened to her."

The anger was returning. Ames caught Brenna's eye, advising prudence. Then he took over the discussion. "Brenna's right, Vic. You're showing your age."

That was the correct tactic. Councilman Ubaldi puffed and blustered and tried to suck in his prominent belly. "Not at all! I just wanted to get these things straight. If you're on the team, that doesn't mean you're piloting, does it, Saunder?"

"I may be." Brenna would let him think the answer was moot. But when Prototype III was ready to go, no one was going to keep her away from it!

"Well . . . I don't understand pilots. Never did. You're crazy, all of you." It was Ubaldi's last shot. He grimaced and slowly raised his hand, adding his *yes* vote to the rest. Ames, then Bolotin, and it was unanimous. Bolotin looked long and hard at Ames. Brenna sensed an undercurrent flowing there, secret exchanges. She thought of the assassination attempt on Ames. There had been other near-misses, aimed at other Council members, in the weeks

213

since Colony Days. Terran Worlds Council was under a lot of pressure, and so were its rivals in the reactionary parties on Earth. What did any of that have to do with Breakthrough Unlimited's franchise? Brenna didn't know, but she felt sure that significant look of Bolotin's was somehow involved with her *and* with those pressures.

The concluding rituals were over in minutes. The Council's secretaries cued terminals and sent the records to T.W.C.'s offices out in the colonies. Agreement forms spit out. Signatures were written on the screen surfaces and duly entered in the books. Signed, sealed, and granted. The franchise!

For one year.

Nobody gave Brenna the rush, but she knew others were waiting. There would be a brief recess while aides set up the next applicant's meeting with the Council. Ames used the opportunity to escort Brenna out of the Council's chambers. She paused to thank the various members she passed along the way, shaking hands, being the proper, gracious businesswoman who appreciated T.W.C.'s confidence in her project. Even Ubaldi shook her hand, grudgingly. Brenna knew that gesture wasn't for her sake; she was merely a symbol for Todd Saunder and "McKelvey's kid." When they were finally outside the main room, Ames gave Brenna a rare smile. "I told you. Give Vic and a few others a chance to gripe, and then they'll vote your way."

"Thanks to your powerful persuasion, General. Thank you."

"Want to know what really turned the trick?" Brenna nodded, and Ames went on. "That stuff Morgan sent. Bowled them over. Awesome amount of data there. He's been busy."

"Yes, he has." Brenna, too, had been awed by the amount of research Morgan was churning out via the ComLink terminal in his isolation chamber. Awed, and worried. Several times on the flight to Earth and during the ten days she had spent on Earth since then, she had called Dian and Dr. Ives, asking them if Morgan was okay and not overdoing things too much. They had assured her he was coming along as well as could be expected—as the pat phrase went. Keeping him from working caused him more problems than allowing him to use the vid. So they simply kept a close eye on him and let him go ahead.

Morgan *had* said that what he could do best now was think. It consumed very little of his precious energy reserves. No distractions. A man set apart and therefore intensely focused on his work. This had paid off, for Breakthrough Unlimited's franchise application.

Several Space Fleet troopers were following Ames as he and Brenna strolled along the corridor. It seemed very unlikely that any murder-bent fanatics could attack the Councilman here, within Terran Worlds Council's own building. But Brenna didn't blame Space Fleet for taking precautions. Ames stopped at a window-wall fronting the Pacific. To Brenna's surprise, the old general took her hands and regarded her fondly. "You *are* going to fly her, aren't you? I thought so. You've got that look. Your aunt had it. So did your dad, believe it or not, when he was younger. Damned good flier, Todd Saunder. Mariette, too. Runs in your family. Got your backup pilots picked? Count on that Russian. He's reliable all the way."

"I know. Yuri's the best," Brenna said. Yuri Mikhailovich Nicholaiev was also a former Space Fleet pilot. Was Ames merely being loyal to his troops, even after they had left the service? No, Yuri *was* reliable, a rock Brenna could depend on.

"A bit of advice," Ames said, lowering his voice so that the nearby troopers couldn't hear. "Don't let your cousin invest *too* much."

He wasn't talking about Morgan. "Stuart's made a donation. We're grateful. That's as far as it goes," Brenna said firmly. Ames nodded, seeming reassured.

He peered out the window-wall at the breakers pounding the offshore rocks. Seething white water filled the tidal pools directly below the enormous window. When the pools drained, the waves sucking out, glistening black stone shone in the bright southwestern sunshine. The last time she had been in Terran Worlds Council's Western HQ of the North American Union, the sea had been calm, a dark wasteland, shimmering glass, stretching to the horizon.

"Beautiful, isn't it?" Ames asked. "Always did like this location. That's why I insisted we build here, because of that view. Roll on, Pacific! When it looks like it does today, it reminds me of the time we assembled here in 2040, going on out to the South Seas to enforce the Trans-Pacific Armistice. Your uncle Pat worked that one out.

Crooked dealing under the surface, but it got the war stopped, at least. He deserved credit for that. Ah, but you don't want to listen to a broken-down old war horse reminisce, girl . . ."

Reminiscences about other Saunders, the famous older generation. No, she *didn't* want to listen. She wanted to build her *own* fame, and someday people would reminisce about knowing *Brenna* Saunder!

"Are you going directly to Saunderhome from here?" Ames asked.

Brenna nodded. "I'm taking a flier out to Mojave. I'll be meeting Yuri and my junior pilots there. They've been doing a media tour for a week. I promised them some R and R and rubbing elbows with the high and mighty at Aunt Carissa's party."

"Great speech your dad gave yesterday! The Ambassador's, too. Tell him I said so, will you?"

"Won't you be there?" Brenna was genuinely surprised.

Ames shook his head. "T.W.C. business. Can't make it. You have a safe flight." He pointed commandingly at the Space Fleet troopers, picking out two of the guards. "See that the lady gets to her flier safely." They saluted him, just as if he still wore his rank. Once a Space Fleet general, always one. As Brenna and the troopers stepped into the elevator to the roof, Ames waved and said, "Give your dad my regards."

The rooftop hangars were a luxury Brenna appreciated. Terran Worlds Council copied from the best—Saunder Enterprises, which in the Thirties had brought back the convenience of parking air transport on the roof. Brenna's escort walked with her from the elevator to the nearby flier shelters. Trees and flowering shrubs lined the way, or appeared to. They were holo-mode illusions, very good ones. There were too many problems growing foliage in a place like this—too much UV getting through the depleted ozone layer, too much heat and pollution created by the congestion of forty million people in the valley surrounding the T.W.C. building. Yet not only this rooftop but every available open patch of ground for hundreds of square kilometers boasted green, growing things, mirages that moved with the breeze and were impervious to drought and brush fire and even created their own shadows, faithfully matching the Sun's position as it crossed the sky.

Green and comforting and real—until you tried to touch the trees and flowers and your hands closed on empty air. The real trees were much farther out, in unpopulated lands and superhorticultural domes.

"All checked out, Miss Saunder," the flier attendant said, touching his cap. Brenna palm-printed the voucher and signed, though that wasn't expected. The Space Fleet troopers stood around gossiping with the attendant while she climbed into the one-seater and made a hasty run-through of the systems. She had handled these little ships since she was ten. Old stuff. Safe. Steady. A limited range, of course, but then she was only going from So. Cal.-L.A. out to Mojave Spaceport.

Brenna nudged the controls, passing her hand over the screen, activating Traffic Guidance. The flier lifted and sidled out over the edge of the roof. Perspective enlarged in a split second, from a meter to a hundred meters, the hazy, crowded streets suddenly revealed below. The nearby rooftop "foliage" didn't stir in the breeze the flier made as Brenna edged past it; the stuff was programmed into the weather bureau only, with no entries for outside effects. Brenna held the flier at a hover and signaled "Okay" to the attendant and the troopers. Then she pushed the small craft around, circling, heading northeast.

A few quakeproof towers, like the Terran Worlds Council building, poked above the bluish miasma covering the megalopolis, but most of the ground structures were cloaked in a smoky veil. Brenna was glad the flier had its own filtering system, could go on total life-support if necessary. She had been on foot in that stuff down there, once or twice in her life, and didn't care to repeat the experience. The big toxic-waste scandal of 2015 had sup-posedly been the first million-people killer to poison the valley's air, and there had been frequent similar incidents since then, unfortunately, including one this year. Thanks to her reading in the history tapes and Derek's studies for his Hiber-Ship assignment, Brenna knew that this area had *always* been hazy, even when its population density was near zero, centuries earlier. Use of fossil fuels had com-pounded the natural problems, of course. But fossil fuels weren't used any more; the precious resources were needed for other things, and fusion and solar energy had taken up most of the slack. Yet the haze remained. There was always *some* combustion going on when you collected this many people in one place. Their life processes alone generated a thick atmosphere . . .

Derek. The simplest things brought him to mind, even aimless thoughts about geography and history. He had called the SE shuttle while Brenna was en route to Earth. Their parting quarrel hadn't been forgotten, nor had what they'd shared for years. He had called nearly every day since then, not letting her put him out of her mind. As if she could! Brenna smiled and set the flier for cruise speed, relishing the leisure. She wasn't due at Mojave Spaceport for another hour, and it was only 150 kilometers away.

She climbed up into the sunlight, peering down through the haze. So. Cal.-L.A. was a better place to live than most on Earth. If you *had* to live on Earth, you could do much worse than this. At least they had water; on the flier's rear scan screens, Brenna saw a tabular iceberg delivery coming into the harbor, and melt-crew workers swarming all over the floating mountain. Enough fresh water, brought from Antarctica, to quench the thirst of millions and irrigate their crops. Hydro farming was essential. This fertile region had to raise surpluses for those in the glacier-racked climates. The entire scene below fascinated Brenna as a visit to any exotic locale would. A trip to Earth was food for the mind and stimulated the imagination. It tended to make "space brats" more appreciative of what they had, out in the colonies, too. Luna's buried city, Copernicus. Goddard Colony and other space stations. The Martian frontier, carved into the red rocks. Challenges to mankind's ability to adapt. When humanity finally traveled out to *really* alien worlds, that experience in adapting would be vital. She was glad she didn't have to live on Earth, though. A nice place to visit. No, an *interesting* place to visit, but . . . That was elitist, true. But at least the colonists were offering Earth an alternative. Her people could leave, if they wanted to—if they had the courage.

The flier was crossing hectares of suburbs now, cross patches of row upon row of buildings and skimmer transports. She peered down, watching a skimmer train scooting along its rail, heading for the coast. SE Trans Co, hauling passengers. Every time one of those passengers boarded and touched the ident plate and put a fare in the accounts, a percentage of that went to Brenna.

But she had put her share of those riders' fares in pawn, at least for the next year . . . as long as the franchise held.

Could they do it? One year. Only one year. They had worked *three* years after the last, fatal accident before they dared risk it again. By August 2076, Breakthrough Unlimited would *have* to prove out, or—

The ground and sky exploded.

Brenna was flung violently against her safety harness, horizon lines tumbling. Her ears were ringing from an overwhelming blast of noise.

Reflexes took over.

Rolling. Counter! Go to manual! Move!

Screens began sputtering, tendrils of smoke curling around the edges of the console. The automatic systems weren't putting the internal fire out. Brenna hit another manual circuit, overriding, her hands everywhere on the board at once.

The flier, over on its side, starting to complete another full revolution and another . . .

Brenna stood on the emergency stabilizer controls and found a bit of power left at her command. Gingerly, telling her stomach to shut up and settle down, she trimmed.

Carefully! Or the tortured ship could go to another mode, a worse one!

Steadying . . . steadying . . . the roll slowing . . .

Atmosphere shrieked past the canopy as Brenna held the flier, refusing to let it start another sickening spin. She had it now! Brain in top gear and working frantically.

All the normal systems were dead, the faithful screens blank. What kind of mechanical failure could blank *all* of them? Brenna was on eyeball mode alone, flying by the seat of her pants, and with very little to control the crippled ship *with*. She craned her neck quickly, looking back over her shoulder to port and starboard. A falling cloud of propellant was sifting down onto the outer suburbs behind her. Her fuel. Brenna reached for the emergency switchover to reserve, then hesitated. She couldn't say what instinct made her stop. The way the flier was handling, the main tanks must be nearly empty.

Well, I've handled one of these dead stick before . . . wonder where that term originated? "Dead stick." No stick here. Glide signal controls, like every modern surface craft . . .

Her mind raced through manuals she hadn't studied on a vid in years. She needed altitude. She wasn't going to get it, unless she picked up a thermal off the desert ahead. How far? Before all hell had broken loose, the ETA had read ten minutes. That could be a long way, in a ship flying this low and practically starving.

"Mojave Spaceport Traffic Control, this is SE Flier Three-One. Do you copy? I have an emergency . . ."

The audio circuits were supposed to hold no matter what happened on board the flier. Apparently they hadn't. There was no response. No sign that the little ship was sending anything to the landing area ahead.

Brenna felt keyed taut, exhilarated. Hands very steady, she balanced the controls, stretching the flight, taking in the landscape on either side and down her glide path. The end of the suburbs, coming up. Scrubby open ground not yet invaded by housing or the horticulturalists. Salt pan. Heat waves rising in distorting curtains.

Beautiful little flier! Steady! Taking the abuse and hanging on!

What *had* happened? Brenna had no time to speculate. An on-board explosion of some sort—knocking out the systems, almost crippling the flier.

Almost, but not quite.

The ground was getting uncomfortably close. Brenna forgot all the regs and training. Estimates would have to do. Approximate airspeed—200 kph and dropping. Deadly dangerous, landing this craft with *full* controls at anything higher than 150 kph.

She wasn't ready to bring the nose up yet, though. Brenna had to get more distance out of the flier. She darted a glance sideways and down from the cockpit. Maybe a hundred meters to the baked surface. Not enough altitude, but the best she was likely to do.

Nurse it. Keep it aloft. If there had been a way to put an arm out the side and "swim" it through the air, Brenna would have done that to help the flier stay airborne.

Eight minutes. Still stretching. Each minute cutting that hundred meters down by ten or so.

Somewhere, deep in the more primitive parts of her brain, Brenna knew she should be gibbering with terror.

She was fractions of seconds from sudden death. One slip, one errant wind gust catching the flier, and it would be all over.

It wasn't going to happen. She had control. Ride her on out. Steady. Steady . . .

Other ships were closing in around Brenna, bracketing her. Breaking the regs, flying as low as she was. Escort? Another hasty side glance to check idents—Space Fleet! This wasn't their territory. They had ships posted on Earth, but only for the Council's convenience. Now, however, they were running rescue, helping a disabled ship into port. But this wasn't an asteroid base or Goddard Colony or a Kirkwood Gap satellite! There would be more room to maneuver, out in space, than there was here, coming in too fast toward an ancient lake bed!

The com was useless. Brenna used hand signals to tell the accompanying Space Fleet pilots that she had nil automated control. They answered the same way. "We will nursemaid you in, SE Flier."

"Just stay out of my way when I touch down," Brenna muttered, worried about distractions or hitting a wing tip and cartwheeling and one of the would-be rescuers making it a grand smashup nobody could walk away from.

The landing strip, ahead. She wasn't on the glide path. It didn't matter. She hadn't a prayer of sideslipping the half-kilometer to get *to* the glide path. Brenna hoped the escort had radioed ahead and warned Traffic to clear the approach. There was certainly nothing *she* could do to avoid other craft!

Thirty meters off the hard desert surface now. Kilometers of open space ahead of her. She didn't let herself breathe easy yet. Brenna brought the flier's nose up by hairbreadth intervals, easing the airspeed down, feeling the drag when the sturdy craft began to lose her airworthiness.

Twenty meters . . .

Ten . . .

Five . . .

No skids were down. Those controls had been blasted, too, in whatever unknown disaster had crippled the ship. She would have to go in on her belly, dead straight and as smooth as possible, to make it.

Brenna blessed the cooperative air currents, bracing herself, the nose of the flier at optimum angle. Without vid screens, she could only tell by intuition when touchdown would come.

She did. Exactly. A kiss. A hard one. But smack on target where she wanted it, on the strongest part of the underframe. The flier settled and continued to slide, hideous scraping noises shaking the entire one-seater.

Skidding forever, it seemed. Brenna had made longer powerless touchdowns in a simulator, though. She didn't anticipate, balancing her weight to help the flier finish the descent in style.

When the craft stopped and sagged over onto her left wing, it felt like an anticlimax.

Brenna took a deep breath, then unsnapped the safety harness. She cracked the canopy. Desert heat poured into the cockpit. She had thought it was melting hot within, during that hair-raising dead-stick landing. But it was much hotter outside, on the landing strip.

The escort was landing, now that she was safely down. One of them had followed Brenna in, at a safe distance. The pilot was taxiing up, cutting power ten meters aft. By the time the pilot got out and ran toward Brenna's flier, Brenna was doing her walkaround, looking over the disabled aircraft. She felt like kissing the one-seater. Sirens were wailing. Emergency vehicles thundered toward the cripple and the landed escort at flank speed, stirring up enormous clouds of dust. The Space Fleet escort pilot trotted up to Brenna as she completed her circuit of the ship. "Miss Saunder? Traffic lost your signal on their screens. They notified us immediately. You okay?"

Brenna nodded absently. She turned and stared at the emergency vehicle screeching to a stop a short distance away. Firemen and medics piled out at a gallop. Yuri Nicholaiev was in the lead. Brenna waved a cheery greeting to him.

"Brenna! Are you all right?"

His frantic concern and the Space Fleet pilot's amused her. "I'm fine." Brenna patted the flier's cowling. "Afraid she isn't, though. Look at that." Brenna pointed to a gaping hole in the craft's skin. A knife might have ripped through the metal, severing key control linkages and propulsion feed lines all in one deadly slash. "Wonder what happened? I never saw in-flight mechanical failure that looked like *that*." Yuri bent over, peering up at the damage, fingering some of the dangling metalline connectors. Firemen were spreading out around the flier, using their gauges, testing for radiation and explosion potentials. "She's clean," Brenna said. "Lost most of the propellant back there. Didn't matter, though. She's a forgiving little ship, fortunately."

Yuri's expression was changing from puzzlement to hard anger. He crawled out from beneath the flier, standing up and dusting his hands. The Russian looked intently at the Space Fleet pilot, who had walked a few paces away. The rest of the escort was landed now, and his fellow pilots had hurried to the scene of potential disaster. The military pilots had their heads together and were talking softly. Brenna frowned, questions beginning, amid the triphammer rhythm of her heart and the cold sweat of relief drenching her. What was Space Fleet doing here? She might have expected a Saunder Enterprises Security Flight Force team to rush out to help her, if they had known she was in danger. She might even have expected Protectors of Earth's Civil Enforcement Flight Division to send some of their expert emergency backup pilots. Space Fleet? That didn't make sense. The chief pilot had said Traffic knew she was in trouble the moment her screens went out, when the explosion happened. That was damned fast detective work for Mojave Traffic Control. Or . . . someone had tipped them off and put Space Fleet on the alert. That meant someone *knew* what was happening.

"Yuri?" Chills mixed with the exhilaration chasing through Brenna's veins. The Russian was still staring at the Space Fleet pilots. If there was a silent language former servicemen could use to communicate with those in the Fleet now, Yuri was reading their minds. He didn't like what he was seeing. When he finally turned to her, Brenna asked lamely, "Joe and Adele and Shoje?"

"They're waiting in the V.I.P. lounge or maybe the tower, by now. When we got the news, I was closest to the door. And we couldn't *all* ride the crash wagon. The firemen will radio them that you're okay."

"Yes, I am. But the flier isn't. She was sabotaged, wasn't she?" There. She had said it. The unthinkable, impossible thing. Brenna saw her own shock and outrage mirrored in Yuri's green eyes.

"The tower said it was a probable malfunction." Memories of Prototypes I and II in that phrase. Yuri lowered his voice to an aching whisper. "It looks like she was cut open with a mini-mine. Those are very precise, not heavy firepower. But nasty."

"Maybe they didn't want to blow me out of the sky, just make it look like an accident," Brenna said, speculating with him. Anger overrode her fear. But she was shivering, cold to the marrow.

Yuri grinned, a bit shakily. "If that is so, it did not work. You are a top pilot."

Brenna looked at the huddle of Space Fleet pilots, thinking. Sabotage! Space Fleet tipped off, right on the spot, seemingly trying to help her. Or maybe to make sure the sabotage attempt worked properly? Why? No, it couldn't have been Space Fleet. They had no motive. But they might be involved in countermeasures against whoever *was* responsible. The Fleet was a trifle sloppy, if that was the case. They had almost lost Terran Worlds Councilman Ames at the Colony Days gala. If this was related to that conspiracy by the crazies, they had come in too late to do another potential victim—Brenna Saunder—much good. She had saved herself by damned skillful flying and the grace of a lovely little ship. But . . . why was Brenna Saunder a target in the same category as Councilman Ames? For starters, they were both Spacers. That was good for megatons of fanatics' hate right there! In a cockeyed, mixed-up way, all of this was making a kind of ugly sense.

The chief Space Fleet officer broke away from his huddle and approached Brenna and Yuri. The man's face was a rigid mask. "Miss Saunder? You're not hurt?" She assured him again that she wasn't. "Then, if it's okay with you, we'd like to take over. Permission to contact the general?" He didn't need to explain *which* general. Ames. Not Ubaldi, the reactionary. "This affair ought to be handled . . ."

"Discreetly," Brenna finished for him, growing bitter. Politics! Again! "What can I say? You've got the Spaceport Authority in your pocket, too, I'll bet." Brenna shrugged. "Okay. You can bottle it up. I won't tell Com-Link. On one condition—*you* don't tell my father. He's got enough worries. Agreed?"

224

"Consider it done, Miss Saunder. We don't want this news spread around any more than you do."

Brenna didn't let him off the hook. "But I want to know what you find out. Tell that to the general, huh?"

The pilot's face was flesh-tone marble. "That'll be up to him, Miss Saunder. Sorry you had a scare." A scare! Space Fleet had a lovely way of understating the case! "We'll check out your shuttle before you leave for the Caribbean, to be sure there won't be any repetitions." He saluted her, very crisply, as if she ranked him. Brenna didn't respond, but Yuri returned the salute with an ironic smile. The man met Yuri's gaze, and the thinnest suggestion of an answering smile touched his mouth. Then he wheeled around, barking orders at the emergency team. They confiscated the damaged SE flier, towing her toward the far side of the field, not to the Saunder Enterprises hangars. Brenna and Yuri watched the group until flier and firemen and pilots were hidden by the billowing dust.

Just like this situation! Obscured in dust!

Mojave Spaceport in August was always murderously hot. Brenna was cooking in the mid-morning sunlight. Yet she was freezing. She couldn't stop shivering. The reaction embarrassed her. She worried that Yuri would think the close call aloft had stolen her nerve. It hadn't. But what was happening now was rattling her badly.

Very softly, Yuri asked, "By the way, did we get the franchise?"

His sly tone, sitting on his intense curiosity, made her laugh. "Yes! A one-year deadline."

"That'll be enough," Yuri said confidently. Then his expression darkened once more. "Maybe that is what is behind this. Earth First fanatics and the Hiber-Ship supporters. We will make Hiber-Ships obsolete . . ."

Brenna didn't want to talk about that aspect of the race for the stars. Her mind was rushing over the events and what the Space Fleet pilot had said. "Can we trust Ames? *Really* trust him? He's been our booster, but . . ."

"You can trust him." No qualifiers, no reservations. Brenna hoped that wasn't Yuri's old Space Fleet loyalty talking, but present-day common sense. He studied her thoughtfully. "Brenna, do . . . do you wish to cancel this trip to Saunderhome?"

"Hell, no!" The question roused her out of the last of those post-crisis shivers. "Think of the talk *that* would stir up. We want to keep this under wraps. Just a little trouble on the flight into Mojave, right? Don't even tell Joe and the others. Besides, I promised the kids a party at one of my aunt's famous affairs. We can't disappoint them. You all earned it, during last week's media stints. Let's go!"

She threw an arm over Yuri's shoulder. He smiled and fell into step beside her, his arm around her waist. They walked toward the emergency vehicle, intending to hitch a ride back to the tower—two swaggering Breakthrough Unlimited pilots united against the "Earthling" ground crew. Brenna revved up her emotions, biofeedback working. She wanted them to think she was cocksure, and in moments she *was*—no pretense. Somebody had tried to stop her, and he had flunked. Whoever was behind that sabotage and whatever he hoped to gain by it—it wasn't going to work, now or ever. This elite bunch of Spacers was on its way to ultimate success, in one short year from now!

CHAPTER THIRTEEN

✪✪✪✪✪✪✪✪

Saunderhome 2075

IT was incredibly easy to get full, fast clearance for departure from Mojave Spaceport Authority. Too easy. Brenna had a lot more trouble putting off the junior pilots' questions than getting the clearance. No one from Traffic brought forms up on the monitor screens; no inquiries as to why Brenna Saunder had brought a flier in on a nonglide strip area. No accident reports. No red tape at all. The nameless Space Fleet pilot, and his general, certainly had taken care of everything, as promised. Mojave was positively eager to get rid of the Breakthrough Unlimited bunch. Brenna wryly wondered if they were afraid trouble was following her around and might hit again—while she was on Mojave Spaceport property. As soon as Space Fleet gave someone the high sign, the Authority was ready for Brenna's group to board the trav-carts and get to the SE hangar. She declined, preferring to walk the half-kilometer between the V.I.P. lounge and the waiting shuttle. Space Fleet said okay; that must mean the shuttle was free of "devices." No more nasty surprises! And the "kids" had given up asking questions, too, finally!

Brenna relished the exercise. After the adrenaline-drenching her system had taken during the fight to keep the flier aloft, she had had to sit still and be ultra-cooperative with the spaceport personnel. Now she stretched her legs, almost loping along the tunnel.

Brenna complimented her companions on the public appearances the four had been putting on for Breakthrough Unlimited around the globe. "Caught as many of your shows as I could. You sure kept busy! And you looked great," she said, hurrying down the ramp into the main parking section. Voices echoed off the soaring roof of the hangar.

"We just tried to follow Morgan's style," Joe Habich said modestly. The others nodded agreement. They meant it. They weren't trying to flatter. They genuinely idolized that man in the isolation room on Mars.

"Hiber-Ship Corporation stole some of our time," Adele grumbled. "They stole some applicants for Breakthrough we had almost convinced to sign up, too."

"It's a touchy time for us to recruit," Brenna reminded them. "Morgan and I had to go through the same thing when Prototype I failed. It takes a lot of guts to sign up with a project that's suffered a spectacular mishap. We only get the best ones," she added with a smile that included all four. Recruitment was a lousy job. She had done her share of it. And they would have to keep it up, casting their nets in anticipation of the years to come. Once they made the breakthrough, they would need a *lot* of personnel. Habich, Zyto, and Nagata would then be "old-timers." They could brag, then, with justification, that they had followed the dream when others had hesitated.

"Did you know they've already signed up several hundred volunteers for *New Earth Seeker II* and *III*?" Shoje Nagata asked incredulously. "I cannot see why so many

227

flock to be frozen and wake up in the next century, to colonize a planet they have never seen."

"Well, at least some of them are willing to leave Earth," Brenna said. She felt obligated to give Derek's dream its due, too.

"That's the star route for the fainthearted," Joe retorted. "They'll never even know they've been in interstellar space."

Brenna didn't correct him or argue that it took a certain kind of courage to trust your life to cryo stasis. Not an FTL pilot's courage, though! Someone made a crack about the male-female ratio on board the Hiber-Ships, and the joke was bad enough so that Brenna joined the laughter without even thinking about Lilika Chionis and Derek's other nubile shipmates. By the time their quintet reached the SE shuttle, they were giggling helplessly and elbowing one another. The mechanics and check-in personnel at the boarding elevator gawked at them. That stimulated even more laughter. The pilots knew the joke. The outsiders, including their fellow Saunder Enterprise colleagues, didn't. The in-group nature of the crude anecdotes made them special, like the tight-knit and cocky group of pilots themselves.

The shuttle was one of the new, light, Mach 6 models, an eight-seater. They piled their hand kits onto the three extra seats and started hooking up their safety webbing. Brenna headed for the first seat, then stopped and glanced at Yuri. "You've never flown her all the way to Saunderhome, have you? Be my guest." Yuri's smile was ingenuous, showing how delighted he was with the opportunity. Brenna didn't reveal the real reasons for her magnanimity—delayed reactions from the wild flight-for-life catching up with her. She was quite content to take the second seat and ride backup. The temptations of handling the speedy ship might have been a bit much for the trainee pilots. However, Yuri made a quick takeoff and kept her under steady control. He even resisted the urge to buzz the traffic tower. The programs were on the boards, but Yuri switched her to manual, enjoying himself. They arced up toward their vector, heading east by southeast.

Brenna hadn't been on a PR tour this past week. She had had to meet a lot of the "right" people, though, prior to the franchise hearing. She sank back in her couch now, muscles loosening. With Yuri at the helm, there was no need for concern. If he required help, he would ask for it, unlike a good many pilots.

The kids and Yuri had turned over a list of thirty possible future employees—would-be pilots, techs, mechs, medical personnel, a bit of everything they needed. And the Terran Worlds Council session had gone easier than Brenna had expected—except for that slight contretemps of a sabotaged flier afterward. No more business for a while. The selling job was over.

At least until August 2076.

What if . . . ?

She tried to shut off that train of thought. Worse coming to worst. Another failure. The franchise lost. The financial wells run dry. More injuries. More deaths. And Breakthrough Unlimited out of business. Graviton spin resonance drive would revert to Space Fleet's labs, where it would probably be filed, indefinitely, because of interstellar politics. Nakamura might keep working on the matter-antimatter drive, with poor promise of success. Little wonder Hiber-Ship Corporation was gathering recruits. They had proved cryogenic stasis worked. Their recruits *would* travel to the stars—or at least to one particular star, and to other planets.

Brenna didn't know which threat scared her more— mankind not achieving faster-than-light travel for centuries to come, or someone like Nakamura achieving it before *she* did. There would be only one winner of this race, and time was running out for Breakthrough Unlimited's crack at the finish line.

The shuttle was above breathable atmosphere now. The sky was almost black. Sunlight reflected dazzlingly off the wings. As the Mach speeds climbed, they were telescoping time zones. The angle of the Sun's rays increased as they chased the clock. Traffic at these altitudes was minimal, only a few intercontinental and private, quasi-nation shuttles like this one, and a scattering of Space Fleet ships. They lanced across the continent. A map flowed past them, below. Green markings on the nav screens showed the outbound vectors from Orleans Spaceport. One of the visual scans framed a view of a single-stage spaceship rising from the spaceport, heading up and out. The interplanetary craft was bound for Goddard Colony and Lunar Base

Copernicus. Golden fire spewed from her tail, lifting the massive ship out of Earth's gravity well. Brenna watched her go with regret, wishing she and Yuri and the other pilots were aboard her. They weren't due for departure for another couple of days, though. Then they would take the regular Saunder Enterprises space shuttle up to parking orbit and pick up the Mars-run ferry there. Not many spacecraft, these days, were built like that big bird now disappearing down range above Brenna's ship. They were too expensive, those single-stage monsters with old-style engines. Experts predicted they would all be modernized or phased out within ten years. There was a glamour about them, but their days were numbered.

Ten years. By then, many interplanetary transfers would be from a parking orbit to a faster-than-light ship —which would leave the world's vicinity and reappear, scant days or weeks later, in the neighborhood of another star!

The terminator was out over the Atlantic, creeping toward them as the shuttle started her descent. They were dropping down into a more congested section of the sky. Brenna took over traffic monitoring to free Yuri for piloting. "Air-Sea Rescue Surveillance ship at plot 34G-8, proceeding northwest. The Orleans-to-Buenos Aires shuttle's bisecting our vector twenty kilometers aft . . ."

"I see them," Yuri noted. "Approaching loss of signal. Plots are on the boards. We are cleared for atmosphere re-entry. Everyone strapped in?" A formality. They weren't passengers. They knew the safety regs.

It was always an eerie sensation, losing audio, an Earth-flight effect. It wasn't a problem near satellites or planets with tenuous atmospheres. After the steady chatter on the com, the sudden wipeout gave the effect of a door slamming between the ship and the rest of humanity.

That must be what it was like to enter faster-than-light space. The labs had to come up with sub-space radio soon, or it was going to be a rough deal, talking across the light-years while *Homo sapiens* explored the galaxy.

Out of stress zone. Acquisition of signal. Orleans Traffic connecting with their ship. New plotting data rippling up on the screens. Brenna glanced at the chronometer: 5:18, local time zone. They had beaten the sunset, thanks to Mach speeds. Saunderhome came on the monitors. "SE

Shuttle, we have you in visual scans. You are cleared to approach on strip East Five. ETA, twelve minutes."

"East Five, Saunderhome," Brenna said. "We copy. See you soon."

The island complex was straight ahead of the ship's glide path. Brenna cued the viewports, dropping the shields so she could see in "clear," not on the screens. She had made this approach so many times, ever since she was an infant sitting on Dian's lap! Brenna dimly recalled other landings, when she was strapped in a child's safety webbing and standing up to see better—breaking the rules and getting scolded. She had strained to see over the cockpit screens. Todd and Dian had talked to each other, grown-up jabber that meant little to a toddler. But she seemed to hear her father saying, as if it were days ago, "Look! They're rebuilding Saunderhome. It's almost like it used to be, before . . ."

Before his mother had destroyed it in that murder-suicide disaster of 2041. The holocaust that killed Jael Saunder and her older son had also wiped out the original Saunderhome. Nothing was left but a deep bay in the coral reefs to show where Ward Saunder had built his island kingdom. There were other islands, though, not too far away, and they had survived. When the scandal settled down, and Carissa Duryea Saunder was emerging from the mess smelling like a rose, she had hired the best marine engineers and architects and ordered them to re-create the lost palace in the tropic sea. And they had. The new Saunderhome was much bigger, sprawling across an archipelago of once-barren natural islets and man-made reefs. From the air the new complex looked rather like an octopus surrounded by a broken wheel—the outlying hurricane walls and wave power generator cofferdams. Within those impressive seawalls, along three sides of Saunderhome, landing strips stretched out like welcome mats. Ships lay anchored at the docks; Saunderhome was a legitimate port, rivaling many full-sized nations' harbor facilities. Most travel to Saunderhome, though, was by air. That had always been so. But comparing the current Saunderhome with holo-modes of the original had told Brenna that air traffic was now much heavier, to and from Carissa's castle, than it had been thirty-four years ago.

231

"Do you wish to take her in, Brenna?" Yuri asked deferentially.

"You're doing fine."

Yuri Nicholaiev had never landed at Saunderhome, but no one observing him would have guessed that. Touchdown was flawless. He brought the ship to a stop right in front of the service hangars.

Brenna could see a lot of activity over on the main island. The pilots climbed out of the shuttle, letting servants load the big luggage onto trav-carts. Brenna offered to give the junior pilots a walking tour and sent the trav-carts off to deposit the suitcases in the cabanas. Nicholaiev had visited here before, but he tagged along interestedly as Brenna pointed out the sights. Saunderhome was famous from countless vid documentaries and newscasts, of course. Up close and real was another matter. Joe, Adele, and Shoje tried not to rubberneck, but they couldn't help it. This place—and the island that had once stood here—was the stuff of myths.

Pedestrian and trav-cart bridges connected the landing strips and the sheltered inner islands. Guest quarters consisted of cabanas or bungalows set along curving arms of the main complex. White beaches, lapped by crystalline waters, fronted every cabana. Saunder Enterprises Security patrolled the grounds, as unobtrusively as possible. Gardeners kept the foliage at its peak. The tropical plants would have pleased any drama producer, a perfect setting, and all completely real. Brenna showed the pilots a businesslike building on the far side of the complex, just barely in sight. Waterways linked that area with every other one throughout the archipelago. "That's Sea-Air Dolphin-Assisted Rescue Division," Brenna explained. "They have a permanent base here, just beyond the outer line of palms over there. It's a handy location for them. They're near the sea lanes, where their services are likely to be needed. And since Saunderhome is a quasi-nation and Carissa gave them the land in perpetuity, they won't have any problems with politics. One of my aunt's good deeds," Brenna said, not hiding her cynicism.

"The charming little bridges, the precisely cared-for gardens and groves, remind me of—" Shoje Nagata broke off, reddening. "I . . . I did not mean to compare . . ."

"Why not?" Brenna said amiably. "Carissa's architects

232

copied Japanese structures and landscaping. Your home islands provided the model. This is the imitation."

"Most skillful. So beautiful!" The others chimed in with similar compliments. They understood the intra-familial friction between the Saunders. But they couldn't hold back their praise, sincerely impressed.

Brenna led the way through an arcade of palms and flowers to the guest quarters. Servants stood at every door, eager to please. The pilots blinked when they realized they would each have a separate small house for their exclusive use. Brenna ignored the fawning help and sent the maid assigned to assist her away. She used the cabana's shower to scrub off travel sweat and ease tension, then dressed in the fashionable clothes she had brought to wear at this event. Normally, she didn't bother with the trends among Earth's designers. But she had made a special effort to find out who was "in"—and bearable. That hadn't been easy. SE's Earth-based experts had finally pointed her to one of the new United Ghetto States stylists who was coming up with striking concepts. U.G.S. wasn't decadent, and its fashions had a vigor and freshness Brenna rather liked. She studied her reflection in the mirror, approving. Flowing green, diaphanous draperies did nice things for her hair and complexion. Not bad! She wished Derek were here. But if he were, they might never get to the party at all!

The other pilots had showered and changed, too, and met Brenna outside the row of cabanas. They were watching the party on the lawn of the main house. A sparkling moat separated the guest island from the central one. Again servants offered the use of trav-carts, and again Brenna refused. "It's only half a kilometer or less. We aren't helpless. Come on."

They walked through a miniature jungle lining the shore. Saunderhome sometimes reminded Brenna of her father's solarium, though this was a hundred times larger and far more ostentatious. Birds of bright plumage scattered and flew in wheeling flocks and settled again amid the trees. Pet monkeys jumped and swung on vines and chittered at the humans walking below them. The bridges over the moat let Brenna's pilots see the fish darting through filtered water. The place was a tropical paradise, pruned, tidied, and completely shorn of its wildness. Beautiful, and artificial, as were the grassy slopes of the main island—and the islands themselves.

A ComLink reporter—one of the properly behaved ones —awaited them on the shore, just beyond the blue-water moat. He had been assigned to do spot interviews of Carissa's illustrious guests, including Brenna and her entourage. He knew his place and how to ask the right questions. His woman assistant adjusted the reporter's camera pendant for the best lighting effect, and he took pains to introduce each of the pilots and talk about their flying careers. When he talked about Breakthrough Unlimited, the tone was upbeat, no inane inquiries about whether Morgan would be flying on the next test flight or anything like that.

"The franchise hearing went well, we understand. Then you don't anticipate any problems in meeting the Terran Worlds Council's deadline?"

"We're getting very optimistic reports from our metallurgy specialists. The new hull material will be ready for testing in October."

"I take it you'll be hoping to fly the test craft, Joe . . . ?"

The setting for this "off the cuff" yet carefully planned interview was perfect. Saunderhome, that magnificent castle, was the backdrop. A just-rising nearly full Moon hovered on the horizon behind the palms. Halo-lights were starting to come on as night descended. Brenna hoped the reporter's tiny button mikes were picking up the distant calls of tropical birds and the high-pitched cries of the dolphins from the Sea-Air Rescue Station. With luck, Breakthrough Unlimited might even get a few more prospective recruits out of this "candid" session.

The reporter finally had enough footage and let them go. The junior pilots were visibly disappointed. They had been enjoying the spotlight. Then they saw some of the famous people on the terrace and willingly gave up being hams for the moment.

No robots to wait on the guests here. Instead, there were a great many human servants, eager to fetch and carry and deliver drinks or sandwiches. Saunderhome had a staff of dozens—more, if the Saunder Enterprises security police posted here were counted. Todd or Dian occasionally made scathing remarks about not being able to move at Saunderhome without tripping over maids and butlers and general help. Carissa insisted she needed an enormous staff simply to take care of the establishment—and besides, she was doing her bit to alleviate North American Union's constant unemployment problem. Carissa always seemed to have an answer like that, one to underline her altruism and concern for the public welfare, especially where that concern also worked to Carissa Duryea Saunder's benefit.

The hostess was holding court near the edge of the terrace. Brenna saw Quol-Bez towering above the small group of celebrities, and T.W.C. diplomatic guards standing nearby, trying to look like ordinary servants. The guest list appeared to consist equally of vid entertainers, Earth's most flamboyant politicians, and a selection of "special people" Carissa deemed worthy of invitation to her reception. She held receptions at the slightest excuse. This time she had a good one—honoring Ambassador Quol-Bez and her brother-in-law.

Todd saw Brenna coming up the grassy slope and made his escape from the cluster of society types. He trotted down a row of wide flagstone steps and embraced Brenna, then shook hands with the pilots. "You made good time. When I spoke to Norm Ames, he said you'd left this morning. But I wasn't sure you could get clearance straight on through . . ."

Brenna studied him warily. Her father didn't mention the franchise renewal. It was possible he hadn't asked General Ames about that. And Ames, knowing his old friend's attitude about FTL and Brenna's involvement in Breakthrough Unlimited, apparently hadn't brought the subject up, either. Nor, it seemed, had he let Todd Saunder know someone had sabotaged his daughter's flier and nearly killed her. Brenna began to breathe a little easier. Perhaps Ames *was* trustworthy.

"I saw your landing," Todd said, waving toward the airstrip, now hidden by trees and twilight. "Nice job."

"Yuri had the controls. He was showing off his Space Fleet training." Nicholaiev grimaced. The halo-lights heightened his color. He was actually blushing as they praised and teased him.

The ComLink reporter and his assistant were setting up a broadcast booth on the beach nearby. Voice-over chatter butted into conversations. "Good evening, Listeners. This is Karl Laszlo, speaking to you from beautiful Saunderhome, NAU. Tonight the lovely and gracious President Emeritus of Protectors of Earth, Carissa Duryea Saunder, is holding a grand celebration in honor of Ambassador Quol-Bez of the Vahnaj planets and ComLink President Todd Saunder. In a few minutes, we'll be bringing you some spot interviews with several celebrities attending this lively affair. Later on, we'll enjoy a spectacular performance by the famous Dolphin-Human Sea-Air rescue teams stationed here at Saunderhome. Director of Rescue Operations Lujan will give us a description of the daring tricks the dolphins and their human partners perform while saving . . ."

"Let's get away from here," Todd Saunder suggested, wincing. "Too much noise." He pointed toward the terrace. "Let me introduce you young folks to your hostess. I don't think you've ever met my sister-in-law, have you, Joe? Adele? Shoje? Come along."

There were a lot of delays as they made their way across the grass and up the flagstones. Everyone knew the Saunders, and anyone in their company was worth meeting, in the opinion of a lot of the guests. By the time the junior pilots had shaken hands with vid stars, up-and-coming sports figures, and some of the glamorous new crop of world politicians, they were slightly dazed. They were treated as super-celebrities—which was even better than going on a PR tour and pitching for the cause of faster-than-light travel! They preened and strutted, until Brenna and Yuri were grinning fondly at their friends. Not too many years separated the older pilots from the "kids"; they were in their early twenties, while Brenna and Yuri were crowding thirty. But the gap in experience re gatherings like these was enormous. Yuri Nicholaiev had been with Breakthrough Unlimited since its beginnings, and he had rubbed elbows before with many of the guests attending Carissa's party. He, like Brenna, was fairly blasé about all these big names.

They were finally clear of the crush, moving up the slope toward a canopied area near the mansion. The three-story-high window-walls of Saunderhome were catching the halo-lights and reflecting the glow—a second form of moonlight to rival that streaming from the heavens. The eerie, cold-blue illumination turned faces and forms pale. The lawn and the terrace steps seemed crowded with ghostly figures, people shimmering in unnatural light. Brenna was glad to see that her dress withstood the effect well. The artificial light merely deepened its color to a mysterious-looking sea green.

The usual cordon of SE Security and diplomatic corps guards surrounded the V.I.P.s under the canopy. They weren't wearing uniforms, but they stood out sharply from the relaxed party-goers. Only a few people at a time were permitted into the elite inner circle. The guards didn't strong-arm anyone; they simply stalled the person until they had decided it was okay for him or her to enter the little pavilion. Ostensibly, this was for Quol-Bez's protection. Since these guests had been thoroughly checked *before* they had been invited, it seemed more likely the setup was some of Carissa's snobbery, a form of separating the upper castes from those not quite so upper. Todd Saunder had spoiled the effect by leaving the area under the canopy and wandering around the grounds on his own. Quol-Bez and his aides were more of a captive honor group. They stayed put, nodding, shaking hands, being introduced and shown off.

"Brenna! My dear! So good of you to come!" Carissa cooed as Brenna drew close enough for her aunt to recognize her.

"Aunt Carissa . . . you're looking well," Brenna said, lying politely.

The women embraced, carefully, not touching any more than they had to, their lips kissing the air centimeters away from each other's faces. Brenna knew better than to muss her aunt's frilly high-fashion gown. Carissa treated her niece with the same rigidly correct courtesy.

Brenna's father was leading the other pilots through the ritual. They shook hands, complimented Carissa on her elegant party arrangements, said how pleased they were to be there. Brenna thought everyone sounded like a badly programmed computer. No imagination in any of the pat phrases.

Stuart Saunder was holding court a few steps to Carissa's left. He was unusually subdued, his expression bleak. A pretty, rather nervous-looking young woman was at his side. She wasn't of the same mold as Stuart's interchangeable collection of bed partners. Brenna wondered who the stranger was. The poor thing appeared terribly ill at ease, as if wishing she could escape. Brenna shared the sentiment, but she *had* to stay, thanks to kinship.

Carissa suddenly turned to the young woman. "Oh, I don't believe you've met Felicity Emigh, of the Orleans Emighs—my daughter-in-law-to-be." Carissa waved her bony hands, drawing attention to the fortune in jewels she wore on her fingers. "Here, step forward, dear. Let them see you." As obedient as a puppet, Felicity jumped, shaking hands and accepting the good wishes offered her.

Brenna was stunned. Daughter-in-law-to-be? Carissa had pulled a real shocker. She must have been negotiating this match secretly. Now that Carissa had introduced the puppet woman, Brenna remembered seeing Felicity's picture on society vidcasts about various Earth social events. Felicity Emigh had never done anything of note. She seemed to be a cardboard person, strictly for show, with no substance. Of course, the Emighs were rich, though not nearly up to the Saunders' level. Who was? Old John Emigh was said to have made his fortune during the aftermath of the Crisis of 2041, so in a way he owed his wealth to the Saunders. Jael Saunder *was* the Crisis of 2041! But as far as Brenna knew, none of Emigh's heirs showed any of his traits. They were content to blend in with the scenery and spend the money he had cut throats, figuratively, to win. Marrying a daughter off to Stuart Saunder was one way of consolidating Earth's wealth and making sure there would always be enough money to keep Felicity in luxury.

What about Stuart? What did he have to say about any of this? Not much, if his expression was an indication. Brenna stole a sidelong glance at her cousin. Stuart sipped his drink and absently responded to the congratulations the guests heaped on him. He looked hypnotized. Was he on some new illicit chemical? Carissa had tried to dry up his sources, and had always failed. Brenna couldn't tell if he was numb or simply sunk in despair. He certainly wasn't the image of a happy bridegroom-to-be.

Felicity? Obviously she was the type who would do what Daddy told her to. She didn't reveal any opinion about this match at all. Maybe she *had* no opinion. That would make her an ideal daughter-in-law for Carissa. A lump of pretty clay, to be molded the way Carissa Duryea Saunder wanted it to be.

Brenna thought about Stuart's discarded mistress and

238

illegitimate child. Not *bought* off. *Cut* off cold. Carissa had engineered that. She owned the judges and she had the power. Stuart's mistress and child had been banished, all their legal claims wiped out. Now Carissa was going to get him married off to a wealthy nonentity. *Her* choice, this time, not Stuart's. The mother-son warfare that had been going on ever since Stuart was old enough to say, "No!" was over. Carissa had won.

"Why, we've decided to have the wedding at Christmas," Carissa was telling a guest who had asked. *"We."* Not *"they."* She probably hadn't bothered to consult the happy couple. Mommy knew best, anyway. "It'll be so lovely here, at that time of year . . ." Carissa was fluttering, very happy. Her maid had brought one of her pet dogs, and Brenna's aunt was using the tiny beast as a prop to hold the audience's attention. The fashionably clad dowager empress, the just-right hairdo, the still-slim figure, the face a bit too firm to be believable—but corrective surgery could do wonders!—and the purebred little terrier. Carissa, to the nth degree.

"I feel so sorry for that girl," Todd whispered in Brenna's ear. "That's a marriage made in the computers, and in the accountants' ledgers. Carissa's done it again."

Brenna whispered, too. "How on Earth did she force Stuart to agree to this?"

"Mutual pact, I hear. Shh! Stuart's watching us. I'll tell you all about it when we have some privacy . . ."

People milled around the pavilion, nibbling at the fancy food, ordering exotic drinks from the butlers. Several high-ranking guests were in earnest conversation with Ambassador Quol-Bez. Todd wandered over that way, in order to rescue the Vahnaj from his own politeness, if necessary. Brenna noticed Yuri Nicholaiev and Chin Jui-Sao chatting affably. She smiled. There had been times, during *Homo sapiens'* not-too-distant past, when Yuri's and Sao's ethnic groups hadn't been on good terms, to put it mildly. Millions had died during national collisions and struggles to preserve "honor" and "face." Some of that animosity lingered still, even in the final quarter of the Twenty-first Century. But that didn't affect Yuri and Sao at all. They were Colonists. The squabbles and old national conflicts of Earth seemed remote to them. They had their eyes on different goals, and Earth's horizons were pitifully limited.

Those two, in easy conversation, summed up the best of Terran colonial life styles, for Brenna. Her junior pilots were mingling nicely. Joe was talking computers with an inventor from the Northern European Democracies, and Adele and Shoje were listening intently to a famous entertainer's outrageous stories.

Then, too close to ignore, Brenna heard Stuart complaining. "No, I will *not* dance with her, Sweet Mother Carissa. You can lead this castrated bull to the slaughterhouse, but I'm damned if I'll dance with the butcher who's going to put a ring through my nose."

"Stuart, you will," Carissa said, her voice almost lost in the yapping of her noisy little dog. Stuart heard her, though. So did several other people. Carissa's husky, tearful-adolescent lilt was unmistakable, even when it was coated with icy steel. Carissa dominated the confrontation. Stuart's posture had always been awful, and dissipated living hadn't improved him. He slumped unattractively, every line in his rapidly aging face showing. Of the two, his mother looked healthier and younger. Without taking her eyes from his, Carissa raised a finger. "Come here, Felicity. You and Stuart are going to dance."

Other conversations continued, a soft murmuring all around and through the pavilion. But everybody was also watching this little battle, trying not to be too obvious. Nobody dared back one or the other of this branch of the Saunder clan. People tried to stay out of their way, fearing them.

"Dammit, Mother . . ."

Felicity trotted up, ready to do her duty for her future mother-in-law. Brenna thought the least Felicity Emigh could do was salute. Or perhaps prostrating herself at Carissa's feet would be more appropriate. Carissa gestured to a flunky, and smarmy, safe, and out-of-date popular music began to waft from hidden audio systems. Several couples took the hint, making halfhearted efforts to dance.

Brenna had never seen Stuart's haggard face look so ugly. Hatred, not dissipation, was twisting his once-handsome features this time. He reached out and savagely pulled Felicity toward him, making her gasp. Too fast and far too roughly, Stuart whirled Felicity around, dancing across the terrace with her. It was apparent to all who were watching

240

that he would rather be strangling his hapless fiancée. SE Security hastily got out of Stuart's path. Felicity's expression tightened with fear, but she hung on desperately. Too afraid to try to break free!

Brenna felt, rather than heard, the gossip beginning. There would be no account of the incident in the media. No reporters were present except security-cleared ComLink employees, and no guest who carried gossip outside Saunderhome could ever expect a repeat invitation. Plus, "unlucky" things were likely to start happening to him or her, for "betraying" Carissa's favor. But they would gossip, just the same, among the social circles the Saunders and Emighs inhabited.

And everyone knew *these* Saunders were related to the Mars Colony Saunders—Todd, Dian Foix, and their daughter, Brenna. Brenna wanted to sink into the grassy lawn and disappear, chagrined even to be in the same place with such people as Carissa and Stuart!

Across the pavilion, Ambassador Quol-Bez was looking at her, sympathy in his large black eyes. He understood. Even less than a member of the family, he couldn't express his personal opinion of Carissa or Stuart. He had to put up with them. They were powerful people among the Vahnaj Ambassador's hosts. A diplomat was paid to be polite. It was enough to know she wasn't alone, that Quol-Bez appreciated the situation and wasn't snickering at her embarrassment. She had never felt so friendly toward the alien.

"Brenna? We meet again."

She glanced up, startled. Terran Worlds Councilman Yan Bolotin was standing beside her, his hand held out to take hers. "Oh, sorry, sir. I didn't see you. Small world! T.W.C. meeting all finished, huh?"

Bolotin nodded. The Hiber-Ship Corporation badges on his uniform caught the lights vividly. The tiny fabric copy of the photon ramjet interstellar craft seemed a painful reminder of Derek and the only other major competitor of Breakthrough Unlimited's reach for the stars. Bolotin gazed across the lawn, watching Stuart and Felicity going through their charade. Carissa's dog was yelping, punctuating the syrupy music. The effect was discordant and set Brenna's teeth on edge.

"Glad you got the franchise," Bolotin was saying. "I mean that. I can tell you, now that I'm no longer presiding over the meeting. Ames can get terribly partisan at times, of course. So can I. But we're all Spacers, when you come right down to it." He was nodding again. Brenna envisioned him riding aboard the first Mars Probe, part of the crew who had flown to the red planet in '45, with her aunt and uncle. A brave pioneer. A Colonist. A Spacer. One more of her father's contemporaries, a legendary figure from the past who had lived into present times and was still active and very much involved with bringing the future into being. For Yan Bolotin, however, the future was in cryogenic stasis ships, not faster-than-light drive. Yet he had said he was glad Brenna had gotten her renewal on the test-area franchise.

"Thank you," Brenna said, with sincerity. Yan Bolotin was one of the main ramrods of Hiber-Ship Corporation, but he wasn't an enemy. He could have made things rough for Derek, when he had turned the ferry around so that he could be with Brenna after Morgan was hurt so critically. Instead, Bolotin had merely chewed out his popular young officer, then forgiven him and granted an extended leave. In effect, they *were* all on the same side, the one resolved to go on out into the universe, even though their methods were different. "I'm glad you approve, Councilman," Brenna said. "After all, without Breakthrough Unlimited to compete against, Hiber-Ship wouldn't have much of a horse race going, to keep volunteer enthusiasm at a peak."

He smiled at her. Bolotin had that look of eagles Ames had spoken of. If a test pilot hadn't bought it in a crash, perhaps he or she kept that look for the rest of life. "We enjoy a horse race, true," Bolotin said. "Not everyone does, though. Or maybe it's more accurate to say they want to win so much they try to rig the odds. Let's keep this a fair contest, shall we, Brenna?" The former navigator touched his Hiber-Ship uniform cap politely and strolled away to greet other guests.

Brenna stared after him. What had that last remark meant? She sensed that Bolotin knew about the sabotage of her flier; he had probably learned about it from Ames. But there was something more in his reference, an allusion she

242

couldn't puzzle out. Rig the odds? Wasn't that what somebody had tried to do to her flier—blast it, and Brenna, out of the sky? But Yan Bolotin had hinted the situation was reversed. He had implied it was Breakthrough Unlimited that might play dirty in order to win the "race." Victory at any price. And in space, losing a race could be deadly.

CHAPTER FOURTEEN

✪✪✪✪✪✪✪✪

The Tower in the Sea

BEWILDERED, Brenna stared as Bolotin wandered across the lawn, mingling with the other guests. She wondered what, exactly, he'd been hinting at. The simplest way to find out, of course, would be to track him down and demand an explanation. But Brenna saw no graceful way to do that, and she doubted the old pioneer would give her the answers if she did. Maybe talking in such cryptic terms made the "horse race" more intriguing to him. She sighed and rejoined the throng.

Servants cruised the grounds constantly, keeping everyone supplied with refreshments. With only Todd Saunder's network allowed into the party, these world leaders and celebrities knew their reputations were reasonably safe. Their excesses wouldn't become public knowledge. That tempted quite a few of them to overdo matters. As a result, by morning some of the guest quarters would hide scenes of misery. Carissa's personal physician and the Saunderhome med staff would be busy.

Conversation was the main entertainment, though the upcoming dolphin-human rescue team show was arousing some interest. Sadly, Brenna thought of Morgan and herself and Derek and a devil-may-care SE guard who had been willing to dance with Morgan, last fall. They had stirred up some excitement at one of Carissa's parties *that* time. But that wasn't going to happen again. Carissa had barely asked about Morgan, no more than the absolutely necessary queries and a few clucks of sham sympathy. She didn't want to be bothered with such unpleasant matters. She contributed generously to Earth's charities. Misery wasn't allowed to touch her personally, however. She found it distasteful.

Speak of the devil . . .

Brenna's aunt floated toward her, a maid and a set of flunkies in her train. The terrier curled over her pale arm, yapping. "Brenna, my dear, I've been having the most wonderful chat with your friends. They're such lively young people, these pilots! So dashing. And Yuri is terribly droll. I just love his cute accent . . ."

Yap! Yap! Yap!

Carissa's conversation was usually studded with these doggy Greek chorus comments. She, or one of her flunkies, carried Carissa's terriers around constantly, like a jeweled ornament. Brenna didn't know if this current favorite was an original purebred pet or a clone. Whenever one of Carissa's dogs died, she would order a replacement from her labs—a puppy bred from the same bloodlines wouldn't do. Carissa wanted a genetic copy of her precious "Snipperkins" or "Jumpsy." Certainly she could afford the staggering expense of cloned pets—dogs, prize cattle, dolphins, and, as the poorly kept family secret proved, human children.

"I never think of Yuri's having an accent," Brenna mildly protested.

"Oh, but you've known him forever, my dear. Of course you're used to it. It's so charming, the way he positively dotes on you and Morgan . . ."

Yap! Yap! Yap!

With difficulty, Brenna kept herself from swatting the growling, nasty-tempered little bitch. "Uh . . . the party looks like a great success, Aunt Carissa," she said inanely.

"Oh, yes! Your father's speech was the highlight of P.O.E.'s summer session. And of course everyone wants to meet Quol-Bez whenever he's on Earth." Carissa frowned prettily. "He spends so much time away from here, these days. Your family really shouldn't be so dog-in-the-manger with him, my dear, keeping him up on Mars for weeks on end. Hush, Whoozums. Mommy wasn't talking about you. You have a nice velvet cushion, not a smelly old manger!" Brenna felt a bit as if she were coping with a malfunctioning gyroscope. At times, Carissa's chitchat wandered all over the landscape. "Did you notice that the Southwestern African Nations' Premier came? The first time *ever* to one of my receptions! I'm so thrilled! It's quite a coup, you know. Theresa Wachs has been trying to lure him to one of her charity balls for just years! Perhaps he heard that you and your young friends were going to be here. You know, the glamour of spaceflight and all that sort of thing. Maybe it was the influence of your African fellow. What's his name? Bena, or something like that."

"Beno. Tumaini Beno," Brenna corrected her. "I hardly think that's the reason. Tumaini was born in the Affiliation of the Rift. They aren't clannish with the southwestern nations."

"No? How confusing! I assumed they'd all get along with one another. Did you know Beno's wife is active in the Serene Future League, my dear? I wonder if that doesn't cause bad feelings. That Serene Future bunch is so oriented toward back-to-nature . . ."

Brenna didn't want to talk about Aluna Beno. She tried to turn the conversation. Compliments did the trick. Superb party. Beautiful dress. New hairdresser? Splendid coiffure. In a way, the compliments were deserved. Carissa put on a good show. She was the reigning socialite of Earth, her power steadily increasing. That climb to the pinnacle hadn't been easy, thanks in large part to Stuart's scandalous appetites for sexual and narcotic thrills. Carissa *and* Stuart would be a great deal wealthier than they were if she hadn't had to buy off appalling numbers of would-be blackmailers and jurists.

Carissa insisted on taking her niece on a tour of the grounds. One clawlike hand clutched Brenna's arm, the other cuddled the yappy dog. Brenna submitted as gracefully as possible. It was easier than arguing. Her aunt gestured theatrically, pointing out new additions to the annexes and mansion. Carissa walked in a cloud of rare perfume. If not for the automatic bug traps, she would probably have trailed a cloud of insects as well, attracted by the heady scent. The aging society queen's hair was piled up in an elaborate style, laced with gems—real jewels, not synthetics. The jewels Carissa was wearing would pay for half a Chase spacecraft. Her makeup was extreme, but that was the current mode—purpled lips and gold-flecked cheeks and eyelashes. Brenna looked naked, by comparison.

Her aunt kept up a running stream of passing greetings to her guests as she walked along. "Haddad! So nice to see you. You know my niece, don't you . . . ? Enchanting evening, Mrs. President . . . So happy you could come, Excellency . . ."

Yap! Yap! Yap!

"Giannina, you've been a stranger at Saunderhome . . . Congratulations on your election, sir . . . What a beautiful gown, my dear! . . ."

Yap!

Now and then, between these effusive exchanges, Carissa pumped Brenna for family gossip. Brenna didn't satisfy her, being much too closemouthed. "No, I didn't attend the Protectors of Earth ceremony this year. I watched it on the vid, Aunt Carissa. Yes, Dad's speech seemed to go over very well . . . Mother? Oh, she's just fine. She's staying with Morgan while Dad and I are here . . . Yes, Morgan's coming along okay. He sends his love," Brenna lied shamelessly. Simpler to lie than to respond to a pointed question with an awkward silence. "The elections? I really don't have an opinion. I'm not an Earth citizen, you know . . ."

There were people of wit and intelligence at this affair, people Brenna would have enjoyed meeting and talking to. She began to realize she wouldn't be allowed to do that. Carissa monopolized her, leading her from one small group of guests to another, the silly chatter never stopping. Brenna was tempted to manufacture an excuse and duck out. Yet this was only an occasional nuisance. She was standing in for Dian, and Dian loathed Carissa and her airs even more than Brenna did. If mother could put up with it, so could daughter.

Brenna gazed out over the lawn, at the important people in their costly clothes, moving about in the ghostly halolights. Earth-bound. More than that. These people were planet-bound, mostly. The colonists on Mars and the Moon and the satellites didn't think of themselves in that way—because they didn't *feel* that way. It was far more than Earth's gravity making the difference. So few Earth-based citizens ever left the planet. But colonists regularly took their vacations on satellites or other colonies—and

Earth was usually at the bottom of their list of places they wanted to visit.

Earthmen are content to remain here for their entire lifetimes. And we colonists don't like to come back here. We think they're limited and narrow. I have to beat the bushes for Breakthrough Unlimited supporters, here. I have hundreds of willing investors, elsewhere. But the funding always flows most strongly here on Earth. To keep the flow moving outward again, my pilots and I have to come to Earth regularly and perform, like . . . like those dolphins are going to perform for the tipsy guests.

The Sea-Air rescue teams were starting their show, finally. Many of the guests headed down to the beach to watch, providing the excuse Brenna had been hoping for. Her aunt was obligated to join the crowd, at least for a while. But Brenna had seen the human-dolphin teams in action many times before. It was an entertaining show, yet very familiar. She made her apologies, staying on the upper terrace while Carissa, dog, and flunkies hurried across the grass toward the beach. Actually, Brenna found she could see as well or better from up here. Silvery aquatic mammals leaped out of the water and splashed the guests who stood too close to the shore. Halo-lights made the animals' wet hides shine like polished metal. The human members of the teams body-surfed along behind their dolphins. One woman rode her dolphin, hanging on precariously by a slender cinch. The humans shouted and chirruped to their intelligent sea-living partners, staging a mock race.

"Excuse me, Miss Saunder." Brenna glanced around. A servant, one of the older retainers who had been at Saunderhome for years, was at her elbow. "Your father wished me to relay a message—he said he was a bit tired and was going to lie down in his cabana for a while. He said if you weren't too busy, perhaps you might drop in." Brenna thanked the man and looked around the area, spotting her people. The junior pilots and Yuri were watching the dolphin show. Yuri was a good scoutmaster. He wouldn't let the green members of Breakthrough Unlimited go overboard on Carissa's potent refreshments. Quol-Bez and Sao and most of the other distinguished guests were either watching the dolphins or sitting or standing around and talking, enjoying the evening breeze. A few couples were even dancing to the corny music. But Brenna didn't see Stuart or his bought-and-paid-for fiancée anywhere. Maybe Stuart was sampling the merchandise before the wedding. More likely, considering his patent dislike of the woman Carissa had chosen for him, he had bowed out as soon as he was out of his mother's reach. Brenna might have done her cousin a favor by providing another handy target—someone Carissa could lord it over and demand attention from. Apparently he had made his getaway while Carissa was towing out her niece about.

Brenna decided to drop out, too, at least temporarily. She would stop at her father's cabana for a while. The easiest way to get there was to go down to the beach and cross the footbridges. But that route was completely blocked by the dolphin show's audience. The other option was the long way around, through Saunderhome. Brenna shrugged and trudged up the terrace toward the mansion.

Saunderhome loomed above the lawn and the flagstone patios and steps. The main house was a soaring edifice of polarized glass and handmade brick constructed into the side of an artificial hill. Carissa had gone to some pains to capture the essence of the original Saunderhome, which had been built into a natural island peak. She had succeeded rather well. More than one vid-drama producer had sought permission to film Saunderhome as an exotic locale for fictional adventures. If Carissa knew the producer, or thought cooperation would be to her benefit, she sometimes agreed. The place was like a fairy-tale castle, a blend of ultramodern decor and jungle wilderness.

Lights shone on all three floors. Some guests were in the public rooms of Saunderhome, watching the vid or holo-modes or live theatrical presentations. The polarized glass softened interior effects, so that all the people and furnishings visible through the windows became golden, smoky shapes.

Brenna nodded absently to the SE security guards who snapped to attention as she entered the main house. There was no door. Air pressure, precisely engineered, separated exterior from interior. Cool, dehumidified air was invigorating, a welcome contrast to the languid, tropical evening.

In the main entry, glass and metal rose to a cathedral ceiling that was pierced with high windows, now letting in the moonlight. Gradually Brenna's eyes adjusted to Saunderhome's gloomy, muted hall lights. She suspected Carissa kept that setting because so many of her guests—and Stuart—used mood enhancers and chemicals which affected their vision.

The public rooms on either side of the entry were pleasant little refuges from the heat and the noisy dolphin show. Brenna nodded to some of the people sitting on the couches and the sling webbing as she moved on down the hall. When she got beyond the public rooms, the halls were empty, except for a few servants and guards. At one point she passed a servants' station and overheard a couple of the maids chattering.

"Well, if you ask me, that Emigh woman's a fool . . ."

"Aaaw, it's the money. Who wouldn't marry him for money?"

"*I* wouldn't!"

"Good thing! He ain't likely to ask you . . ."

"That little heiress is goin' to wish old Mrs. Saunder didn't ask *her*, when she figures out what she's got into . . ."

One of the women noticed Brenna and pinched her companion's arm to shut off the gossip. Their faces suddenly turned into utterly blank masks, as if they could wipe what they had said out of Brenna's ears if they didn't look as if they could talk. Brenna smiled slightly. She considered assuring them they had nothing to fear from her, but they probably wouldn't believe her. Carissa had a nasty way of finding out when her servants were getting uppity; quite a few of them had rejoined the ranks of the permanently unemployed because they had forgotten where they were and for whom they were working.

Brenna took the escalator up to the gallery and walked across to the north annex. The aerial tunnel was glasswalled, like those connecting the three Saunder Estates on Mars. The scenery, though, was totally different. On Brenna's right lay the moonlit sea, blackness dancing with bright diamonds atop the waves. To her left she could see the curving lower levels of the hill and Saunderhome, and beyond those the terrace and the beach and waterways. People clapped their hands and opened their mouths and swayed to and fro, but she couldn't hear what they were saying or doing, couldn't hear the music. The gallery was totally soundproofed, cutting her off from all outside noise.

The descending escalator carried her down into the north annex. There were some guest quarters here, but a lot more servants' rooms and utility areas. Brenna rarely came through here except to avoid Carissa or Stuart or, as she was doing tonight, to take a roundabout way to reach the opposite island. Her sandals made faint slapping sounds against the tile flooring, echoing along the corridors. There were no windows here, no scenic outlooks on the Caribbean or the party. If Brenna hadn't known her way, she could easily get lost in this maze of interconnecting rooms and halls.

Brenna heard singing, piping, childish voices. She stopped, listening to the familiar nursery rhyme. No one knew where that song had originated, and few people today realized what the words were really all about. Brenna knew, however, and she winced. She was drawn by the baby voices, tracking them by the song. In an alcove off the corridor she found four toddlers skipping in a ragged circle and chanting:

"Oh, Lady in the tower, the tower in the sea!
Look out! The knight is coming, to set the people free!
The Lady's in her tower. Oh, see the Lady frown!
The knight will burn her tower up . . .
And all . . . fall . . . down!"

The children acted out the final words, giggling and tumbling to the floor in a heap of chubby arms and legs. Then the biggest toddler saw Brenna. His laughter choked off abruptly. He pulled the others to their feet and lined them up in a ragged row, stage-whispering instructions to them. "We be good," he assured Brenna. The little ring-leader made a poignant effort to tidy the two smallest babies' clothing and tousled hair. Apparently he hoped that neatness would make a favorable impression on the "authorities"—adults.

The four looked very much alike, in some ways. All were dark-haired and had strange, pale eyes. Though their features were similar, their personalities were not. The tallest boy looked boldly at Brenna, keen intelligence in his steady gaze. An equally alert but smaller and shyer boy hid behind the leader and sucked his thumb. The other two babies dismayed Brenna. Their expressions were unnaturally sweet yet vacant, with the telltale unresponsiveness of mental retardation.

"Stan' up straight. Say hello," the ringleader ordered, nudging his siblings. The blank-faced pair mumbled nonsense syllables and continued to smile inanely. With a sigh of exasperation, the assertive one yanked his shy brother's thumb out of his mouth and repeated the command. This time, Brenna heard the unspoken added warning in his words: "Hurry up and say hello, or the adult might hurt us." Blushing, the thumbsucker obeyed, speaking clearly. Then he hastily hid behind his brother once more. Possibly, when no adults were present, he was as expressive as the bigger boy. Brenna realized that it must have been the two brighter children she had heard singing the nursery rhyme. The retardates weren't capable of much except following the leaders. Now she knew who these babies were: the clones Carissa's hired scientists had created from the late Patrick Saunder's genes.

Brenna leaned forward, hands on her knees, studying the group's spokesman. He faced her bravely, his sharp little chin raised. Brenna noted that if he lived to adulthood, he would likely be a very handsome man, as his "father," Patrick Saunder, had been. "What's your name?" Brenna asked kindly.

"Anthony," he lisped. When that announcement brought no punishment, the boy pointed to the others in turn. "Bart . . . Carl . . . Eddie." He hesitated a moment, then added solemnly, "Dwake is gone."

Drake. Gone. Dead. How did a three-year-old cope with the sudden death of one of his look-alikes? Brenna recalled Dian's comments, a few months ago, that the fifth clone in this experimental group had died of unspecified genetic flaws. Not even Carissa's wealth could eliminate all the risks in this still-radical technique.

Anthony was watching Brenna with unnerving scrutiny, as if he were probing her mind and trying to anticipate what her next reaction would be.

"Charming little brats, aren't they?"

Startled, Brenna stood up, and came face to face with her cousin Stuart. Baby Anthony immediately shoved his siblings nearer to the wall, then stood between them and Stuart, like a tiny warrior defending his family. Stuart grinned at the children, baring his teeth. It wasn't a nice

251

smile. Suddenly, Brenna was frightened for the babies' sakes. These innocents had been cloned when Stuart and Carissa were locked in a frantic struggle for the controlling hand of the Earth-based Saunder empire. The situation had been complicated when Stuart's mistress claimed that her newborn son was a Saunder and demanded her "rights." Carissa had eliminated those "rights," and the unfortunate woman's relationship with Stuart, with these four little children. Patrick Saunder's carbon copies. Gray-area legal questions. A threat to Stuart's eventual inheritance of all Carissa's awesome wealth. She had won then, as she had won tonight, by announcing Stuart's engagement.

And the babies had lost, never realizing they had been pawns in a dynastic war.

"What did you think of their sweet little song?" Stuart asked Brenna. "Quaint, hmm? Ironic, too. Consider," he waved a pale hand over the toddlers' heads, "that they learned that ditty the way children always have learned nursery rhymes, since time immemorial. By rote. I wonder who taught it to them, here at Saunderhome? They haven't the slightest idea of the significance behind the words, do they, poor little things! Don't know that the *Lady* is their grandmother, Jael Saunder, and the *knight* was Sweet Mother Carissa's sainted husband. Or that Jael's son—the *knight*—burned up her, himself, *and* the *tower*. Did so the year I was born, as a matter of fact."

Brenna glowered at him. She spoke gently to the babies. "Shouldn't you be in bed? It's awfully late for you to be awake . . ."

"Rachel!" Stuart bellowed. Brenna flinched at the blast of harsh sound. The toddlers clung together, gawking up at the man with the drink-hardened face. Footsteps pattered along the hall and several servants rushed up to the alcove, panting for breath. Stuart pointed at the little clones. "Take them away. My cousin insists it's past their bedtime. No doubt it is. Women are so maternal about these things. We mustn't let anything bad happen to them, must we? Stay more alert in the future, or I'll report you to the current lady of the tower." The servants didn't understand the reference, but they understood Stuart's threatening tone. They took the toddlers by the hand and led them

252

away. Baby Anthony kept peering back over his shoulder, his unusual eyes raking across Brenna and Stuart.

Brenna had seen eyes like that before: her aunt Mariette's eyes.

When the children were out of sight, Stuart said with amusement, "You see? You needn't think of me as such an ogre. Why, I wouldn't harm a hair on those precious darlings' heads. That *was* what you were thinking I might do, wasn't it?" Brenna made no reply, on guard. Stuart was obviously drunk, and he was no longer subdued. This was her cousin at his ugly "normal" level, and he was blocking her path.

"What do you want, Stuart?"

Surprisingly, he wasn't flip. His expression was mean, but it wasn't aimed at Brenna, or at the children, she sensed. "Nothing you can give me, Cuz."

She guessed what was deviling him. "I'm sorry. I gather you didn't have any say in the matter."

The arranged marriage. She had offered him congratulations earlier, on the lawn. Now she dropped the pretense and offered him sympathy.

Stuart's smile was frightening. "Oh, I had a choice: 'Sign here.' You wouldn't believe some of the things . . . well, maybe you would. Anybody would who knows her." He made a rude noise. "What the hell does it matter? She's got a surprise coming. New dynasty, she thinks. Wrong!" Stuart's hag-ridden face twisted with terrible hatred. "No more little Saunders from *this* branch of the family. I made damned sure of that. If she thinks Felicity is going to make her a grandmother, she's got a lot of rethinking to do." Brenna didn't know what to say. There didn't seem to be anything *to* say. She stared at her cousin pityingly. Stuart suddenly focused on her, a malicious glitter in his eyes. "Now if it'd been *you*, my pretty relative . . ."

"Stuart, you're disgusting."

"I try." The smile vanished. "But in this case, I'm not stretching the truth . . . *too* much. We could have something, you know . . . we used to play on the beach when we were kids . . ."

"Your memory's faulty," Brenna said, her words dripping ice. "Morgan and Derek and I played on the beach.

253

You came along and caused trouble—the family bully, picking on the little kids."

"Only six years' difference. That's not too much! I was there. You should have—" Stuart broke off, a peculiar mixture of sad nostalgia and anger chasing over his countenance. Brenna had a sudden image of a lonely, and spoiled-rotten, pubescent boy, gazing longingly at the three happy playmates romping on the sand, shutting him out of their games because he was too old and too big and too manipulative. Stuart attempted a smile, a sheepish one. "Ah! Well, we can never go home again, they say. Except I never get *away* from home, do I? Trapped in this damned tower in the sea. There are times when I feel like replaying history for Sweet Mother Carissa." The lady in the tower —burned up by her son. Stuart was no knight, and the only person he wanted to set free was himself. But his hatred was strong enough to make Brenna shudder.

"Let me by, Stuart . . ."

He grabbed her arm, just as he had at Colony Days, his sharp fingernails digging into her flesh. As she had done then, Brenna whirled, and this time she didn't hesitate. She chopped down with the heel of her hand, breaking his grip. Stuart gasped and reeled back against the wall, looking at her with amazement. "I warned you not to do that. I don't bully worth a damn any more, Stuart. Six years *doesn't* make a difference now. You're out of shape and drunk. Don't make me follow through, or you won't be having any romps in bed for a while, child-free fornicating or not!"

"Quite the little rough-and-tumble artist," Stuart muttered. He nursed his sore wrist, pouting. "You shouldn't do things like that. We can help each other. No, listen to me! I *can* help . . ."

"Breakthrough Unlimited doesn't need your money, Stuart. Thanks for the donation to the hospital, but—"

"You *do* need me! You don't realize it yet, but you will." Stuart nodded slyly. "Very well. I can wait. I'm not sure *you* can, Cuz. I've been watching a couple of wealthy industrialists trying to recruit Yuri Nicholaiev to captain their commercial fleet. How long do you think the lure of FTL is going to hold your pilots? Hmm? You're going to need more than faith to get the job done. Why the hell

254

can't you open your eyes? Or would you rather wait until you get your pretty skin fried off, like Morg did?"

"You're drunk," Brenna repeated, her voice dropping to absolute zero.

"Okay. I am. Touchy subject, eh? Keep it in mind, though, Cuz. And when you're hungry enough, and desperate enough, give old Stuart a call. We'll work something out. You'll see." Very tentatively, he reached out. Brenna raised her hand, warning him. But all Stuart did was tweak her chin, to her surprise. The gesture was almost affectionate. Stuart backed away, a bit unsteadily, the liquor affecting him. He waved to her, then ambled off in the opposite direction from where she was going, weaving down the corridor.

Brenna felt unclean, as if she had come in contact with something crawling with invisible and filthy monsters. Reflexively, she scratched her arms. Very disturbed, she proceeded on her way, leaving the annex by the western door and crossing the servants' trav-cart bridge to the cabana side of the waterway. The beach on the Saunderhome side was still crowded, but the path leading to the visitors' area was nearly deserted. Brenna walked under the palm fronds, heading for the most luxurious cabana. Carissa wanted Brenna's father to stay in guest rooms in the main house when he was on the island; but whenever possible, Todd insisted on using a cabana—probably because doing so removed him from his sister-in-law and her son and their notorious quarrels.

SE Security was guarding the door, naturally. Yesterday, Brenna would have said that was needless, that the old days of the Saunders' being in danger from unknown enemies were long past. After what had happened to her flier, she wasn't so certain. The guards nodded and stood to attention and then relaxed to parade rest as Brenna went on into the cabana.

Her father was watching the vid. Brenna saw with surprise that the main picture was a so-called "sports" event —the beginning of the Fourteenth Annual Pan Asiatic Controlled-Violence Meet. Todd Saunder loathed the concept of the Hazlet-proposal arenas. She had never seen him look at one of these modern gladiatorial contests for more than a few seconds before shutting off the channel. He had the audio muted, but the pictures were graphic, needing no sound to tell their story. Todd glanced up at her and gestured to the screen. "Will you look at that? They've already killed a dozen participants. And audience feedback rating is enormous. Hazlet was right; there *is* a lust for blood among some of the populace, disgusting as that seems. It must reach some deep savage streak in *Homo sapiens . . .*"

Brenna sat down beside him. "Why are *you* watching that?" she asked.

"Damned if I know. I guess it touches some deep savage streak in *me*." He turned away from the screen. "Want a drink? Some rye? I forgot. Your generation goes in for different depressants."

"Not all of us," Brenna said. "Stuart won't turn up his nose at anything. And Aunt Carissa turns up her nose at everything. We're a real bunch of misfits, running the gamut, huh?" She had his attention, and Brenna poured out her tale of meeting the four little clones. Her father listened solemnly as he sipped from his glass. Brenna noticed a half-empty bottle on the table. "The whole thing makes me sick," she finished. "Those babies were just ammunition in a nasty legal game. Now nobody gives a damn about them. That boy—Dad, I've never seen a child so young look so cynical. It was scary."

"Yes, I've seen them. I've spoken to Carissa, but it doesn't do any good." Todd took a long pull on his drink. "I think she's going to keep them around just in case Stuart gets any funny ideas . . . again."

"I think he already has." Brenna described her hair-raising encounter with Stuart, laundering the details so that her father wouldn't be unduly upset. She paused and looked at him searchingly. "You said you'd tell me what made Stuart agree to that farce of a marriage. I think I know. Money."

Todd was nodding, very glum. "What else? Money and power. Carissa spoiled him when he was a kid, and lost control of him when he was a teenager. Now it's a battle to the death. He hopes to outlive her. She's trying to make him fulfill her dreams. They use each other without mercy."

"And the losers are victims like those babies." Brenna stared down at her hands. She would probably develop a faint bruise, where she had connected with Stuart's arm.

Nothing worth concern. "Stuart says he's sterilized himself. No grandkids. Carissa's been outmaneuvered. Felicity's wasting her time. I hope Emigh signed a tight pre-nuptial agreement with Carissa, or else Felicity's only reward will come if she outlives Stuart—which may not be too difficult, considering the way he's drinking himself into an early grave." Her own morbid remarks made Brenna slump in her chair, shaking her head sorrowfully. "How did the family get in a mess like this?"

"Not *our* branch of the family," Todd said emphatically.

No. No civil wars between us. But Morgan's crippled. And you and I and Dian can't seem to pull together like we used to, Dad.

"I wish you'd been here earlier," her father said abruptly. "Your mother was on the com."

"Any news?"

"Oh, everything's fine." But he sighed heavily. Brenna was about to ask if indeed all was well, fearing Morgan might have taken a turn for the worse. Then Todd said, "God, I miss her. Miss the boy, too. Even when he's inside that shell. Getting so hard to talk to him. Quol-Bez . . . thank God for Quol-Bez. Morgan relates to *him*. I wish sometimes that . . ." He gazed at Brenna a long time. There was a silent melee raging on the vid screen behind his head. Brenna wondered if the same sort of thing was going on *inside* her father's skull. What was he thinking? "Your mother and I have been talking about having another child," he finally said. "There's still plenty of time for us, you know. We ought to have thirty years or more, easy. Good health. And plenty enough money to support a bigger family. Your trusts are solid, kitten. We wouldn't be taking anything from you." Todd Saunder patted his slight paunch and gazed into empty air, apparently making plans. "I'm going to retire. I mean *really* retire, this time. I'll turn the whole damned thing over to Elaine and the board. The corporation can run itself fine. Dian and I will just stay put, do the whole domestic routine we've never had the leisure to enjoy . . ."

Brenna was stunned. Jealousy and resentment stirred deep within, the instinctive reactions of a suddenly threatened, beloved only child.

Late middle-age parenthood wasn't too unusual, for those who could afford it, and the Saunders certainly could.

Quite a few people opted for just what Brenna's father was proposing, sometimes delaying *all* parenthood until they were in their fifties or sixties and their hard-won career successes were behind them. With the general practice of preserving sperm and ova and DNA cryogenically while people were still young and vigorous, conception could be put off indefinitely. There were always surrogates willing to carry a lab-conceived fetus, for a fee. A number of Todd Saunder's contemporaries had done exactly that. Some men and women were older than he when they started a first or second family. Brenna tried to imagine Dian and her father dropping their active lives and "settling down" into a vid-drama, happily-ever-after, little family scene, with toddlers at their feet. The idea seemed silly. But then she remembered Dian's tired face, that morning when she had told Brenna they wouldn't come to the test of Prototype II because "it'd kill us if anything happened to you." She looked at her father and saw decades of work and worry beginning to etch lines into those kind features.

"Have I been such a disappointment to you and Dian?" Brenna asked softly.

He didn't react to that for a moment, still building dreams in his mind. When he finally comprehended what she had said, he was appalled. "No, of course not! That's an idiotic attitude!"

It seemed to Brenna that his response was too vehement. "Is it? Okay. You can afford it, and you deserve it. How many kids were you planning to hatch, in this new domesticity? There's no reason you and Dian couldn't have a dozen. The surrogates would be delighted to collect their fees. For that matter, you're Aunt Mari's executor. Doesn't that include, legally, her reproductive capacity? Her ova and Uncle Kevin's sperm are on file in the Enclave. Raise some nieces and nephews to take Morgan's place, and a houseful of siblings for me. One big, happy family . . ."

Todd set his glass down hard. He blinked owlishly, raking a hand through his white-streaked hair. "You . . . you really *are* hurt, aren't you, kitten?" He sounded stricken. "We never wanted to hurt you. I'm . . . I'm not expressing myself well. I've drunk too much. I ought to know better. Pat and Mari could handle it. I never can. I turn into a turnip after a couple of stiff belts." He looked ruefully at

258

the bottle, then at Brenna. "It's not the way you pictured it. Not at all."

Brenna wanted to accept that. She wasn't a baby. The might-be younger sibling or siblings wouldn't be usurpers, would they? Wasn't she far past the sort of childish rivalries bigger families were supposed to suffer? Her accusation about Morgan had been unfair, too. Even if Todd exercised his executor's option and reproduced other nephews or nieces from his sister and brother-in-law, they wouldn't be rivals for Morgan. No one, she knew, could replace her or Morgan in her parents' affections.

And yet . . .

"Here we go again, huh?" Brenna muttered. Her father frowned in puzzlement. "Just like thirty years ago. Morgan and I know the family history. Carissa was making political capital out of her widowhood, and using Stuart as The Little Prince, heir of his martyred father. And the in-fighting between the Saunder branches was getting nasty, wasn't it? Aunt Mari and Uncle Kevin had started Mars Colony, and you and Dian were expanding your contacts with the Vahnaj. Aunt Carissa tried to leech onto you, as well as hanging on Fairchild's coattails and climbing the ladder to the P.O.E. Chairmanship. I don't know if it was a conscious decision, but Morgan and I were always aware that Dian and Aunt Mariette decided to have kids just to prove to Aunt Carissa she wasn't the only fecund female among the Saunders . . ."

Her father was shaking his head, looking miserable. Despite his trying to deny it, she had touched a nerve. "We loved you. We *wanted* you. And Mari and Kevin wanted Morgan. Kevin was so proud I thought he'd burst. He always hoped Morgan would go into service, the way he did . . ."

"Instead, it was Derek," Brenna said, turning the knife on herself, willing to share the pain she was dishing out. "But Derek was part of the family, in a way. And there we were. Three little cousins and our playmate, Derek. Balance. One kid per Saunder branch." She took a deep breath and plunged on before she lost her courage. "I'm surprised you didn't want to start a new family when Aunt Carissa had those babies cloned, four years ago. Maybe this is just a delayed reaction? No, it's the marriage, Stuart's marriage. Even if he refuses to sire any kids, it's

259

a one-upmanship tactic by Aunt Carissa. But if you out-maneuver her and have kids of your own—*more* kids—you win. She can't do that herself; she's the perpetual widow, and she won't dare try cloning *again* . . ."

There were tears in her father's eyes. Brenna broke off, ashamed and angry. But she had spoken the truth. They both knew that. Brenna and Morgan *had* been loved and wanted children. The intrafamilial politics got all tangled up with genuine caring. She pushed her own feelings aside. Brenna tried to look at the situation from her parents' point of view. *She* became the parent, speaking with mild reproof. "You know that's the way it was, Dad. And I won't deny Morgan and I benefited, in love most of all. But there's another reason here. Dian mentioned it, months ago." She hesitated while he wiped his eyes and took another sip from his drink. After a moment, he nodded for her to continue with what she was saying. "It's me. And Morgan. And Breakthrough Unlimited. Okay. You and Dian go ahead. Start another family. Start one for Morgan, too; it's also possible for him to have his own children by the same methods you'll use. Then what happens? Say you and Dian get those thirty more years, and even beyond. That's possible, the way the life span's lengthening. Those kids grow up. And they go off on their own. They won't choose to experiment with FTL. Not by then. Something else will attract them. I don't know what, but something. And whatever it is, it's likely to be dangerous. They may die."

Todd winced, cut to the bone by that picture of the future.

Brenna was alone. Her father and Dian and the older generation stood on a canyon rim. Brenna and her generation stood on another, opposite. Between them lay a chasm as deep as Valles Marineris. Probably there were other chasms as well, dividing each generation from the rest, each generation forced to live through different times and customs, each one reaching for its own dreams. Each generation loving—or hating—the ones that came before and those that would follow. Differences, and yet similarities. The goals might change. But would the emotions? Her father had said the younger generation never believed its parents had cared as much as they did. But hadn't the older generation forgotten how it *felt* to care so much about an ideal, a goal? Would the generations be forever alien to one another? Todd and Dian's hope of a second family seemed like a wistful effort to recapture their youth —and maybe to avoid whatever mistakes they had made in raising Brenna.

Or so it looks; but will it, when I'm as old as they are? What mistakes will I make and wish I could go back in time to correct? Or . . . will I be dead and past all chance of replaying history and making it right the second time around?

Brenna tried to imagine herself older. Dian's age. Still healthy and active, but older. Able to shrug at defeats. Able to be maddeningly patient and casual about the absolute necessity of achieving faster-than-light travel. Not to be in a hurry. Not to care so intensely. Not to *want* so much . . .

Impossible!

"We . . . we haven't made any definite decisions," Todd said faintly, almost apologetic. "We just talked about it."

That knife Brenna had turned on herself twisted painfully. How cruel she was! How heartless! Worse than Stuart! She reached out and took his hand. "Dad, no. Don't change on my account. Please. I was selfish. I'm beginning to understand. I *am*. You know, it might even be interesting, having siblings at my advanced age," she said, smiling.

He managed a weak smile in return. "Very interesting, especially if you have kids of your own. That used to happen, in the old days, though not quite in the manner we're talking about."

"I . . . I haven't thought about having children," Brenna said, lying, her voice unsteady.

Todd's smile grew sad. "You will. You may have them on another world, beyond the Solar System, kitten. Someday." He was drunk, but not so drunk that he mentioned Derek and Hiber-Ship. Dian had said they would prefer that future, even if it meant they never saw Brenna again. They'd imagine her alive and happy—and with Derek— far in the next century on a world they would never live to see. Better than sudden death in an experimental FTL ship.

But both were taking chances—both would separate her, inevitably, from the generation that had gone before. And any children her parents had now or that she might have would be the *next* generation!

Impulsively, Brenna kissed her father. "It's okay, Dad. It'll work. We'll make it. However scrambled our family branches become, at least we can get along with each other," she stated with smug satisfaction.

His smile widened, turning sunny. "Rely on it, kitten. That's because we're honest with each other. Nothing will ever change that."

"No, nothing." Brenna stood up and walked over to the table, capping the whiskey bottle. "I'll bet Dian told you to lay off this. So will I. And quit watching that damned controlled-violence arena. It'll give you an ulcer."

"Nag. Just like your mother."

"You going back to the party?"

He shook his head, looking scornful. "Quol-Bez will drop by later on."

"That's good. He's got some sense, not like some of those pickled celebrities. I approve. So would Dian." She kissed him again and patted his shoulder encouragingly. "Turn in early, huh?"

As she let herself out of the cabana, Brenna noted that her father was changing the channel on the vid. A holo-mode color show now filled the wall, and Nineteenth-Century music drifted through the room and out onto the beach. Music two centuries old, to please the man whose sophisticated communications systems linked Earth, her colonies, and the Vahnaj planets. Todd Saunder's motto: Tie the past and the future together and make them work in tandem. Todd Saunder's daughter had a lot to live up to. She would have to make a future in which she would be proud to have any of her unborn siblings—or her own children—grow up.

The subsidiary screens were showing less esthetic images, more troublesome scenes. News, grim, as it usually was from some areas of Earth. Economics, and that, too, was frequently appalling. There were political speeches—always. These inevitably brought back thoughts of Carissa, babbling about the candidates she preferred. Far more than a P.O.E. election was at stake. Behind the candidates were power brokers—like Carissa, and like Stuart. Fortunes rode on votes, and millennia of this sort of thing had

262

taught Earth dwellers to play nasty. The colonies' politics, such as they were, were noisier, but more honest.

Brenna started along the path leading to her own quarters. The area was quiet and she had most of the little lane to herself. The palms cut off much of the halo-lights' glow from the main island across the way. The breeze coming off the sea was refreshingly cool. Brenna walked slowly, thinking over the conversation with her father.

A tipsy guest approached her, heading in the opposite direction. Brenna and the plump older woman met at an especially shadowy spot on the flagstone walkway. Quite suddenly, the woman shed her drunken mannerisms. "Captain Saunder? The general sends his regards."

Brenna peered sharply at the woman. The dim light hid details. The stranger looked like the rest of Carissa's society acquaintances—stylish, wealthy, and inclined to overindulge. But Brenna knew she had nothing to do with the party. Brenna glanced around warily. SE guards were patrolling the grounds nearby, apparently not alarmed to see Brenna talking to a harmless, slightly intoxicated society matron. Why should they be? Even if they knew about the sabotage of Brenna's flier, this chubby older woman didn't look like much of a threat.

The woman giggled, a trilling, foolish laugh, as if she had heard a lewd joke and were reacting. Her sham mirth evaporated, and she lowered her voice to a whisper. "We caught them. Hired. It's going to be difficult to track down the original instigators. But the general has his ideas. He said to assure you he'll take care of it personally." Brenna opened her mouth, then thought better of it. She listened, asking no questions. The woman swayed a bit and giggled, then added in the same *sotto voce,* "It's the Hong faction. They wanted to get even for some bad investments. Your aunt and cousin cut them up pretty bad, recently. Then there's the election, of course. They're tricky. Whatever happened—a close call or your being killed—would have suited their purposes. But now it'll all go flat, because we hushed it up." A vicious, triumphant smile lit up the round face for a brief moment. Then the woman giggled and toddled on down the path.

Brenna tried not to stare after her. The surreptitious message had been delivered quite clearly. Her compliments to General Ames. Brenna drew the capelet of her dress around herself, chafing the goose flesh on her arms. Ames said he always backed the winning side. How did he figure out which one that would be, out of the tangled mess of Earth's politics and financial wheelers and dealers?

Carissa and Stuart—and someone "getting even" with them by sabotaging their relative's flier. That was twisted, sick logic. A Saunder had hurt them—so get even with a Saunder. *Any* Saunder!

Brenna thought about the little clones, about the rivalry between Carissa and Dian and Mariette Saunder that had produced Stuart, Brenna, and Morgan. Manipulations within and without the family. Derek was always muttering about "unnatural" methods of reproduction, such as surrogate gestation and cloning. Well, Stuart had been born by "natural" methods—and wasn't he a wonderful argument for that old-fashioned practice! He had no more filial affection than those poor clone babies did; and at least they had the excuse that they had never known their father or the surrogates who had carried them until birth.

She sighed, gazing up at the soft Caribbean sky. She wanted Derek to be here, to feel his arms about her, to hold him—the two of them, facing the future together. That wasn't going to happen. There would be no late-middle-age families for them, no *first* family. No intra-family feuding. And no joy through the decades of their lives. Surrounded by sounds of surf and laughter, Brenna grieved for that special dream of family that was never going to come true for her.

CHAPTER FIFTEEN

✪✪✪✪✪✪✪✪

Promises: Broken and Renewed

BRENNA's train of thought kept drifting all during the day-long flight down from FTL Station. She had difficulty keeping her mind on the job recently. The message from Derek, just before she had left the Station for the return trip, had added to the distraction she was feeling. Time and again, the support crew or her fellow pilots had to repeat themselves when they were talking to her. It was becoming embarrassing. And her private concerns had nothing to do with Breakthrough Unlimited. In a sense, Derek was a rival for attention she should be putting into her *own* company and her co-pilots' and team's efforts. She shouldn't let thoughts of Derek rattle her concentration this way. There was too much to do, and too little time in which to do it. The deadline. Derek's deadline was closer, however. Hiber-Ship Corporation would launch in March 2076. Cryogenic processing would begin, out there at Jovian orbit. She had known this was coming, since that night before the President's gala. But now the inevitable breaking point was rushing at her. Derek would be entering a cryogenic stasis cubicle, leaving . . .

". . . could save so much time, with a few tips from the Vahnaj."

Brenna roused out of her reverie, looking around. Yuri was piloting the shuttle, lining up for re-entry orbit. Mars was on the screens; Traffic Control, in constant contact. The metallurgy tests had netted a lot of hull samples, which were crated up and riding in the ship's cargo hold; they had put the new hull material through a hundred times the stress it would have to take from the graviton spin resonance drive, and it had held up. The next step, once the oscillator problem was solved, would be a full-scale mock-up and an unmanned FTL test. *Another* one. Yuri and Hector, in the front seats, were talking about the on-going P.O.E. elections on Earth. Earth couldn't seem to hold elections without bribery scandals and a few wholesale riots. From the vid reports, this election was running true to form, to the disgust of the colony worlds.

It was the conversation in the nearby seats that had caught Brenna's ear. The support team was sitting farther to the rear. The other pilots were in the same tier Brenna was. Joe, Adele, and Shoje were rehashing the just-completed test and possible future ones, anticipating the time when *they* would get to handle the Prototype. Tumaini was playing ringmaster to their marathon gabfest. Brenna eyed him anxiously. Tumaini had insisted on going along on this trip. His depression over his wife's leaving him had convinced Brenna to agree, much against Dr. Ives's orders. Now Brenna realized Helen had been right. Tumaini hadn't been up to the long shuttle trips to and from FTL Station or the week of testing in high ecliptic orbit. Medications couldn't quite keep his pain under control. Everyone had tried to make the journey easy for him. But Tumaini resented that as much as he resented being an invalid. Brenna had given up lecturing him; making him mad was causing him more problems than the fatigue was. Soon they would be back on Mars. Maybe he would follow doctor's orders there.

"Sure, nothing to it," Adele was saying. She chuckled like a villainous ident forger in some corny vid drama. "We could just borrow the ship for a few days and run her out to an old hijackers' hangar at, oh, about five A.U."

"Yeah!" Joe Habich chimed in. "What's that one near Hector . . . ?"

Obregón, riding co-pilot, heard his name and looked around, staring at the junior pilots. Joe made a derisive noise. "The asteroid Hector, not you, you cretin!" The older man's face darkened with anger, but he didn't say anything.

Tumaini supplied the answer to Joe's question. "Eighty-five Ores. That's the abandoned hijackers' hide-out you're thinking of. The Fleet cleaned it out in '73."

Shoje laughed and zoomed his hands through the air. "Eighty-five Ores. Right! Perfect. I remember we stopped by there on a rescue run when I was with SE Trans Co, right after the Fleet shut it down. There's plenty of privacy and a big hangar. Might even be some life-support systems left working inside the rock. You could peel the Vahnaj ship down to the alien's FTL drive . . ."

"Yeah!" Habich said again. He winked at his comrades. "Quol-Bez wouldn't mind lending her to us for a little bit. Besides, Sao can console him."

The others made some lewd cracks about that suggestion. Brenna grew angry at the liberties they were taking. It was one thing to dream about "borrowing" the Vahnaj ship and picking her brains—*every* FTL pilot did *that;* but when the younger pilots got into personalities, that was out of bounds. In these past months, since Morgan's accident, Brenna had come to know Sao fairly well. She was about to speak up on the translator's behalf and tell the mouthy hotshots to cut it out, but they were already rushing ahead with the rest of their scenario. "Get every-

266

thing we need to know," Adele said, "and put her right back in her parking orbit; nobody would ever spot the difference."

"Except Space Fleet," Tumaini reminded them, looking amused. "There's a small matter of a well-armed crack division making sure no one can get *to* the Vahnaj ship in the first place. Sort of plays hell with your hijack operation."

The other three were floating in the air, relaxing in a roughly spherical configuration near Tumaini's couch. They scowled like chastened adolescents, and Brenna almost laughed at how petulant they looked. "Maybe," Joe Habich said, "there's some way to bribe them . . ."

That *did* make her laugh, a noisy guffaw that Tumaini echoed. The Rift Affiliation expatriate said, "Now you've really blown your circuits, Joe. You can't bribe Space Fleet. Think! You're not talking about Protectors of Earth's enforcement troops. Terran Worlds Council isn't corrupt."

"*Yet*," Shoje said cynically. "Give 'em time."

From up front, Yuri sang out, "Approaching re-entry burn. Everyone strapped in back there? Helmets in place? Individual life-support regs."

The announcement broke up the idle conversation as the pilots secured their webbing. Farther back in the shuttle, George Li and the techs and mechs had been buckled up for some time. They rarely waited until the last-minute warning, the way the pilots did.

Brenna was relieved that the interruption had shut off the nonsense talk. She had thought getting in harness and going out to FTL Station for some metallurgy testing would work the kinks out of the crew. Instead, it had just seemed to make them more restive. They had been through this before, the unmanned tests prior to the accident with Prototype II. For Yuri, Hector, and Tumaini, this was the *second* time they had had a disastrous setback and looked forward to another tedious succession of tests . . . with no guarantees that the third try at a manned test would work any better than the previous two.

They're itchy and irritable, and I'm exhausted to the bone, trying to keep the lid on everything. I don't know how much longer I can go on whipping myself. I thought the situation would get better, after we were assured of the franchise for another year. It's gotten worse.

Re-entry and landing were nominal, as expected. Yuri was the steadiest pilot, if not the flashiest, among the Breakthrough Unlimited crew. He was the only one who had been flying spacecraft as long as Brenna. Yuri's father, a shuttle pilot from Goddard Colony, had allowed his son to handle the ship, occasionally, when he was a boy.

They set down in their section of Saunder Enterprises landing strips and hangars, and the maintenance crews towed the shuttle into the underground areas. The pilots acted as sidewalk superintendents while George Li's people carefully unloaded the crates of metallurgy test pieces. The conveyors rolled the boxes on into Stress Analysis for follow-up procedures. All the while, in the back of Brenna's thoughts, time was ticking off. She was supposed to meet Derek in the Main Spaceport concourse at 1500, approximately. Two more hours to kill. She wasn't sure she would be any good with ordinary business chores, until then. But just the same, she excused herself and headed for the cubbyhole she and George Li used as a general coordination office. George was still with the Analysis crew, nursemaiding the crates. That meant there was at least a little room in the tiny office. Brenna sat down at a screen and ran up the accumulated messages Tash had set aside for her. She had barely begun when she sensed someone else nearby. Hector Obregón was leaning against the door, arms crossed on his chest, his mustaches drooping. He looked very ill at ease.

Brenna put the monitor on *hold*. "Yes? Some problem out in the hangar?"

Obregón shook his head. "No. All going well."

She wondered if she would have to pry information out of him. What was troubling Hector? Not marital problems, she hoped. Brenna wasn't sure she could deal with another bombshell like Aluna Beno's—or what it would do to Hector if Carmelita walked out. Carmelita? That timid little thing! The image of her deserting or taking *any* initiative was ridiculous.

"Hector? What's the matter?"

Abruptly, he unfolded his arms and held out his hand, offering her a disposa-fiche printout. "This . . . I think this is required. To make it legal."

Totally at a loss, Brenna took the flimsy sheet and glanced

268

at it. She felt as if he had kicked the chair out from under her. The simply stated form was Obregón's resignation from Breakthrough Unlimited. As she stared at him, he became defensive. "I'll stay for the analysis wrap-up on this test, if you wish, of course. I . . . I'll be here until Earth-style year-end, if you need me."

For a long moment, Brenna was utterly speechless. Her mind was as frozen as the readout on the monitor screen at her side. Finally, she found her voice. *"Need* you? What the hell do you . . . Hector, how could you do this? If it's the money . . ."

"No." He paused, then flushed. "Yes. Somewhat. But you can't pay me what they will. It wouldn't be fair to Yuri and Tumaini if you did."

"Who?" Brenna demanded. She wanted somebody to blame. With great difficulty, she was keeping her angry disappointment under control. The shock helped; she couldn't marshal her thoughts *or* her anger very well.

"Goddard Agri-Transshipment Corporation." Obregón avoided her eyes.

At least he wasn't quitting Breakthrough Unlimited to join Nakamura's quasi-nation or Alamshah's. If she were losing Hector Obregón to a rival corporation, that would be the ultimate disgrace. Goddard Agri was a subsidiary of Saunder Enterprises Agri-Services. Realization penetrated the small comfort Brenna took from that fact. The transshipment outfit Obregón was joining was one of Carissa Saunder's many financial investments. In effect Obregón was jumping from the Martian-based branch of Saunder Enterprises to the Earth-based one. A step backward, for a Colonist, even if he would be working out of Goddard. She didn't keep the contempt from her voice. "That's a truck driver's job, Hector. You'll really be putting your skills to work for them, won't you?"

He had been fussing with his mustaches, still avoiding her eyes. Now he looked squarely at her. His expression was a mixture of shame, defiance, and pain that Brenna could almost touch. "I have to," he said. "You don't know how it is."

Despairing, Brenna said, "If it's money, we can work something out. You know that."

Hector shook his head. "It's . . . it's not that. It's . . .

just time for me to move on. I put it off as long as I could, I swear."

Brenna's weariness sapped her, draining away the fight. What was the point? "I can't talk you out of it, can I?" She read the answer in his dark gaze. This wasn't a sudden decision for Obregón. He had been working up to it for quite a while. At least he hadn't made the break right after the accident.

She had been through *that* sort of ripping agony, though —after Prototype I was destroyed and Derek quit Breakthrough Unlimited. There had been others who had quit, these past three years. Lots of them. But losing a pilot was the worst. Technicians and med people were difficult to find, and filling vacant posts was becoming tougher and tougher. But in a sense, every pilot was essential. They couldn't have enough of them. Hector's defection wasn't as severe a blow as Derek's had been, but it was bad. She couldn't afford to lose him. But she understood. Money, yes. And fear. Security for his family. And growing doubts that Breakthrough Unlimited was ever going to fulfill its promises.

Somehow, she found the presence of mind to stand up and hold out her hand. *You're a Saunder.* Noblesse oblige. *Even when you're madder than hell at an unexpected desertion in the ranks. Be gracious to those who aren't made out of the same fiber as the Saunders and McKelveys.* "Well, good luck," Brenna said. Hector flushed still darker, then shook her hand and let go of it as if it were on fire. He opened his mouth, thought better of whatever he had meant to say, and closed it. The moment was painfully awkward. Brenna took no further steps to end it, though. That was a type of vengeance. All these years! And now he was simply walking out!

Without another word, Hector turned to go. He ran into Yuri, who was just about to enter the office. The two stared at each other at a distance of centimeters. Then Hector pushed his way past Yuri, hurrying on out into the hangar. Yuri watched him go, consternation chasing over his face. Brenna sighed. "What now?"

Yuri blinked, flicking a glance at the frozen monitor screen. "I thought perhaps you hadn't heard. It's on the vid. Chairman Hong lost the election."

Brenna had to shift mental gears. Election? Oh, yes.

Protectors of Earth. The scandal about the Earth First Party fanatics hiding in Chairman Hong's entourage and the accusations that he was letting Terran Worlds Council suck Earth's economic lifeblood away. Hiber-Ship Corporation was solidly underway, drawing staggering amounts of capital investment—and Yan Bolotin and the other board members were all Terran Worlds Council members. Breakthrough Unlimited just might do the trick, and *it* was T.W.C.-backed. The colonial fuel depots and trade agreements and ore runs—all T.W.C.-controlled. Year by year, Protectors of Earth was losing ground. And Hong had paid. Brenna shrugged, not even curious enough to ask who would be assuming the Chairmanship now. *Not* an Earth First Party secret supporter, she could be sure. Maybe whoever it was would stamp out that ridiculous dinosaur left over from the political infighting of the Forties. And long overdue! Assassinations . . . and sabotage, she added to herself, remembering. A new regime might make Earth a more hospitable port for Spacers, in the future.

"Hector quit, didn't he?" Yuri asked suddenly.

"Are you here to give me a resignation, too?" Brenna retorted bitterly. She tossed the disposa-fiche on the desk. One look at Yuri's eyes told her she had wounded him in the vitals. "Sorry. I'm . . . I've got a headache. Haven't been taking my gravity compensation medications, I guess."

A lot more than that was causing her headache, and they both knew it. Yuri's hurt at her momentary distrust vanished. He shook his head, very sympathetic. "I . . . I heard them talking to him this summer. He's the oldest. They made him a very good offer."

"They made you offers, too," Brenna said, Stuart's remark about certain guests at the party on Saunderhome coming back to her. A sad smile twisted her mouth. "But you turned them down." He didn't bother replying. There was no need. Yuri Mikhailovich Nicholaiev was a mainstay. He would never quit. They would have to shoot Breakthrough Unlimited out from under him to pull him away from the company.

A sudden commotion in the main room made them both look that way and run out into the hangar. The pilots and several techs were struggling and yelling. Stuff was scattered on the floor, being kicked. Yuri loped toward them,

271

lunging into the confusion, Brenna at his heels. As Tumaini Beno swung his hand in a roundhouse, Yuri ducked and picked the blow off on his shoulder. He grappled with the Mweran, letting punches whistle harmlessly by his head. Other people were pinning Hector Obregón. Brenna stepped on something and looked down at a mess strewn on the hangar floor. Hector's personal kit had fallen or been knocked out of his hands, and the belongings were underfoot. One of the techs was picking stuff up and throwing it back into the duffel, not being very gentle with the things.

Tumaini was hurling Mweran curses as well as punches, words that sounded like *"Nangwaya, chiumbo!"* Fortunately, only a couple of techs understood him. Hector got the general idea, but not the exact terms. All the other pilots were clustered around Tumaini, helping Yuri pin the furious African. Tumaini was starting to cough, his whole body shaking with effort. He stopped trying to get at Hector and bent over, gasping for breath. Even then he swore, switching to English. "Fucking sellout! Go haul cottonseed and rotten fish, you cretin son of a bitch . . . dog of . . ."

Hector fought those who were trying to keep him away from Tumaini. The Mexican's face was almost as dark as Tumaini's. But as Tumaini broke off, too breathless to talk, Brenna saw Obregón leash his anger. He *couldn't* hit a man in Tumaini's condition, even though he had good reason; Hector's lip was split, already swelling. Tumaini had gotten in one hard blow before the others pulled the two men apart, obviously.

The tech finished repacking Hector's kit and handed it to him. She looked as if she hated to touch the thing. Obregón grabbed it, yanking it out of her hand. He glared at them all. Behind the fury, again, Brenna saw his pain. He hadn't wanted to bail out like this. But there was no way to make this kind of break amicably, not after all they had been through together. Obregón slung the kit over his shoulder and butted aside the techs and crew members, practically running for the exit. Nobody went after him or tried to stop him. One or two of the earthier support-team members spit on the floor as Hector hurried by them, and Joe Habich made an extremely obscene gesture at his one-time fellow pilot's back.

Everyone busied himself fussing over Tumaini. That didn't lessen the noise level, but when Tumaini sat down and quit gulping for breath, it gave him something new to curse at. Those oaths, at the people trying to help him, were fond epithets. The ones he had thrown at Hector hadn't been.

There was no use carrying on office tasks. Brenna returned to the small room briefly and shut off the monitor screen. Work would have to wait. The hangar didn't settle down for over an hour. By then the headache tabs she had taken were having a slight effect. Between Hector Obregón's resignation and the news of the P.O.E. elections, Brenna was surprised *anything* was working right. She didn't bother asking how Tumaini and the others had found out that Hector was quitting. Bad news traveled fast. He might even have told his friends himself. It didn't seem to matter now. Brenna left early for the Main Spaceport concourse, not wanting to hear any more angry jabber or to answer further questions about the metallurgy tests.

On the way out of Breakthrough Unlimited, Brenna passed the PR offices. Evanow was holding a basic briefing on the just-completed materials tests at FTL Station. He was good. He succeeded in making them sound like a major accomplishment rather than a tentative step along the way to solving critical design flaws. It should have cheered Brenna to see that Breakthrough Unlimited still qualified as a media event; ComLink and TeleCom and the better-accredited newshunters in the science and transport fields were there, even though the political news from Earth was the current hot topic. But the sight only worsened her fatigue. Demands for news, and her company was producing so little these days. She took the roundabout way toward the spaceport shuttle, avoiding the reporters.

Not all the newshunters were inside the Saunder Enterprises complex, however. Charlie Dahl still didn't have entree. He was hanging around the shuttle platform and saw Brenna and her SE security escort hurrying down the ramp toward the shuttle. "Hey! Saunder!" he yelled, and others in the area, waiting for their trains, heard him and turned to look and listen. "I hear the rats are leaving the sinking ship! Obregón got a better deal elsewhere, eh? Any tips on who's going to jump off the boat next?"

"Want me to shut him up, Miss Saunder?" one of the SE guards offered.

Brenna was tempted. But she had asked for it. She had stopped Charlie Dahl, and he was grabbing his chance to get even. The TeleCom lawsuit was crawling its way through the courts right now. What purpose would it serve to add to Dahl's ammunition against her? He was already claiming she had cut off a legitimate signal during the Prototype II accident. "Ignore him," she said. "He just likes to hear himself talk."

Dahl pursued her, shouting questions all the way down the ramp. Only the shuttle's doors closing in his face rescued Brenna from the harassment.

She appreciated the brief, quiet comfort of the shuttle ride—five minutes' worth of blessed nothingness. Brenna sprawled in the seat of the private car and let her mind go blank. The guards were watching the screens, ready to jump out the door when they arrived at the Main Spaceport. Dimly, Brenna heard them muttering what they would like to do to pests like Dahl. Her aunt Carissa probably would have given them the go-ahead—warning them to be discreet about it. Mustn't cause a mess. Was her way, or Stuart's sidling, slinking-around-behind-the-scenes method, better? No. If Brenna wanted Charlie Dahl squashed, she would do it openly. Of course, that also meant he would know exactly whom to blame for his losing cushy assignments. Brenna couldn't win . . .

The Main Spaceport concourse was unusually busy. Brenna paused at the Debark platform, gazing over the milling crowd. Surely not all these people were here on spaceflight business. Then she saw the excited groups clustered around the big holo-mode news screens. The startling election results from Earth were coming in. The concourse, a hemispheric and colony cross-traffic nexus, was a handy place to congregate and gossip.

A familiar, tall, towheaded man was standing at the far side of the cavernous underground depot. Derek was waving and smiling. He ducked under the courtesy barrier dividing departing luggage loads and took a shortcut to reach Brenna sooner. A concourse employee yelled and started to order Derek to get back where he belonged.

But when he saw the lovers embracing, the baggage handler grinned and looked elsewhere, ignoring the breach of rules.

Brenna managed to catch her breath and fell into stride alongside Derek. This time they took the long way around, earning an OK sign from the baggage handler. Brenna snuggled close to Derek, an arm around his waist. Her headache was completely gone, all of a sudden.

"I missed you constantly," Derek was saying. He was heedless of where they were, nuzzling her hair. "These crowds! Crazy! All because of that election. Doesn't concern them."

"Or us," Brenna said, not wanting to talk about the home world. Goddard Agri was tied to Earth. It was responsible for luring Hector Obregón away from Breakthrough Unlimited. The shock of his betrayal had left an empty spot in her being, as if an old friend had died unexpectedly.

As they stepped up onto the outer walkway, Brenna saw Lieutenant Chionis a few meters away. The Hiber-Ship officer was holding a mini-transcriber and looking around the concourse. Apparently she was searching for Derek, probably in order to give him a message from Yan Bolotin or one of their bosses. "Captain . . . !"

Derek frowned. "What? Lilika, I told you I have a half hour free. If you don't understand that, I'll write it down for you."

"Councilman Bolotin instructed me to—"

Derek stopped her with a gesture and a glare. "You can tell *him* the same thing. I'm not property. Is that clear, Lieutenant?"

Chionis drew herself up very straight. She shot a daggery look at Brenna. Did she blame the Breakthrough Unlimited pilot for this chewing out? Obviously, she did. "Yes, Captain," Lilika replied tonelessly.

"Good! I'll report when I'm due. Not before. Come on, Bren." He led Brenna past his crewmate, heading for the cafeteria.

"If . . . if Bolotin needs you . . ." Brenna began.

"He doesn't. He'll have me full time, starting a half hour from now. I'm entitled to my own life until then. And Lilika knows damned good and well not to butt in when I'm free," Derek said, still annoyed.

275

Lilika. Looking ahead to the time when Derek Whitcomb would be Adam to her Eve, on a colony world thirteen light-years and seven decades distant from Earth. She could simply be anticipating and cutting out Derek Whitcomb's current "Eve," Brenna Saunder. After all, no sense in letting the captain get too attached to someone who would be an old woman by the time he made his planetfall near Kruger 60.

"Yeah, she *does* get out of line," Brenna said. "And her saluting is a trifle sloppy, too."

The cafeteria doors dilated silently ahead of them. Derek peered at Brenna and smiled. "Affirmative and underline. Actually, Lilika *would* salute, if the charter called for military forms like that. Let's get a booth before the late shift lets off at Earth-Mars terminal. They'll be burning with gossip, and every one of them will want a place to sit and soak up caffa."

They slid side by side into an empty place. "Not only that, but the shuttle from Earth will be arriving in about fifteen minutes," Brenna added. "More fresh gossip." He raised a fair eyebrow, tacitly asking how she knew the timetables so well. Brenna smirked. "I own SE Trans Co stock, remember? That's one of our spacecraft."

"Saunder princess." She didn't resent the nickname so much any more. Derek dialed the wall servo for cups of caffeine and some carbohydrates. The orders slid out of the delivery slot, and he sorted them out between himself and Brenna. The cups and the food then sat untouched. He took Brenna's hands, looking at her with that intense expression she knew so well. "I wasn't exaggerating. I don't have much time to spare at all."

"You never do. That's the story of our lives, nowadays." She had hoped, when he had asked her to meet him here, that this reunion would be different from the other recent ones. Now it appeared it wouldn't. When she had returned from Earth in late August, she and Derek had had almost a full week together, a lovely holiday at his place near Syrtis Major. Since then they had gone back to the ships-that-pass-in-the-night routine. What with frequent visits to see Morgan and Brenna's involvement in the new Breakthrough Unlimited program and Derek's in Hiber-Ship's fast-culminating schedule, there had been weeks at a stretch when they hadn't seen each other at all.

In training, for the moment when I know I'll never see him again, ever.

"I don't get any more leaves," Derek said softly. Startled, she searched his face. It was only October. Hiber-Ship's *New Earth Seeker* wouldn't launch until March. It was too soon for Derek to be going out of her life like this. "I've got a ferry pickup at Goddard, a relay from Earth. It's the last of the animal-breeding stock and construction supplies. A lot of volunteers are making the trip then, too, for final orientation. We'll take the long orbit out. Once we get there, in December, after the stops en route at Kirkwood and the Trojan Jovian stations, we stay there. The rest is all set, Bren."

She pulled her hands free, not wanting him to feel her trembling. He could see it, though. No way to miss it. She was so cold her teeth were chattering. Brenna picked up the cup and gulped caffeine, fighting panic.

"Have you . . . thought over what I said in September?"

She nodded. "You said a lot of things. So did I."

"You know what I'm talking about. If you'd just come out and see the ship . . ."

New Earth Seeker. Starship. A *working* starship. Photon ramjet. A sub-light-speed craft. But she could make the journey. Hiber-Ship's prototype had been out beyond Pluto and back again, in the Sixties. Cryogenic stasis had been perfected, working from Ward Saunder's patents, in the Fifties. Hiber-Ship Corporation had overcome *that* objection—a lingering fear from the Crisis of 2041, when Jael Saunder's supporters had demonstrated that the old cryogenic method used in the Antarctic Enclave didn't always work. The new one did. Revival rate, 100 percent. Ramjet *and* cryo stasis—proven. Not theories which killed people or left them hopelessly maimed or broke the spirits of once-dedicated space pilots like Hector Obregón.

The words, and Derek himself, were a siren call. Brenna knew she should run away, figuratively and literally, to escape the lure Derek was casting in her direction. But she didn't.

"I . . . I've seen all the PR literature. I was out at the ship in '72, right after you . . ." She had been about to say, "Deserted me and joined a company that's opposed to everything I believe in." Instead, Brenna said, "After you signed up with Hiber-Ship."

277

"So much has changed. The ship was just bare bones then. She's finished now, and she's beautiful, Bren. The PR vid presentations don't begin to do her justice. I want you to see her." There was an unspoken additional part of that statement. He wanted Brenna to come aboard *New Earth Seeker* and stay—with him. Derek was too wise to say that out loud, though. "I've been up to FTL Station," he reminded her. "Your turn." He was putting a lot of chips on the table in this winner-take-all game of words.

Not recently, you haven't been, Derek. You weren't at FTL Station when Morgan and Tumaini and Rue were hurt. But . . . you came back. You risked your rank and your berth on board that ship to be with me and Morgan. You love me that much.

And now . . . how much do I love you?

"It'll have to be soon, Bren," he was saying. There was a note of desperation in his voice.

No more leaves. Final stages before launch. They would start putting the volunteers in their cryogenic cubicles in a few weeks. The adventure of the century, Hiber-Ship's PR called it. Twenty-five hundred colonists in stasis. Heading out for the stars. Derek would be one of them.

Time, running out. And she had to have time to think, to decide what to do. The temptations scared her. She had always been able to resist them before. What was happening? Was it the nearness of the fatal launch date? *New Earth Seeker* had been years in the building and recruiting, just as Breakthrough Unlimited had been striving to achieve faster-than-light drive for years. But now *New Earth Seeker* was ready, and there was no end in sight for FTL yet. If she delayed, or made the wrong choice, would she be left with nothing? There would be no chasing after Derek's ship, once it had left the Solar System, and protesting that she had changed her mind and wanted to go with him after all!

"Please," Derek said, his whole heart reflected in his face, in those sky-blue eyes. "There's another ferry heading out that way in two weeks. They'd always find a seat for you."

"I can't go," Brenna whispered. Derek appeared stricken. "Not then," she added.

He pounced, taking her hands again, drawing her close. The two of them had been together since they were

278

children. All the emotions were reflexes by now, battering her shaky resolve. "When?" he insisted, pleading.

"I . . . I could make better time in a private spacecraft," Brenna said, thinking hard and fast. "Maybe . . . after the next unmanned test."

"Great! An SE ship? Governor Matsumoto would be delighted. He's fully supporting Hiber-Ship. He'd love to have a Saunder visit."

Brenna nodded weakly. It seemed like the best solution all around. A rendezvous at Jovian orbit. But she would take her own ship, not one of the "enemy's." She had to maintain some balance in this struggle. The siren was coaxing her toward the shore. A friendly shore, or rocks that would shatter her dreams and her hopes for the future? Derek's eyes searched hers, probing her soul. What was he seeing? Her motives? Her faltering independence?

"I don't know what my ETA might be. I'll have to call you. You're not keeping radio silence or anything like that, are you?"

Derek smiled and shook his head. "No, not at all. Call me, any time. I'll be waiting." He raised her hands to his lips, never breaking eye contact, devouring her with love. The buzz of voices around them seemed to fade into white noise. There were only the two of them, lovers and philosophical rivals, twin worlds, double suns, orbiting around each other, neither able to break free, bound to each other.

CHAPTER SIXTEEN

☙☙☙☙☙☙☙☙

Losing Contact

BRENNA sat in the spaceport cafeteria a long while after Derek had left to catch his flight. Lilika Chionis hadn't come to page him. He had kept watch on the time and departed, reluctantly, with five minutes to spare in order to reach Hiber-Ship's launch gate.

The doubts didn't begin immediately afterward. But they set in slowly and insidiously. Brenna toyed with her cup of caffeine and nibbled on the carbohydrates, staring at nothing. Was she so shallow that the moment Derek was out of sight she would renege on her promises? No, it wasn't exactly that. But while he was with her, his presence made her forget so many counterarguments. It had always been that way, to some degree. But until the last three years, it had never been a serious problem because they had thought so much alike, believed in the same things, dreamed of the same goal—reaching the stars. After Breakthrough Unlimited's Prototype I had been destroyed, though, after Kevin McKelvey, Derek's idol, had been killed, the situation had altered. Derek had made his decision, and for the first time he veered away from the track his childhood playmates chose to follow. His course was set. Brenna had thought *hers* was. Now . . . doubts, increasing.

How much of the doubt was due to realistic appraisal of Breakthrough Unlimited's future and how much to her love for Derek? She couldn't tell, but she would have to jump one way or the other.

"It'll have to be soon, Bren . . ."

"Soon," in space travel terms. Derek wouldn't be at Jovian orbit until December, he had said. When would the next unmanned Breakthrough Unlimited test be? She didn't know yet, for sure. A lot would depend on the data they had just brought back re the hull material. Morgan would have to look that over. All she would have to do would be to get an answer out of him, if that were possible. She wasn't so sure about *that* any more, either.

Brenna gazed out the cafeteria "window," a vid-screen view of the spaceport above the concourse. The crater floor stretched to the horizon. Every so often a ship would take off, heading for other ports on Mars or to distant worlds and colonies. The Hiber-Ship ferry for Goddard Colony was one of those launching up into Mars' dark sky. Brenna watched the ship until the vid cameras couldn't hold it in their lenses any longer. Then she sighed and touched the com at the side of the booth. "Saunder Enterprises Central, please." For a change, there was a human, not a computer, at the other end of the line. Brenna laid her hand against the screen's surface, registering her palm print as proof that she really was the person the dispatcher at the other end of the call was seeing. The computers would verify her voice as further identification. "I'd like a sub-surface car ready at the cafeteria gate in five minutes, please."

"It'll be ready, Miss Saunder."

SE Security had checked the car over and was on board to ride shotgun when she arrived. Brenna nodded to the guards, then sat back in the plush couch. The private car could carry thirty passengers, but usually the Saunders used it merely for handy transportation around the planet. If Brenna hadn't been in such a hurry, she might have used a skimmer. However, the weather report wasn't favorable, so that plan probably would have been aborted. "Saunder Estates," she said to the program. The monitor blinked and fed the command into the mass driver car's systems. In seconds, the train left the spaceport, accelerating eastward. The screen showed Brenna that she was passing public trains rapidly, overtaking the Pavonis City express and other transports using the tunnels. Unburdened by excess weight or extra passengers, the small car made the trip from Amazonis Planitia in a half hour. Brenna hadn't asked for flank speed, or the vehicle could have shaved the time by five or ten minutes.

Along the way, she had glanced at some of her correspondence. One look told her that none of this stuff was likely to determine the future course of her life or anyone else's. Brenna was quite suddenly bored and annoyed with the endless demands. She thought of her father, saying he was *really* going to retire. Would she be like that? When had the fun gone out of being a corporation co-president? Or was this just a bad mood that would disappear by tomorrow? Usually, she could gauge her own biorhythms and predict. This time she couldn't. Tomorrow was a blank. She couldn't see beyond now.

The SE guards had been willing to chat, to pass the time during the journey. But they sensed Brenna's don't-touch-me frame of mind and kept their distance.

The car eased to a stop at the Saunder Estates:Mars terminal, and Brenna got out and rode the elevator to the Estates level. She stopped at her own residence first to shower and change. There had been no need to bring her travel kit with her. She kept plenty of spare clothes

281

here. Saunder Enterprises would pick up the kit at the hangars later and clean and recycle the work jumpers Brenna had brought back with her from a week's stay at FTL Station. As soon as she had grabbed something to eat, Brenna went out on the bridge and crossed over to her parents' estate. The intraestate monitor said Dian was at home; her father was in Pavonis City right now and wouldn't be back till late tonight.

She found Dian in the mansion's office, going over some Wyoma Lee Foix Medical Foundation reports. Brenna saw herself in her mother's bored but conscientious run-throughs of financial statements and correspondence. When Dian looked up, it was plain she would appreciate a recess. "Welcome home," Dian said cheerfully. She studied Brenna closely. "You look wrung out."

"Thanks, and I just tidied up, too," Brenna retorted, smiling, and sat down.

"Rough trip?"

"No. That was smooth." Brenna shrugged. "The spaceport's pretty excited about the election news."

"Huh! Coulda seen that one comin'," Dian said with a sniff. "Hong got what he deserved. What's funny is: Aycock lost, *too*. Carissa was backin' *him*. Guess she's getting too cheap with her bribes these days. Too used to payin' off in the old credit exchange."

Brenna propped her arm on one knee, cocking her head and resting it on her hand, gazing soberly at Dian. "Are things really that bad on Earth? I admit it wears thin fast, whenever I go there for a visit, but . . ."

"And what do you see?" Dian asked sharply. "A view from an SE flier or shuttle? Saunderhome? Terran Worlds Council's fancy new building on the Pacific Coast? One of the Saunder Enterprises enclaves in Switzerland or the Philippines? You lead an insulated life, girl. *That's* not Earth." Ugly memories were reflected in the older woman's dark eyes. Legends of the Chaos and the Death Years and the Crisis of 2041. Brenna sighed, anticipating a lecture. "Yeah, it's bad there. Bad enough even *you* almost got your tail feathers singed off, I hear."

Startled, Brenna jerked upright, staring. "Ames. He told you."

Dian pursed her lips, her manner scornful. "He'd damned

282

well better. He owes your father and me. We owe him, too. But he owes more."

"I told him not to . . ."

Dian poked a small dark finger at her daughter, stabbing the air. "He didn't tell your father, and neither will I. Got that straight? But *I* want to know when something like that happens."

"Why?" Brenna asked belligerently. "I'm a big girl now. I don't need you holding my hand and leading me over to the air lock. If that's what you want of me, I think you and Dad *had* better start that second family."

She had caught her mother off guard. Dian leaned back, frowning. "Don't get sassy. Yes, we've talked about it. I think your father's dead-on serious. I'm getting so I like the idea. He said you wouldn't object . . ."

Brenna was about to say she didn't know they had considered her wishes in the matter, but thought better of it. "Dad explained his feelings. I understand." That wasn't a lie, though it wasn't exactly the truth. It served to avoid a confrontation with her inner feelings.

"Get back to the main issue," Dian said abruptly. "You wanted to know why Ames told me. Because *we'd* better know about those things. He gave me a message to relay to you—said to quit worrying about it. He took care of it. Permanently." A shiver chased down Brenna's spine. The statement had an ominous ring to it, like "assassination." Dian was nodding. "You don't ask any deeper than that. But we have to know where we stand. And SE Security should have been notified immediately. We can work *with* Space Fleet. Where are your brains? This isn't a kid's game. You're old enough to know better. When I was your age . . ." Dian caught herself in the middle of that cliché, stopped, and a sheepish smile curved her mouth.

Brenna didn't return the smile. "When you were my age, you'd lived through the Death Years and the Chaos, escaped from the United Ghetto States, had cracked the Vahnaj language code, and helped stop my grandmother from destroying Earth and Goddard. That's a hell of a lot to live up to. Not everyone enjoyed your hair-raising form of education. I muddle along with what I've got, and I make mistakes. I'll probably make more of them. But I'll make them on my own, if you don't mind."

She stood up and started out of the room, hearing Dian's footsteps behind her. But Dian made no attempt to stop her. She followed Brenna out into the corridor and through the domed greenhouse. By the time Brenna reached the outer gate, her temper had cooled. She turned and looked at her mother warily. Dian's guard was up. She glared at Brenna. "It's tough being a legend. Is that what you're thinking? Huh! I know all about that, girl. You'd better get used to it. You're old enough, and then some. Either you can let those legends sour you and turn you hateful, or you can make your *own* legends." In the stubborn set of the older woman's face, Brenna saw a series of dark images receding through the years.

Children of legends. Dian's grandmother was a legend. Brenna's father walked in the shadow of Ward Saunder and the notorious Jael. Morgan had been expected to follow in Kevin McKelvey's footsteps, become governor of a space station, a leader. Morgan knew how disappointed his father had been when he chose not to go into Space Fleet. Even Stuart was haunted by a legend—his father, Patrick Saunder, the golden-voiced orator, the savior of Earth.

Dian was right. It irked Brenna to admit that. She was feeling cornered and uncomfortable when, abruptly, Dian hugged her. Brenna was surprised, then responded to the embrace. Slim, strong arms closed about her tightly for a moment. When Dian let go, Brenna saw that her mother looked upset. Dian covered whatever was disturbing her with tough words. "Yeah, you go do that. Make your own legends. But," and Dian held up an admonishing finger, "you watch your step while you're about it. Hear? Don't try to do it all alone."

She remained by the greenhouse gate until Brenna had crossed the bridge to Morgan's estate. Brenna turned and waved, and after a noticeable hesitation Dian went back inside the mansion.

Brenna stopped to chat with the med aide at the monitoring station. Helen wasn't at the Estates this evening, but by now Brenna was on a first-name basis with most of Dr. Ives's staffers. She wondered if their loyalty would hold up any better than Hector's. No, that was unfair. Hector had stayed quite a while, through several kinds of hell. But his desertion hurt, badly.

"He's doing okay right now, Miss Saunder."

Okay. That handy euphemism. What Dr. Ives and her medics meant by "okay" was, "no crises; patient is holding his own as well as can be expected." As the summer months had ended and September and October had passed, Brenna had begun to realize—as Helen and the surgeons must have known right after the disaster—that Morgan would never recover. He was under an indeterminate sentence. A plateau was satisfactory, from the doctors' point of view; it meant he wasn't losing ground. Brenna sensed that, eventually, Morgan *would* lose ground.

"Doing okay," considering he had been broken into pieces and seared and put back together again with spare parts.

Brenna continued on into the visitors' alcove, where she found Ambassador Quol-Bez. She wasn't surprised. He was as much or more of a "regular" here as the medic team was.

Quol-Bez stood with his skinny arms behind his back, hands clasped. His broad, gray face was screwed up in concentration. On the other side of the transparent wall, Morgan had moved his chair-bed to within a meter of the pli-material, but he wasn't touching it. He wasn't looking at Quol-Bez, either. He was staring at an array on his monitor screen. Brenna recognized the readout: the latest test figures on the hull material. George Li and Yuri must be sending them through from Amazonis Spaceport. Didn't Morgan ever stop studying Breakthrough Unlimited's data? Apparently not. After all, there wasn't much else for him to do.

Brenna felt like an intruder. Neither the Vahnaj Ambassador nor Morgan took any notice of her. Brenna got the impression the two of them had been occupying the same positions for hours. Morgan wouldn't strain his frail body by merely lying in the chair-bed and gazing at the figures on the monitor. His concentration had always been good. Now it was awesome, since sensory deprivation cut off his contact with the outside world. What was Quol-Bez getting out of his own extended silence? Did his being here qualify as a "visit" to the invalid? This wasn't the first time Brenna had come in on this sort of scene. Quol-Bez would spend hours here, standing and looking at Morgan and saying nothing.

The continued stillness, excluding her, stirred resentment. Finally Brenna cleared her throat to announce her presence. Quol-Bez's snaky neck craned, and he peered around at her in surprise. "Brenna! I did not hear you. My apologies for my rude-ness." The Vahnaj turned back toward the pli-wall. "Morgan, Brenna is here with us."

Morgan kept on staring at the vid display until Brenna grew worried. "Perhaps I'd better check with the attendants . . ."

Quol-Bez's three-fingered hand fell on her shoulder lightly. "No, that is not needed. He is aware of your presence."

"Is he?"

Quol-Bez smiled. Not his pointy-toothed grin. This was a sad, closed-lips smile, somehow distant. Goose flesh prickled on Brenna's nape and arms. A discussion, ages ago, sprang up in her mind—she and Derek and Morgan talking about an occasional atavistic reaction, like shivers and goose flesh, caused by two beings from radically different evolutionary paths coming into contact. Quol-Bez sometimes felt shivery when he was around *humans*, too. Wasn't it all a matter of angle and point of view? Who was the alien? The other being, of course—it was whoever you *weren't*.

As if he had read the thoughts in her mind, Morgan slowly moved his head on the stera-gel pillows. Those inhuman eyes looked through her, at things Brenna couldn't see. There was less of Morgan in that gaze, each time she saw him. Brenna tried to ignore the unnerving stare. She nodded her head in greeting, exaggerating the motion so that Morgan's computerized eyes would detect the movement. "Been reading the data, I see. The hull material collapsed right where you said it did. Pins down one more item on the probable cause. Of course, it also gives us another very expensive pile of junk—crates full of it, stacked up in the hangar."

One of those awful stillnesses followed. Brenna fidgeted, watching Quol-Bez sidelong. He didn't seem bothered by the lack of a response from Morgan. That faint smile still played around his mouth.

After what seemed like an interminable wait, Morgan responded. "I've ordered three more test frames and a full-scale Prototype. They'll deliver the frames to FTL Station in January, the Prototype in April."

Money. A lot of it. Time. A lot of that, too, and that was even more precious. Terran Worlds Council's deadline was an angry red calendar date in Brenna's mind's eye. So was Derek's March departure date aboard Hiber-Ship's *New Earth Seeker*.

"I'm paying," Morgan said. Talking was an obvious strain. His voice wasn't as close to normal-sounding as it had been. He was losing ground there. And breathing was an effort. The extra breath required for speaking taxed him visibly. Brenna felt guilty that she had said so much earlier. Morgan behaved as if he were obligated to answer her unspoken questions about the funding. It didn't take telepathy to guess that Breakthrough Unlimited was hanging on by its fingertips, financially!

"That's not important," Brenna said and meant it. She had lost sight of the goal. FTL at any price.

And what a price Morgan had paid!

A year ago, Morgan would have had a cute comeback: "Sure. What do we care? It's only money. So sell a few more asteroid ore cargoes. What do you think you're my partner for? Just to look beautiful?"

Now he said nothing. Another aching silence dominated both rooms. Brenna could hear the hyperbaric chamber's machinery operating beneath the floor. The mannequin form that was Morgan lay in the chair. When Brenna thought he had lost interest in seeing or talking to her, his chest rose and fell rapidly several times. "The oscillator redesign is underway," he finally said. "I hired Tobiyah's firm to do it for us."

Brenna exclaimed, "A redesign? But . . . that's a major update! Why didn't you tell me? How long will it take?"

This time he answered her almost at once. "Till April." If he had been able to show facial expression, he would probably have grinned and then reminded her that he had already told her the Prototype wouldn't be delivered until April. The new oscillator, a new test ship. He sucked in air for a few moments, then added, "The mini-models will be ready in January, for the unmanned tests. I didn't consult you because you were busy. We have to get it ordered now."

April. Derek would be in cryogenic stasis by April. On his way to the stars.

"It'll work," Morgan said simply. "I've got the data matching now." He didn't say anything else. He rolled his head back, looking at the screen once more, a man-sized doll, barely capable of movement. Only his brain still worked the way it used to. Better, perhaps.

Quol-Bez was almost as motionless as Morgan, standing there in one place for hours. A man dependent on machines for his every breath and for his eyesight and voice and movements, and an alien being who came from an entirely different evolution and culture than *Homo sapiens*. But they seemed to be on each other's wavelength, and no one else had a receiver. Everyone else—including Brenna—was out in the cold.

Brenna was Morgan's arms and legs. Manage the test runs. Take a trip out to FTL Station. Take a trip to Earth and stroke-the-sycophants and kowtow to Terran Worlds Council. Be the front-office partner, cope with the supply problems and scut work, accept resignations tendered. She was like Morgan's servo mechanisms, a workhorse, not a partner who could sit down and talk to him as she used to. Even a few months ago, they had had more conversation than *this!*

Those strange eyes looked toward her, impaling her. Lifeless and artificial eyes, but controlled by a keen, passionate intelligence. He didn't speak. But she understood. *"No, you're not a robot. You're my cousin. You're here. That counts, Brenna. You still come to see me, when most of my old friends don't."* Involuntarily, Brenna took a step back, frightened by the intensity of that stare.

Had she been angry at the silent rapport between Morgan and Quol-Bez? Or speculating about telepathy? Well, what if it were true? Wouldn't that be wonderful for Morgan? What did he have in the way of friendship now? Not very damned much at all. Brenna and her parents. Loving people, separated from him by immeasurable difficulties in communication. The family tried to keep operating on the old basis. Baby-sitting Morgan, trading off schedules so that one of its members was always at the residence. Yet they couldn't really touch him or give him what he needed and wanted. Brenna glanced at Quol-Bez again, fascinated, envious, even a bit jealous.

288

Her jaw ached. She had been gritting her teeth, hating herself for her selfishness. "Morgan? It's okay. About the oscillator."

He didn't move his head, but his eyes were on her. She watched him marshaling his strength, breathing heavily. "It'll work. Don't worry. I won't let anyone else be killed." A pause. An unspoken addition: *And no one else will be condemned to a living hell such as I'm in.* His words were raspy with the effort of talking. "I said I'd put the pieces back together and make it work. I will. When the new oscillator's ready, will the pilot be ready? FTL doesn't forgive mistakes. You have to make up your mind, to go with it or not."

Implications hammered at her. Somehow, he knew about her doubts. As long as her feelings were torn, she would be risking herself and the ship. Morgan realized Brenna would demand the right to pilot the next Prototype. He was setting her an ultimatum. He had the key. And he was a partner with full voting rights. He could cancel out her vote, legally. Besides, the other pilots idolized him, trusted the conclusions Morgan was reaching on his data studies. Brenna wouldn't be able to go against them *and* Morgan.

He was silent again. Brenna sensed the rapport between him and Quol-Bez. It all but shimmered in the air, penetrating the pli-wall. Human and alien. Sharing something no one else could. "Rest," Quol-Bez said. Brenna was startled at hearing him speak. The Vahnaj swiveled his head and looked at her kindly. "You know he speaks harshly out of stress. You must not think he does not love."

"Of course," Brenna replied uneasily. "I understand how it is . . ."

The tall figure swayed. Quol-Bez's long tunic and cape rustled. "You Saunder-kin *do* under-stand. You com-mun-i-cate. This is the . . . your craft. What is the word? Ah! Your com-pan-y. Breakthrough. Todd has told me of his male parent and the de-vices he created. In-ven-tions. Ah! These advanced your species. My friend Todd em-ploys these de-vices. So do you and Saunder-kin Dian and Stu-art and Ca-rissa. And Morgan. This is all com-mun-i-ca-tion. Touch-ing."

Sunset was falling across Valles Marineris, outside Morgan's room. The dying fire in the sky reached past the dim lighting in the isolation chamber and limned Quol-Bez's tall form. The effect made Brenna blink, seeing the Vahnaj as a supernatural creature.

Communication. Touching. That was what faster-than-light travel would mean, too. Interstellar touching between species, touching on a mass scale. Hundreds, then thousands, of humans would travel to the stars. They would meet thousands of Vahnaj and other beings. Quol-Bez wouldn't be an intriguing oddity among humans any more.

If only Quol-Bez had let humans examine his FTL-equipped Vahnaj ship before the accidents.

I cannot give the ship to you. And you cannot take it. Do not risk such a thing. It would end in terrible catastrophe.

Had she imagined that warning? Or had Quol-Bez been reading her mind and putting his thoughts into her brain without speech? And just what did the warning mean? Morgan had hinted at the same thing. A booby trap on board the Vahnaj ship? The Vahnaj might not think of a protective device in such crude terms. But that *could* be the situation. Morgan had pointed out the logic to her, when he was still indulging in what passed for normal conversation.

"Morgan has left de-ci-sions to you, Brenna," Quol-Bez said suddenly. "You do not see this, but it is so. He cannot reach."

"He reaches you." Brenna hadn't meant that to sound accusing, but it did. "And you reach him."

Quol-Bez made no reply. He bowed politely and turned back toward the transparent wall. For a moment he was silhouetted by the sunset. Then the light winked behind a distant peak and the effect diminished.

Brenna waited for a while to see if either of them would say anything further to her. They didn't. She gave up and stalked out past the monitor station, moving on down the corridor and out into Morgan's living quarters. She stood in the darkened main room, in the fading sunset, clasping her arms tightly about herself, shuddering. Without realizing she was doing so, she whispered, "Damn, damn, damn . . ."

"It is deep pain, is it not?" A voice came from the shadows. Brenna jumped and turned toward the hidden figure. Chin Jui-Sao touched a light relay, revealing herself. The glow from the nearby panel was muted, not competing with the red fire outside the balcony window. Sao was sitting in a corner, her feet curled up beneath her. "I did not mean to intrude on your privacy," she said. "It is apparent you are disturbed. If you would wish to be alone . . ."

Brenna waved her hand tiredly. "It doesn't matter. I don't care, not about anything. Not right now." She walked toward Sao and perched on the edge of a divan, facing the Chinese woman. For the first time, Brenna realized Sao had been crying. Her cheeks were still wet. "What's happening to Morgan?" Brenna was talking to herself as much as to Sao. "I'm losing him, and I don't know how to stop it. How can you lose someone you've known all your life? We were babies together, kids together."

She didn't expect an answer, but she got one, of sorts. "It is no less painful when you lose someone you have known only months—when you comprehend you never had that person at all." Anger was in Sao's voice.

Brenna dragged herself out of her depression, regarding the smaller woman thoughtfully. She leaned forward, putting an arm around Sao. Very gently, Brenna said, "You love him, don't you? Morgan thought you did."

"I love Morgan, too. But . . . yes, I love . . . Quol-Bez." Sao pronounced the name timidly, as if fearful of being chastised for such forwardness. "He does not love me . . . *cannot* love me . . . not as I would wish."

Brenna eased herself down beside Sao, cradling the translator's head on her shoulder, wanting to comfort them both. "To love one's . . . employer . . . is not good form," Sao said, sniffling. "I was trained not to . . . I had not wanted to show the Ambassador my . . . my feelings."

"It happens," Brenna replied with a rueful smile. "And sometimes you simply can't shut those feelings off, no matter how hard you try. I know that too damned well. It's hopeless, isn't it? You can't have what you want—and you can't let go. You hang on, and you torture yourself, and you torture the one you love, too. Spirit of Humanity knows why we humans do these things to ourselves!"

Sao hid her face in her hands, rocking back and forth. "It is worse! You do not know! His . . . his superiors . . . they entered his being, before . . . before he left Vahnaj. His mental capacities and intelligence are intact, but he

291

must not . . . cannot . . . certain vital emotional and glandular functions . . ."

Aghast, Brenna demanded, "Are you saying they gelded him, like some sort of animal?" Was *that* the explanation for the rapport between Quol-Bez and Morgan? Morgan's brutal unmanning was due to the horrible burns he had suffered. But if Quol-Bez had been robbed by his own kind . . . !

"No, no! Not that! I do . . . I do not think," Sao replied, raising her head. Her expression was desolate. She lowered her already-soft voice to near-inaudibility. "We touch. We we have . . . made love. But it is . . . not complete. There is always an emptiness. Always."

Brenna wasn't sure what to say. "Maybe it has to do with his alienness, Sao. We're different species, after all. That has to be a very big . . . uh . . . problem." Prurient curiosity stirred. Brenna was vaguely ashamed of that human weakness. But she wasn't the first to wonder about human-Vahnaj sex. Sensationalist newshunters had gathered large audiences by just such extrapolations, before Terran Worlds Council's diplomatic watchdogs had clamped the lid on those gross programs. From then on, speculation remained private, gossiped about, but not a subject for the media to discuss. Sao had personal knowledge, however. Did Sao's bosses at T.W.C. know? They must. Perhaps they discreetly looked the other way, believing it best not to interfere with the Ambassador's intimate relationships. He was not, after all, theirs to command. Terran Worlds Council was eager to stay on good terms with the Vahnaj *and* their Ambassador. There could be human empathy in their attitude as well. Humans could imagine themselves the sole member of their species, in an alien culture. Who would blame a being for taking the solace of a sex partner in such a situation, even if the bedmate was of a different species? They might wink and nudge one another—and keep their mouths shut as a diplomatic courtesy to Quol-Bez.

Chin Jui-Sao was living the fantasy of thousands of human women who had been fascinated by Quol-Bez since he first arrived in the Solar System. Yet Sao was miserably unhappy. For her, the sexual liaison was a tragedy, not a joy. She was suffering far beyond the ordinary disappointments of an inept lover. From her account, there was no physical mismatch at all. The failure was something beyond bodies and orgasms, an indefinable joining of spirit that Sao wanted but wasn't going to get.

Rapport. Missing. Not there.

Sao gripped Brenna's arm. "Do you not see? They are the same, Quol-Bez and Morgan. They cannot touch other beings. Not *real* touching. And . . . and even if Quol-Bez returns to his own people, he will now forever be apart from them. What they took is . . . is irreplaceable."

Brenna tried to smother her outrage. The Vahnaj had altered Quol-Bez's ability to relate, not only to humans, but to his own species as well! "Yes, I've seen the rapport between Quol-Bez and Morgan," she said. "It's been going on for weeks now."

Sao nodded. "It has its roots in Morgan's injuries."

Isolation. Sensory deprivation. Whatever the Vahnaj had done to Quol-Bez to make him "immune" to emotional involvements with humans—and with other Vahnaj—wasn't working the way it must have been meant to. Their surgery, or telepathic castration, or whatever it was, was being canceled out because of what had happened to Morgan. Brenna imagined an alien organ or a portion of a Vahnaj brain that was vital to communication among the Vahnaj, linking them to other creatures of like emotions. The Vahnaj had cut it away from Quol-Bez, though.

That made a cruel kind of diplomatic sense. The Vahnaj were still feeling their way into this interstellar crossspecies relationship. For all they had known when they assigned Quol-Bez to an embassy in the Solar System, the humans might take him prisoner and try to brainwash or torture him to extract secrets the Vahnaj didn't want revealed. As Morgan had once said, the Vahnaj surely weren't fools. They had anticipated that possible threat and taken steps to prevent it, "altering" their Ambassador. Not castration, Sao insisted. No, it wouldn't be anything so crude or so easily understood by the human mind. Quol-Bez was evidently a functional male, and cross-species problems didn't interfere with *that* sort of contact. Sex was on a strictly physical level, nothing more, to Sao's grief.

Yet something else had happened, quite apart from a sexual affair. The Vahnaj *hadn't* anticipated that Quol-Bez would become good friends with Todd Saunder and his "kin-family," especially Todd's severely injured nephew.

They couldn't have predicted the devastating accident and the strange new energies to which Morgan had been subjected. Had those wounds opened avenues in his brain that were normally closed to the rest of mankind? Quol-Bez had hinted at that. A door now open, and a brain now able to accept Quol-Bez's touch? Intimate *emotional* contact—the very thing Quol-Bez's superiors had sought to prevent—and despite the "surgery," Quol-Bez had retained enough ability to make that contact.

Telepathy? Two-way telepathy, perhaps?

The Vahnaj FTL ship was off-limits to them. Probably booby-trapped. But maybe there was another way to plumb its secrets. Had Morgan found that way?

Mind to mind. A human mind, trapped in a crippled body, but determined to solve the riddle of faster-than-light travel. A Vahnaj mind, forbidden to reveal how his species had developed that technology. Forbidden to reveal it in words, by speech. But what if he—unintentionally—revealed it during the linkup of human and Vahnaj minds?

Guesswork. All of it. Sheer wishful thinking and speculation.

But if it were *true* . . .

Morgan was absolutely sure he had figured out the flaw in the Prototype. He just might have, all on his own. A brilliant mind, a crack space pilot, and no more outside distractions. Total concentration. And maybe the problem-solving included a little help from a Vahnaj friend. That exciting premise might be the one good thing that would come out of so much pain.

Sao got to her feet, pacing restlessly. Brenna followed the Chinese woman across the room and out onto the enclosed balcony. They stood gazing out over the rim of Valles Marineris and into the evening sky. Sao seemed to be making her peace with herself, drying her tears, withdrawing inside a stoic shell.

The stars were shining, and the Martian moons reflected a small amount of light. An afterglow lingered from the sunset, an eerie light shrinking toward the horizon. In that pale radiance, Brenna saw Mars' rugged mountains and the steep walls of the rift. Her world. It was one among billions of inhabitable worlds, worlds near enough to Earth's norms for *Homo sapiens* to call them home.

The stars—a sky full of jewels, and promise. Sao was looking at the stars, too. The men she and Brenna loved came from the stars, or wanted to go to the stars. Nothing could help Sao's pain. Even on Vahnaj, she and Quol-Bez would never share that special closeness she desired.

And what was out there, among the stars, for Brenna Saunder? Could she hope for happiness? Morgan had told her to choose. Choose the right road. Hiber-Ship? Breakthrough Unlimited? Forget the stars for years. Join Derek and enter a stasis cubicle and begin a deathlike sleep on the way to a distant world. Or trust Morgan. Believe that the flaw was found, would be corrected. That *this* time the faster-than-light ship would pierce the barrier and hold the universe captive.

And if she did that, Derek would go on his slow, steady way to the stars without her. Without Derek, was there any happiness—out there, here on Mars, or anywhere else?

CHAPTER SEVENTEEN

⊗⊗⊗⊗⊗⊗⊗⊗

New Earth Seeker

THE two Chase ships eased into FTL Station's dock. Tethers and fueling linkups attached. The storage-bay air locks opened, and tech crews began removing the orbiting drones the pilots had retrieved from the test-run area. The pilots clambered out, swimming on their safety lines. Maintenance had their mini-skidders ready, and the four returning pilots rode them over to the Station.

The welcome was subdued, compared with those Brenna had known in the past. She couldn't blame the support crew and media pool reporters like Ife Enegu for being wary. After all, they had waited out plenty of unmanned tests over the years in which Breakthrough Unlimited had been operating. This one might be a bit different, technically, but the earlier excitement had worn off, blunted by too many disappointments. Nevertheless, as the pilots came out of Debriefing with George Li, Enegu and the other ComLink and TeleCom people asked the right questions, trying to maintain the old enthusiasm. "The boards said it was a nominal faster-than-light hop," Ife Enegu called to Brenna. "That means it exceeded the barrier?"

Brenna nodded, rather wishing she could turn this part of the routine over to George. She had a timetable the media didn't know about. Brenna wondered, a bit anxiously, if the newshunters would notice a certain reserve in her co-workers. They were aware of her plans, though the details weren't public knowledge.

"Yes, the unmanned test vehicle made a perfect hop to approximately five A.U.—that is, in popular terms, 'beyond' the asteroids. And she returned safely, right on programmed schedule, all data intact."

Noyes of TeleCom—who had taken advantage of Charlie Dahl's *persona non grata* status to move ahead with his company—couldn't resist a pointed reminder: "This isn't a full-sized faster-than-light spacecraft, though, is it?"

Joe Habich and Yuri and the other pilots scowled at him for a split second before resuming their nonchalant, superpilot poses. Brenna shook her head. "No, it's a model. This was a test of the new oscillator system Morgan Saunder McKelvey has worked out in cooperation with Tobiyah High-Tech Engineering . . ."

The media personnel made note of her easy, confident stance, impressed. Brenna hoped they wouldn't read beneath the I'm-in-charge manner and see how tired she was and how much she shared the TeleCom reporter's skepticism. She couldn't seem to recapture that cutting edge. Worse, over the past weeks, under the barrage of steady com calls from Derek, she had begun to wonder if she really *wanted* to. That kind of uncertainty was dangerous, to the people she cared about as well as to herself. She had caught the surreptitious glances aimed her way, through the waning months of '75. They were worried, questioning glances, but no one confronted her. What was unspoken could be canceled out, as if it had never been.

The press conference wound down. George Li tied the loose ends, explaining technical terms to the laymen. His staffers stroked the network personnel who had made the long trip up here for the test. They hadn't seen much from their booths in FTL Station—just the data and remote scans from the test-run area, and then a miniature version of a Prototype FTL ship disappearing from view. Three minutes later, the small vehicle had arrived at her destination at five astronomical units out from the Sun. After a suitable pause to dispatch her drones, take her own picture and pulse, the test vehicle had returned. Bingo. Nothing to it. There she wasn't; there she was. Test completed. Faster-than-light travel achieved, no sweat. *Unmanned* FTL, though. Little wonder the reporters and crew weren't as excited as they could have been. This was old stuff. Here we go again, ho-hum.

Yet it *had* worked. Morgan had predicted strengthening the hull material and redesigning the oscillator to exceed resonance point would cure the fatal problems with Prototype II. It seemed he was right.

But they had thought that with the previous unmanned test flights, prior to Prototype II's blowup last April, and look what had happened!

April 2075 to January 2076. And it would be April again before a full-sized oscillator and a beefed-up, crew-capable test vehicle would be ready. Months, spinning away. Morgan's birthday had come and gone, and Brenna would turn a year older by the end of January. And was she really any closer to reaching the dream than she had been?

"What's next on the agenda?" Ife Enegu asked. She had privileges, being an SE reporter, that the rival networkers didn't. She hung around the pilots' ready room after the press conference had broken up, gathering further details for her story.

"Well," Adele Zyto said, "Shoje and Joe and I will be going out to the completed hop point and opening up the station there. It's been closed since . . ." Her voice trailed off. Closed since Prototype II's disaster. Adele cleared her throat. "We have to check out the instruments and get her ready for the next stage, which is a manned spacecraft test. It's standard procedure to have a rescue Chase ship and emergency medical personnel standing by at the point the manned vehicle will emerge from, when Prototype III makes the FTL jump . . ." Standing by, in case of another tragedy. Breakthrough Unlimited hadn't used the station, saving money. But now . . .

Brenna left the room, not wanting to put off questions

297

if Enegu was indiscreet enough to ask them. George Li would say the right things, make reasonable explanations. Brenna headed for her cabin. Adele's gear was packed and ready for loading on the Chase craft the young woman would fly out past the main asteroid orbits. Brenna's gear, too, was packed. She would be taking a different Chase craft, for her own use, and setting a slightly different vector out from the Sun. Brenna cleared her message screen, sending through the last by-the-rules notes awaiting her okay. Then she slung the kit over her arm and turned toward the corridor.

Yuri Nicholaiev blocked the way. "I have to talk to you," he said, closing the door, cutting them off from the constant buzz of activity throughout the Station.

His expression alarmed Brenna. The worst possibilities sprang into her mind. "What is it? Did Helen call? Is Morgan . . . ?"

"No, no, nothing of that sort," Yuri said quickly, pained that she had taken fright.

"Then . . . is something wrong in Control? George . . ."

"Would you care?" The instant Yuri had said that, he looked as if he wished it back. For a moment, he held a hand over his mouth. He turned pale. "I . . . I know you would care if anything happened to a team member. I am sorry I spoke so thoughtlessly. I did not mean to sound . . . angry. But sometimes it is confusing, when I remember what you intend to do."

Brenna stared at him. She had the strange impression she was seeing Yuri for the first time, though she had known him for years. Subconsciously, she must have been aware of this hidden part of his personality, the intensity now revealed in his strong face. She had pretended it didn't exist. And he had encouraged that attitude in others, including Brenna.

"Yuri, I cleared this leave with George, and with Morgan . . ."

"What did Morgan say?" Yuri pressed her, hopefully. What was he hoping for? An ally, in Morgan? Against Brenna's plans?

Brenna didn't want to recall that conversation, a week ago. It had been as awkward and one-sided as all conversations with Morgan were now. Also, Quol-Bez had been at Saunder Estates, further hampering any effective give-and-take between Brenna and her cousin. When Brenna had stated what she was going to do after the unmanned vehicle test was over, Morgan had looked through her, reading her as if she were a monitor screen. Brenna dredged Morgan's terse comment out of her memory and repeated it to Yuri. "He said I had to live my own life. I am. My leave time is my own."

"Is that what it will be, Brenna? Leave?"

In more than five years he had never spoken in that tone, accusing, almost possessive. Brenna tried to laugh but failed. "What is this? I'm not answerable to you."

His green eyes were sad. "No, you are not. Not to anyone. Not to Morgan or the crew. But I wish . . . you should not go to the Hiber-Ship," Yuri blurted. Obviously it had required enormous courage for him to spit that out. And now that he had, he was braced for her reaction.

Brenna's temper flared. "Should not? Yuri, I'm a free citizen. I have fully authorized pilot's regs. I *own* Breakthrough Unlimited—Morgan and I do. I can use any ship I please to go anywhere I please, including taking a trip to Hiber-Ship Corporation's launch point . . ."

"And will you come back?"

Yuri Nicholaiev could bullshit a media session as well as the next space pilot. He had done his share of smiling when he didn't feel like it and talking optimistically when he and every other crew member knew a recent test had been a catastrophe, not a whopping success. But all that was gone. There was no distance, no mask of upbeat words and smiles, between him and Brenna. Everyone on the Breakthrough Unlimited team knew that Brenna was on vacation, and they knew where she was planning to go. But not one of them had mentioned it to her, until this minute. None of them had referred to that deep worry that had to be on everyone's mind.

Will you come back?

They knew her love for Derek, knew *New Earth Seeker*'s launch date, that time was running out, permanently, for the relationship. It was inevitable they would wonder if a very *big* rat wasn't going to desert the Breakthrough Unlimited "ship." Hector Obregón hadn't been the only one to resign. In the past two months Breakthrough Unlimited had lost sixteen techs, mechs, and med personnel to other space-oriented companies, despite

299

Brenna's offers of higher salaries and more perks if they would stay with Saunder Enterprises. It was getting hard to find good replacements, too. The team members who remained were on the defensive, more chauvinistic and supportive of their organization than they had ever been, whistling to keep their spirits up, lest they panic. Brenna's defection would be a terrible blow. Little wonder Yuri Nicholaiev was bringing up the subject on the team's behalf.

"I have no intention of entering a cryo stasis box," Brenna said flatly. She tried to maintain her anger and resentment. She was entitled to that. These questions were highly personal. Yuri had no right to cross-examine her.

Didn't he? Hadn't he earned that right, with his unflagging loyalty? There was a great deal more than company loyalty in his expression and stance, though. Yuri gazed at Brenna sadly, wanting to believe what she was saying, but not quite able to. "I hope you mean that. We cannot go on without you. Morgan will continue to pay and analyze results. George would try to lead us. But it would never be the same."

"We went on without my aunt and uncle and Cesare," Brenna reminded him. The words hurt them both. "I'm *not* irreplaceable, Yuri—not that that needs discussing. I *said* I wasn't going there to join up. I . . . I'm going out there to . . . to say . . . good-bye to the man I love." That was another statement that hurt, an agony of fire and ice, twisting within her soul.

Yuri's eyes held hers. "Captain Whitcomb is not the only one who loves you, Brenna. Remember that. Please . . ."

He had no chance to go on. The door dilated, and Tumaini Beno walked in. "We need you in Control, Yuri. George is setting up the schedule for the retrieval flight, and he wants you on cap com. Oh, Maintenance called, Brenna—they have your ship refueled and resupplied and ready to go."

She took a tighter grip on her kit and swam past Yuri. Reluctantly, he moved aside, clearing the aisle to the door. Brenna clung to a stanchion and paused. The implications in Yuri's last statement had affected her deeply. She felt guilty yet warmed by that new burden of knowledge. Brenna wanted to speak to him, but Tumaini was an unwanted witness. Perhaps that was best. What Yuri had said needed to be thought over at length.

Brenna smiled at the men. "Well, I guess I shouldn't keep Maintenance waiting or clog up the hangar docks, huh? You and the kids will be needing the maneuvering space when you head out to pick up the vehicle, Tumaini. Listen, I'm depending on you old-timers to keep the kids in line while I'm on vacation."

Yuri nodded, very morose. Tumaini glanced at him sharply, looking startled and uneasy. Had he guessed what Yuri and Brenna had been talking about before he had butted in? After a noticeable hesitation, Tumaini forced a grin. "It is taken care of. You have a good leave. Keep in touch!"

"I will."

Brenna floated on out into the corridor, sculling through the air, heading for Suitup. She glanced back over her shoulder and saw Yuri and Tumaini hovering in the hall just outside her cabin. Tumaini was saying something to the Russian, but Brenna was too far away to hear what it was. Yuri didn't appear to be paying any attention to his friend. He was staring after Brenna, an invisible tether binding him to her, through his eyes. Brenna jerked her head around, moving too fast, bumping into the curving wall. Seconds later she was in the access tunnel and couldn't see Yuri any longer. She suspected it would be a lot easier to shut off the sight of him than to forget some of the things he had said.

No one at Maintenance made much of her planned destination. They knew it, of course, from her flight plan and the required supplies they had stowed aboard the Chase craft. But only Yuri had pressed Brenna about the matter and let his anxiety show. The obligatory pre-flight run-through was by the book, George Li personally handling the com and wishing Brenna a smooth trip. Then she was away from FTL Station and heading outward. Her Station fell behind on the visual scans and grids. Soon she was alone, cruising out from the Sun amid a night full of stars.

The team would be leaving shortly in Chase Two and Three to open up the hop point station, in distant orbit. They would be conserving fuel. Brenna knew she ought to do that, too, since she was going as far out in the

Solar System as Shoje and the others were. Impatience drove her, though. She had set aside a special fund to pay for the expense of this journey, and she had been waiting since October to make this rendezvous. Brenna fed more power to the sleek little ship. Travel times began to shrink. The computers would feed the updates to Space Fleet Traffic en route. There would be no problem, as long as she didn't stray from her vector.

The trip out was a long one, the days boring. Brenna's craft was equipped with a spartan sleeping area, and she carried six weeks' food and water supplies. She wouldn't need that much, of course, but those were the regulations for a spaceflight of this duration. Air was no problem; it would be recycled by the mutated oxygen-generating microorganism inside the life-support system. So she had little to do but oversee the automated programs and monitor the com.

Derek's calls continued to arrive, as they had on a steady basis ever since he'd left Mars in late October. "October" was a term from Earth's calendar. Mars' seasons didn't match Earth's, and the red planet's years were almost twice as long. But a lot of the Solar System's economics and trade was still linked to the home world, even though that setup was rapidly changing. Terran Worlds Council was working out a coordinated, universal clock and calendar that would adjust to suit local needs throughout the Solar System. T.W.C.'s carefully calculated schedules allowed Derek to call during Brenna's on-board waking periods, each twenty-four-hour day.

Those calls! Derek looking at her from the screen. That voice she loved so much, beckoning her like a male siren. She understood the tactic and accepted it gladly. She seemed to be racing toward a fairy-tale ending for their romance. Brenna deliberately blocked out reality—that this would be farewell, not happily-ever-after.

The standard com chatter changed as she passed the "busy" areas beyond Mars. She refueled at Kirkwood Orbital Station, spending an obligatory hour or two with Administrator Krowa, to be courteous; the woman was eager to entertain a Saunder, and Brenna had a hard time making her getaway without being rude. Soon the Kirkwood Station fell behind, as had the inner asteroids.

Earth-bound vid viewers saw models of the home world's

colonies and envisioned that space really looked like that—crowded clusters of asteroids, for example, whirling in their orbit around the Sun practically bumping into one another. In actuality, very few areas in this vector even approached that misconception. As far as Brenna's navigational system could tell, she had more elbow room than she knew what to do with.

Exchange times for audio and video were beginning to stretch. It took increasingly more minutes to complete the circuit from her present position to Mars and back. Brenna didn't bother with it very often, though she checked in with Saunder Estates:Mars faithfully every twenty-four-hour period, to be sure Morgan was okay.

Six days . . . seven days . . . she was in "empty" space now. Only a few eccentric-orbit asteroids—potential moons which Jupiter would probably capture sometime in millennia to come—occupied this region. There wasn't a lot of traffic. On the Sunward side, far behind Brenna, the mass driver ore ships plied the space lanes, ferrying cargoes to Mars and Earth. Along the same route Brenna was taking, Hiber-Ship's ferry caravans had carted supplies and volunteers out to Jovian orbit. But most of those preparatory trips were finished; *New Earth Seeker* was readying for her historic journey to the stars. Far beyond Jovian orbit, so far that Brenna's nav screens didn't even record them on the grids, Space Fleet patrols and pioneer ships were traveling to and from the Saturnian realms. New colonies were starting up on the ringed giant's moons. Jupiter and Uranus had rings, too, of course, but Saturn's remained the most spectacular in all the Solar System. What a view the colonists on those moons would have from their life-support domes! Brenna had been out to Saturn once, when she was twenty; she had tagged along on a Space Fleet run with her father, with Derek acting as their liaison. ComLink had been cooperating with Space Fleet then to set up an interplanetary communications system. Brenna had found the experience exciting, imagining ways to make the journey faster. Breakthrough Unlimited had snapped up graviton spin resonance drive experiments, after Space Fleet had given them up, partially in expectation of the glory—and the profits—that would accrue to whoever cut that long trip to the outer planets down to nothing.

Derek's group was thinking in far different terms—of leaving the Solar System altogether and starting the whole colonizing procedure elsewhere.

They were both impatient to see the stars. Humanity, toddling out of its backyard, finally, though earlier progress *had* been impressive. Within a century mankind had gone from interplanetary voyages which took years to those which consumed mere fractions of that time. The *next* big jump . . .

. . . would be Hiber-Ship's *New Earth Seeker*, the first manned vehicle to leave the Solar System.

Eighth day. Brenna's vector brought her in "behind" Jupiter, though at a considerable distance out from the awesome world. She was millions of kilometers away, but Jupiter's disk loomed in her viewports. There were no colony settlements on Jupiter's near-satellites yet. The radiation problems generated by the planet had so far frustrated Earth's would-be pioneers. But those, too, must eventually yield to *Homo sapiens'* technology. Brenna hoped that dream would be fulfilled more easily than Breakthrough Unlimited's had been.

She shut off that line of thought hastily. She had had entirely too much time to think, even though she'd cut the travel time extensively. Often she'd considered canceling, turning back, daunted by the enormity of the problems. She kept remembering Yuri's woebegone face when he had begged her not to leave and asked if she were coming back. And she didn't dare think about Morgan and that accusing, silent stare he had given her when she announced she was going to see Derek at *New Earth Seeker*'s orbit.

Her tracking monitors sharpened a view on Hiber-Ship Jovian Base, masking Jupiter out of their calculations. Grids shaped around a large cluster of man-made objects. Brenna's destination point. Matsumoto's Jovian Orbital Station was over the visibility horizon, at present. This "Station" was strictly temporary, unlike the Orbital Colony. Jupiter's disk drifted farther and farther to port. Brenna fired thrusters according to program, decelerating precisely on schedule. Though she itched to take manual control, Brenna let the computers handle nearly everything. This was no seat-of-the-pants lark, flying through heavy Earth atmosphere, or a Chase ship cruise through empty space. The man-made complex ahead contained asteroid-sized structures, a lot of them. There was constant mini-skidder and cargo barge traffic between the orbiting objects, and it was dangerous for a newcomer—hotshot space pilot or not—to zip through congestion like that. Out here, she obeyed Hiber-Ship's traffic systems scrupulously. This was their bailiwick.

"Hiber-Ship Jovian Base, this is Saunder Enterprises Craft Fifty-five. Do you copy and track?" Brenna signaled.

After the lengthening communications gap from Mars, FTL Station, and even Kirkwood Orbital Station, it was a bit of a shock to receive an instantaneous answer. "SE Craft Fifty-five, we copy you loud and clear. You are on our boards and cleared to dock at Construction Shack Seven. We have your guidance locked in. Welcome!"

Brenna sat back, letting remote automated systems take over her ship. She didn't enjoy being a mere passenger, but it gave her leisure to look things over while she approached the mammoth multicity in space. She had been here in '72, but, as Derek had said, things had changed. People had changed, too, in the interim. When Brenna had visited the project, she had been more defiant than curious, ready to heap scorn on *New Earth Seeker,* if for no other reason than that it had lured Derek away from the dreams she and Morgan had shared with the former Space Fleet pilot. *New Earth Seeker* hadn't looked like much at all then. Brenna had studied holo-modes of the now nearly completed interstellar ramjet before she had left FTL Station, but they hadn't prepared her for the astonishing growth that had taken place.

"Mankind's greatest adventure!" Hiber-Ship boasted. The complex looked the part. The dots on the monitor screens enlarged until each structure was visible to the naked eye. The constructs were enormous, the supporting sections nearly as large as Goddard Colony. For months they had housed the work gangs and collected the incoming supplies and the volunteers in training. Hiber-Ship had built as much on site as possible, constructing and installing the cryogenic stasis boxes and machinery here, pulverizing nameless asteroids for materials and refining them in these mills and factories. There had been other industrial output as well, of course, to make the project economically feasible. The bulk had gone into *New Earth Seeker,* one of the most farsighted investment efforts in mankind's his-

305

tory. Earth-based companies like Bolotin's Alliance Manufacturing had spent heavily to bring *New Earth Seeker* into being. The recruitment, the concept, and the about-to-be achieved success had channeled off not only funds but a volatile and restless portion of Earth's population. High Aggressiveness rating on a psych profile didn't keep anyone off the roster. Medicine could harness that, to a colony's benefit, and the challenge had attracted a great number of volunteers who might otherwise have died to no purpose in Earth's controlled-violence arenas.

"Earth's brightest and best . . ." *And* the ones who wanted to take hold of the future with their bare hands and tame an unknown planet.

Hiber-Ship Jovian Base was home for five thousand people. Twenty-five hundred of them would be aboard *New Earth Seeker* when she set forth. The rest were here to build not only this starship but the ones that would follow. Hiber-Ship Corporation was becoming a self-supporting operation, thanks to the mining finds in near-Jovian orbits.

Brenna floated in her safety webbing, watching. Traffic pulled her ship in slowly, weaving through the obstructions. Planetoid-sized collections of housing pods and storage facilities hung in nothingness, surrounding her. Shiny metallic bugs darted among the gigantic structures—ships like Brenna's and space sled mini-skidders running errands and delivering small cargo. If any one of the orbiting warehouses or dormitories touched its neighbor, dozens of ships would be crushed to atoms. But there was no danger of that. Everything obeyed the laws of physics, moving inexorably along a path laid out by gravity and velocity, the entire complex following mighty Jupiter in its course around the Sun.

Construction Shack Seven filled Brenna's viewports and screens now. Her ship appeared to be sliding down a long, brightly lit tunnel—the docking area. Forward thrusters fired delicately, and Brenna lifted a few centimeters forward out of her couch as the Chase ship braked. Motion was timed to milliseconds. Tether snakes reached out for the incoming craft. Chase One's forward momentum now matched that of the Shack. Brenna heard the magnetic anchors clamp onto the hull. Lines tightened, easing the berthed spacecraft into the bay Traffic had reserved. Brenna had never seen the procedure better handled anywhere.

Permission to come aboard was granted. By the time Brenna reached the air lock, the Debark access tunnel was fitted snugly against her ship; she could float directly into a pressurized environment. She was still in free fall, at the hub of the Construction Shack. Seven was a parking lot for incoming ferries and Space Fleet patrols who used the Hiber-Ship Base as a convenient refueling station—and thereby helped Hiber-Ship's financial balance. From here workers and *New Earth Seeker* crew members rode skidders or satellite jumpers over to the interstellar ramjet.

As Brenna swam out into the arrival area, Derek hurried toward her. He gauged his speed expertly, sluing to a stop, one hand on a safety bar and the other closing around Brenna's waist and drawing her to him. "You really did come!" he exclaimed.

"I said I would. You *knew* I would. I don't make promises I can't keep," Brenna said.

She wished their spacesuits didn't separate them. But there could be no privacy, even if they took the suits off. Arrival Bay was busy. Many other people floated by them or drove small cargo carriers past on their way to the loading areas. Intercom chatter, coming through Brenna's helmet, was a steady, murmuring presence. None of that really mattered, though. It was all unimportant. What counted was seeing Derek. She had traveled all the long distance to be this close to those turquoise-blue eyes and that smile that rivaled sunlight, to be this close to *him*.

Derek reached out as if to touch her face. He, too, had forgotten where they were. A sheepish expression spread over his features. His gloves and Brenna's faceplate made actual touch impossible. Derek glanced at the passing crowds. "It's pretty busy here. Did you have a rough voyage? I can arrange for sleeping quarters in the transient cabins section here at Seven, if you . . ."

"Uh-uh! I've had a week to rest in," Brenna said. "I'm fresh. You said you'd take me on a tour. When do we start?"

Balancing in the air, Derek put an arm around Brenna's shoulders. He led her along the safety rail toward the mini-skidder area. "All right! Let's pick up a sled. We're already in our pressure gear . . . nothing to slow us down."

307

The skidders were parked at the far end of the Construction Shack's hub. Along the way, Derek responded to dozens of greetings and wisecracks from the workers. There was no mistaking his status at Hiber-Ship Complex. Not many of these people would actually be riding *New Earth Seeker* out of the Solar System, but they plainly respected the young captain who would be one of the leaders of the stasis ship. Derek Whitcomb had served the corporation well; he was famous and popular, and about to go into the history tapes.

"Got a two-seater checked out for you, Captain," the dispatcher said when they swam into the skidder berths. The hangar crew made a quick visual survey of Derek's and Brenna's spacesuits, to be sure they were fully equipped for the ride across to *New Earth Seeker*. Once cleared, Derek and Brenna climbed aboard the little space scooter. Brenna felt as if she were reliving her childhood days at Goddard Colony. She wedged herself into the second seat. There was barely room for her legs and shoulders inside the cockpit. Derek identified himself with Base Traffic Control, set flight course, and they shot out of the hangar into space.

The skidder was a frisky vehicle. Brenna begged to take the controls for a few minutes. Derek indulged her, since Traffic had override powers and could take them back if they got in trouble. Brenna enjoyed the brief, exhilarating piloting excursion, but she soon returned control to Derek. She wanted to watch the sights en route.

They cruised between city-sized structures. The skidder had some freedom of movement, and Derek did some hotshot flying, never endangering his own craft or others, yet coming in close to give Brenna a good view. Now and then, Jupiter popped into sight suddenly, as they zoomed out from behind the bulk of a construction shack or depot. Then the minuscule two-seater broke away from that grouping and started across a comparatively open area. Twenty kilometers away, *New Earth Seeker* waited. Even at that distance, she filled Brenna's eyes. Jupiter, in a dangerously close approach, must dominate one's vision and senses in just this manner. The stasis ship wasn't sleek and enclosed, the way old-time vid-style space dramas pictured a starship. She was an awesome collection of gleaming spheres held together by kilometers of struts and tunnels. Laser control systems bristled from the outer perimeter. The scoop that would pick up interstellar hydrogen and use it for fuel was incomprehensible, too enormous to be accepted as a man-made device. The thing bulged ahead of the stasis ship like part of a planet sheered away from its core and chiseled to suit a god's artistic pleasure. That was the only "pretty" detail about *New Earth Seeker,* however. She wasn't neat and buttoned up, as an FTL ship would be. Yet the sight left Brenna dazed with admiration.

"How do you like her?" Derek asked proudly. The mind-boggling starship might have been an infant, and he her doting parent.

"She's beautiful," Brenna said, with sincerity. Derek swiveled in his seat and gave her a glowing smile.

"Skidder Two-Four-One, you are okay for Level Thirty-five . . ."

"Thank you, Control. ETA, ninety seconds."

Like a swooping bird, the skidder paralleled the orbiting stasis ship's track. Derek was doing a flyby, letting Brenna inspect the myriad tunnels and spheres and connections. There were shuttle craft attached to the main spheres— each shuttle as big as a standard SE passenger spaceship, and each was a completely self-contained planet lander. They would be carried for decades, waiting, their on-board computerized self-repair systems maintaining them at peak operational efficiency. When the ship arrived at its destination, the shuttles would be needed. The enormous main ship could never enter atmosphere. She would assume orbit around her target world, and the colonists would board the shuttles for descent to their new home.

Everything was ready. The final countdown had begun. Hiber-Ship Corporation had picked the best brains, drawn investments from some of Earth's and the colonies' most powerful people—including Brenna's aunt Carissa. They had recruited from the bravest and most adventuresome stock of humanity—volunteers like Derek Whitcomb. And now the ship they had worked ten long years to build and the crew that had taken five years to reach full roster were ready to depart.

The skidder dived in between two of the spheres, maneuvering carefully. Each sphere was half a kilometer in diameter, with ten meters of strutwork between it and the

309

next sphere in line—leaving plenty of room for a skidder to land. A hatch opened at the base of one huge globe—a hangar door, large enough to admit five skidders abreast at once, but the portal was no more than a spot of sudden light amid the shadowed surface of the sphere. Derek had made the flight countless times, and his sure touch on the controls showed that. Brenna recognized the pilot's tricks —tripping the hatch-close relays before they were actually inside the hangar, not lowering the skids until the last possible moment.

"Showoff," she muttered fondly as they coasted to a stop. As Derek had planned, the hatch *hadn't* closed too soon and cut them off, and they *hadn't* done a belly slide but had landed perfectly.

They clambered out of the hangar and into a nearby locker room, where they discarded their suits. *New Earth Seeker* was solidly on her own life-support systems by now. The air was recycled but oxygen-heavy, quite breathable. From the locker area, Derek led the way up a ladder. The ship had gravity, not Earth pull but the equal of Mars'. *New Earth Seeker* was so enormous Brenna hadn't been conscious of the gravity-creating spin when they were approaching her. Instruments and logic had told her Hiber-Ship would provide gravity for the workmen's comfort while they were putting the finishing touches on the spacecraft.

The ladder ended at a catwalk. Brenna and Derek had been climbing up between the hulls of the sphere, and now they paused to look out into the main part of this ship's section. Concentric levels, lightly suspended from interior strutwork, held coffin-sized containers and accompanying cryogenic machinery. Techs worked their way through the maze, checking stasis settings. In each container there was a body, a man or a woman in seeming sleep—or death. They didn't move, didn't breathe. The casings secured them in a coldness rivaling Mars in winter. Once *New Earth Seeker* was underway, most of these cryogenics areas would shut down external heating plants; those were on only for the workmen and techs. The people inside the cases wouldn't need warmth, and the stasis equipment operated just fine at conditions near absolute zero.

Brenna gazed at the scene, involuntarily shivering. The faces were serene. These weren't condemned criminals,

310

resisting their sentence of frozen imprisonment. Every one of these colonists had gone willingly into a stasis cubicle. In time, there would be more than two thousand of them, scattered throughout the silvery spheres. Sleeping—a sleep that would last for nearly a century.

And one of those calm-faced, confident sleepers would be Derek.

CHAPTER EIGHTEEN

⊗⊗⊗⊗⊗⊗⊗⊗

Choices

DEREK hadn't pulled any punches and hadn't softened his pitch. He had begun the tour in the place Brenna had the most reservations about. But from the cryogenic storage area, he escorted her to an adjacent sphere to see things that were easier to take. Derek skipped stuff that might have interested an Earth-oriented vidcaster. That was run-of-the-mill, old hat to a space pilot.

The propulsion system tour fascinated her, when it would have been over the heads of the average tourist. Derek pointed to the connecting channels lacing through the outer sections of each sphere. "The Isakson photon pulse regulators. Links everything all together. We'll reach seventeen percent of c in only six months."

"Impressive." Brenna whistled. It was indeed. She compared the facts to Breakthrough Unlimited's progress and squirmed inwardly. For all Breakthrough's successful un-manned tests, they had never proved their theories by breaking the light-speed barrier with a manned voyage program. Hiber-Ship had done so, more than six years ago, with a trip beyond Pluto and back again, and with cryo-genic stasis volunteers revived, living, and volunteering to go into stasis *again*, for this much longer trip. Brenna gestured to the kilotons of machinery filling the sphere's interior. "That's not propulsion equipment."

"No, it's for colonization—the heavy agricultural tools

and land transports we'll need when we make planetfall. Come on, the next sphere's even more interesting."

It was. Brenna stepped out of the connecting tunnel into a garden of Eden. There were levels of grass and trees, cleverly engineered to turn with the sphere as it rotated independently and made its own gravity. The central area of the sphere held a holo-mode "sun," one that generated a useful spectrum and stimulated photosynthesis. Animals, specially bred for adaptability to odd gravity and environmental conditions, roamed the artificial meadows or lolled in the warmth of the "sun." She saw cattle, sheep, swine, several horses, and a few domesticated dogs and cats. The scene resembled a mythic re-creation, even though there were no lions to lie down with the lambs—in fact, no lambs or *any* other juvenile animals, only adults. The beasts, probably because of their genetic makeup, were coexisting in remarkable harmony. The animals were proof that *New Earth Seeker*'s colonists looked forward to a world where they would have few terraforming needs, as humans did on Mars. It was plain Hiber-Ship also anticipated a colony that relied on food animals and some beasts of burden and useful pets. "You aren't expecting these poor things to keep on chewing their cuds or gamboling on the green like this for seventy-five years?"

Derek smiled. "Negative. Remember the brochure tapes? These are the last of the breeding animals. We won't put them in stasis until just before departure. This area's a popular relaxation one, and we're maintaining it in its natural state as long as possible." He nodded, and Brenna noticed other "tourists" on catwalks at the opposite side of the sphere, enjoying the bucolic panorama. "When it's time, the vets will tranquilize them and put them in stasis. Of course, this isn't a tenth of our full stock."

"Adaptable multi-populations, via cryo-stored animal sperm and ova," Brenna said. "And already-fertilized prize embryos, ready for implantation when you arrive. Makes sense," she admitted, giving Hiber-Ship planners their due. Quite a few reactionaries—quaint Earth First Party adherents, mostly—back on Earth had objected strenuously to this procedure. Brenna couldn't imagine why. Humans had been eating meat produced by artificial insemination and embryo implants for nearly a century now, as well as from animals produced by cloning methods. Presumably a great many humans never stopped to consider where their protein was coming from, however, or how that tasty morsel came into being. In the majority of Earth and colonial markets nowadays, food production was high technology, coming off assembly lines of syntha proteins, cloning, and implant husbandry, an output of trillions of kilograms. What difference did it make that Hiber-Ship Corporation had rounded up samples of live animals and their genes and embryos from prime domestic stocks to set up its first colony in style? The reactionaries saw nothing contradictory in espousing assassination-oriented attitudes at the same time that they ranted against "unnatural" means of preserving life and letting humans and animals reawaken years from now, near a distant star.

There were more spheres, more astonishing accomplishments. Again and again Brenna replied with honest praise to Derek's eager hints for approval. The tapes didn't do *New Earth Seeker* justice. Brenna wasn't sure any mind could take it all in. This was humanity's most successful collective technological achievement, to date.

The brochures had explained that it would take five weeks to complete all the cryogenic procedures. The animals would be far down on the list, to allow those crew members who were still ambulatory to enjoy them. The high-rating techs and the space-trained ship's crewmen, like Derek, would be the last to enter cryo stasis and the first to be awakened by automatic systems resuscitation. They would be needed to oversee the orbital plots and the gradual reawakening of the rest of the colonists, many years from now.

At one point in the tour, when Derek was showing Brenna through the operating navigation section, Brenna noticed Lieutenant Chionis eyeing her. This time Brenna couldn't mistake the angry resentment in the woman's glance.

They climbed more ladders, passed through more tunnels, toured more spheres full of equipment and people and animals. Brenna lost track of how far they had come. Her directional sense told her they were making a circuit and were now heading back toward the sphere where they had begun the tour. They must have covered two or three kilometers, at least. Low gravity made that easy. Brenna didn't feel at all tired. Growing excitement gave her additional energy. Part of the excitement was the ship's grandeur. The concept was contagious and beginning to sway her. The greater part of her excitement, though, was spending so much time with Derek, in his own territory, and sharing his joy. He was in his element, at his absolute best. Brenna was his lover and *New Earth Seeker* was his mistress, and they weren't rivals, for once! Brenna and Derek had been together, touring the ship, for nearly two hours, and they hadn't had a single argument!

Once a crewman tried to interrupt them, murmuring something about the message center. Derek had shut the man off savagely, refusing to be bothered. "Take it to Carlos or Ned. I'm not on duty. Is that clear?" Derek steered Brenna out of the room, annoyed by the crewman's presumption. That was the only harsh note throughout the excursion.

Derek finished the show in one of the observation arena bubbles, up top in the Nav Control and Guidance Systems Sphere. Plexi viewports, not scanners, gave an outlook on the universe. The effect was staggering. Brenna could see a 360-degree sweep, looking back along the awesome length of the starship toward the Sun, toward Jupiter and the constant race of satellites over its broad face and its nearly invisible tracery of rings. Then she could look "anti-Sunward" toward the stars. Derek stood close beside her, enjoying the view as much as she. "I know," he whispered. "It's breathtaking. Think what it'll be like out there."

"You'll be in stasis," Brenna said. The idea was depressing. One of those solid, coffinlike boxes; Derek locked inside, asleep, unaware. One of thousands. *This* was Derek, this warm, strong, beloved person embracing her.

"It doesn't matter," Derek said, shrugging. "I'll wake up a month before the passengers. We'll have plenty of time to enjoy the ride when we're approaching planetfall." He had no doubts whatsoever. He was sure he would climb out of that stasis box and resume his life. The proofs had been demonstrated again and again. In truth, he had far less reason to be worried in *this* ship than Brenna would if she ever climbed into Breakthrough Unlimited's Prototype III!

Brenna wanted to believe. She *did* believe. Rows of proofs. Armies of Hiber-Ship experts. Ten years of solid,

314

replicable results, and years before that, testing everything in the labs. They couldn't have gotten so immense a project moving if they hadn't convinced humanity's rulers. Politics was involved in it, undoubtedly—the politics of economics and exploiting the gas giants and the outer planets of the Solar System, which Hiber-Ship was doing very well; the profits fled Sunward, to Mars and to Earth, and the volunteers kept coming. Politics to show the Vahnaj that Earth *was* capable of reaching the stars. It had taken incalculable foresight and hope for the future for Hiber-Ship to set these wheels in motion. It was unlikely Yan Bolotin or the older sponsors would ever ride one of these colony ships or live to see the distant settlements their recruits had established. That was for mankind's future generations. A plan on a cosmic scale, extending forward by centuries, not by years.

Uninhabited worlds. The Vahnaj guaranteed that, said they would be protected from exploitation by any other species. It was a handout, but Hiber-Ship and *Homo sapiens* had swallowed their pride and were taking it. Because it gave humanity the stars.

"Brenna . . . ?"

"You won't be conscious when you hit your peak acceleration," she said sadly.

Derek admitted the fact. "No. We'll all be in stasis. That's just the way *Seeker* operates."

"You'll be frozen—" Brenna caught herself and corrected the term before Derek could protest. "Okay. Stasis isn't exactly freezing. That still means you won't be awake. You won't see our Sun recede or your new sun grow as you approach it."

Gently, Derek grasped her shoulders, holding her close by his side. He kissed her, and then they gazed out the port, into infinity. They wanted each other, and they wanted the stars.

"No," Derek said. "But there's a world waiting for us, a new world, a whole marvelous adventure no one on Earth has ever known. I want to share it with you, Bren. It's never going to be complete for me if you aren't there. I want what we have at this moment to last forever."

So did Brenna. To know the future. To wake up, with Derek, when Earth and Mars and the universe were older. But not to age herself. To conquer time and an unknown planet. She had been too young when Mars was being colonized, and the terraforming efforts on Venus wouldn't yield results for another hundred years, if that. But by then she could be helping tame a world no intelligent being had ever explored. She and Derek, under an alien star.

His hands were caressing, quickening her pulse. "You planned this," Brenna said, tugging playfully at his beard. "You shameless fornicator."

Derek suddenly grew very solemn. "No. This isn't some silly vid-comedy routine, Bren. It never has been and never will be. I want you. For all our lives. All the quaint old forms."

Brenna was racked by exquisite sensations, fear and physical desire mingling. "It sounds so lovely. If only . . ."

"It will be. We can make time stand still, Bren." His mouth met hers, and Brenna responded eagerly. The words, the moment, the shared sexuality—it all fitted together perfectly, as Derek said it would. She was convinced. For this one precious instant, she was convinced. "We're going to have a wonderful future together, out there," Derek murmured.

Brenna had drifted out of place, out of time. But she couldn't continue at this intoxicating level. Reality intruded: memories of other people she cared about, a project to achieve faster-than-light spaceflight. "It's such an enormous gamble."

"It's worth it," Derek said with a tolerant smile. "Think of what's waiting for us."

"But what if . . . what if you're partway there and FTL is discovered?" That problem had been debated loud and long. It wasn't merely that FTL was, at the present moment, an unproved theory that had made the difference. Those who had gone with the Hiber-Ship philosophy had to accept the whole package. Derek did.

"We go on. It's in the charter." Brenna stared at him wonderingly as Derek added with serene confidence, "We demand the right to colonize the Kruger 60 system. It's part of a sub-section in the Earth-Vahnaj treaty, Bren. Every one of us signed the agreement."

Refusing to be rescued, even if their venture should become obsolete!

"But, my God, Derek, think how many things might go

316

wrong along the way. You could *need* help. Equipment malfunctions . . . you could arrive at your colony world with too many dead humans and animal or plant stock to set up a viable culture . . ."

He held Brenna close, soothing her as if she were a frightened and foolish child. "Look who's talking about malfunctions!" He didn't mean that viciously. He was merely making obvious comparisons, and so far, *New Earth Seeker* was proving out a lot better than Breakthrough Unlimited. "You can be part of it. The first Terran independent colony."

"Oh, Derek! What's the point? You're torturing us both. Even if I agreed, there wouldn't be any room for me. The roster's complete."

"There's room."

A cold tingle crept along Brenna's skin. She wriggled free of Derek's arms. "What are you talking about?"

"You're on the list. Your entry's been approved. A cubicle has been reserved for you."

Brenna studied that handsome face. Suspicion was a Martian dust storm, rising up and engulfing her. "What about all the tests?" Those were awesome. Genetic tests. Physical fitness tests. Educational background. Mental attitudes suitable for pioneers on an alien world. Each applicant had to pass them all. But Brenna read the answer to her question in Derek's eyes. In essence, Brenna Foix Saunder passed all those tests without ever having to submit to them in person. She had qualified as a top pilot long ago. As for the rest of the record, a Saunder was almost public property. Hiber-Ship Corporation had contacts with Carissa Saunder. There wouldn't have been any problem. The publicity, for the *next* stasis ships, would be tremendous. A Saunder, aboard *New Earth Seeker!* The acceptance board would wink at the letter of the law, in Brenna's case.

"I put your name in," Derek confessed. "It's *always* been on the list, ever since I enlisted in '72. I always hoped . . ." He tried to take her hand, but Brenna wrenched away.

She paced back and forth, arms crossed beneath her breasts. "You planned this! The whole thing!" she exploded, her anger building. "Almost four years, since you enlisted—and all this time you've assumed that naturally

317

I'd come to my senses, eventually, and fall into your arms. It never occurred to you to ask how I felt before you signed me aboard this oversized coffin-carrier, did it? Don't I have any choice in the matter?"

Derek lunged toward her, seizing her shoulders, forcing her to face him. Unless she resorted to violence, she couldn't break free. "No! It wasn't manipulation. And you have a choice. You've always had one, my love." Everything he felt was in his eyes. "Who could make you choose anything you didn't want? That's one of the countless things I've always loved about you—your damned stubborn streak. All Saunder and a kilometer wide. Bren, it *is* your choice. I'm just telling you that you *have* a choice, that it's not too late for us."

"My being a Saunder wouldn't have anything to do with Hiber-Ship's decision in the matter, would it?" Brenna demanded. "I'll bet! They've got potential investors lined up for a whole series of stasis craft. It'll be a lovely selling point if they can brag that they bagged *me* to go along with Captain Derek Whitcomb and a ship full of prize physical specimens. Can't you imagine the newshunters getting hold of that? *True Love Conquers the Stars.* If a Saunder buys it, it must be profitable, huh?"

Derek didn't deny the accusation. His superiors had kept the possibility under wraps. If they had released the news prematurely, and Brenna *didn't* join *New Earth Seeker's* crew, the lawsuit would be historic.

"Affirmative. But I meant what I said. Bren. Please?"

She threw up her hands, beating at him feebly until he released her. She needed space and time to collect her wits, and Derek wasn't giving either to her. "It's . . . it's a hell of a jump, philosophically and in all other ways."

"The only real difference between FTL and Hiber-Ship stasis is technique. Both ways point to the stars. But cryogenic stasis and the Isakson photon drive are sure, safe . . . and they're *now*."

Brenna looked over his shoulder, at that tantalizing sight out the viewport. "I don't know. I can't just . . . just make up my mind. The propulsion system is pitifully slow but proven. Colonizing a world from scratch intrigues me. I could even accept cryo stasis. But there are other elements . . ."

"Such as having my children?" Derek guessed. He

318

studied her, smiling patiently. "I know. Childbirth will be a big jump for a lot of women already on the crew list, too. But it's been going on for millions of years and likely to continue. In the Solar System, or elsewhere."

"Under primitive conditions," Brenna said with a shudder of revulsion.

"We have expert physicians accompanying us. It's not a naive, back-to-nature utopia we're going to build in the Kruger 60 system . . ."

Brenna shook her head. "It's primitive, compared with what we're used to."

"What some humans have become used to," Derek corrected her. "You travel too much in elite society circles, Bren. Not every woman reproduces via a surrogate."

That old argument. Brenna flared, "It's common and approved, even recommended for women who have difficulty carrying a child to term. For half a century or more . . ."

"For wealthy women," Derek said, stressing the elitism in practices Brenna had always accepted. "Dian could have carried you to term without difficulty. Mariette Saunder could have done the same for Morgan. They chose surrogates because they were busy."

"How dare you pass judgment? *You'll* never have to make that decision!"

"No. I'm just pointing out that that isn't necessarily the only way or the best, Brenna," Derek said in his most charming, come-let-us-reason tone.

"I'll remind you of that while you're pregnant . . ."

"Dammit, Brenna! I don't want to argue. Since you want to play that game, you can speculate that your mother and Morgan's might never have chosen to reproduce at all if they hadn't been trying to get even with Carissa. Family feuding, to the nth degree . . ."

"Shut up!" Brenna yelled, cut to the bone.

Imperturbable, Derek went on. "It's true, and you know it. Is that the modern and non-primitive method you're defending? Think about it." His voice softened. "Brenna, is it so selfish and primitive for me to want you to share my life, to want you to bear my children?"

Brenna felt cornered, though they were standing in the center of the observation deck. "Me and how many other women? Lilika? Who else? Hiber-Ship's charter was always arranged for polygamy."

"A form of it, only temporary, to mix the gene pool until the colony's well established," Derek said with a shrug. "That has nothing to do with love."

"Maybe Lilika isn't quite that casual about it."

"Spirit of Humanity!" Derek threw his head back, staring up through the dome, silently praying for strength. "That! If sex is all that concerns you, you shouldn't be starving. Why be so dog-in-the-manger? Are you trying to claim Nicholaiev hasn't obliged you when I wasn't available?" Something in Brenna's expression made him stop and blink. Derek appeared genuinely taken aback, visibly shifting mental gears. "No?" He seemed confused. "Why not? He's been as obvious as a moonstruck lover on a vid comedy. If you're *not* falling into bed with him regularly, you're torturing the poor fool. Not that he minds. He'd follow you anywhere, just like one of Carissa's pet dogs. Your pet FTL pilot. Nicholaiev won't even complain when that damned FTL ship gets him killed—as it inevitably will—"

The wall screen by the door clicked on. An alarm buzzed, demanding attention. Derek crossed the observation blister in three long strides and hit the reply cue. "Get the hell out of here!" he thundered at a startled crewman's image. "Leave us alone! Is that clear, mister? It's no emergency, or you'd have gone full signal! So take it and freeze it—now!"

The screen went blank. Derek stood still, fists clenched as he took deep breaths, commanding himself to regain control. When he was calmer, he looked at Brenna.

"You're wrong about Yuri," Brenna said with icy detachment. "If you used that as a license . . ."

"I am *not* involved in a sexual relationship with Lilika Chionis or any other woman but you! You may not believe that, Bren, but it's true. I'm not saying there haven't been occasional hedonistic indulgences, but those were meaningless."

So far.

Brenna didn't say that out loud. But she thought it. Derek Whitcomb, the stalwart, handsome spaceship captain. Extrapolate a successful mission, no deaths, no malfunctions during that long journey to the Kruger 60 system. They would make planetfall. The dedicated pioneers would begin carving out their future on a new world. There was a heavy imbalance toward females in the crew roster. Chances were very good that the dashing Captain Whitcomb would be invited to spread his genetic qualities around freely and enrich the new colony's mix.

Could I endure that? How jealous can I be? Could I be satisfied with being his first choice, his preferred bed partner, but sharing him with others? Knowing the Hiber-Ship charter obligated Derek to impregnate other women and acknowledge paternity of their children as well as any I might conceive?

Derek said wearily, "Face it—it isn't the sex that's bothering you. It's cryogenic stasis. It works, Brenna. Repeat: It works. You're living in the past, thinking about Jael Saunder's pulling the plug on those corpses stored in the Enclave in Antarctica. Dammit, that was Dark Ages cryo science. The woman's dead, but her superstitions are still running your life."

"My grandmother was right to question cryo stasis in her day," Brenna replied. "Don't ridicule her. The technique *didn't* work in the Thirties, even though science claimed it did. She had no way of knowing what future developments would bring . . ."

"Are you listening to yourself?" Derek asked scornfully. Behind his head, Jupiter seemed to be painted against a black curtain, appearing to move slowly past the viewport as the gigantic ship revolved to create gravity. "Jael Hartman Saunder was a monster. That's not my opinion, Bren; that's history. The Saunders who come after her have to live down her deeds, not admire her and follow in her footsteps. But that's what you're trying to do, my love. You're as obsessed about Breakthrough Unlimited as she was about controlling Earth through her older son's political ambitions. You *and* Morgan. He's as obsessed about FTL as you are, and it's left him a cripple."

"And you can't stand to look at him," Brenna shot back ruthlessly. Derek winced as she went on. "You're his best friend. And the sight of him turns your stomach. You're grateful to be leaving, aren't you? Abandoning Morgan, the way you're abandoning Earth."

Derek closed his eyes a long moment. When he opened them, he said with blunt honesty, "Yes, I'm a coward

321

about pain and crippling. I see Morgan, and I see myself in his place. I'd rather die than survive and be the way he is. That's my weakness, Bren. I'm not proud of it. But I tried to overcome it. I really tried. Did I abandon Morgan? Or did he abandon me? He wouldn't talk to me or look at me—or at anyone else. He prefers the Vahnaj. So be it." Derek's face was open, soft with love and yearning. "I can't help Morgan any more. I can't save him, and he doesn't seem to want me around. With him, I never had a chance. I can save you, though."

Brenna choked on a sob, shaking her head frantically. "I can't run out on him! I don't know how *you* can! He needs us."

"Does he? Or do you need *him?*" Derek's gaze held her, probing her mind and heart.

The room was icy. Brenna chafed her arms, trying to restore some warmth to her shivering flesh. She knew the observation deck's temperature was in the comfortable range. The cold she suffered came from within. "The reason he prefers Quol-Bez is . . . I think Quol-Bez may be a sort of telepathic catalyst. Without his friendship, Morgan would have gone mad. As it is, he's focusing on the graviton spin response drive, finding solutions none of us could. He's gone beyond the team, beyond the engineers. And he can spend every waking minute concentrating on the problem, because of his sensory deprivation." Brenna paused, then went on. "He's dying, Derek." Derek's expression was bleak. He knew, but hadn't wanted to look squarely at that truth. "He hasn't got many years left," Brenna said. "Helen said five, maybe, seven if she gets lucky. His lungs are deteriorating, and the muscle atrophy has only been slowed down, not stopped. Without faster-than-light travel, he'll never see the stars, Derek. I owe him that. At least to *try.* When Breakthrough Unlimited jumps out to the Vahnaj star systems and beyond, it'll be because of Morgan Saunder McKelvey. I want it to happen in *this* generation, while Morgan's alive and can reap the honor he's entitled to."

Derek was silent a long while. When he spoke, his voice was so soft that Brenna had to strain to hear him. "Is that what you believe? Is that why you're risking everything? For Morgan's sake?" The volume rose, and the words turned into a cruel accusation. "Or are you merely trying to assuage your guilt? I suppose getting yourself and the other pilots killed would do that. But how many times do the Saunders have to atone for past sins and mistakes? You're still atoning for Jael Saunder, and paying back your aunt Mariette. Now you're paying back Morgan. It never ends. The Saunder way—fighting an endless battle with hopeless causes. I guess . . . I guess it's too late." He hung his head for a moment, then exclaimed, "Nothing stops a Saunder! Right? Well, thank the Spirit of Humanity that my people are going to be clear of the holocaust. I thought you'd eventually come to your senses. But no. We won't contact Earth again until we make planetfall. I'm glad of that. By then maybe we'll be picking up the signals and can find out if there's any human civilization left back here, or if the Vahnaj wiped you out."

"What the hell are you . . . ?"

The door opened. A red-faced crew member marched in, braced for war. She saluted stiffly and spoke before Derek could stop her. "This *is* an emergency message of sorts, Captain. There's a Class A signal for Captain Saunder on the box in Central. It's on a diplomatic channel."

Derek snorted in contempt. "All right. You delivered the word. Dismissed. If Captain Saunder wants to take the message, she'll come down to Communications. Now get out."

"Yes, *sir!*"

As the woman scowled and hurried out, Brenna felt that her brain was being stirred like soup. Derek's harangue and the crewwoman's confusing message were using her mind for a battleground, and no one was winning, especially not Brenna.

"Class A . . ."

"I assume that means Quol-Bez or the Terran Worlds Council got wind of what your bunch is up to," Derek said bitterly. "Not that it probably matters, not with all your money and the politicos mixed up in it." He raked his hand through his fair beard. "Goddamned Saunder pride! You just *had* to have FTL, at any price! And you certainly can pay the price! Nothing gets in your way, does it? Not Morgan, or that poor sap Nicholaiev, or idealistic dreamers like Tumaini. The hell with the Earth-Vahnaj treaty, too." He stopped, finally, like a man waking from a hysterical rage and finding out that the target of his wrath had disappeared. Derek darted a sharp look at Brenna, his brows drawn together in a deep frown. "Don't pretend you don't know."

Brenna realized she was hyperventilating. She made a deliberate effort to slow down her breathing. She tried to focus on this fury and confusion Derek was dumping on her.

Derek waited for comprehension to dawn in her face, for some guilty emotion to peep out behind her bewilderment. When it didn't, he exploded in exasperation. "Oh, come *on*, Bren! I know when I'm being pumped for info. They weren't very subtle—Tumaini, and Habich, and the other two. They've been digging away since summer —going to 'avenge Morgan,' as they put it. Crazy kids! And Tumaini's not thinking right, hasn't been since the accident and Aluna's walking out on him. Why shouldn't they all be screwed up? You and Morgan taught them to be as obsessive and unbending as you are. When Morgan got hurt—"

"What the hell are you talking about?"

Brenna's scream shocked Derek, cutting off his tirade. "The Vahnaj ship, of course. Quol-Bez's private ship. You've been drooling over it ever since he arrived in the Solar System. Your kid pilots are going to hijack it and cure your ship's glitches . . ."

The battle within Brenna's mind went critical. In the split second it took for her dizziness to dissipate, all the thousand tiny fragments seemed to fall together, magically assembling into a nightmare.

"They pumped you for info. And you were supposed to decoy me out here."

Derek shook his head violently, suddenly on the defensive. "No, it wasn't that way." It was his turn to be impaled by an accusing stare. He didn't handle it very well. He repeated, frantically, *"No!"* He reached out, and Brenna stepped back, avoiding his touch. "Bren, you have to believe me. When Tumaini . . . he said he didn't want the same thing to happen to us that happened to him and his wife . . ."

"And what about Adele and Joe and Shoje?" Brenna said furiously, heading for the door. Derek broke into a run, loping after her. He should have been able to overtake her easily, but he kept running into objects along the cat-walk outside the deck. Brenna didn't slacken her pace. "Where's Communications? What *else* have you been keeping from me, in your tender concern for giving me choices about what to do with my life?"

At that moment, Brenna spotted a You-Are-Here placard directory and quickly oriented herself within the huge ship. She swung left and started down the ladder there. Above her, Derek struggled down the rungs, skipping several and dropping the last two meters, galloping in her wake. The lower corridor was wide enough for them to walk abreast. Derek ran alongside Brenna awkwardly. "Tumaini never . . . hell, Brenna, what they intended to do was practically an open secret. I thought you were in on it. And when you came out here, I hoped you'd changed your mind."

"They couldn't cope by themselves," Brenna said, not breaking stride. "They need help to get past the Space Fleet ships guarding Quol-Bez's craft. You're talking conspiracy, and a lot heavier stuff than my pilots have got. Who else is in on this?" Her adrenaline was racing. She didn't feel shaky or short of breath at all. Anger and fear fed her energies. Other members of Hiber-Ship's crew were in the corridors. They ducked into alcoves or side rooms as Brenna and Derek flew by, staring after the couple.

"They knew plenty," Derek insisted. "Somebody's been giving them Space Fleet info. They knew stuff *I* didn't have the clearance to get." He had to stop when they came to a narrow passageway and walk on Brenna's heels until they emerged at the far side of the bottleneck. There were more ladders to climb, and he continued to press his case while in motion. "I'm as much a pawn in whatever they're up to as anyone else. Charlie Dahl said it was all in the family and the price was right."

Brenna swung around, and Derek choked off his protests abruptly. "Charlie Dahl? He's in this, too? Why? To see my outfit get smeared?"

They were nearing the center of the sphere, working their way through a maze. Brenna followed the arrows, plowing on determinedly toward her goal. On the threshold of Communications, she slammed to a halt. She peered at Derek and sputtered. "Stuart. Of course."

Stuart, at Colony Days last year, slyly egging Brenna on

to challenge Quol-Bez about the Vahnaj ship. Stuart and his crocodile tears when the accident happened. Stuart, accosting Brenna at Saunderhome after his ugly confrontation with his mother about the marriage. Stuart saying, "You *do* need me! You don't realize it yet, but you will . . . you're going to need more than faith to get the job done . . . when you're hungry enough, and desperate enough, give old Stuart a call. We'll work something out . . ."

She hadn't called him. And he hadn't waited. Intuitively, Brenna knew her cousin was at the bottom of this, and that his machinations had little to do with her or the race for the stars. He was getting even—somehow and in some way no one else could understand—with Carissa.

Derek was still at her heels when Brenna rushed into Communications. He pleaded with her, heedless of where they were. Duty officers stared at them. "Brenna, maybe I did make a mistake. I know Tumaini wouldn't want to hurt you. Neither would the others . . ."

"They're just greedy, like me. I taught them. Isn't that the way you put it?" Brenna said acidly. She shot him a murderous glare. "Is Yuri supposedly in this, too?" Derek shook his head negatively. He looked miserable. "I didn't think so. *He'd* have told me. And *he'd* have stopped them if he'd known what they were up to."

"Here's the tape, Captain Saunder," a tech said, handing Brenna the chip. He pointed to an unused office. "You can play it in there, if you wish."

Brenna didn't try to keep Derek out. She fed the chip into a readout terminal. The Vahnaj Ambassador appeared on the screen. Brenna recognized the background; Quol-Bez was recording the message at Saunder Estates:Mars. "Brenna, for-give intru-sion. Morgan has ex-plained how to lo-cate you. There is . . . urr . . . diffi-culty. The hypothetical risk we have spoken of has oc-curred. I do not wish this to become an *affaire*." The French word sounded odd amid his high-pitched, growly English. But the deadly serious import of what Quol-Bez was saying riveted Brenna. "You understand. Councilman Ames will co-operate. We are in-formed you may be able to . . . urr . . . effect pre-ven-tive medicine, as it were."

Sao had been doing a good job, teaching him human idiomatic expressions. Brenna had no trouble reading the message hidden in the tense words. As Derek had said, the hijack was underway. Councilman Ames and Quol-Bez were trying to prevent an interstellar diplomatic incident. This message would reveal nothing to the people along the communications link, but it told Brenna a great deal—more than she wanted to hear.

Quol-Bez's broad face twisted in distress. "Councilman Ames will provide . . . urr . . . will expedite what is necessary. If you will contact Space Fleet posted at your location, all effort will be made to assist . . ."

Warnings hammered at Brenna. A familiar scenario—the wishful-thinking plot to "borrow" Quol-Bez's ship, then put her back after discovering her FTL secrets. And Morgan—*and* Quol-Bez—telling Brenna emphatically that it couldn't be done. But Tumaini, Joe Habich, Adele, and Shoje were going to try to do just that. They hoped to "avenge" Morgan, solve the problem of faster-than-light travel, and give humanity the stars. Instead, they were going to die, horribly, in an alien ship rigged against theft: *"I cannot give it to you. And you cannot take it. Do not try."*

CHAPTER NINETEEN

✪✪✪✪✪✪✪✪

The Bait Is Taken

THE message ended. Quol-Bez's image dissolved. Brenna knew he had wanted to say more, but didn't dare while they were on an open, unscrambled circuit. She would have to do what Quol-Bez had recommended—trust Terran Worlds Councilman Ames and Space Fleet. They would have diplomatic channels, coded. She had to make contact with them as soon as possible. But not from *New Earth Seeker.*

"I've got to get to my ship," Brenna said. "Will you take me to her, or do I hitch a ride with someone going that way?"

"Quol-Bez is using you to do his dirty work. He's no better than Stuart and you know it," Derek protested.

"Does that mean you won't help me?"

The door to the larger room was shut. No one could overhear them. "I read between those lines as well as you did," Derek said. "Whatever Stuart and the others cooked up has already started happening. You can't stop it, so why try?"

Brenna spoke rapidly, pouring out her tension. "I'll trust you to keep your mouth shut about this, at least for seventy-five years, Derek. If my people steal that ship, they may indeed create an interstellar incident. I don't know how *that* part of it will work out. But one thing's guaranteed—if they tamper with it, they'll die. Maybe you don't give a faint damn what happens to them, but I *do*. That ship's booby-trapped, and I don't want Tumaini and the kids to be killed."

Derek barely reacted to what she was saying. He sighed. "I'll take you over to Seven, if that's what you really want. Be sure it is, Bren."

"For God's sake! Haven't you been listening? It's *my fault!* I should have guessed what they were planning. It's my responsibility. They're doing this for Breakthrough Unlimited, and for Morgan. I owe it to them, and to Morgan, to save them, if possible," Brenna explained angrily. "Their lives are at stake, *and* humanity's future."

"Humanity *in the Solar System*. Maybe it deserves what it'll get."

Brenna stood with arms akimbo, gaping at him in disbelief. "An interstellar war? Are you saying anyone deserves *that?*"

"I doubt it'll go that far," Derek said, maddeningly casual. "Don't the Vahnaj constantly tell us how civilized they are?"

"There are limits to their patience, I'm sure. But that's right. I forgot. None of this concerns you, does it? No matter what happens, it won't be *your* problem. You're bailing out, abandoning us."

"It needn't be your problem, either, Brenna."

"I must be hearing someone else!" Brenna cried. "Not you! You've never been callous, Derek. Come with me now. You can help me get those kids out of this mess before it's too late. They respect you. If Hiber-Ship's most popular recruitment officer joins in the rescue operation, they'll have to know we're acting in good faith and it's not a bluff. Derek?"

The roles were reversed. She was the one begging, and she wasn't getting through to him. The barriers were up, as impossible to break down as that of light-speed.

"I have a launch schedule." Derek saw the horrified shock that simple statement caused. "It's your choice, Brenna. That hasn't altered." His voice was gentle, that soft and aching tone that normally destroyed all her resistance. "I'm thinking of the rest of your life. Of *our* lives. I want you at my side, out there on the new world."

Brenna plucked the message chip out of the viewer, turning it around and around between her fingers. "Compromise goes both ways, Derek." She faced him squarely. "I *am* selfish. I couldn't live with myself in that kind of future—waking up light-years from Earth and remembering that I ran out on my species, and on people who love and trust me."

Derek's countenance was empty. "I thought you loved me. I love you." Very slowly, he reached for the intercom. "I'll have someone escort you from the access hatch to Construction Shack Seven. Do you need me to show you the way to Suit Storage?"

A knife ripped through Brenna's soul, the jagged edges cutting brutally. Cutting Derek out of her being—but not completely. Great gaping wounds were left. Derek was mixed in with the blood and the pain. She would never be able to separate them. Some part of Derek Whitcomb would always be with her, a deep agony she couldn't forget.

"No. I can find my way back—alone."

Brenna looked at him one last time, imprinting Derek's face and form on her retinas and brain. Then she ran out through the communications section, heading for the access hatch down below. She didn't let herself think about Derek or the irrevocable decision she had made. Four friends were in desperate trouble and didn't even realize how close they were to death.

The Hiber-Ship crewman who ferried Brenna back to Construction Shack Seven kept stealing glances at her, plainly curious. But he didn't ask questions. When she swam across the big hangar, hurrying to get to her Chase

329

ship, others watched her with similar curiosity. Brenna could guess what was on their minds. At first she had been afraid they had listened in on Quol-Bez's message. Then she knew that they were reading her behavior as an aftermath of a lovers' quarrel.

The ultimate in lovers' quarrels! But this time there would be no reconciliation.

No! Shut off the memory. Shut off everything but the vital task at hand.

As Brenna reached the tunnel leading to her ship, four Space Fleet troopers blocked her way momentarily. "Miss Saunder? Intelligence. The general sends his regards . . ."

Even this far away from Earth and Mars! Terran Worlds Council's reach was awesome. But then it had an entire species to take care of, and dozens of colonies. T.W.C. was tangled up in this situation, much deeper than outsiders knew.

"I'm in a hurry," Brenna said.

"We know. You'll need this." One of them handed Brenna a small iridescent wafer. She recognized the device —military code matrix, top-secret. She had seen holo-modes and descriptions of these—but never the real thing— much less held one in her glove. Brenna frowned, studying the four men. Her father called their sort "wallpaper people," the kind of faces you couldn't remember the moment they were out of your sight. That no doubt made them excellent intelligence officers. They could have been androids, totally without any distinctive characteristics. Even their voices were passionless, very even in tone. "The Ambassador will contact you."

"Are you going to escort me?"

"No, Miss Saunder. Orders. Low profile. The general requests your cooperation."

In exchange for extending the franchise and backing Saunder Enterprises for decades, Councilman Ames now expected a payoff. Keep the scandal hidden. Handle this delicately. No major calling-out of the Fleet. All Brenna Saunder had to do was stop a catastrophe in the making and cram the lid back on it before the political mess blew up in someone's face.

One of the blank-faced intelligence officers moved closer to her. "We're expediting. Your ship's been refueled, Miss Saunder. We added a booster."

Brenna exulted. Top power! With a Space Fleet booster primed onto Chase One's potential, she would come close to matching anything in space—anything, save the Vahnaj ship if it went to faster-than-light speeds.

"Thanks," Brenna muttered. Clutching the code matrix wafer, she kicked off and sailed down the boarding tunnel. There were no maintenance people in sight. Space Fleet had secured the bay for their operations: adding a booster, and who knew what else, to a civilian ship. Brenna raced through the boarding routine, grateful for years of practice. As she snapped the safety webbing, she heard an on-going murmur on the Traffic Control screens. An out-of-frame argument was in progress. Then a Space Fleet officer moved into view. Her face was just as unreadable as the intelligence officers'. She was probably part of the same espionage team, and she had suddenly usurped Hiber-Ship's traffic controllers' position. "This is Class A-One Priority," the officer said, quashing the last complaints from the civilians in the control section. "Clearance for this launch only." The woman was reading her boards expertly, moving small traffic out of Brenna's way. Brenna saw an unnaturally clear field, straight from the launch tunnel. "You are okay to depart, SE Chase Ship . . ."

Brenna switched to manual, taking charge of the helm personally. The blast along the cavernous, well-lighted docking bay was dangerously fast for such close quarters. Every scrap of her experience came into play. She was part of the machine, as she would be on an FTL test run, peeling out of the tunnel and curving away on a wild vector.

She dropped the top-secret matrix wafer into the com slot and activated the systems. Brenna didn't know how long it would be before Quol-Bez or Councilman Ames responded. They must be frantic to know what was going on. They had smoothed the path for her as much as they could, with Space Fleet riding roughshod over Hiber-Ship Base's regulations. Yet Quol-Bez was on Mars, and Councilman Ames might still be on duty on Earth. Both planets were light-minutes from Jovian orbit, and time was the thing in shortest supply for all of them right now.

Chase One was a comet! Brenna opened the propulsion systems up wide, her hands everywhere on the guidance system, feeding new programs. The sleek little craft shot

Sunward, fast leaving Hiber-Ship Base behind. Brenna avoided the computerized links, only using her on-board monitors for the heavy stuff. She didn't know who was in on this, but the fewer signals anyone outside could pick up from her ship, the better.

She had never felt such power at her fingertips. Booster systems! The limit in sub-light-speed velocity, for human technology, so far. Brenna scanned the maps, locking in her destination, clumsy in her haste.

The com winked on. Split screen. Quol-Bez and Ames appeared side by side. In actuality, they could be on different planets, millions of kilometers from each other. The images were unsteady, affected by the coding devices. Brenna heard a faint, eerie echo—the scrambled audio and video signals, as they would sound to anyone without a decoder wafer. The voices were a bit distorted to Brenna, but understandable. They talked over each other's words, each eager to tell his story.

"Sorry about this, girl. No time to prepare you," Ames was saying.

"Ver-y dif-fi-cult, Brenna. They must not. I do not wish ... the ter-ri-ble con-se-quen-ces ... and the treaty ..."

There was no point in Brenna's talking back to them. She was too far from signal origin. It would take too long for the exchange. She would have to wait until their message was complete and see if anything needed to be said, then relay everything at once—and wait another interminable interval for their reply. The laws of space and distance.

"Heavy territory," Councilman Ames said, veiling his meaning as much as possible, despite the code. "We have a problem. I imagined you've guessed it. We ... uh ... were fooled by some *hijackers.* Excellent fakes and top-secret materiel involved. We didn't know the *merchandise* had been removed until an informant tipped us off." *Merchandise!* Quol-Bez's Vahnaj ship! "We've been able to pinpoint the time at which the *removal* occurred. Those who pulled the trick on us are using ... uh ... disguises." That was what Ames had meant by top-secret materiel. The Vahnaj ship and those who had stolen her—riding a Breakthrough Unlimited Chase ship—were now hidden even from Space Fleet as they made their way to an unknown destination. Unknown to Space Fleet, anyway! "Uh

332

. . . we rather hoped you could act as an intermediary for us. We're willing to negotiate a ransom as soon as possible. The Ambassador tells me you understand the necessity for fast action. It's essential this not . . . uh . . . get out of hand. We've been hailing them constantly. The parties haven't responded, and we are unable to locate them due to the . . . disguises." Councilman Ames let some of his true feelings slip past the code talk. "I hope to hell *you* know where they are, or this whole thing is going to come apart on us, if it hasn't already!"

Brenna was already way ahead of him, putting the puzzle pieces together, the overheard scraps of conversations to which she should have listened. She aligned her nav systems as fast as she could. She had to reach her destination before Joe, Adele, and Shoje started tampering with the Vahnaj ship.

"We'll keep hands off. The Ambassador requested it specifically. It's your baby, girl." Ames hesitated. "We hoped Tumaini could tell us . . ." He had broken his own rules. Now that he had let the name of one of the conspirators slip, he went ahead, trusting the code matrix to protect the message. "Unfortunately, some cretin tried to corner him, and Beno made a run for it. He didn't make it. Sorry. I promise you the officer who stepped beyond his orders will pay, girl. I dislike incompetents . . ."

Brenna was suspended in high vacuum; nothingness swamped her marrow and brain.

Tumaini. No . . . !

Ames was still talking. ". . . well planned, I'll give them that. And somebody fed them a lot of help and secret equipment to pull this off, too. Beno used a holo-mode to make Space Fleet Traffic think two of your Chase ships were on that routine mission out to your mothballed FTL hop station. Had their flight plans filed right on time. Cute. Then we got the tip and knew who the hijackers were—but by then it was too late. If Beno just hadn't run . . ."

Tumaini Beno, drawing potential pursuit away from his comrades, and dying for it. He had sacrificed himself, taking the risk, for the greater cause. Nausea and grief boiled within Brenna. Tumaini, dead! She realized, too late, that he had been the ringleader, not for evil purposes, but for the goal of Breakthrough Unlimited. Faster-than-light travel at any price—even at the cost of his life. He

333

had shown the others the way: *"After all, what can they do to us after we crack the Vahnaj ship's secrets? It'll be ancient history!"* She seemed to hear his voice, that strong Mweran accent. Tumaini was the junior pilots' second idol, next to Morgan. What would his death do to them?

And treacherous conspirators had led them into this. Unknown agents with their own ugly motives, whispering, "Go ahead! You can do it. Count on us. We'll steal the devices you need, play hijacker. Grab the Vahnaj ship . . ."

Brenna furiously brushed away angry tears, concentrating on the job at hand.

Chase One's added boosters gave Brenna a bit more power, pushing her into the couch, the acceleration climbing toward two gees.

Elapsed time? Okay. On target. Maybe a bit ahead. She would have to start decelerating approximately five hours from now. At least she knew the junior pilots were coming from farther away than she was. Fortunately! She *had* to get there before they had a chance to . . .

If only she had a graviton spin resonance drive aboard this ship! A *working* FTL drive! She could get there hours ahead of them and be waiting when they pulled in.

Dreams.

Brenna prayed that dream wouldn't turn out as badly as so many others had for her over the past months.

Quol-Bez was talking to her. "Brenna, this must be pre-vented. Councilman Ames in-forms me that our friends have already used the sub-light drive on my vessel . . ." Despite the terrible situation, Brenna grinned. Top pilots! They had cracked the secrets of the alien's sub-c propulsion system and put its controls to work. Score one for Joe and the team. But they weren't likely to make many more such successful scores. They would be cocky, after that initial success, and think they could figure out *any* Vahnaj machinery. "Once the faster-than-light systems are opened," Quol-Bez went on, "cer-tain actions must be taken, or . . . I fear our friends will not know that." No, only a Vahnaj would. And Quol-Bez wasn't riding with the three young pilots, couldn't warn them what not to touch and order them off the ship before it was too late. "In-ex-or-able, Brenna. In your time se-quence, ten min-utes. It is de-signed to limit . . ." *Homo sapiens* to their own Solar System? "The *opui-sir-can* func-tion will not

334

en-gage." Vahnaj FTL drive. Forbidden. And deadly. "It will . . ." The alien broke off, wagging his head from side to side. The solemn gesture was more frightening than anything else he might have said.

"They'll go up like a miniature nova," Councilman Ames put in, pulling no punches.

Brenna was tightening the vector, hoping to cut off travel time. She put a reply message through the code matrix, even though Ames and Quol-Bez hadn't ended their signal. Obviously they weren't going to tell her anything else of use. She could find out the details later . . . she hoped.

"I'm on my way. Councilman, hold off the dogs. My people are sharp. If they sniff Space Fleet, they'll try to make a run for it. Let me go in alone. It's the only way, the only chance . . ."

Quite suddenly, Morgan appeared on the monitor screen. The shimmering, coded image softened the effect of the too-pale skin, the tracery of veins, the mannequin's face, and the eyes that never blinked. But the force behind the stiff features and the artificial voice was Morgan. For a heartbeat, he was back with her again, unchanged. "Brenna, the flaw is gone. We can't lose you, too. Please! Take care. Don't . . ." He had to pause and gulp for breath, his failing lungs shutting off his attempt to speak.

Brenna fought back fresh tears. This wasn't the time. She added a few words to her coded message. "I will, Morgan. You, too. Don't worry. We new dogs know a lot of old tricks, remember? Stand by. Will complete message after the test run."

There was no need to veil her intentions in talk like that. But somehow it felt better. Test run. A test with one purpose—survival.

Brenna muted the com. The code wafer even quieted Space Fleet's normal traffic chatter. The computers were keeping track of where ferry ships and patrols were running. Brenna saw she need have no worries about collision; she was far off the regular vectors by now, and getting farther below the ecliptic every minute.

Pieces of the puzzle and bits of past conversations—dovetailing. ". . . *run her out to an old hijackers' hideout . . .*"

Eighty-five Ores. One of hundreds of pockmarked

335

lumps floating endlessly through the Solar System. This particular chunk of rock was conveniently close to Lower Quadrant Sector Eleven, where Quol-Bez's ship had been parked. *Too* close! And Brenna was too far away.

Under normal flight speeds, she couldn't reach the unnamed asteroid in less than eighteen hours, even though she was heading Sunward and had help from Sol. Now, with the boosters, she was chewing the ETA down by quarters of an hour at a time.

Joe, Adele, and Nagata didn't have the advantage of Space Fleet propulsion boosters, and they were nursing an alien spacecraft alongside Chase Two. They would be moving carefully, not wanting to attract undue attention to their masking devices.

How did they ever think they were going to get away with this! She would ask them later.

Eight hours to rendezvous . . .

Seven and a half . . .

Six . . .

Shaving the seconds, cutting corners wherever possible, ready on deceleration stage.

Com silence shattered. Another message, coming in on a different transmitter from Quol-Bez's and Councilman Ames'. Yuri. His image wavered like the others, but the color was sharper. He was a lot closer to her than the Ambassador or Ames had been when they broadcast their messages.

"Brenna, Morgan told me. I will be there . . ."

She tried to tell him it was no use. He couldn't close the gap in time to do any good. Nothing changed. His vector was a third line, arrowing toward Eighty-five Ores. Win or lose, he was rushing to meet her.

Three hours . . .

Two.

In all the years of her childhood and adolescence and adulthood, Brenna had never hated the vastness of space. She had always reveled in those infinite horizons. Now she cursed the distances.

She began talking ahead of the ship when she was one hour out and closing. The slow-moving asteroid wasn't visible yet, except as a bracketed grid on the nav monitors. But Brenna prayed one of the three eager young pilots had left a circuit open. She spoke in clear, not trusting her juniors to be listening on a guarded channel.

"Chase Two, this is Brenna. Do you copy? I am on course direct to your position. ETA, forty-two minutes. Do you copy? Dammit, Joe, answer me! Adele! Shoje!"

She kept it up almost ten minutes before she received an answer. The asteroid was coming up on her visual scans fast. At two gees, it had taken her five hours to slow down. She couldn't risk plowing into Eighty-five Ores. *That* would throw the whole mess into the fire! What had Ames said about a miniature nova? If she collided with the hijackers' abandoned hide-out, she would likely trigger off not only her own ship's power plant but those in Chase Two *and* the Vahnaj ship—all together, in one magnificent final display.

"Brenna?" Adele Zyto peered at her incredulously. The image was crystal clear, the voice painfully loud, since Brenna was practically on top of them.

"Get out of there! Now! The damned thing's going to blow if you try to tear it down!"

Joe Habich was leaning over Adele's shoulder. He, too, gawked at Brenna as if she were the last person he had anticipated seeing. "We thought you were . . ."

"I'm not! I'm here, coming in fast. Get into Chase Two and bail out of there right now!"

"How did you . . . ?"

Brenna wanted to scream imprecations at them. Had they tampered with the alien ship? Was it already too late to save them and save herself? Ten kilometers and closing. At this range, she would be engulfed in any explosion by an FTL drive. Brenna could see the small asteroid and detect the rocky hangar hollowed out of the cosmic dust mote. There were lights showing behind the life-support barrier. Brenna envisioned the three pilots out of their Chase ship, perhaps out of their spacesuits, wandering around in the once-busy hijackers' lair, congratulating themselves on pulling off this crazy stunt.

"Never mind! Listen to me. That ship's rigged to blow if you dig into her guts. I thought you knew it. Your contact with those crooked politicians damned well knows! You've been set up. Now, get *out* of there . . ."

All three faces were on her com screens now. Brenna

watched a split-second shift take place down there on that rock—amazement, doubt, and then consternation and signs of panic. Belief! Thank God—they *believed* her!

"Get out!" Brenna shrieked. "Have you touched that ship?"

"We . . . we just opened her FTL unit . . ."

"When?"

They hadn't been watching the time, of course. It had never occurred to them they might be starting a countdown for their own deaths. The Vahnaj ship's drive wasn't engaged. Therefore she couldn't be dangerous. Right?

Brenna was yelling at them. They were running, slapping helmet faceplates down, sealing Chase Two, firing her up.

Ten minutes, Quol-Bez had said. Brenna trusted him. He would have no reason to lie. He wanted to *save* lives —the lives of Morgan's young friends and admirers.

Chase One was still closing with the asteroid, forward momentum almost down to that of the overgrown rock. The life-support doors were opening—and a great cloud of accumulated debris exploded out in the escaping air. For a nanosecond, Brenna's heart stopped. She thought it was the prelude to a fireball, one that would wash over her and the other Chase ship and devour them. Instead, she realized the junior pilots had carelessly triggered explosive decompression within the hangar in their haste to get out. Chase Two soared ahead of the billowing junk, making her escape from the hijackers' hide-out. And behind her, borne out of the hangar by the exhausted atmosphere within, floated the Vahnaj ship.

Following Chase Two! As if she had a murderous will of her own and wasn't going to let them get away without punishment for their crime! Ames wanted to save the Vahnaj ship, if possible. Brenna simply wanted to save *them!*

Brenna screamed at her navigation panels, reprogramming frantically. Vernier thrusters fired, altering her course. So slowly! Gradually, she was paralleling the Chase ship's escape vector. Brenna had the power to outrun them, with the boosters Space Fleet had added to her ship. But she hung alongside Chase Two, nursemaiding, darting horrified glances at the figures on her screens.

338

"Light her tail!" Brenna roared. "Get moving!"

"We . . . we were powered down . . ." Joe explained, desperation making his voice crack a trifle.

"Let me . . ." Adele was the steadiest of the three, overriding their confusion. Brenna saw the acceleration rate starting to build.

How long did they have, though?

They were still on top of the damned asteroid—and the Vahnaj ship was still pursuing them, tumbling, blasted at right angles to the hollowed-out rock.

Five kilometers . . . ten . . . fifteen . . . eighteen . . .

They had just crossed the twenty-kilometer line when the Vahnaj ship exploded. The tidal wave of fire and shock Brenna had feared was overtaking them. She didn't know if she could outrun it, even if she opened Chase One up.

She didn't try.

The universe tossed wildly, the Chase ships pitching in the surge of debris and new energies. The waves were invisible but awesome, shaking the sturdy spacecraft, threatening to turn their own guidance systems against them.

Brenna stood in the safety webbing, fighting for balance. Her middle ears protested. Her stomach lurched, almost filling her throat and mouth.

The cockpit was a dizzying smear of glowing screens and fairings and panelings sliding around and around—as *she* was doing!

The emergency on-board computer guidance controls tried valiantly to steady the tossing ship. Verniers and main propulsion systems fired in strange sequences.

Pitching and yawing and about to roll, totally out of the hands of humans or computers . . .

Brenna got hold of the manual switches, clinging to a stanchion. Somewhere, Shoje Nagata was crying, *"Tobi-dasu! Hai!"* The shout hurt Brenna's already-aching ears.

Falling, forever. No. Not forever. She *was* in free fall, but there was order, a detectable path to this falling through orbit. The roll tendency was damping. Yaw was ending. Pitch, too. All three horrendous breakouts in the ship's flight pattern—coming back into her hands.

Brenna seized the weakness in her metal steed, gently taming it with the manual keys. Carefully! She was a good

339

test ship, and spirited. Very responsive to control, and to outside forces battering her.

The webbing holding her was no longer squeaking and strained to the limits of its tolerances. Brenna hung limply from the safety lines, too busy to tighten up the restraints.

Hull integrity? Solid. Life-support? Nominal. Guidance systems? Badly rattled, but repairing themselves. Computers and com? Recovering from the assault.

Exterior scans showed Chase Two steadying down, too, seconds later than Brenna's ship had. Once that would have made her smile with pride, that she had outstripped them in pilotcraft. Now Brenna simply felt relieved.

Radiation counts were dropping into safe ranges. Residual debris cloaked both ships, traveling with them like mist off an Earth ocean or like a Martian dust storm. The junk was starting to thin out, very slowly. Here and there Brenna began to see stars peeking through the dirt and floating shrapnel.

A shaky call came through the intership com. "We . . . Brenna? You okay?"

The visual screens were steady enough so that she could nod and know they would see her. Brenna wasn't sure she trusted her voice yet. Her mouth burned with the taste of stomach acid. She cleared her throat gingerly. "Okay. We made it."

Three faces on the monitors, three expressions of awe-struck guilt and delayed-reaction horror. Adele gasped, "We almost . . . we didn't think . . ."

"No, you didn't," Brenna snapped. Then she caught herself. It was partly her fault. They had dropped enough clues. She should have paid more attention to them, and to Tumaini. Now it was too late for him—but at least three others had been saved.

Yuri's com signal broke into their exchange. The computers noted that he was still three days away from their position, even though he was coming at top speed. The danger was over, and he would be angry and grieved that he hadn't been able to take part in it, Brenna knew. And he would blame himself, as she was, for not having discovered the plot sooner.

"Brenna? I am relaying to Morgan. Can you . . . ?" She put him out of his misery, ending the suspense as quickly

340

as she could. The distance between them, and the signal lag, didn't lessen his intense relief at hearing the good news. "*Nichevo!* I hoped that . . . *nichevo!*" he repeated, overwhelmed. Then, very sadly, he said, "Space Fleet has told me. If I had realized what he was going to . . ."

"Tumaini knew you were too reliable, too sensible," Brenna said. "He also knew how dangerous it was. He wanted to spare you."

New horror was seizing the junior pilots. They read the truth behind the brief conversation, hardly daring to ask for a confirmation. "Tumaini?"

"He's dead." There was no way to soften that. On the monitor, Brenna saw Yuri bowing his head, his shoulders heaving with suppressed pain. She recalled the last time she had seen Tumaini—who had been eager to rush Brenna off on her trip to Hiber-Ship Jovian Base. And Tumaini watching Yuri warily, afraid his friend had guessed the secret plot. Brenna heard herself lecturing them fondly, in a teasing tone that now stabbed her with remorse: "I'm counting on you old-timers to keep the kids in line." Had Tumaini taken that as a hint that she, too, might suspect what he and the junior pilots were up to? She would never know. And Tumaini would never see his sons reach maturity. Rue Polk and Mariette Saunder and Kevin McKelvey . . . and Tumaini Beno, added to the growing list of Breakthrough Unlimited's casualties.

"Brenna . . . ?" Shoje Nagata, his Oriental face stiff with shame.

"Don't say anything more. By now, Space Fleet's back on our channel and listening to every word. The three of you are going to have a hell of a lot of explaining to do. And you'd better wait until I hire a good Saunder Enterprises law team to help you out."

Yuri was nodding as if he would like to crack the trio's heads together—but was too happy to see them and Brenna safe to hold onto his anger. The young pilots were chastened, shaken by grief and their close call, only now beginning to comprehend the magnitude of the mess they were in.

Brenna checked her exterior scan monitors. The rainbow cloud of alien metals and twinkling Vahnaj-manufacture plastic was dissipating, separating into individual orbits that would circle Sol endlessly. Junk. All that was left of Quol-Bez's wonderful ship. The secrets of Vahnaj faster-than-light space travel—gone. The only ship in the Solar System capable of FTL had been destroyed. And this time, there wasn't even a working model of Prototype III ready to take her place and challenge the stars.

CHAPTER TWENTY

❁❁❁❁❁❁❁❁

Judgments

BRENNA had never realized it until now, but a temperate zone blizzard on Earth was just as awesome as one of Mars' famous dust storms. She stared out the window at the megalopolis below, shrouded in whipping winds and white flakes. It hadn't been snowing when they had arrived at Terran Worlds Council HQ in New York-Philly. The storm had started while the Council's Diplomatic Treaty Hearing had been in session. If Brenna had been super-stitious, she would suspect the heavens were making a comment on her junior pilots' chances with the Council. They and her lawyers and the Vahnaj Ambassador had been closeted with the Council for three hours now. There couldn't be that much evidence. Everything was on the Chase ship's tapes: there was also a flood of corroborating testimony from Space Fleet and a captured group of Earth-based conspirators. Joe Habich, Adele Zyto, and Shoje Nagata had been more than willing to cooperate. Tumaini's death, and the realization of how they had been duped and used by forces behind the scenes—people with no genuine concern for faster-than-light travel—had chas-tened the three thoroughly. Grieving and contrite, they had marched in to take their medicine.

Brenna wondered if Space Fleet had collected the junk left after the Vahnaj ship had blown up. The Space Fleet cordon which had closed in on Brenna's ship and Chase Two after the explosion hadn't challenged them, but they had been in custody ever since—Brenna very courteously treated, the junior pilots a lot less so. It was only Councilman Ames's intervention, and Quol-Bez's, that had allowed her to contact her legal firm.

Three weeks to reach Earth, loafing along. Space Fleet had been stalling. That was obvious. Politics again, Brenna suspected. They must have been rounding up conspirators while the surviving FTL pilots were being escorted to Earth to stand up before a Terran Worlds Council hearing. Brenna hoped they had kicked over all the rocks and found the murderous types who had set up this plot!

"Why did we have to come here?" Stuart grumbled. The room was well heated, but he was beating his arms about himself. One of his flunkies threw a cloak over Stuart's shoulders. Stuart didn't thank him, but he clutched the fabric about himself, glaring at the white flakes dancing against the window-wall. "It's too damned cold. Must be another glacier outbreak." Yuri and Brenna and the flunkies regarded him with pitying amusement. "And why the hell do we have to stand around waiting like this? Who do they think we are?"

"Witnesses and participants in a major political plot," Brenna said.

Stuart shot a frightened glance her way. His lawyer cautioned him to say nothing, not even to another member of the Saunder clan. At the other side of the room, Carissa was being consoled by her aides and hangers-on, all of whom agreed it was simply beastly of T.W.C. to demand her presence at this stupid hearing in the middle of winter. It was treachery of the worst sort that Protectors of Earth hadn't rescued her from the summons. What *was* Earth coming to?

"Shut up that damned dog!" Stuart roared.

That had about as much effect as yelling at the blizzard would have. The terrier in Carissa's arms simply yapped louder, competing with the irate Saunder scion. Brenna couldn't resist digging at him and adding to Stuart's misery. "Look on the bright side. They *could* have insisted on holding the hearing on Mars. Eos Chasm is lovely at this time of year . . ."

The door to the inner chamber opened, and the junior pilots, followed by the legal staffers, exited. One look at their faces told Brenna the session had been exceedingly rough. She had wanted to share it with them. So had Yuri.

But the Council had demanded a private hearing. What had happened behind those doors?

"Could have been worse," the chief counsel told her, trying to put an optimistic face on matters.

Joe Habich smiled ironically. "Yes. It could have." Shoje's face would crack if he let down his guard and revealed his feelings. Adele was plainly on the verge of tears and fighting them desperately. They had come through the nerve-shattering situation near the asteroid with flying colors. But this was a problem they couldn't beat by top-notch piloting and courage.

"Pilots' regs lifted for eighteen months," Joe said, before the lawyers could spell out the judgment. "The Ambassador made them waive the fine. Good thing! We couldn't pay it."

"*I* would . . ." Brenna started to say.

Adele snapped, "No, you wouldn't!" Her face was flushed with shame. "You've been through enough for us. You, too, Yuri. They sucked us in with their lies. It's what we have coming for being so stupid . . ." The others were nodding ruefully.

A Space Fleet squad stood by watching them, waiting. Shoje tilted his chin up bravely, squaring his shoulders. "We are ready." He turned to Brenna and Yuri. "We have agreed, as part of our punishment, to cooperate to the full extent with the Fleet. We're going to a briefing. It . . . may be a very long discussion." Brenna admired his aplomb. She and Nicholaiev shook hands with their fellow pilots, wishing them good luck, frowning anxiously as they left the room, hemmed in by Space Fleet troopers.

"Well, that's out of the way," Stuart said sourly, wriggling inside the makeshift cloak he was wearing. Yuri glared at him and took a step in that direction. Brenna caught the Russian's arm, shaking her head.

"Such an imposition! I shall certainly lodge a protest with . . ." Carissa began whining.

Yap . . . yap . . . yap.

The inner doors opened again. A high-ranking aide summoned those in the anteroom. "It's about time!" Carissa complained and led her retinue inside. Stuart lagged, unable to think of a way to bolt and get out of the dilemma. Brenna, Yuri, and Brenna's accompaniment of SE Security and legal staff brought up the rear. The Council hearing the testimony was small—only five members. But they were among the most powerful people in the Solar System, Ames especially. Carissa's employees fussed around, getting her seated properly. They were shocked when the Council ordered the terrier removed. One of the employees, looking unhappy, carried the yelping dog out to the anteroom. When the door shut, a welcome silence fell over the main chamber.

"I do hope this isn't going to be tedious," Stuart said.

Yan Bolotin sternly told him to be quiet. The Earth-based Saunder legal team rolled its eyes collectively, anticipating trouble for its clients.

Ambassador Quol-Bez and Sao weren't sitting at the Council table. They were perched in special chairs at the side of the room, at right angles to Stuart and Carissa. Brenna smiled at them; Quol-Bez smiled in return. That seemed encouraging. He had already applied some muscle on the junior pilots' behalf. What else was he going to do? Obviously, in any crisis involving the Vahnaj ship, he should have the deciding vote.

"We've studied the depositions and the evidence," Bolotin said. "I don't believe there's any need to be formal. This is a judgmental hearing."

"My client doesn't accept the authority of this Council to pass judgment on her behavior," Carissa's weasel-faced lawyer protested.

Councilman Ames grinned nastily. "Who said we were passing judgment? Could it be that you have a guilty conscience, my dear?" Carissa's mouth dropped open. She forgot to simper and wheedle with that little-girl voice, for once. Ames's manner toughened. "If you *want* to make this a court test, we'll oblige you. But take my advice, 'Rissa, you're going to be a lot better off taking what we dish out here in this room. And Stuart . . . well, we'll get to you."

They did, cutting the red tape and the nonsense ruthlessly. The assembled lawyers were aghast, white-faced, as the Council explained the events behind the hearing. As pale as the lawyers were, Stuart was paler. In contrast, Carissa was reddening. Brenna grew worried her aunt might suffer a stroke or faint.

It was a jumble of intrigue and interwoven plots. Brenna listened in stunned amazement.

345

At the Colony Days gala Chairman Hong had said, huffily, that Terran Worlds Council wasn't going to be involved in the business practices arbitration between Alamshah and Nakamura Kaisya; and Councilman Ames had then warned him that if the Progressive Expansionist Coalition kept pressuring Space Fleet's contractors, T.W.C. *would* get into the fracas. Progressive Expansionists had, with P.O.E. egging them on. And Terran Worlds Council had taken over—one more chunk of authority P.O.E. was losing to its space-oriented governing rival.

Apparently, that was the point at which Carissa and Stuart had gotten mixed up in the mess. Obliquely. And on different sides, of course. Brenna recalled Councilman Bolotin's reminding her that she shouldn't rig the odds in the horse race. Now Yan Bolotin explained that he had mistakenly believed Brenna, too, was involved in her aunt's and cousin's schemings. He apologized. Yuri sat with his arms crossed, nodding in grim satisfaction, an "I told you so" expression on his face. Last summer, Brenna had been swimming amid sharks and hadn't known it:

"It's the Hong faction. They wanted to get even for some bad investments. Your aunt and cousin cut them up pretty bad, recently. Then there's the election, of course ... Whatever happened—a close call or your being killed —would've suited their purposes. But now it'll all go flat because we hushed it up."

The plump, matronly secret agent at Carissa's party had believed that. But things had worked out differently. The sabotage of Brenna's flier had gone unnoticed. A small defeat. That had only made the plotters more desperate. And there was a very great deal of power and money at stake—Stuart's and Carissa's among those.

Brenna grew dizzy, hearing the recital. Agents, working a roundabout way, making contact with Tumaini Beno and putting a bug in his ear about stealing the Vahnaj ship. An independent agent, Stuart's lawyer yelled. No one contradicted him, but the Councilmen smiled knowingly just the same.

Meanwhile, at the other end of this tug of war, other "independent agents" associated with Carissa's candidates in the election were prodding Protectors of Earth and the Progressive Expansionist Coalition.

Both factions wanted to wipe out Terran Worlds Coun-

346

cil's power and turn back kilotons of economic advantage to Earth. And somehow, they had cut each other's throats, pushed the wrong buttons, hired the wrong thugs and assassins. Fanatics were difficult to control, it seemed. Erratic. The assassination attempt at the Colony Days gala was a terrible miscalculation. No wonder Stuart had made such a quick disappearance! He had been scared, not of the assassins—but of being thought part of their plot!

No wonder Carissa had gone to such pains to commandeer her niece at the reception in August—lest Brenna talk to some of the wrong people and start putting two and two together about the sabotage of her flier and certain financial machinations involving Saunder Enterprises: Earth. Even so, Brenna had exchanged words with Yan Bolotin and that matronly secret agent. Her suspicions had been aroused, but not pointed in the right direction. The conspirators hadn't realized that, though. They had rushed ahead with their complicated plotting for fear Brenna would discover what was cooking and give them away.

Instead, a disgruntled TeleCom reporter had stumbled onto the scheme and galloped to the nearest Terran Worlds Council intelligence source he could find. Whatever else he might be, Charlie Dahl was a good newshunter, and he knew critical mass information when it dropped into his lap!

The irony was, he had blabbed and tipped off the plot in an attempt to get back at Brenna Saunder—but Brenna Saunder had had nothing to do with the crazy conspiracy against Terran Worlds Council and the space-oriented industries supporting them!

Charlie Dahl—like a good many humans—thought the Saunders were all alike. Hurt one, and you hurt them all.

Brenna almost laughed out loud. She got her amusement under control and listened to the conclusions. Across from her, Stuart had turned the color of snow. Carissa had tried sobbing and sham fainting and hysterical pantings. But the Council had plowed right ahead, sending its resident physician to look over the aging President Emeritus of P.O.E. The doctor had stated Carissa was fine— agitated, with good reason, but in superb health.

"You keep your hands clean," Ames summed up. "We

know what went on, of course. But for right now, it suits us to let it just sit there. Do I make myself clear?"

The Earth-based Saunders regarded him with fear and loathing. The Councilman *had* made himself clear. He had a weapon to hold over them for the future. So did Terran Worlds Council. Power plays. Protectors of Earth's downward slide out of power would continue, and accelerate. Terran Worlds Council's ascension of the throne would continue, and accelerate. And from now on, the dowager Saunder queen and her rebellious, degenerate son would stay on the sidelines and count their wealth—no more— if they were wise. Carissa blubbered about Earth First Party and insane space pilots and thefts of sacrosanct Vahnaj property . . .

Quol-Bez finally spoke up. "I have explained to my government, Mrs. Saunder. We will a-bide by the treaty. They understand."

The Councilmen leaned back, nodding smugly to one another. Case closed, at least from their point of view. From Brenna's, they had shown the bewildered listeners just a glimpse of secrets beyond a heavy door—and they weren't going to show them any more. Space Fleet confidential info. Politics. Knowing where the bones were buried.

Brenna studied her aunt's face, and Stuart's. *They* knew where the bones were buried! And they were terrified that Ames and Bolotin would dig them up and spread them out for all humanity to see.

The Council had won. Carissa and Stuart—fighting each other as much as they had been fighting the offworld government body—had lost.

So had Tumaini Beno. So had the Vahnaj, who were now short one FTL ship.

Breakthrough Unlimited had never been the target of their hatred at all! Stuart's sly hints about helping Brenna out and doing her a favor—all scheming to turn the tables on his mother. *Again!* Was he never going to stop trying? And was Carissa never going to stop trying to keep him, and her pet politicians, under her thumb?

No.

Stuart lunged to his feet and charged at Carissa. Only fast action by the elite Space Fleet guards protecting Quol-Bez and the Councilmen prevented Stuart from overwhelming his mother. They held him until the moment of fury had subsided, at least a trifle.

"Your fault! Always your fault! Never let me be!" Stuart shrieked. "Well, it's not going to work. I don't care what they've got on us. You're not going to hold me . . ."

Carissa shook her head at him, making small tut-tut noises. "Don't be silly. Displays like this never gain anything."

Stuart pulled an arm free and pointed at her. "You can take Felicity and throw her to your dogs!" His dissipation-lined face twisted with ugly rage. "She'll get more from them than she will from me. Oh, I'll tumble her quite merrily, Sweet Mother Carissa! But you can wait a long time in hell before she gets any kids from me. Forever! Do you hear me? It's over. I'll outlast you *and* her. I'll outlive you both, and *then* who'll have the final laugh? Huh?"

The lawyers were whispering to one another frantically. Bolotin was hammering for order, scowling. Councilman Ames sat back, exchanging a look of tired patience with Quol-Bez and Brenna.

Carissa never stirred from her chair. She waited until Stuart had run out of steam. Then, in a voice that chilled Brenna, her aunt said, "Will you outlive me, my dear? I wonder. Not the way *you're* going."

Stuart's face crumpled. "I will! I *will!*" He sounded like a petulant child. People gaped at him in disgust.

"If there is nothing further to discuss, you can consult with my legal firm," Carissa said. She rose, not asking permission, and swept out of the room gracefully, leaving astonishment in her wake.

"We'll do that," Ames muttered. "As Todd is wont to say—rely on it."

Yan Bolotin dismissed the hearing, warning Stuart's lawyers that they were to keep their client, and his mother, in readiness for further questions, should the need arise. Then he waved them out of the hearing room. Stuart's flunkies had to help their boss along. Brenna and Yuri stayed behind for a few moments to speak to Quol-Bez and Ames, thanking them for their leniency toward the junior pilots. The matter would be hushed up. Space Fleet wasn't eager to have its faults exposed. How would it look if it was known the conspirators had penetrated military

349

secrets and used them to help the Breakthrough Unlimited pilots steal the Vahnaj ship? Ames assured Brenna that wouldn't happen again. She recalled Dian's counsel—when the former general spoke in that tone, it was better not to ask exactly what he meant.

Tumaini was dead. The Ambassador's ship destroyed. Three good pilots in disgrace, out of flying for a year and a half.

And none of it had been aimed—really—at the Vahnaj Ambassador or at his ship or at Breakthrough Unlimited at all!

Brenna swore under her breath. Politics! Why did the Saunders persist in getting mixed up with it? Politics had destroyed part of the former generation. Carissa ought to have known what would come of it in *this* generation!

When Brenna and Yuri went out into the anteroom, they found Stuart carrying on about the dirty deal he had gotten, ranting about Carissa and the Council. Brenna shrugged and interrupted him. "That's what comes of playing in the controlled-violence arenas, Stuart. Some of the contestants are out for blood. They don't think it's amusing when people get killed and property is destroyed and an interstellar war hangs in the balance."

Beneath Stuart's flaccid, pasty-pale skin, there were good bones, the shell of what had once been a handsome face. Brenna had seen him in his teens, before his rebellions and hell-raising had ravaged his looks, and his hopes of an easy inheritance from Carissa. What a waste! A good mind. Wealth beyond counting. Potential to influence future history. And he was throwing everything away on sensuality and futile efforts to escape Carissa's clutches.

"Look, we can work together on this, Cuz . . ."

"I gave you my answer on that last summer, Stuart. God, but you learn slow!"

Stuart's voice rose, cracking. "They're going to make me pay for that damned alien's ship!"

"Restitution. Of course. Price of being naughty."

Stuart actually pouted for a moment. The effect was ridiculous. "That's the way you're going to be, eh? You'll be sorry. I'll manage. I can pay the fine. And when I come out of this . . ."

Beyond Stuart, in the doorway of the main chamber, Quol-Bez and Sao were watching and listening. Brenna could read their thoughts without any need of telepathy. She felt burning shame that they had witnessed this, and that they knew Stuart was related to her.

"That's all it means to you, doesn't it? Money. Your silly problems with Carissa."

"Money *is* everything, Cuz . . . the *only* thing—"

He didn't get to finish. Yuri Nicholaiev brought his fist up hard and connected with Stuart's pointed chin. The older man collapsed, sprawling on the floor. Bodyguards moved—Brenna's and Stuart's. Then they froze. They didn't know what to do. Brenna stared admiringly as Yuri loomed over Stuart's prostrate form. His fists were still clenched, waiting for another opportunity. Stuart had been stunned speechless for a few moments. As he regained his wits he clutched his face and screamed. "You can't get away with this! I'll . . ."

"Have your agents kill me, the way you killed Tumaini?"

The fierce accusation silenced Stuart. He crawled away from Yuri, his aides helping him to his feet. "Don't you touch me. Eli! Eli! This man hit me! I want you to sue him for everything . . ."

Brenna touched Yuri's bicep lightly, conveying approval. Then she took a step toward Stuart. Stuart flung up his hands defensively, looking as if he were about to scream for help. "Do that, Stuart. Sue him. Won't that look good in the media? Brave test pilot grieving for his friend is insulted by Stuart Saunder. Saunder shows no remorse for criminal acts. Shall we hire Charlie Dahl to do the story? He'll crucify you. And I'll help him, even if it *is* Charlie. Crawl! Go on! Your best way out of this is to go home to Carissa. Your *only* way out."

She had struck him a mortal blow. He would keep trying to break free, and he would keep failing, and eventually he wouldn't try any more. He would sink deeper into degeneracy, and Carissa would tighten the leash—the noose —until he strangled on his own self-hatred. The aging playboy would never fly away from the nest. Carissa had broken him.

Stuart gagged, hands over his mouth, and his flunkies hustled him out of the anteroom.

Quol-Bez approached Brenna and Yuri. Sao nodded to the Russian, silently applauding what he had done. Now that he had his temper tamed, Yuri was taking an inordinate interest in his knuckles, looking embarrassed.

"What will you do, Brenna?" Quol-Bez asked.

No preliminaries. Reading her mind? Again?

The blowup with Stuart had been a catalyst. Brenna knew what lay ahead, what path she would follow, as she had never known before.

"Go to Mars. Talk to Morgan. Try to put Breakthrough Unlimited back together. We'll have a working ship in April, and I'm going to test her."

"Ah! The re-place-ment ship you will provide me with," Quol-Bez said lightly, trying to make a joke. Then he grew serious. "You must not grieve for the decisions that have been made. It is done. I made my de-ci-sion—to come to your worlds." And what that had cost him! His own species, removing part of his being! "Morgan made his, to ex-per-i-ment with graviton spin resonance. You must make your de-ci-sion."

"I already have." Brenna was aware of all eyes on her. Yuri's sympathetic stare, Sao's knowing one, and Quol-Bez's enormous black eyes, product of evolution under a distant star. *"New Earth Seeker* left orbit this morning."

Derek. Leaving.

"Be sure it's what you really want."

It wasn't. But she couldn't have both things she wanted. She had had to choose. As Quol-Bez had said, he had made his choice—to live among aliens. Derek had chosen to leave the Solar System in cryo sleep. Morgan had chosen to risk his life, and had paid, was still paying.

Now it's my turn.

Brenna gestured emphatically to Yuri. "Come on. We've got a shuttle to catch, and a light-speed barrier to crack. The only way the Ambassador is going to visit Vahnaj now is on *our* ship. Let's prove her out!"

CHAPTER TWENTY-ONE

❀❀❀❀❀❀❀❀❀

Breakthrough Unlimited

THEY had objected, long and loud and with barely a letup. Brenna had dug in her heels. George Li had resisted, arguing. Helen Ives had gotten into the act, even though she wasn't the duty med officer at FTL Station any more. Yuri had been especially vehement against the plan.

Only Morgan had been on her side. Or *was* he?

Brenna had brought them the tape Morgan had made. She hoped it would clinch her case. She could overrule them all, of course. But it would be a much better experiment if they would cooperate willingly. Stony-faced, they had watched the tape of Morgan

"It's feasible," he had explained. Diagrams spun out on the monitors as he spoke. Some of the crew hadn't been able to look at the screens while Morgan's image was there. Like Derek, it hurt them too much, and they remembered too well what Morgan had been like before the accident.

"All mechanisms can be operated by servos. The major purpose in the two- or three-man crew is spreading the glory around." It required a great deal of effort for Morgan to pronounce that many words, but he took the trouble, for Brenna's sake, knowing how badly she wanted this. And yet the glance he had given her showed he was seeing far beyond surface desires. Morgan didn't see her face as a *face* any more. He read other things. When he spoke to anyone, it was important. He couldn't afford to waste his strength. "I'm giving Brenna my proxy on this one, George, Yuri. She has the final vote. The ship's ready as she stands. It's Brenna's option . . ."

Brenna didn't want to rehash the protests. George Li: "We need more unmanned tests." Yuri: "We need to recruit more people." Dr. Ives: "It's sheer lunacy to go without six months' simulation."

The arguments had raged. And all the while Brenna had felt Breakthrough Unlimited trickling through her fingers like Mars' sands. After the fiasco of Quol-Bez's ship, they had lost nearly two dozen team members. People were afraid of being caught in a Saunder Enterprise collapse, or they were simply giving up.

The new, full-sized, fully equipped FTL ship had been delivered late in March. Tobiyah High-Tech Engineering had beat its deadline on the oscillator redesign.

It was April. The deadline was in August. Everyone argued against an immediate manned trial. Morgan showed Brenna the data—and then seemed to back away.

"Nobody else will be hurt—or killed—testing one of our ships."

One way to make sure of that was to eliminate anyone who wasn't a co-owner. Brenna couldn't say when that wild idea had taken hold. But it was embedded in her mind now, and she wasn't going to give it up for anyone —even if she had to operate the entire test by remote computers.

"Set it up," Brenna ordered finally. She had heard them all out, and she had decided. They looked at her with dismay. Several times, these past few weeks, Brenna had overheard a comment from members of the Breakthrough Unlimited team. ". . . changed . . . getting awfully set in her own ways . . . like she's a different person . . ."

Not different. Older. One birthday hadn't made the change. A lifetime of hurting and mourning was doing it.

As Morgan had said, the procedure was possible. The third faster-than-light ship, with its new oscillator and much-strengthened hull material, was at FTL Station. Brenna had never stopped physical training and fitness exercises. She had gone by the book for years. Maybe that was the problem, she decided. She trusted Morgan's research. Nearly a year of thinking—nothing *but* thinking. Now it was time to prove out what he had learned.

No simulation. No big PR push. Pool reporters like Ife Enegu would be there, on command. Saunder Enterprises' ComLink still possessed enormous clout—more than it had, since the decline of some of the Hong conspiracy supporters who had been funding Nakamura and Associates and Alamshah's network. Still, it was going to be a small show. Expectations were low. Brenna found she didn't mind. The push for glory no longer seemed the important thing.

I promised Morgan I'd take care of everything. And I promised Quol-Bez I'd provide him with another ship. Either this does it, or . . .

Even though the team had agreed, it took a while to arrange everything. Brenna remained in daily contact with Morgan. She was used to seeing Quol-Bez or Sao on the monitor when she called Mars now. She spoke to them as often as she did to her parents or to Morgan—*far* oftener than she spoke to Morgan, in fact.

She and Morgan had said all they needed to say. Morgan's most vital contribution had been made. It was the one irreplaceable ingredient. The ship would work. Without fail. Guaranteed.

Somewhere, Brenna had heard that before.

She didn't let herself dwell on the past. Work was a panacea. She pushed it just to the brink of exhaustion, then quit before her doctor pulled a medical-emergency routine to shut the preparations down. Brenna was walking a tightrope across high vacuum. All the years of spaceflight and the long-nursed hopes for Breakthrough Unlimited seemed to be fitting together at last. The keen cutting edge wasn't there. Something else had taken its place. She didn't know if it was the fact that Derek was gone out of her life or that she was accepting Morgan's permanent isolation, finally. But the results were visible to others, and they shaped Brenna subtly.

Not cocksure. Not bragging and strutting, the ace space pilot, laughing at danger.

Brenna Foix Saunder. Morgan Saunder McKelvey's partner. Co-owner of Breakthrough Unlimited. Pilot of . . .

"We're not going to call her Prototype III," Brenna had announced a week before the test. George Li and Yuri and the rest had been shocked. Before they could drag it out into discussions, Brenna had said firmly, "No. We're not. No superstitious nonsense about third time's the charm. I won't have the media using that. This is a new breed of ship. She needs a new name. She's *Saunder Enterprises FTL One.*"

They had rolled the name around on their tongues, murmuring to one another. Some of them still didn't like it. But nobody was willing to make it a major cause. The new name was etched into the nav systems and identity circuits in anticipation of registry with Space Fleet.

The routine. Once more. Good-luck messages from Grieske and Ames and all the other familiar dignitaries. Watchful waiting. Would Breakthrough Unlimited pull it off, *this* time? Brenna didn't blame anyone for skepticism. She was amazed anyone was optimistic, actually.

No message from her parents. She had thrashed that one out, too. They didn't speak of it when she was with them. She existed, and their love for her existed. Breakthrough Unlimited did not.

A last message from Morgan. "Take her out to Jupiter and beyond, Brenna." He would be watching, in his isolation room on Mars. His future lay with her. His only hope of seeing the universe.

Brenna went through Suitup procedures without enthusiasm. Yuri kept up the logical arguments as long as he could. Brenna finally cut him off. "I'm going alone, Yuri. And you're flying Chase. That's *it*. Who else have we got? We're not exactly overburdened with experienced pilots!" They had taken on two possible future hotshots, but neither was ready to handle a Chase ship yet, much less ride co-pilot on the FTL craft. And it would be months before Habich, Zyto, and Nagata could consider coming back to work for Breakthrough Unlimited.

The newcomers, and a bare-bones emergency medical crew, were posted out at the completed hop point; that was as much as Brenna could afford.

She softened, reading Yuri's desperate concern. Brenna hadn't put on her helmet yet, and she surprised the others in Suitup—and Yuri—by leaning forward and kissing him. He turned bright red as she smiled. "That's for luck, for both of us. Maybe I'm superstitious after all. Let's go!"

Still blushing, he managed to get out a hearty *"Valjaitje! Da!"*

Brenna had been through the whole routine before. This time it was special. She had dropped away from FTL Station before. She had peeled away from the base and set a ballistic course anti-Sunward, racing for infinity, before.

But then she had been riding Chase. This was the first time she would be in the main ship. She had wanted it desperately, once. Now she simply accepted.

Automatic. Reflexes. All the run-throughs and checks.

"Nominal on pressure, George. Life-support is optimum. Power consumption well within predicted range . . ."

Yuri, with one of the new pilots riding in the second seat, was flying nearby, opening up some distance, per the test schedule. Thirty kilometers. Easy rescue distance.

If I'm going to end up like Morgan . . . at least I won't take anyone with me.

Cold, calculated confidence. She had never felt so calm. Shouldn't the excitement be feeding itself? Her biomed readings were flabbergasting the doctors back at FTL Station.

"I am approaching test-point start," Brenna announced tonelessly. She allowed herself no hope, and no doubt. This was it. No special Space Fleet boosters on her ship. Those wouldn't be needed. Graviton spin resonance drive was going to work. In a few minutes, she would surpass, by many times, the very best speed that Space Fleet could get out of its spacecraft.

"Graviton spin resonance drive . . . switch on." There was no switch, of course. The terminology was traditional, though. Brenna watched with strange detachment as the graph lines started to go vertical.

Just as they did when I was monitoring from Chase One, and Morgan was piloting Prototype II.

A different ship. A different oscillator. A different pilot. "She's at the top . . ."

"Spirit of Humanity go with you, Brenna!" Yuri shouted. The energies were interfering with the com signal. She saw his likable face blurring out of recognition. Only the audio remained, full of static but understandable. "Bring us back a souvenir." He added, with painful sincerity, "Bring us back *you.*"

Brenna raised her hand over the controls that would engage the graviton spin resonance drive. She was aware of no forward motion at all. Time seemed to stand still. The systems were steady. The new oscillator showed no stress.

"Bring the frequency *above* the resonance point," Morgan was telling her, "and she'll do the job."

Her hand swept forward. No turning back.

Amplitude—under control. Frequency—at the level Morgan selected. Length of pseudo-speed hop—fourteen times the speed of light.

357

Gauges that had never been used suddenly registered impossible energies and distances. No speed gain. Not in *real* space. But the ship was removing the barriers of time and infinity. The barrier field between the hulls was at near-singularity—and holding!

The universe appeared dim, stars visible but seen through an illusionary veil.

The hop ended. Brenna checked the exterior scans.

Jupiter was a disk, "below" her and off to the starboard. Two minutes before, Jupiter had been a dot, identifiable mainly by navigational grid plots.

SE FTL One waited, in effect. She had dropped back into normal space. Her speed was what it had been before Brenna engaged the drive. Off to her port, the scanner screens picked up the small Breakthrough Unlimited emergency rescue station and the standby Chase ship waiting nearby. For the first time in Breakthrough Unlimited's hectic and tragedy-filled six years of existence, they were seeing a *manned* FTL ship materialize in their section of space!

Brenna touched the com before they could. She could hear the crew yelping and howling in delight, over on the adjacent ship and on the little satellite. A skeleton crew. All she had been able to afford or hire. They had been loyal. And *now* they were part of a success! She suddenly loved them and wanted to share her joy with them.

"Relay back to FTL Station and Mars. Send coordinates of successfully completed hop. Time: 1237 Mars Central. Notify Yuri and George Li that the field engaged perfectly—and I feel great. I am now proceeding with further FTL jumps . . ."

That *wasn't* by the book! The lure was irresistible, however. Brenna moved her hand over the oscillator controls once more. The universe dimmed. Seconds ticked away. She could cut in and out at any moment she chose. At five and a half astronomical units. At six. At eight. The temptation overwhelmed her. She let the minutes pass. Twenty A.U. Thirty A.U. She was now at the position, near Neptune's orbit, where the Vahnaj messenger beacon had first been contacted by Todd Saunder, before Brenna Foix Saunder was born.

Forty A.U.

Fifty.

Brenna stopped the advance. Slowly, she opened her helmet faceplate, then removed the helmet. She tugged at her suit's seals, opening those as well until she sat in her pilot's jumper, vulnerable to explosive decompression or fire. A spacesuit hadn't helped Morgan in that sort of holocaust. She wasn't going to depend on it to help her.

Anyway, it wasn't needed.

She was outside Pluto's orbit. She was outside the Solar System. There was enough fuel on board to travel another fifty astronomical units before she reached the point of no return.

Far enough, for a first successful FTL jaunt.

A . . . first . . . successful . . . faster-than-light . . . jaunt!

Brenna threw back her head and laughed, the sound booming within the cockpit, a cockpit large enough to house three pilots. She was alone, with the ship, and with the universe.

Brenna floated in her safety webbing, laughing, tears streaming down her face. She reached out, closing her hands on the air and bringing them to her breast.

The stars!

The entire universe!

Such a simple phrase! As Morgan had said, *"It works."*

Brenna didn't know how long she had been sitting—floating—there. She had no more tears. She was hoarse from laughing. Joy and pain mingled.

"For you, Rue. For you, Tumaini. Aunt Mari. Uncle Kevin. Cesare. We made it. All of you made it with me. We're here. And it's just the *beginning!*"

Finally, Brenna set up the computers. Delicately, the straight-space-travel thruster systems realigned the sleek, buttoned-up craft, turning her nose toward a golden star —the Sun. So far away! The Sun *was* a star, seen from out here beyond Pluto!

Ballistic trajectory. She mustn't exceed her scanner's reach. One short hop at a time. She would have years in which to experiment. New inventions that Saunder Enterprises had to come up with to smooth out this operation. Sub-space radio. Scanners that could search beyond ten astronomical units. A whole new method of navigation.

The Vahnaj will have to help us now! Share their star maps, as we've shared ours with them.

You'll have your ship, Quol-Bez! You can go home to

Vahnaj, via Saunder Enterprises Transport Company, if you want to! Stuart can't pay you back. But I can! My ship will be just as good as the one you lost. Better!

Brenna retraced her route. The Sun and Jupiter grew in the scanners, then Jupiter dwindled once more as she passed it, heading Sunward. The last hop was critical. The orbital plot had to be precise. She was using the computers' calculations, advancing the point at which she had left FTL Station's near-vicinity—and the Chase ship's.

"Stay put, Yuri," Brenna begged. "Right where you should be. I don't want to come out of a pseudo-speed hop on top of you. By the book, just the way you always are . . ."

Except when he was losing his temper at the mighty Stuart Saunder!

SE FTL One winked back into the "real" universe. Chase One was forty-five kilometers off the port bow.

Not bad! A drift of fifteen kilometers, when she had been millions and millions of kilometers outside Mars' orbit and back again.

The computers' calculations needed a bit of fine-tuning, though. They would need to do better than that. Put a ship right where it was supposed to be, to the last meter.

It could be done. It *would* be!

A cacophony exploded from her com screens. Yuri Nicholaiev, yelping like a madman. And from the Station, whole groups of team members, crowding toward the monitors, dancing up and down and singing and crying.

Brenna knew the feeling!

George Li leaned toward the screen, shouting to make himself heard. "We just got . . . just got your relay from Jovian orbit, Brenna. You did it!"

"*We* did it," she corrected him, smiling from ear to ear.

Yuri was mouthing "I love you," not caring who saw him. His new co-pilot was pounding him on the back, creating fearful problems for them both in the effects of action and reaction.

Nobody had noticed that she wasn't wearing her helmet or suit—that didn't seem important now. They would have to work up a whole new set of safety regulations. A whole new way of thinking about space and the universe . . . and about *Homo sapiens'* place in that universe.

"I've got a message to send to Breakthrough Unlimited HQ on Mars," Brenna said.

George Li straightened up, forcibly quieting his aides. He tried to speak seriously, but his wide grin spoiled the stern manner. "Yes? Anything at all! The data's going through right now. The media are screaming for an immediate update."

"This is personal." Brenna felt tears falling again. She didn't wipe them away. Death could know he had looked her in the face. She didn't care. This time, she had beaten Death, and conquered the road to the stars. "It's for Morgan. Tell him he was right. We new dogs *do* know some old tricks, and some new ones, too. Tell him . . . we own the stars. We're big kids now. We can leave the backyard of Earth. We can go anywhere we want to! We won, Morgan! We *won!*"

And on Mars, a man forever trapped in his artificial body, seeing with eyes that weren't his own, would understand. Brenna prayed it was worth it to him. She could never give him back what he had lost. But she could give him this, the thing they had both dreamed of for so long.

Hiber-Ship was obsolete. Mankind wouldn't need to enter cryo stasis and sleep its way to the stars. Not seventy-five years to a nearby star—now seventy-five *days!*

Too late, for Derek and for the other twenty-four hundred colonists on *New Earth Seeker*. They were on their way, dinosaurs, extinct before they would reach their destination.

Problems to be solved. What would Quol-Bez and the Terran Worlds Council do about Hiber-Ship? What would the Vahnaj do with their Ambassador, who had been altered so that he couldn't fit in among his own kind any more?

The stars, in her hands.

And Derek, forever beyond her reach.

Brenna slumped in the webbing, trying to gather herself to complete the operations procedure and return the ship to FTL Station. Not yet, though. She was crying too hard to see the screens.

CHAPTER TWENTY-TWO

✿✿✿✿✿✿✿✿✿

Outward Bound, At Last!

"On this glorious occasion, we must pause to reflect where we have been, and where we will be going . . ."

Brenna had always thought speechmaking in free fall was a spectator sport. Watching orators bob about awkwardly, trying to control their movements *and* get the most mileage out of their platitudes, was better entertainment than most vid comedies. She didn't begrudge the dignitaries their moment, though. She smiled for the media. Dozens of holo-mode camera pendants took her image and preserved it and sent it to Mars and Earth and the colonies. Day side and night side made no difference, as billions of human beings watched their vid screens, enthralled at what they were seeing.

But *all* they were seeing was a bon voyage gathering. The *real* party would be a private one—out there, beyond the "rim" of the Solar System.

". . . day of glory, for Saunder Enterprises, and for mankind. We will remember this day, and our children will commemorate it forever . . ."

Forever was a long time. Brenna Foix Saunder would settle for being remembered in her lifetime. A hundred years? That seemed about right. Long enough to roam among the stars and learn and love.

FTL Station was jammed. People who rarely ventured into space floated beside those who were thoroughly at home in this environment. Team members, friends, and relatives, well-wishers, important people who now wanted to be hangers-on. They had clamored for a ticket to this event. They wanted to say they had been here. This would happen only once.

The first Earth ship to travel to a Vahnaj planet.

Brenna caught Quol-Bez's glance and returned his wise smile. *SE FTL Five* would be carrying a diplomatic pouch from Ambassador Quol-Bez to his government. Brenna had offered, many times, to take the Ambassador with her, as supercargo. After all, she had promised him a ship to replace the one her misguided young pilots had accidentally destroyed. Quol-Bez had gently refused. Chin Jui-Sao had watched him solemnly, loving him, worried for him. And Brenna had wondered if she would ever really understand this gentle alien being from the Vahnaj stars. Not even Sao could reach him. Only Morgan could do that.

Morgan. She had fulfilled her promise to him as best as she could. He couldn't survive an interstellar voyage as lengthy as the one Brenna was about to set out on. But earlier this year, she and Yuri and their new trainee Breakthrough Unlimited pilots had helped Dr. Ives's medics convert the cargo area of *SE FTL Three* into a spacegoing hospital. They had still been using Morgan's first design on the oscillator then, and it had taken almost twenty-four days to travel to Proxima Centauri. Morgan had stood up to the trip rather well, though Helen had been adamant that he mustn't try that again, not until he was stronger. Morgan and Helen Ives and Brenna knew that wasn't going to happen. But Morgan *had* visited another star system. He had seen—after a fashion—a sun and its planets far beyond Earth's Solar System.

"I promised you the stars, Morgan. I guess we'll have to settle for just one star, for the present."

Morgan hadn't complained. Quite the contrary. Through the pli-wall protecting him from direct contact, he had gripped Brenna's hand gratefully. The computerized eyes had revealed a kind of joy.

And now Morgan Saunder McKelvey was busy on a *new* project—FTL radio developed from *Homo sapiens'* technology. Everyone was betting he would solve that riddle, too, in the same way he had broken the problems with the graviton spin resonance drive. In more ways than one, Morgan's name would go down in history. They were the cousins who were giving the entire universe to mankind.

Brenna's parents were at FTL Station; it was the first time they had been there in more than four years. Smiling, holding hands like young lovers, bursting with pride as they watched their daughter accepting the plaudits of the crowd.

George Li and the crew were looking as pleased as punch, enjoying their own share of the adulation. The loyal ones. The ones who had hung on through thick and thin and the bad times . . . and now, the good.

Councilman Ames, grinning slyly at Brenna. *"I always back the winning side."* He had this time, too.

Councilman Yan Bolotin was also there, looking wistful. He was a good loser, even though Breakthrough Unlimited's success was costing him untold amounts of investment capital. Hiber-Ship Corporation was abandoning all work on the *New Earth Seekers* and was dickering, instead, with Saunder Enterprises to convert cryo stasis hibernation ships to faster-than-light drive. That would take some time. Brenna would have to deliver Ambassador Quol-Bez's diplomatic pouch to Vahnaj; the Vahnaj government would have to make some adjustments in the Earth-Vahnaj treaty. Humanity was now a full partner. Trade would begin.

Vahnaj no longer could look down or patronize.

Brenna glanced at Quol-Bez again, wondering. Rapport. Had Quol-Bez broken some Vahnaj rules? *Had* he unintentionally planted ideas in Morgan's head, ideas that aided Morgan in modifying the flawed graviton spin resonance oscillator? Brenna would never know. But she suspected the Vahnaj wouldn't be expecting to see a mission from Earth, in an FTL ship, show up on their doorstep quite so soon after they had assigned Quol-Bez to a backward group of planets around a star named Sol. Quol-Bez's future as a trusted diplomat might be as uncertain as Morgan's.

No matter! He would always be welcome among humans. His magnanimity in the matter of his destroyed ship had earned mankind's affection and respect. An accident. Three too-eager, lied-to young pilots, and a heroic older pilot who had given his life to protect them. ComLink had taught *Homo sapiens* not to fear the Vahnaj. And Todd Saunder's network had smoothed the reputations and polished up the deeds of the family for two generations. At Brenna's request, her father's interplanetary corporation had done the same for three contrite young fliers—who very soon would have their pilots' regs re-established!

Someday, when they got the sub-space com system really working, Todd Saunder's ComLink would be interstellar as well as interplanetary.

It was time to go. Most of the dignitaries didn't try to shake hands with Brenna and Yuri and the crew; they were learning their lessons about action and reaction. Brenna's parents risked that, though, and pulled it off quite successfully, embracing her. Spacers! Old hands at this! George Li and the others who had stayed with the program through its darkest days ignored awkwardness, too.

"Spirit of Humanity go with you!"

"Take our good wishes to Vahnaj!"

The faces that *weren't* in the crowd seemed just as significant as those that were. Carissa had sent the expected form message, no more. Stuart hadn't even sent that. The Earth-based branch of the Saunders was eclipsed, in disgrace, being swept under mankind's rug in favor of a new and glorious Martian branch of the illustrious family . . . Carissa and Stuart, hiding in their tower in the sea.

Charlie Dahl wasn't there. He was recuperating from a skull fracture in a hospital in Brasilia. One of his celebrity interviews had turned out very badly. Brenna had thought it couldn't happen to a nicer guy. She didn't miss his presence at this happy occasion in the slightest.

Hector Obregón wasn't there, though he had sent sincere good wishes. He had bailed out too soon. His name wouldn't be in the history tapes. Yuri Nicholaiev's would.

Aluna Beno wasn't there, but nobody objected—and she was doing much better for herself on Earth than any of Tumaini's friends would have dreamed. The media loved Aluna Beno, the woman who was making a career out of telling her tragic story: "My husband was murdered by Protectors of Earth fanatics!" Just what the gypsy news-hunters panted for.

Cameras, everywhere, watching as Brenna, Yuri, and the three lucky crewmen who would accompany them boarded the skidders for the ride to the hangars.

They were expert at this now. The only difference this time was the attendant publicity surrounding the diplomatic pouch—and the ship's destination: the Vahnaj near-planet.

Graviton spin resonance had been improved. No doubt

365

once the military finished elaborating on the patent, it would be even better. Breakthrough Unlimited had always known Space Fleet would be right there, eager to pick the civilian team's brains, after it took the risks and achieved results. That was the way things were.

"Engaging standard drive . . ."

"Say hello for us," George Li's cry came over the ship's com.

A privileged message from Brenna's parents: "Be careful, kitten." "Huh! Just behave yourself when you meet the Vahnaj. Remember, you're a Saunder."

There was no message from Morgan. Not necessary. Brenna carried him in her heart, always. Partners. As long as Morgan lived. There had been more discussion, recently, about his siring children from his cryo-stored reproductive tissue. Brenna approved. A second family for her parents, a first family for Morgan . . . and maybe one for Brenna. A whole new generation of little Saunders and McKelveys!

"Leaving Station . . ."

Opening up space. The noise and the civilian hoopla behind them. The pilots settled down, going through the routine. The glory was great. But *this* was what it was all about—switching on graviton spin resonance drive and ripping a hole in the fabric of time and space.

"Mission beginning. Time: 1450, Mars Central. September 17, 2076."

The universe dimmed. They were leaping out toward Jupiter, condensing days of old-style space travel. In last year's model, the oscillator had been limited to fourteen times real-space light-speed. The improved version could jump to twenty times c. Distances, out there, shrinking so fast the science experts couldn't keep up with the developments. They would reach the outermost Vahnaj world in slightly over seven months—less time than it took to gestate a human child!

At the rate things were going, another FTL ship, with a still better oscillator, could pass them along the way. But that wasn't going to happen. Quol-Bez and the Terran Worlds Council had agreed on the new treaty terms; no further ambassadorial mission would be sent until this one had been completed. Brenna Foix Saunder's team would have the honor of being the first humans piloting a spaceship into Vahnaj planetary territory.

"Deviation is in the comps," Yuri reported. The other crewmen looked around curiously. They had been told about this, but weren't in on the reasons behind it.

SE FTL Five was beyond Pluto's orbit now, timing her pseudo-speed hops delicately. The next jump was a short one. The shiny, oblate FTL ship had seemingly come to a stop. She winked out of non-space and into real space.

Ten kilometers off her starboard quarter, *New Earth Seeker* rode against the eternal darkness, moving at an imperceptible rate, compared with *SE FTL Five*'s capabilities.

Brenna gazed at the view screen, reducing the scan so that she could see the whole planetoid-sized hibernation ship. Yuri said, "I'll go with you."

Brenna didn't argue. She was grateful for Yuri's presence on the skidder. This stop en route had been in the program from the beginning—her option and Yan Bolotin's request. There would be other FTL ships coming along this same path on a regular basis. That was part of the new treaty. Brenna could have turned the duty assignment over to one of the disinterested new pilots in her crew, but she hadn't. Only Yuri would know just what this short side venture would mean to her. She didn't want a big audience, since she was uncertain how she would react.

New Earth Seeker was programmed to be wary of possible collision factors, but Yan Bolotin was a controlling figure in Hiber-Ship Corporation. Brenna and Yuri had the proper code sequence. The hangar hatch opened readily for their tiny intership sled.

Yuri had never been aboard this monster. He stared in fascination for a few moments, then followed Brenna up the ladder to Main Control. They went through the prescribed checks, relaying the data back to *SE FTL Five* and to the Solar System. That would confirm the figures Bolotin's group was already receiving, and alleviate some of their worries.

The necessary checks done, Brenna and Yuri could have gone back to *SE FTL Five*. But Brenna made her way down a tunnel to one of the enormous spheres, remembering the tour the last time she had been aboard this interstellar colonizer.

Bolotin had let her see the registers. He had sympathized. But he had stuck to his guns. The colonists had been aware of this possibility when they signed up. It was always in the charter. Derek had told her that. Even if faster-than-light travel was discovered after *New Earth Seeker* had launched, the colonists were not to be disturbed. They would continue on their long journey to the Kruger 60 system, unaware.

Brenna lowered herself into the sphere containing the piloting crew's cryo cubicles. Yuri clung to the ladder, not descending any farther, watching her anxiously. There was no spin on the photon ramjet now, no gravity needed to make those on board feel comfortable. Brenna floated in air, sculling with her hands, hovering beside the cubicles. She looked into the still faces. Outside row. First file. Cubicle ten. Lilika Chionis. Cubicle nine. Derek Whitcomb.

Cubicle eight was empty.

Brenna remembered Yan Bolotin pointing to the screen, indicating the spot on the register: "Reserved for Brenna Foix Saunder."

There had always been a place for her. Derek had always hoped—up until the final moment, when she had made her choice.

Derek was a statue, cold, serene, vid-star handsome. He would remain thirty years old for the next seventy-four years. Brenna Foix Saunder would not. Lilika Chionis would still be young and beautiful in three-quarters of a century. She, not Brenna, would be Derek's Eve, his first wife, on that alien, uninhabited world these people would civilize.

Brenna had thought she would weep. She didn't. The tears had been spent, months ago. What they had had was gone, locked in memory. It must stay there, as long as life lasted.

"Brenna . . . ?"

She raised her eyes, meeting Yuri's worried gaze.

"It's okay. I can manage." Brenna looked once more at the man in the cubicle. "He wouldn't appreciate it if I spoiled his plans. They worked so hard for this. We'll protect them. And when we're busy or getting older and too tired to do that, a younger bunch of FTL pilots will play watchdog. Nobody's going to foul this up for them. We'll make sure they get to Kruger 60 safe and sound . . ."

368

Yuri nodded, very solemn. His glance shifted to Derek's cryo cubicle, and the Russian slowly saluted a fellow, former Space Fleet officer. Brenna laid her gloved hand on the edge of the case and whispered, "Good-bye, Derek. Spirit of Humanity make you happy."

She didn't speak on the skidder trip back to *SE FTL Five*. But by the time they had steered well off from *New Earth Seeker* and engaged the graviton spin resonance drive again, Brenna was able to smile a bit.

"It's a trust," she explained to the new pilots. "Space Fleet will take over the job eventually. But for now, it's ours. They're space pioneers, too, in that ship." The pilots were wide-eyed, impressed.

Listening to the old-timers, Brenna thought, laughing inwardly. Yuri and she *were* old-timers, to this wet-behind-the-ears bunch of hotshots! Old-timers, at age thirty.

Well, there was a lot of life in *this* old-timer! She wasn't going to waste it loafing along at sub-light speeds. "Let's go meet the Vahnaj," Brenna said.

SE FTL Five was bigger, roomier, and better equipped than anything in her model class built before her. Seven-plus months not spent in luxury, but they weren't uncomfortable. And they weren't bored.

Infinity, out there. It was taking a long time to travel to the nearest Vahnaj world—yet they wouldn't be a year older when they got there. Incredible speed! The temptation to roam off the vector was tremendous. Somehow they resisted it.

They picked up alien signals. Not only the Vahnaj used these star lanes. Brenna heard new languages, recording them, imagining how her mother's linguistics teams would revel in these treasures. She was hearing the voices behind those names Quol-Bez had mentioned so long ago—the Whimed, the Trannon, the Ulisor. Other peoples. Other cultures. A whole universe full of them!

And now she had the ship that would take her to meet them!

It wasn't until they were approaching orbit around the destination world that the elapsed calendar time made an impression on Brenna. She had marked it off automatically, thinking in terms of the whole journey and how far they were from point zero and point arrival. Yuri Nicholaiev noticed Brenna's expression and said softly, "Yes. It is the same. April twenty-eighth."

"Two years too late for Morgan and Rue and Tumaini . . ."

"They are with us," Yuri said. Brenna took that solace, holding it tightly in her heart. Let it be so. They had deserved it, those brave pilots of Prototype II. They had always hoped that date would be immortal. Now it was. April 28, 2077: the day the first human-piloted FTL ship arrived at a Vahnaj world.

The com lit up. The Vahnaj had learned *Homo sapiens'* frequency preferences many years ago, when Todd Saunder discovered the beacon messenger the alien beings had sent out into the galaxy to search for other intelligent life. Since then, they had sent an Ambassador, forgiven the destruction of their Ambassador's private spacecraft . . . and perhaps begun to wonder if the humans weren't a bit quicker to catch on and faster to develop than the Vahnaj government had anticipated.

Brenna had been polishing her fluency in Vahnaj all the way from high ecliptic Mars orbit. *"Thor-i-saduo,* Vahnaj. *Pla chur SE FTL Five,* Earth . . ."

The pilots leaned toward their screens, intrigued by the image appearing there. Not Quol-Bez's. Another Vahnaj's. His face was browner, his sideburns lighter colored, and his teeth weren't as pointed as Quol-Bez's The *second* member of the Vahnaj species human beings had ever seen. And very soon they would be meeting him face to face— him, her, and many, many others.

Formal and informal, frequent social relationships with an extraterrestrial civilization!

At last!

"Thor-i-saduo, Eff Thee Ull Fife, Earth . . ." The Vahnaj welcoming them sounded mildly surprised to have been addressed in his own language.

Brenna grinned mischievously. He was soon going to be even *more* surprised! She hadn't wasted her time. She had a lot of questions to ask. Brenna was going to find out, for one thing, if dangling the bait of an FTL ship in front of "primitive" sapient species was a learning tactic or a taunt. Carrot on a stick, or the tortures of Tantalus? She wanted to believe the former, but if it was the latter, that was okay, too. Because this time Tantalus had reached up and taken the bait and wrested it away from his tormentors.

Hang onto your pride, Vahnaj. Here we come!

"*Nyo-re-sterla*, Vahnaj," Brenna said, smiling victoriously. "The Ambassador sends his regards."

The saga of the Saunder family will continue in Book Three of *Children of the Stars*, LEGACY OF EARTH, soon to be published by Del Rey Books.

ABOUT THE AUTHOR

Juanita Coulson began writing at age eleven and has been pursuing this career off and on ever since. Her first professional sale, to a science-fiction magazine, came in 1963. Since then she has sold fifteen novels, several short stories, and such odds and ends as an article on "Wonder Woman" and a pamphlet on how to appreciate art.

When she isn't writing, she may be singing and/or composing songs; painting (several of her works have been sold for excessively modest prices); reading biographies or books dealing with abnormal psychology, earthquakes and volcanoes, history, astronomy—or almost anything that has printing on it; gardening in the summer and shivering in the winter.

Juanita is married to Buck Coulson, who is also a writer. She and her husband spend much of their spare time actively participating in science-fiction fandom: attending conventions and publishing their Hugo-winning fanzine, *Yandro*. They live in a rented farmhouse in northeastern Indiana, miles from any town you ever heard of; the house is slowly sinking into the swampy ground under the weight of the accumulated books, magazines, records, typewriters, and other paraphernalia crammed into it.

JAUNITA COULSON'S CHILDREN OF THE STARS SERIES

A STELLAR-BOUND DYNASTY; UNITED BY BLOOD, DIVIDED BY GREED.